D0275032

# THE HONOURABLE
# LIFE OF
# THOMAS CHAYNE

*By Cynthia Jefferies*

The Outrageous Fortune of Abel Morgan
The Honourable Life of Thomas Chayne

a&b

# THE HONOURABLE
# LIFE OF
# THOMAS CHAYNE

CYNTHIA JEFFERIES

Allison & Busby Limited
11 Wardour Mews
London W1F 8AN
*allisonandbusby.com*

First published in Great Britain by Allison & Busby in 2019.

A CIP catalogue record for this book is available from
the British Library.

First Edition

ISBN 978-0-7490-2339-3

Typeset in 11/16 pt Adobe Garamond Pro by
Allison & Busby Ltd.

The paper used for this Allison & Busby publication
has been produced from trees that have been legally sourced
from well-managed and credibly certified forests.

Printed and bound by
CPI Group (UK) Ltd, Croydon, CR0 4YY

# CHAPTER ONE

I should first relate that the year 1624 saw my birth, on the 23rd of a cold February day. My mother told me that I arrived much before my time, to a landscape covered with deep snow, and more falling from the sky. The best doctors and midwives should have been there to aid her, but the weather and my sudden arrival conspired together to leave my poor mother with no help other than her servants.

Her maid, who had been engaged because of her skill at dressing hair, told my father, who unusually happened to be in residence, that one of the kitchen servants had attended several births, but my father would allow no peeler of carrots to be at the nativity of his heir. The bone-aching cold did galvanise him into ordering the fire to be hastily lit in his wife's chamber, but in spite of the excellently seasoned ash and oak logs that had been carefully chosen and laid there in anticipation, they had hardly any time to make an impression on the temperature of the room before I arrived with indecent haste.

It would not have been surprising if I had exited this life almost as soon as I had arrived in it, being born small, chilled and hungry, but my mother had lost her first infant, and was not inclined to lose another. In the absence of a wet nurse she scandalised her husband by putting me to the breast. Not only that, she also insisted on me lying close with her in bed, instead of being put in the cold ancestral cradle. Of course, this state of affairs didn't last long. As soon as the snow allowed, a flurry of experts arrived, and I was whisked away, to be raised in a more seemly manner, but I do believe that not only did she bear me, but also it is likely she saved my life.

During those few days together, as the room warmed and we both grew stronger, we must have formed an unhealthily close bond. That was my father's opinion about the great reluctance with which she gave me up. I think now that perhaps he was jealous of the love she had for me, as well as his determination that I should fit the life I was born to. I cannot remember even one occasion when both of my parents and I were fondly as one. My father seemed to hate any sign of affection between my mother and I, and my mother too discouraged it, in obedience to her husband, and also I like to think in order to spare me a little of his ill humour. It was different for my younger brother Hugh. Our mother could tousle his hair and our father would smile. If I sat at her feet and she did it to me he would complain that she was making a fool out of me, and order me to sit elsewhere. Perhaps he loved me, in his own fashion, but I never saw any sign of it. I certainly longed for his love, and never really grew out of that longing. I honoured him, respected his great station, having as he did the ear of King Charles, and did all I could to spark some sign of fondness from him for me, but his lack of feeling, in the end, obliterated my love for him. I feared him, yes, and yearned for his approval, but in the end I could not love him, however much I wanted to. It was a way, I suppose, to guard myself from his lack of feeling, though it never stopped my yearning. I did love my mother, more perhaps than was wise, but I knew she loved me, and felt almost sure that her reticence was imposed by her husband. All the same, in spite of my natural ebullience, my mother's distance was a cause of great sadness to me, because I was an affectionate child by nature.

Of course my father was away a lot, at court, and my first few years were spent in the nursery, so my father was then seldom in my thoughts. In fact, my first real memory is of Hugh's arrival. I was two years old and earned a smack for poking my finger into his eye when we were introduced. Early childhood memories are like flashes of half-forgotten dreams, and my next vivid memory must have occurred when Hugh was almost walking, and so I suppose I must have been about three.

'You bad, wicked boy!'

Hugh loved his wheeled contraption. Whenever our nursemaid put him into it he would set off, careering across the floor in a haphazard, directionless fashion, his little feet drumming the boards. I loved it too. It changed my brother from a creeping creature to one who could look me in the eye with the promise of adventures to come. Perhaps it was adventure I was looking for, or maybe I was simply curious at how his contraption would handle the stairs. It certainly didn't occur to me that my behaviour was either bad or wicked, nor did I see any danger in my antics.

The door must have been left ajar by mistake. I am sure I was not able to unlatch it, but I could certainly pull it wide. With great good fortune, one of Hugh's wheels got stuck, and so his walker only clattered down the first step, lurching Hugh sideways and almost throwing him out. I remember so clearly his laughing face, close to mine while I tugged unsuccessfully at his chariot, trying to free the wheel. Then there were the screams of the nursemaid, who had been repairing yet another of my torn gowns, the lifting of Hugh from danger, and me being dragged in confusion from the top of the stairs. The commotion even brought my mother to see what was amiss. The result was that I never saw that particular nursemaid again. Of my own punishment I remember nothing, except that I was made to pray forgiveness for something I did not understand. It seemed the adults thought I wished my brother to die. In truth, Hugh and I were very close all through our childhood, and although we have not met for many years, I still think of him often.

As we grew, we discovered that life was not all play. A tutor was engaged, and for a while I sat alone in the classroom, learning at first to read and write my own language and then Latin and Greek. By the time Hugh joined me I had my own pony and was learning to enjoy the hunt as well as my books. Hugh was not a natural scholar, but I am, and so we often found ourselves secretly in the role of teacher and pupil, as I strove to help him avoid a beating for not managing his lessons. I always wanted to protect him and I continue to thank God that he survived the dreadful times that were to come. But that all lay in a future I had no conception of then. Indeed, I doubt any at that time would have imagined the difficulties that lay ahead.

# CHAPTER TWO

In my tenth year, my father decided to take me to court in the expectation of presenting me to the King. I always think of that occasion as the start of my adult life. It was when I began to find myself as a person in my own right instead of simply being my brother's guide and playmate. I cannot say I looked forward to the journey. I hardly knew my father, and feared him, but being of an optimistic nature I did hope that spending time alone together might help him to know and like me better. I was keen to impress him with my conversational skills, but things did not happen quite as I had hoped.

'So, you see, Thomas, how important it is to be knowledgeable about all factions at the court, if I am able to advise His Majesty wisely.'

We were in my father's coach, still at least two hours from Whitehall, and I was already weary of my father's attempts to educate me about politics. I wanted to ask about the beggar on a board at the inn where we had changed horses. Had he lost his legs in some accident, or had he been born without any? But I didn't voice my question. It, like the others I had asked, would bring irritation and dismissal, not an answer. The last question, about the name of the great tree we had passed a while ago, had prompted a withering rebuke. My father had glanced at it briefly and then turned to me.

'Trees are for foresters, Thomas. I'm told you have a good brain in your head. Use it to learn about things you will need to know, not frivolous nothings.'

I was angry with my father, and secretly wondered if he even knew the answer to my question. But I was also gratified that he acknowledged my intelligence. I did still want to please him. I could tell, however, that if this was ever to happen I would need to commit all the names of the men he spoke of to memory, as well as their opinions and alliances. It was not his fault that I found such things crushingly tedious. Maybe, once we arrived at court, I would be able to put faces to the names, and everything would fall into place. I would try a better question, on his subject, to show I had been listening.

'So, Father, are all these men members of the privy council?'

Too late I realised I had made another mistake. His frown betrayed his true feelings, although his voice strove to keep his temper under control.

'Of course not! It is vital for the King to have trusted advisers outside the council. It is a mistake to think that the privy council contains all the best brains, or even most of them. Though that,' he added swiftly, 'is not to be voiced in court, nor anywhere else, particularly by a beardless boy.'

Maybe a year before I would not have realised how angry and frustrated he was at not being a member of that inner circle but now, suddenly, I could see it. With that insight came the extraordinary knowledge, like the pounce of a hawk, that like me he was not entirely master of his life, and that his frustration coloured it. I gazed at his profile under my new hat, and decided that when I was grown, I would never put myself in a position where I had to do as I was told. Kings might be our masters, but why put oneself so directly under them, when a life of hunting and hawking, servants to carry out our wishes and comfort aplenty was ours at home? I was, after all, just a boy, but was learning that life was more complicated than I had thought. I had been told much about duty, responsibility and the destiny that was mine, but the word 'ambition' had never been mentioned. Mine had always been to gain my father's affection; now, for the first time, to me he looked less powerful, and much less worthy of my embryonic ambition. Was a man who worked at what frustrated him and could not even name a tree someone I should respect? I glanced at his florid complexion, his greying moustache and his bulging stomach, and with the devastating logic of a ten-year-old, decided that I would never turn into him.

At court I was allowed to watch King Charles and his queen dine. I wondered that they could enjoy their food with so many gawping at them, but they seemed indifferent to their public. All sorts of people came to stare, comment to each other and go on their way. The sight of so much food made my stomach argue for sustenance, and so I was relieved when Their Royal Highnesses rose from their table and disappeared from view. The common people left the palace, but we took a different route. I would soon have been lost, but my father was very familiar with our surroundings. He took me to a side room, where several people were eating together. They hailed my father as a friend, and made room for us at the table. While they talked, I ate. A girl not much older than I, sitting opposite to me and splendidly dressed, smiled at me.

'You are Thomas Chayne,' she told me, as if I might not know.

'I am,' I agreed, swallowing hastily.

'Have a woodcock,' she said. 'They are very good.'

'We have woodcock at home,' I said, taking one. 'And I like them very much.'

It was far more interesting talking to this girl than listening to my father's impenetrable conversation with his friends, but it wasn't long before the gentleman next to her pushed his plate away and got up.

'I must go,' the girl said, hastily wiping her greasy fingers on her napkin. 'My husband has business elsewhere.'

I stared at her like a fool. I had assumed, if I had considered it at all, that he was her father, bringing her, like me, to court for the first time. And yet, I suppose he was not so very old. I got up and gave them both the best bow I could with my stool so close behind me. I hoped I had not done anything to offend him. He had done no more than nod at me when I first sat down, and had not engaged his wife in any conversation at all. I wondered how she had known my name, but then felt even more foolish. She and her husband must know my father well, and had known he was going to bring me to court. She had spoken politely to me but I had not so much as enquired her name. I felt abashed by my rudeness, but by the grin she gave as she took her husband's arm I suppose she must have forgiven me.

A few minutes later the whole company broke up as they went about their business. There were meetings, and committees, petitioners and huddles of friends discussing who knew what. Some greeted my father, and made comments about my likeness to him, which secretly appalled me. One of the ladies caressed my cheek. I did not much like it, although my father smiled indulgently, which he most certainly would not have done if she had been my mother. I bowed and smiled, nodded and replied to the inane questions asked of me as best I could. I could tell that most of the people were little interested in me. They were simply being polite. After this awkward progress we entered the room where King Charles sat, speaking to two gentlemen. We approached a little, and then waited for the discussion to end. Before it had, the King looked up and, seeing us there, smiled and beckoned us forward. I had been taught how to behave in front of my monarch, but found I was very nervous.

'Thomas!' It was my father he spoke to, not me. But then he regarded me with a keen eye. 'And this is your son.' My father bowed again and I did the same.

'Your father is a great addition to our court,' he told me. 'His knowledge of the mood of the people is often right, and I rely on his good judgement. Will I also be able to rely on you, in time to come?'

I did not think he required an answer, but I mumbled something and bowed again. Before I had raised my head he was speaking again to my father.

'There is a meeting this afternoon about the tax that has been proposed. I would like you to attend and give me your opinion afterwards. You may leave the boy here. No doubt the ladies will enjoy his company.' He turned back at once to his earlier conversation and it was obvious that we were dismissed.

I tried not to convey my alarm at the prospect of my father leaving me with all these strangers, but I suppose he must have noticed. He was not used to reassuring me but made a gruff attempt. Pulling me away by the sleeve, he deposited me near a group of gentlemen playing cards.

'I will return when I can. Don't forget your manners.'

I watched him out of the room, wishing I was at home with my mother, my brother and my pets. Alone of all the people in the room, I knew no one. I was perfectly able to behave in a proper manner if I was spoken to but could not begin to think of initiating a conversation myself. Everyone was occupied in one way or another, and so I stood miserably by the wall, watching, and feeling invisible.

However, after some minutes, which felt like an hour, I did recognise someone. It was the girl who had spoken to me during our meal. There was no sign of her husband, and she was with a couple of other girls. After a few moments she spied me and came to me, bringing her friends.

'It's young Thomas Chayne!' she said in a teasing voice. 'What are you doing lurking by the door?'

A shrug has no place in a book of manners. A shrug combined with a slight bow and an embarrassed blush must have made me look as stupid as I felt, but she was not a cruel girl.

'This is Alice, this is Mary and I am Elizabeth, as you know,' which of course I did not. It was kind of her to be so informal.

'Come with us,' said the one called Mary. 'We are going to practise our parts. You can help.'

'I'm terrible at remembering my lines,' said Alice. 'Do come. You can prompt me.'

Elizabeth grinned. 'Your father and my husband are at the

16

same meeting. They will be ages. What else are you going to do? Come on.'

I needed little encouragement.

Much later, on the way home, my father neglected to ask how I had passed my time, huffing instead about the meeting, and telling me how difficult it had been. I hugged my own afternoon to myself, keeping it until I could boast to Hugh about my adventure. When my father was gone again on business I told my mother too, sitting at her feet in her room, with the sunlight warm on my face and the silk of her dress cool against my neck. I had enjoyed a glorious time, being treated like a pet by those beautifully dressed women. The rehearsal for Her Majesty's masque had been enormous fun and I had thrown myself into it. With the words on a paper thrust into my hands, I prompted where needed. The masque would not be performed for some weeks, and it was just as well. Lady Alice was indeed terrible at remembering her lines, no matter how many times I helped her out. I did not have the masque clear in my mind, but these three had been cast as nymphs. Mary's role seemed to consist mainly of her gazing up at the moon, while Elizabeth had a whole verse to recite, and did it almost flawlessly. I, of course, would not be there to take part, or to see it, which felt a great pity. As well as prompting, they had me play all kinds of extra parts, whether made up for their amusement, or in fact to stand in for props that Mr Inigo Jones would supply on the day, I could not tell. I was not used to the company of girls, but they made my presence seem like a treat, and enormous fun. I had not laughed so much, ever! I even saw the Queen. She paused in the doorway to watch for a moment, waving us to continue as we all scrambled to acknowledge her. I, being already on my hands and knees, taking the part of a swan, could not decide if my position was humble

17

enough or not. By the time I had got to my feet to bow she had gone, with a nod of approval to her nymphs before she moved on to inspect, perhaps, others rehearsing for her masque. I still remember that day with great fondness.

I don't mean to convey that my home life was as sad and drab as the afternoon at court was joyful and full of colour. The older Hugh and I got, the more licence we had to ramble over our estate on pony and foot, when lessons were done for the day. We two fought and made up, came home dirty and grew closer each day. Our mother was at pains to teach us all the formality we needed, but when father was away, in her private quarters we could play chess or cards, read aloud or tell stories, and best of all, laugh at jokes. There was much merriment, but it was a separated life, with formality and sober duty in public. I was, I think, fortunate to have been born a merry and demonstrative person, and have always been quick to laugh, but that brought its own frustrations as I often had to master my mirth and assume a purposeful expression. But that afternoon at court taught me that my father's insistence on sober behaviour was not the only way for well-brought-up people to behave. There was no impropriety in the behaviour of the young ladies, simply fun and high spirits. If the Queen could encourage the enjoyment of her masques, with her husband reputed to be righteous and faithful, how could it be wrong? From that day on, I decided to no longer think of those times in our mother's company as a guilty secret. It was, I decided, for whatever reason, my father's error, not ours. Even unto embracing our mother. If Hugh was allowed to, then why should not I? After I had told her of my afternoon at court I stood up and hugged her. The fact that she returned my embrace so warmly told me that in spite of her past reticence she welcomed my affection, and that we had made a pact of sorts. Perhaps she had worried that as a little boy I would not be able to restrain myself in company, especially that of my father, and wanted to spare me his ire. But I was old enough now to understand. The artificial stiffness that had kept us physically apart melted away. It was easy to be formal when I knew that I only had to wait until my father was gone back to his dreary business at court.

# CHAPTER THREE

My court experience did more than show me that affection and fun were not wrong in company; it also pricked my interest in girls. Not having any sisters, they were a foreign species to me. Our servants were not allowed to be familiar with my brother or I. Indeed, my father once dismissed a kitchen girl for smiling at Hugh. He was a very tyrant as far as propriety was concerned. I can only think that he had informed his tenants of his wishes because when we came across any girls in the village, or local boys for that matter, they busied themselves in looking elsewhere. I don't think Hugh or I thought it was strange. We had never known anything different, but that day at court introduced me to the delights of playing with others, in particular girls, and I did not forget it.

But those girls at court were different from any I saw at home. In their silks and ribbons, not to mention their jewels, they were exotic, exciting creatures to me. Yes, my mother wore silk on occasion, but her movements were stately. The girls at court ran, twittered and giggled when not required to be formal. The very sound their clothes made as they moved was different to any I had heard before. Their feet, peeping out from the hems of their dresses in their embroidered satin shoes, were a wonder to me. The little heels on their shoes drummed like woodpeckers when they ran and their dresses susurrated like leaves in a breeze. They delighted in gently teasing me, and I lapped up every saucerful of fun, stored it away and took it home to where the girls were heavily shod and whose clothes were rough, and almost silent.

My father didn't repeat the exercise of taking me to court. Perhaps he thought his duty had been done in presenting me to the King. At any rate, my life resumed its parochial pattern, except that girls seemed more interesting than they had hitherto. And then, at sixteen I found myself in love. For over a year I was in heaven. Of course our liaison was foolish, but my heart was entirely taken by a local farmer's daughter, Mistress Catherine Walke. It was unwise of us both, but youth is seldom sensible in such matters, even with a father like mine. She was, of course, below me in station, but for all that the daughter of a prosperous, land-owning farmer. Her father rented some extra land from us, and we had grown up knowing each other by sight. By the time Christmas had come and gone we were past saving.

How cunning is love! How it creeps up and ensnares a body. We had no need of secret signals in order to meet. No lace handkerchief waved from a window, nor any midnight trysts. We had since early childhood met in plain view at church every Sunday, and also when Hugh and I were on our regular ramblings, because Catherine often crossed our land, going to and from the land and buildings her father rented from ours. At first there was no more to it than the gradual exchanging of polite greetings instead of ignoring one another, as had been the case when children. Such behaviour was proper for adults but we were ripe for disaster. One day, when Hugh was in bed with a slight fever I went alone to the path through the trees. I knew what time she was accustomed to pass along it so I loitered in my callow way, leaning with studied nonchalance against a towering beech tree. I was nervous. I wanted to say more than 'Good day', but what could I say to her, or she to me? I was like a fly, drunk on a honey cake. As soon as I caught sight of her dress, a moving shadow in the patches of sunlight, I bent down and began to scrabble ridiculously in the litter of dead leaves.

'What are you doing?'

She was upon me and I looked up at her laughing mouth, loving it and everything about her, but feeling far from the romantic I wished to be. I wanted to kiss that mouth, having seen men in the village gather their wives and sweethearts into their arms and do just that, but I had no idea how to begin.

'I lost some coins, and was finding them,' I said, brushing the damp mould from my hands. I made to stand up but caught my foot on a root and almost fell. She laughed again and stepped backwards to give me the space to recover my balance. If she had not looked me in the eye once I was standing, I think we could have, even then, remembered who we were and how it must be. But our eyes did catch hold of each other, and that first, fleeting intimacy led eventually to so much more that we both knew was forbidden. I could not cross the space between us that first time, but over the following days we drew nearer to one another until we were breathing each other's air. I feel sure someone must have stolen a kiss from her before. She had more idea about it than I, but was hardly the wanton. It took a while before we did more than kiss, although those kisses ignited a fire that consumed us both in the end.

I had to tell Hugh. He was indignant at being told to go ahead of me when Catherine appeared on the path, or that I felt like walking alone that day. Indignation changed to awe when he knew the truth, and the risks we were both ready to take. But he loved knowing our secret, and loyally held it until it was a secret no more.

By the height of the summer of 1641 we had sworn eternal love and made the firm though impossible decision to marry. If necessary, we would run away together. She was certain her father would understand, and although I was much less sure of my own parents' gentle understanding I was utterly determined Catherine would be my wife. We exchanged vows in the woods one hot summer evening. Such foolishness! But such sweetness too. It seemed important to shed our clothes entirely, rather than the half-dressed, fumbling lovemaking we were used to. I can remember it as if it were yesterday, though not why being naked had seemed so vital to our vows. It was the first time I had seen her body clearly, and she mine. We became shy all over again, and serious, as if we were doing something very grown-up. Then, the sun hot on our skin reminded us of our passion. I remember the fecund scent of the mossy ground we lay upon, and the sun edging its brilliance ever lower through the branches, illuminating our warm nakedness with spots of constantly shifting light. Afterwards I lay beside her, with my head on her breast.

I thought I should perhaps say to her, 'What if there were a babe?' But we had not spoken of it before, and it had not come to pass. I formed the words in my head, but could not utter them.

For shyness, or because if I said it she might deny me in future? I think it was a little of both, and in addition it was a woman's matter. Not for me to speak of it.

We lay for a while longer, drunk with love, but then a cloud covered the sun. Catherine shivered, both with the lack of warmth and the sudden fear that we might be discovered. We scrambled into our clothes and spent a while picking leaves and twigs from our hair. We could not bear to part, but knew we must, and so we told each other that it would not be long before we were together for ever.

It was full autumn by the time I realised she was seriously unhappy. We had talked and talked of what to do. We could never quite decide how to tell our parents of our decision. Should we call a joint meeting? But that was frightening in the extreme! I simply could not imagine the six of us sitting down calmly to discuss the future. We must each tell our own family, but should I tell mine before I had formally asked her father for her hand? My duty was certainly to do so. I was still only sixteen and not free to marry without my father's permission. What if he prevented it? In a small corner of my mind I knew for certain that he would. He had never shown any interest in taking my feelings or opinions seriously. The prospect of his heir marrying beneath him, when there were daughters with fortunes and dynasties to join elsewhere, would rile him to explosive anger. We would never be joined with his blessing, so how to proceed?

One afternoon Catherine arrived with a book in her basket. It was her mother's herbal, the same one I knew to be in our house.

'What's this for? Do you mean to physic me?' I was trying to tease her to get a smile, because her face was even more doleful than the last time we had met.

24

She flopped down onto the fallen log we had made our own and handed it to me. 'I am so afraid, Thomas! I have a lump in my belly. I'm afraid I'm going to die like Mistress Foley did last winter.' Tears began to trickle down her cheeks and I put my arms around her.

My heart began to thump in my chest. 'You're not going to die, Catherine. Mistress Foley was old and . . .'

'Young people can die of lumps, Thomas. You know they can.'

Indeed, a boy of eight had died that spring, of a lump in his neck.

'I've been wanting to look in Mother's herbal for advice, but I never get enough time alone at home, so I brought it with me.' She began to cry in earnest. When she was done I put her gently from me and opened the book. I had no idea what to look for. There were so many remedies, and each had so many uses. Should I look for those under the sign of cancer, or those that were prescribed for internal problems? Could Catherine's problem be exclusive to women? They did, I know, have disorders unique to their gender, but what they might be I had little idea, and I was loath to question her. I didn't want to set her crying again, and frankly, I was embarrassed to ask any intimate questions, even if I had known what to ask.

'Surely,' I said, 'you should tell your mother. And you should see a doctor. If money is a problem I can pay.'

'Don't be foolish!' she said. 'How could I explain that you have offered to pay?'

'Of course you are right. I'm sorry. I wasn't thinking. But I do not know how else to help you. You must consult someone in the village if a doctor is out of the question.'

She clung to me. 'I am so frightened, Thomas. What if they say it must be cut out? I couldn't bear it!'

I didn't think I could bear it either, but I could not say that. 'It's almost certainly a small matter,' I said. 'You probably just need to be purged, and soon will be fine again. But you must go and see the herbalist, or tell your mother. She will know what you must do.'

She looked at me with such fear in her eyes that I knew my talking was not enough.

'I will study my mother's herbal too,' I said. 'Between us we will make you well again. I promise.'

We neither of us had much appetite for loving that afternoon. Soon, after a last, clinging embrace I watched with anxious love as she picked her way along the deer track towards the main path through the woods. Almost out of sight, she paused to free her skirt of a troublesome bramble. She turned then, and gave me a last, sad little parting wave. I kissed my hand, blew her the kiss and then she was gone.

# CHAPTER FOUR

Parents hold all the playing cards when it comes to their children. I think now that Catherine must have confessed to her mother about me, while so distressed about her health. It is easy for secrets to spill out under those circumstances. For the rest of that week I was unaware of any change in our situation. I did as I had promised and studied the herbal kept in our house. Under other conditions I would have found it a surprisingly fascinating read. But I was looking to cure my love of an unspecified disease, and there were too many questions to answer. I was frantic with worry, and there was no one I could speak to as I considered it unseemly to discuss my mistress's health with my brother.

Catherine and I had agreed to meet the following

Wednesday afternoon, but before that, on the Saturday, my father came unexpectedly home. Time has hardly dimmed the memory. First, Hugh was summoned and given a thorough whipping for knowingly keeping my secret. Then I was summoned. If he had thought to cow me by treating my brother so harshly, he was mistaken. Rather than make me meek, his behaviour set such a fury in my head I had difficulty in speaking coherently. He did not, however, request explanations, and my protestations of love simply made him more vicious. I had always known the risk to me, but our father's cruelty to Hugh made me hate him more than I thought possible. I could not prevent tears of pain running down my face during my own punishment, but I was thinking of Catherine, and planning, as each blow landed, to run away with her that night. Hugh could come too. I would look after them both.

Such naivety! Of course we were securely locked in our room. How could it have been otherwise? With great generosity Hugh forbore blaming me for his hurts. Indeed, he was anxious in case I believed it was he who had betrayed us. I am quite sure he had not. At fourteen he was impressively steadfast. I told him I had decided to leave with Catherine as soon as we were released. I did not know how, but I was utterly determined. Of course, Hugh would not go with us. He was more naturally dutiful than I, and besides, he had not fallen in love. However, he offered all the help he could give when the time came. He offered to take a message to Catherine as soon as he could, and so all that evening, while nursing our hurts, we plotted my future like the children we were.

The following morning, Hugh was taken to his lessons with our tutor, but I was left in our room. A little later my father

28

entered. I tried not to shrink from him, and stood defiant, but he gave me no opportunity to speak. All he said was this:

'She has been taken away. It will be worse for you both if you try to find her. I cannot forgive you for treating one of my tenants with such contempt, so you will have to strive hard to eventually regain my regard. That is all.'

Not long after that, I found myself bundled into a coach with two of my father's servants. It was clear they been charged with preventing my escape. For a while I sat silent, my stomach lurching even more than the coach, trying to make more escape plans. My captors were not inclined to speak to me, but after an hour or so, by my reckoning, I could not prevent myself from trying to get a response.

'Surely it would be no harm to inform me where we are going?'

Something in my voice must have awakened pity in them. They looked at each other and after a moment one said, 'We are taking you to university, sir.'

I was astonished. I had asked my father to send me to Oxford several times. I had a great interest in many subjects that our tutor knew little about and longed to attend the university at Oxford, but my father had always refused, saying that there was time enough for that. Now I was going to get my wish, under circumstances that could have scarcely been less welcome.

I comforted myself by realising that Oxford was not so very far. If I could discover where my love had been taken, all was not lost. All the same, I had no idea how I could find out. Hugh and I had wasted the time we'd had together. Instead of planning wild escape plans for Catherine and myself we should have worked out how Hugh and I could communicate in secret, should we need. At the very least we should have devised a code to use in letters, much as spies are reputed to do. We had not done that, and now I would not be able to write to him of anything but the most insubstantial news from university. Would he think to get a letter to me when he found out where Catherine was? Would he be *able* to find out? Indeed, would he even be told where *I* had gone? We had not thought to be isolated from one another. I could not write and ask Hugh or indeed my mother for any information, and there was no one else to ask. A thousand thoughts ran through my mind but all was tangled and imprecise. To feel sorry for myself would be childish, but however hard I admonished myself, self-pity insisted on pricking my eyes. My father had banished me from home, and had not even allowed me to make my farewells to the people I loved most in the world. How could I bear it? But of course I bore it, and, false knave that I named myself, I couldn't help looking forward to Oxford.

It was the first time I had stayed in that city. I couldn't deny my pleasure at seeing those wonderful buildings, and country fellow that I was, I couldn't help gawping at the citizens and students in the streets. I would be one of their number, which held the promise of new friends and a new way of life. I insisted to myself that I would hate every moment away from my Catherine, but the lure of the university was too powerful to resist.

My lodgings were comfortable, even though my father's two servants showed no sign of leaving me to enjoy them alone. It seemed my father did not trust my studies to immediately dilute my attachment to Catherine. No matter. I had expected as much. Indeed, their company was not unwelcome for the first few days. After all, I knew no one else.

On the morning of the first day after our arrival they handed me a letter. It was from my mother. In it she did not admonish me, but begged me to make the most of my time at the university, and not to waste it by sighing, which would do no good to anyone. She didn't mention Catherine by name, but told me a certain person known to me was not in any more physical danger than any other of her gender. *She will,* her letter went on, *with the help of your father's generosity, very soon make a good marriage, one suited to her station. There is no need, nor is it advisable for you to dwell any more on the situation. Youth is hasty, but maturity follows. Pray to God for forgiveness, work hard at your studies and know that time heals all.*

I read that letter many times, holding as it did both good news and bad. Catherine was, it seemed, in little danger from her ailment, for which I thanked God, but my father was going to use his considerable influence over his tenant to get her married with indecent haste. How better to take her away from me for ever? Knowing her lost, I felt relief at having been sent away. For how could we have borne it, living in the same place, me seeing her wed to another man, and her knowing me unreachable? This letter, far more than the whipping and banishment, turned me from a warship in full, angry sail to one hopelessly becalmed, directionless, sails hanging loose. But my mother's gentle tone and reasonable advice, the more times I read it, fell by slow degrees like a salve onto a wound. Indeed, I began to wonder if my mother had also loved and lost, before she was wed to my father. She and my father had made a dynastic match. Love would have had no part in it, and, I told myself caustically, still did not. But she would have been kept much closer by her family than my Catherine had been by hers. There would have been no opportunity for her to experience the dalliance we two had enjoyed, but it was entirely possible that she could have loved another from afar.

For a while I was kept very short of funds, with my captors overseeing every expenditure. I chafed at that, as every student did who was poor, for whatever reason, but for me the restriction did not last all term. Soon enough, my father's servants informed me that they had been recalled by him. I was to be allowed to manage my own affairs, and must write to him regular accounts of my life in Oxford. I would have an allowance, and if I overspent I must apply to him for relief. I did not intend that to be necessary!

I began to turn ever more willingly to my studies, accepting what must be. And there was much to enjoy. There were students of all ages, stations and abilities. Some boys of my station looked down on the poor scholars, and I confess I was inclined to do the same. It seems odd to me now, that while I had been prepared to marry beneath me, I resisted debating with the sons of merchants. I had not thought that the sons of dyers, smiths or builders would have anything of import to say to me, but I was wrong. Their fathers might dwell beneath mine in lands and occupation, but these students were there entirely through ability, rather than wealth or influence, and that made them interesting fellows. I had never been bested in an intellectual argument, having only my younger brother as a schoolmate. Now I was put on my mettle, because almost everyone wished to shine in debate, and some had been taught by better men than had I. Richard Darte was only a grammar-school boy from London. He was a scholar, the son of a glover, and several times he had made better arguments than me. He could have been annoying, but his clear argument and nice modesty as he made his points commended him to me, while his manners were better than some of the wealthier students. I found I could not help but like him, and somewhat to my surprise we found ourselves natural friends. His circumstances had made him determined to achieve as much as he could at the university and beyond.

'For although my father's work is honourable, and he has some standing in the community, I do not intend to follow my father into trade,' he told me one afternoon as we walked to the inn where several of us liked to meet. 'I will write a great philosophical treatise, be invited to court and advise the King.'

'Then unless I can come up with a better career we will be there together,' I told him. 'For my father is determined that I should follow him into politicking at court, but I do not wish to do what my father expects.'

Not doing what one's parent expected became a constant theme for us, and whether accident of birth, or inclination, should rule. We both voted for inclination and ability, deciding to make our own way, while having little idea how to achieve it without penury. There was for us a certain heady power in learning, or at least so we imagined. In our arrogance we worshipped our intellect, as young students are sometimes inclined to do, in a mutually congratulatory manner. It makes me laugh now to think of it: we considered ourselves so much higher than ordinary men. We knew so little, while thinking we knew much, but our ridiculous posing did no harm while it lasted. Soon enough we settled down and learnt a little humility once we realised how we only tiptoed at the edge of knowledge. I won extra regard from Richard for the very thing that had so incensed my father, namely following my heart against his wishes, which included, had he known of it, making Richard my best friend instead of cultivating higher-born students who had young sisters to marry. We were indeed the very epitome of renegades!

I think neither of our fathers would have wished us to get into fights with the city boys, but there was much animosity between the two, and while frequenting the taverns we often had the opportunity of breaking a few simple-minded heads. Fortunately, no real harm was done, and our swagger faded as our love of learning took over. There were some students who remained arrogant, but fortunately that was not our natural behaviour. As Christmas approached, in spite of our great friendship, we both began to look forward to going home, I with a little trepidation. I had received several letters from both my mother and Hugh, but nothing more pertaining to my lost love, and I had not dared mention her in my replies. Would she be in the village, a married woman, when I returned? If so, I would be bound to meet her in church, or at least see her from a distance. How could we manage ourselves? And surely she would blame me for not rescuing her.

But my father had other plans for me. I was not, he informed me by letter, to go home, but was to travel to Norfolk, where I was to stay with the family of a friend of his. The estate was large, and I was to take the opportunity to study the running of it, as well as make myself useful where I could. With the letter was a chest. It contained gifts for the Earl's family, and lengths of fabric to be made into suitable clothes of the latest fashion for me, to celebrate Christmas in a great house. Richard's eyebrows disappeared into his dark thatch of hair when I showed him the contents.

'You are so far above me you are almost beyond my sight,' he said with a sigh. 'Look at all the linen, too!' He had but two sets, which over the time we had been in Oxford had suffered much from our brawling.

When he went out I took my hitherto best linen and wrapped it around with one of the ribbons I had bought for my mother's Christmas gift. I bought her a marmelet of oranges instead, and presented my gift of linen to Richard the morning I left for Norfolk. I had a little trouble in making him accept the gift, but I told him I looked forward to him wearing it when we next wrestled.

'For it will give me something stronger to tear,' I said. 'And you know how I like a challenge!'

In the end he had the good grace to accept my gift, and I received his, a pamphlet of bawdy songs much sung in some Oxford taverns.

'You will have no excuse to be anything less than word perfect when I see you next,' he said with a grin.

'I will practise them every day!' I said. 'But I fear my singing will have to be sotto voce where I will be staying.'

My tailor had turned the fine wool and velvet into two of the most fashionable of suits, which Richard and I both greatly admired. I had sent my gifts to my family: the marmelet along with several other edible delights for my mother; a book of poetry for Hugh; and a volume of philosophy the bookseller assured me any right-minded man would cherish, for my father. I liked it, but suspected he would not. Perhaps he and Hugh could swap the gifts about if they were so inclined.

The roads being bad at this time of year, I was to ride, guided by his lordship's man, with a pack animal being provided for my box. I hoped no mishap would come to the glorious contents before I had a chance to wear them. To my surprise there were two men to accompany me, but they were for my safety, not my restraint.

'There is much unrest in the country, as you know,' said one, in an accent I had not heard before, never having been to Norfolk.

There had certainly been talk in Oxford, but I had not paid it much heed. It seemed to me that king and parliament had been at odds since he had first called it, and I was impatient that the two could not find a way to be reconciled. Of course, the execution of the Earl of Strafford earlier in the year had been a shock. I wondered several times if he had been one of the men talking to the King when I had been presented as a boy, but I had never seen his portrait, and would not have recognised him. No doubt if I had been with my father now, he would have drummed into me all the details and reasons for and against the recent bad mood in London and elsewhere, but I was not with him, and was no more interested in politics than I had been before.

Two hard days of riding without incident got us to Cambridge, and the following day took us north through the mud towards Ely. It had been raining for several days, but that afternoon the clouds cleared away and I saw the cathedral, which seemed to swim in the watery landscape. The horses, tired though they were, pricked their ears and stepped into a more lively pace, knowing they were almost home. We were soon riding through the Earl's estate, but the rain came on again and I was little inclined to look about me. When we reached the house, however, I could not help but be impressed. It was a building of great grace and balance. The huge windows looked out onto formal gardens, and the large, smoking chimneys promised warmth to my sodden body. I was heartily glad to dismount and hand my reins to the lad who ran to receive them. Indoors, I was taken to my chamber, a handsome room with a good fire in the hearth. Soon, my box stood nearby and a servant unpacked while I toasted my cold feet. Not long afterwards, warm, dry and wearing one of my new suits, the green wool, with lace at the throat and wrists, I presented myself to the family.

# CHAPTER FIVE

I confess I had been missing my mother and brother all the way to Norfolk, as well as wondering about my lost love. They would be at home, making ready for Christmas, seeing friends and having fun, while I was forced to spend the festival with strangers. And yet, when I nervously entered the room, I was aware of a warm, lively atmosphere, with lots of chatter. In spite of their nobility, the whole family, Lady Mary and her three daughters, greeted me with the greatest friendliness.

'I'm sorry, the rain must have made your journey very trying, but you are here now, and we will do our best to make you merry,' said the Lady Mary. 'My husband has been called away on business, but we hope he will return in a few days. Meanwhile, you will have to make do with us.' She brought forward a young woman standing to her left. 'This is my eldest daughter, Eleanor.'

She was eighteen but looked older. I wondered if she was unwell. I unkindly thought her a dumpy girl, very unlike her delightful sisters. She gave me a rather awkward curtsey, but her smile was friendly enough.

'Alas, Eleanor's husband is also attending the King, so we are a very female company. This is Aphra, my second daughter.'

Aphra looked, I thought, to be a little older than me but I soon discovered that at just sixteen she was slightly younger.

'And this is the baby of the family, Aurelia.'

Aurelia frowned as she curtsied, but almost instantly grinned at me. 'We will entertain you very well,' she said. 'You won't have time to be homesick, and I'm seven. I'm not a baby,' she added rapidly. 'Do you like shuttlecock?'

'Really, Aurelia,' said Aphra. 'Poor Master Thomas is exhausted with his travels and you propose to tire him even more!'

'I didn't mean play it *now*.'

'I haven't played for a long time,' I told Aurelia, unable to hold back a smile. 'But I used to like it. If this rain stops . . .'

'Oh no!' she said in a hurry. 'We play in the library when the weather is bad. It's perfect for it, and Mother says it is important to take exercise, even in inclement weather.'

I couldn't help laughing, she was so earnest. 'In that case,' I said, 'I will make sure to play with you at the earliest opportunity, if that is agreeable to the rest of your family.'

By the time we had eaten and the two younger girls had shown me a good portion of the house, I was feeling quite at home. When Eleanor and Aphra excused themselves shortly after Aurelia had been taken to bed, I thought it advisable to make my goodnight as well, but Lady Mary stopped me.

'Stay a moment,' she said.

I sat back down. She looked suddenly so serious I wondered what was amiss.

'If my husband had been here he would have said what it is now my duty to say in his place.' She regarded me steadily, and after a few seconds I found myself unable to hold her gaze.

'You are here because your father thought it wise to extend your time away from your home, but he did not want you to have a Christmas without a family to share it. We are happy to have you here, and will do all we can to make your stay agreeable, but I wish you to know that there is to be no repeat of the unfortunate behaviour that led to you being sent to Oxford.'

I found myself blushing. I was so embarrassed I couldn't find any words to speak, but bent my head and mumbled into the fine wool of my suit.

'My daughters will never be alone with you. There must always be one of our women in attendance, or myself. My husband and I wish you to know that we do not think ill of you. It is easy to lose your heart to someone unsuitable when you are young. We are not unsympathetic to your feelings, but if there is any hint of improper behaviour you will be sent immediately back to Oxford. Do you understand?'

I looked at her then, though I still felt the heat in my face. 'I promise I will not behave improperly. You will have no reason to send me away. And I thank you for your generosity in having me here.'

She nodded. 'That's good. I'm glad. So it will not be mentioned again, will it?'

'No. There will be no need. I will remember.'

She smiled. 'In that case, do you play cards? It is not late, and you might like a small glass of wine.'

Lady Mary didn't allow the awkwardness between us to

continue for more than a few minutes, and I was grateful to her for that. If I had immediately gone to bed I would still have felt that awkwardness in the morning, but she made it vanish over a good game, amusing conversation and a glass of wine. The girls must have been told something about their mother's private conversation with me because they were careful not to find themselves alone with me, but all was done so naturally that I didn't feel myself particularly singled out, and their early bedtime was not repeated during the rest of my stay.

The women of this family made it easy to like them, and very soon I began to feel as if I had known them all my life. Christmas is a time of much social celebration, which meant that they were invited to other great houses. They took me about with them and soon I had other young men to converse with. I was invited to hunt, play cards and even take a small role in a masque. In fact, I believe I was of some assistance in escorting the family, being the only male, as their men continued to be away with the King.

Having written to inform Richard where I was, I soon heard from him. He was in London with his family, and wrote of unease in the city, with many people very much against the King, and his French, papist queen. He asked if I would like to visit him. His parents would be happy to meet me. I missed his company but was sure my father would not countenance such a visit. Besides, it would have been deeply discourteous to my hosts in Norfolk to abandon them, so I regretfully declined.

In Norfolk, apart from the various discussions when we were in company, the family kept largely away from politics, and I was happy to follow their lead. I think Lady Mary was concerned for her husband, but she was at pains not to show it in front of her daughters. I suppose I should have worried about my father, as part of a court that seemed to be so roundly disliked by a noisy portion of the King's subjects. But we concentrated on the exchange of presents, attending church and the singing of Christmas songs.

In early January I had a letter from my father, commanding me under no circumstances to visit London, and also not to consider returning to Oxford until he had given me leave to do so. I showed the letter to Lady Mary in some confusion, but she was reassuring.

'You are welcome here for as long as your father wishes it,' she said. 'It makes sense not to travel about the country while the mood is uncertain. We are a long way from Oxford, and further from your home in Gloucestershire. Things will no doubt be resolved before too long. Until then, let us enjoy your company. I do hope Eleanor's husband is able to return before she is brought to bed. I know she longs for her husband to be near when the baby is born.'

She laughed at the expression on my face. 'You did not realise she was with child? Don't be embarrassed. Young men, and not such young men, often do not notice. Perhaps her condition will explain why she is less lively than her sisters these days.'

That afternoon, it being another very wet day, Aphra and Aurelia decided to set up various activities in the long gallery, which also held the Earl's large library. When we sat down after a game of skittles, the girls set me to cutting up apples for us as refreshment. Aurelia took the little knife when I had finished and spun it on the table.

'To whomever the knife points, that person must make a confession!' she announced.

Aphra rolled her eyes most amusingly, and groaned. 'Can't we eat our apples in peace?'

The blade had come to rest pointing at Aurelia, and she took no notice of her sister. 'My confession is that I ate the last of the gingerbread!'

Aphra and I laughed. 'I wonder you dare confess such a thing,' I teased.

The next spin pointed at Aphra. 'I saw you take it!' she said to Aurelia.

Aurelia pretended to be outraged. 'That's not a confession!'

'Yes, it is,' said Aphra. 'I confess I saw you. You took two large pieces. And you should thank me for not telling on you to our mother!'

Aurelia spun the knife again and this time it turned towards me.

'You don't have to play,' said Aphra, seeing my hesitation.

'It's all right. Um . . . I confess that I didn't realise Eleanor was with child until your mother told me this morning.'

The girls stared at me, and for a moment I was afraid I had been too indelicate. Then Aurelia gave a most unladylike whoop of laughter. 'How could you not have noticed?'

Aphra glared at her.

'It's all right,' I said with a laugh. 'Your mother said that, like me, many men don't notice such things, but I did and do still feel foolish about it.'

'That was a magnificent confession,' said Aurelia generously. 'We've all known for a long time, but to begin with, poor Eleanor was quite convinced there was something wrong with her stomach. Even the doctor couldn't be sure until the baby quickened.'

I had been laughing along with Aurelia at my lack of observation, but then a thought took my breath away, like a bad fall from a horse. Aphra, noticing my sudden confusion, took up the knife. 'That's enough now,' she told her sister. 'It's not really seemly to speak of such things in company. Go and set up the skittles again. I want to see if you can beat me this time.'

With an apologetic glance in my direction she hustled her sister away. I selected a book at random from the shelves and took my leave of them.

'I am going to read in my chamber for a while,' I said. 'Unless I can be of any further service to you this afternoon.'

Having been released, I retired to my chamber but the book lay unopened on my bed. I stood at the window and looked out at the bare trees, dripping rain onto the dark earth below. Catherine had thought she was seriously ill, but Mother had seemed to contradict that. Was it possible . . . ? When did a baby first quicken? How long before she would have known, and if she were with child, when would the baby be born? Had it already? I had never taken any notice of such things, but I was fairly sure it took less than a year to breed. Did I have a son or daughter somewhere?

I cannot explain how I felt. There was a swelling in my chest, and I could not sit or stand still. Although it was still raining a little I went with all haste to the stables, and commanded a horse made ready. I rode him out gently, but could tell he felt as I. He chafed at the bit, and tossed his great head impatiently. He was a big animal, had been cooped up in the stable all day, and needed exercise. As soon as we were out on the track I gave him his head. I scarcely felt the drizzle in my face as we galloped down towards a small copse by the lake. Around the lake we went, then uphill until we could enter the woods. I pulled him up to a walk, wary of being caught by low-lying branches. The trees were still dripping, but my hat stopped most of them from drenching my head.

What should I do? What *could* I do? All I knew was that I wanted desperately to know if I was a father or not. My love for Catherine had been slowly fading as I came to terms with the fact that she was lost to me. Now it came roaring back, or perhaps, more accurately, it was desire for a possible child of my blood that had me in its grip. How could men carelessly father children, and then refuse to acknowledge them, as I knew some did? I had always assumed that I would marry and breed children one day, though had not thought to be a father so soon. But if I had a living child I wanted to see it, to acknowledge it, to support it in some way and to give its mother the care she would need! I could not prevent the tumult of feelings that assailed me.

My horse made his own decision when it came to a turning in the track. He wanted his stable now, so I let him take us back. The rain had stopped, and although it was too late for winter sunshine, the afternoon was not bitterly cold. I could walk for a little in the garden, before I returned indoors. Perhaps that would settle me enough to at least give a semblance of peace on my face before I faced the family, even though I was still inwardly in turmoil. To my dismay, as I walked away from the stables in the direction of the garden, two figures emerged from the house. It was Aphra and a servant. Aphra came eagerly towards me.

'I saw you return on Arthur and hoped to catch you before you went indoors.'

'Is that his name?' I said. 'I did not think to ask it of the stable boy.'

'I named him when I was a very little girl,' she said. 'He was so big I thought he must be a king of horses.'

I smiled at her. 'Have you ever ridden him?'

'Not I! He was my father's horse, trained for war, but now Father has a new one, and poor Arthur must stay, dreaming in his stable.'

'Like King Arthur in his cave,' I said.

She nodded. For a few moments we walked together in silence with the maid following on behind. Then she spoke all in a rush.

'I hope you don't mind me coming out to you in this way, but Aurelia is being impossible. I simply had to go for a walk, and hoped to do it in better company than with an annoying child.'

'Then I am glad you found me.' I was not ready for female company, but I could hardly tell her that.

She looked back to make sure, no doubt, that her servant was at a suitable distance. When she spoke again she was direct, as all her family were. 'I could not help but notice our conversation in the library disturbed you.'

'It was nothing.'

'I should tell you that although Aurelia knows nothing of what brought you here, our mother spoke at length about it to me.'

She paused, and I turned away to hide my embarrassment, but she had not finished.

'I just wanted to say that if you wish to talk to a friend I would willingly be that person. I am not a foolish child like my little sister.'

Her voice had been low, and I doubt the servant could have heard, but I could not think what to say in reply.

'Perhaps I should add,' she continued, 'that until a few months ago I was to be married this Christmas, only he died of a fever in September. I don't know what it is to be a parent, but I have felt the pain of love denied.'

I could not prevent my outburst. Nor did I wish to. Anger made me speak. 'I am heartily sorry for that, but what would you have me do?' Seeing her expression, I went on in a lower voice. 'If there is a child, I wish to know, and to acknowledge it!'

She gave a sharp intake of breath. I had said much more than I should. It had been the height of indiscretion to choose

Aphra to tell, but she had put herself in my way, and I had been unable to master myself. Probably I would now find myself packed off back to Oxford, but I was too much in turmoil to care. I strode along the gravelled path, caring little to avoid the pools of water that threatened to drown the stones. I hoped that Aphra would leave me without another word, but she did not. She made haste to catch me up, her little shoes crunching and splashing their way along.

'Thomas. Stop!'

I did so, but could not look at her.

She spoke in a low but urgent voice. 'I cannot tell you what I would do in your place for I am a girl, but I can tell you what I would wish if I were the . . . lady.'

I did look at her then.

'May I continue?'

I nodded, curious in spite of myself.

'My mother told me that the person was to be married before Christmas. In that case, I feel sure her husband must be in full knowledge of the facts, and has shown himself willing to take her, and her babe, if there is one. If I were her, however I felt, I would want my life to achieve some peace after earlier storms. Do you not see how impossible it would be for her husband if you demanded a role?'

'But if there is a child, I am a father, and I would wish to take responsibility for that!'

She reached out her hand, and briefly touched my sleeve. 'We cannot always do what we wish, but what we must. Think of her. You have, I think, not come into your fortune yet, so have no means to help her. You can surely best be of service by giving way, and by giving thanks for the good man who has wedded her, and will care for her.'

'If he *is* a good man.'

'You can pray for that too.'

I felt my eyes fill with tears and fought to keep them from spilling. 'Indeed,' I said. 'I already do.'

We walked on for a few minutes without speaking. The light was going from the sky, and soon we would have to return indoors. In unspoken agreement we turned at the top of the path and retraced our steps. The house was dark against the sky, but candles were being lit in several of the rooms, lighting the great windows with a soft radiance. For a moment, a few rays of the sun broke through the clouds at the horizon, and then they were gone. I shivered, and began to walk more quickly. Aphra matched me step for step, holding her cloak around her. Just before we reached the door she touched my sleeve again.

'I will pray for it too, Thomas. And do remember that I am your friend.' She turned to her servant. 'Come on, Frances. I fear it might rain again, and Mother will scold!' She shot me a brief smile and then hurried in. I wanted to thank her, but was too late. I made sure I did so at the next opportunity.

We had been friends before, but now there was a greater and welcome understanding between us. She had also calmed me more than my ride had done. Sweet Aphra was wiser than me, for all her youth, and I was pleased and grateful to have such a friend. I don't know if she spoke to her mother about our conversation in the garden, but there was no reckoning from it. Indeed, if anything Lady Mary seemed more comfortable at her daughter and me spending time in conversation. I was still at pains to behave properly at all times, and we were never alone, but the servants, and even Lady Mary, gave us enough space for our discourse to be at least partly private. I mustn't give the impression that we were always in serious discussion. Most of the time Aurelia was with us, and there was much ridiculous chatter and lots of laughter. But sometimes, when Aurelia had been taken to bed, Aphra and I would start discussing the natural sciences, or poetry. She wanted to know what I had learnt at Oxford, was prepared to dispute with me, and she had the best of me on several occasions. We got on enormously well.

There was word from our fathers and Eleanor's husband just after Christmas Day. Separately, they informed our household that there had been more trouble between the King and his parliament. As a result, the King wished to be further away from London. There was no word of where the court would go, but there was a definite feeling of disquiet in the letters. The men would, of course, stay with the King, and my father asked if I could stay a while longer in Norfolk. Lady Mary was just assuring me that I was welcome to stay as long as I liked when Eleanor gave a startled whimper, and rose from her chair. Of course I rose too, and so did Lady Mary, who went at once to her daughter.

'Come,' she said to Eleanor quietly after they had exchanged brief whispers. Without further discussion she led her daughter from the room. Little Aurelia looked concerned.

'Is she all right?' she asked her remaining sister.

'Of course!' said Aphra, rather abruptly. She turned at once to me. 'Will you allow Aurelia to entertain you while I leave you for a little while?' I nodded, but Aurelia was not content.

'Where are you going?'

'Just stay there!'

Having not realised that Eleanor was pregnant, but now knowing, I guessed that her time being very near, perhaps it had come, and that the older women wanted the child kept away.

'Come and teach me a new card game,' I coaxed her. Seeing her set face, I added, 'Or if you prefer, blind man's buff.'

'But there's only you and me!'

'Well, but I will promise to stay within your reach.'

She considered it. 'Then we will play. But if I don't catch you in five minutes we will stop. You mustn't make it too difficult for me.'

'I promise I won't.'

It was the beginning of a very long night. Lady Mary sent her apologies and commanded us to eat our meal without them. Aphra and I felt the seriousness of the situation, but Aurelia was all excitement at the prospect of becoming an aunt, once she had been told what was happening. However, she had thought it would all be over in a few minutes, so was very disappointed when her bedtime came and went without any news. None of us could settle to anything. When Aurelia was eventually taken, protesting, to bed, Aphra and I sat a while, but our conversation was desultory, for all we could think of was of Eleanor's travails, and for them to be safely over. Having been unsettled by the atmosphere in the house, I also became more concerned about the reasons for my extended visit. Both of us could find plenty of reasons to fret, and neither of us could think of a distracting subject. In the end, Aphra got to her feet.

'I find I cannot settle until I have spoken to my mother and seen my sister again,' she said.

'Of course. I understand your concern. Please tell your mother that if there is any service I can do, I am more than willing to do it.'

Being left on my own, I again read the letter my father had recently sent.

*Due to the unrest in the country you will not be likely to celebrate your birthday with your brother*, he wrote, not mentioning my mother. *But with this letter come some items for you to share on that day with your hosts, and my gift to you.*

So I would be here for at least another two months! Surely he could not consider the country too dangerous for me to get back to Oxford? I loved being there, wanted to resume my studies and be with my Oxford friends, especially Richard. But it could not be helped. At least with the Earl's letter written in a similar vein to his family, warning them to take care, I could not think that my father was still trying to punish me.

So it happened that I celebrated my eighteenth birthday away from home, but with the very best second family I could have wished for, now extended with a sweet little babe too. The weather was dreadful that month; some days brought sharp frosts and icy winds, others, heavy rain with watery sunlight that appeared as if in apology at the end of the day. I was glad of my buff coat when I went out, but mostly we stayed indoors, the whole family spending much time in the library, where we were all kept occupied in admiring the infant boy.

On the morning of my birthday they all gathered around while I opened the box which contained the presents from my father. At the top were plenty of sweetmeats of all kinds, which I gave to Lady Mary for us all. Underneath, wrapped in cloth, were my gifts. They were not at all what I had expected, not that I had any particular expectation of generosity from my father. These, however, were certainly generous. The smaller parcel held a pair of pistols, with all the materials to carry them and cause them to fire. I had never had a pistol, and viewed them with interest and a keen desire to try them. The girls and their mother murmured, whether in admiration or at a loss for words, I could not tell. At the bottom of the box lay a handsome hanger and well-worked belt. This was even more to my liking. I had been taught swordsmanship, so felt comfortable with it, and proud, as I tried it on. It was, I could tell, a serious weapon, a long way distant from the toy sword I had worn at my breeching as a little boy.

'You will be able to defend us from the mob!' said Aurelia, with great glee.

'Indeed I will,' I replied with a smile. I looked at Aphra but she was not smiling.

'I hope you will not need to,' is all she said.

At the end of March another letter came from my father, who was now with the King in York.

*Take leave of your hosts, and ride home with all haste*, my father's letter instructed. *Before you go, take instruction on how to fire your weapons. Trust no one on the road, but put your faith in God.*

# CHAPTER SIX

I read my father's letter several times, becoming more alarmed each time I did so. *I find myself unable to return, and need you to represent me on urgent business,* he wrote. *If Lady Mary will furnish you with a good horse I will recompense his lordship for it. Keep your wits about you and remain armed at all times. Speak not of your family loyalties or of politics to anyone. Make all speed, but take care not to drive your horse beyond his stamina. A swift horse can save your life in extremis. Write to me when you get home. I trust letters will be there for you and your mother by the time you arrive.*

I took the letter to Lady Mary, who had the same day received letters from her husband, who was also with the King in York.

'My husband commands me to give you a horse,' she said, her calm voice going some way to soothe my severe disquiet.

'Perhaps the one you have been riding would suit you?'

I gave her a bow. 'Thank you. Indeed it would, for I think we understand each other well.'

'Good.'

I mentioned my need for instruction for my pistols and she told me to wait.

'I am just about to summon our steward. He will be able to provide you with the best person. I will also order your packing done, if you select what you will need on your journey. Everything else can go in your box, and pray God it will follow you safely on a sturdy animal.'

'My father has not told me why so much haste is necessary.' I could hear the wobble in my voice, and hoped she could not. I was near to tears, and inwardly berated myself for my childishness. Was I not a man of eighteen? But I was untried, and it would be a long, solitary journey home.

'Perhaps there is no specific reason,' she said. 'Except for a general anxiety about the mood in the country.'

I had handed her my letter as I might to a parent, so she could read for herself the request for a horse and instruction in the use of my weapon. She read it intently, gave me a look of affection and handed it back.

'He does say there is business to attend to at home.'

'Yes.' I looked at the letter doubtfully. 'I wonder what it can be.' She could not enlighten me, and did not try.

I returned to my chamber and packed the saddlebag I had used on my journey here. My father had never given me any real responsibility for anything, but had only given me duties to obey without question. With the serious tone of the letter and the sword and pistols as birthday gifts, a rising feeling of panic ran through my body. At the same time, I could not deny that an amount of excitement was there too. I had done my penance. Suddenly I was being treated as an adult by a father who had never really treated me as any more than an irritation. He appeared to be giving me some responsibility, and so, in spite of my stomach's rebellion, I knew I was more than ready for it – assuming I could safely negotiate the long journey without getting lost or into trouble. I also longed to see Hugh and my mother again. Maybe, I allowed myself to hope, I might discover if I were a father or not. I would not forget Aphra's advice on that matter. I would not be anything other than discreet, but to *know*, that was the thing.

I spent much of the day learning all that was necessary about my weapons. I needed more practice, but by the time the short day had come to an end I was ready enough, and in a fever of anxiety to face my fears and be gone. Lady Mary counselled me to wait until daylight.

'I will send a man with you, to serve and protect you. He will be at the door at first light. Meanwhile you must eat, and rest before your journey.'

'Thank you.' Those two words hardly sufficed. I could have thrown my arms around her and kissed her, but of course I didn't. Her expression, however, gave me reason to suppose she realised my feelings very well. On reflection I realised that she would never have let me go unaccompanied. I like to think it was not entirely that she had been charged with my care these past months, but also because of the affection she felt towards me, of which she had not made a secret. Whatever the reason, I was heartily thankful, and my trepidation at the journey faded to nothing.

Aurelia had already gone to bed, but Aphra had not. She waited until her mother had left the room before coming close. She looked away from me and spoke low, so that not only the servant couldn't hear, but also that I struggled to make out what she said. 'I wish you did not have to go.'

Before I could reply she was gone.

I sat on for a while, drank a glass of wine and paced for some time in the library. I was not willing to admit to myself how much I would miss Aphra, especially now I was about to depart. I retired to bed, but for a long time couldn't sleep. At last I fell into an uneasy doze, and was woken before light by a knock on my door.

A servant brought light, and water for me to wash. I dressed quickly and went down the stairs. All was quiet. On the table were bread and meats, as well as some beer. I made my solitary breakfast and received a parcel of food for my journey. I asked for paper and the means to write, and left a quick note of thanks to Lady Mary for her hospitality, also sending my wishes for the continued health of Eleanor and that of the babe. I left it on the table and told the servant that he should give it to Lady Mary when the family was up, and at a convenient moment for her.

I could not hear rain on the windows, so could hope the weather was at least dry. I was buckling on my sword when a slight noise made me glance up. There, holding a candle and wrapped in a woollen robe, was little Aurelia. Her hair was awry and I guess she had leapt from her bed not two minutes earlier.

'I wanted to say farewell!'

Before I could prevent her she threw herself at me and gave me a warm embrace. I could not help but hug her back, but as soon as I could, I put her from me.

'I am glad,' I said. 'I wanted to say farewell too, but thought it would be too early for you to rise.'

'Something woke me,' she said. 'And I knew I had to come straight away. Now I must go back to bed before mother hears and scolds me.' She turned and made her way back to the door in her bare feet. At the last she turned again. 'Make sure you come back,' she said. 'I will be very cross with you if you don't!'

With a fond smile I watched her skip up the stairs and disappear into her room.

I had been assured by the groom that there would be furniture on the saddle to hold my pistols, so they waited by my modest pack. My boots were on, and I was wearing my buff coat against the cold. I put on my cloak and took up my hat. The shutters had been pulled back, and already I could see a slight paling of the night. At any moment, no doubt, the servant, Mark, who seemed a steady fellow and was to accompany me, would be at the door with my horse. I went out into the hallway and there, hurrying down the stairs, fully dressed but a little unkempt, was Aphra!

'I came to say goodbye,' she said like her sister. 'But I know I must not hold you up.'

'I am happier than I can say that you have come,' I said, realising how true it was. 'I would have been very sad to go without taking my leave of you. I have already had a brief visit from Aurelia.'

'Really?' Aphra laughed. 'She is a law unto herself, that girl.'

'And delightful, as you all are.'

I saw her cheeks redden and moved to lessen her confusion. I went to the table and picked up the note. 'Please give your mother this, which I wrote, not expecting to see any of you.'

'Thank you.' She hesitated. 'And would you wish me to write to you, with news of my family from time to time?'

I felt my heart lift. 'I would like that very much! For I wish to know how the baby Henry does, and I will especially miss our conversations and debates.'

'In that case, perhaps we can prolong them, at least for a while, on paper.'

'Then I look forward to debating with you by letter.' I paused for a moment. 'Your mother has been kind enough to give me Arthur for my journey.'

For the first time she smiled, and the smile was mirrored in her eyes. 'I'm so glad! He will keep you safe until we meet again.'

For a moment I thought she was going to embrace me as her sister had done, but she did not. There was nothing more to say. I bowed to her, and put on my hat. A servant appeared with news of the horses' arrival. I looked at Aphra and gave her a smile. She returned it, but this time it seemed with courage rather than pleasure.

'Pray God go with you!' Her voice was suddenly loud. Even the servant turned to look, but she was departing up the stairs like her sister, without a backward glance.

I went into the grey morning, greeted Mark and mounted the horse, speaking his name so I would not forget.

# CHAPTER SEVEN

The weather was dry to begin with, and the road passable without too much difficulty. However, the next day, the weather turned against us and was inhospitable the rest of the way home. At first it was no more than a light drizzle that sent the smell of sweating horse and wet leather into my nostrils. By early afternoon rain had turned to sleet, and then snow. On the third day we were not so very far from Oxford, but the snow came on so hard we were almost blinded by it. I could recall no nearby trees to shelter under, and the way was featureless and bleak. We were soon, men and horses both, turned from dark to white, the only colour in the snowy world the fast-increasing mud being churned by our horses' hooves. My hands in their handsome gloves were soon so chilled that I marvelled I could still grip the reins. No travelling clothes could keep us warm in the constant snow, blowing as it did with cruel spite into every chink. We had to find shelter, which was why, with eager gratitude, we made at once for the barn that suddenly reared like a ghost out of the storm at the side of the road.

In my naivety, I eagerly dismounted and pushed into the barn before Mark could warn me. I had not considered for one moment that others might have taken the same shelter, and my carelessness almost cost me my life. For ragged men were within, and in a moment they had my horse's bridle, and a knife at my throat. I had no room to draw my sword, and my pistols were not primed, nor were they to hand. The ruffian's blade was on the side of my neck and I knew I was very near death.

The touch of steel on my neck filled me full up with fear, and although it was but moments, time seemed to slow down, as if to make me feel entirely each of the last few seconds of my life. Some things became so clear it was as if I watched them through a lens. The snow melting on Arthur's forelock, and his rolling eye, his head jerking away from the grip of the man who would steal him. The stink of the man's rotting breath, and the wet sore at the corner of his mouth. As he pulled me close like a lover I felt my boots slip on the straw-covered floor as I fought not to fall. He wanted me down, and dead, and was near to getting his wish.

A sudden scream came from one of his fellows, and at once ceased. It must have been him that fell against the other side of my horse, making him rear. My adversary had to choose between control of Arthur or of me, but the plunging of the horse pulled the hand with the knife away from me and it jerked into the horse's neck. Then the horse screamed and, suddenly released from the knife, I was that brawling Oxford student again, one who knew the value of a kick. My boot connected with the ruffian's knee and his leg gave way. He went down, pulling my horse's head with him. He should have let go of the bridle. Arthur's hooves, shod in iron, were much better weapons than my boot, and he knew how to use them. I saw our opponent's face stove in as he fell, and his frantic rolling away to try to protect himself before Arthur struck him again, but I was certain he could be no further danger to us. I gentled Arthur, though I was trembling much more than he. I thought to remount him, but before I could, another figure barged past us and out of the door before I could do a thing.

It was my first real fight, and I knew I was lucky to be alive. I could not stop my shivering. I was shamed by it, and held onto Arthur's wet, steaming body to try and disguise my shaking. Mark must have seen the extent of my fear, but he kindly said nothing, affecting not to notice. He made a quick examination of the man Arthur had attacked, and the rest of the barn, before speaking to me.

'We are safe now,' he said. 'There were but three of them.'

I thanked God to have had my first experience of fighting in the company of a well-schooled war horse and an experienced servant. Between them they had certainly saved me, for my servant had slashed at the ruffian on the far side of my horse, killing him with a blow to the neck. The third man had tried to make his escape, but the servant had dispatched him too, and so he lay just by the door, his blood staining the still falling snow. Only my horse was hurt. The smeared blood on my hands alarmed my man, but I was able to reassure him as to my health, and the cut on Arthur's neck was fortunately not deep. The servant dragged all three ruffians a good way outside. I should have helped him, but found I could not, only staring with horrified indecision at the one Arthur had so injured. He groaned horribly while leaving a smear of red in the churned snow, being the only one still alive.

'What should we do?' I asked Mark.

He shook his head. 'Kill him if you want,' he said. 'But he will be dead soon enough, without our further help.'

Not being able to decide if I was being cowardly or merciful in leaving the ruffian to die alone, I pressed some clean snow onto my mount's neck instead, which soon stopped his bleeding and gave me the opportunity to calm myself.

We thought it best not to unsaddle our horses, but there was water in the barn, and we had oats with us. As the horses snuffed and huffed at the straw on the floor, we two made ourselves as comfortable as we could. It was cold, but we were out of the wind and there was a heap of straw, into which we thrust our frozen legs. During our shelter in the barn I discovered that the servant loaned to me had fought on the continent before entering his lordship's service. He was much alarmed by nearly having failed to keep me safe, while I praised him for his care.

'I made a grave error in not warning you against entering so fast,' he said to me.

'I am embarrassed to have done so,' I said. 'I will not make that green mistake again. You have not only saved me, but also instructed me to be more wary in future. And so I thank you.'

By the time we were somewhat warmer, and the horses rested, we discovered the snow had stopped and the afternoon was clear but frosty. Already the mud and snow churned up at the entrance to the barn had become stiff, and the fresh snow crackled as we led our horses out into it. We were not so very far from Oxford but it was a slow business getting there. With the snow obliterating the road, we at times were hard put to know quite where it was, and we dared not set our mounts to any more than a walk in case they stumbled into a hole and became lame. At last, as the sky began to grow grey we could see the towers and spires of the city ahead and managed to reach our inn before it was quite dark.

The next day was no better. A thaw brought mud with the consistency of porridge, which we slithered through all the way to Gloucestershire, and home. Still, we managed to reach the house not long after dark, with no serious mishap, and for that I was most grateful. If we had been in a coach I daresay we might not have made it in a fortnight, and most likely not at all. As it was, it took no more than four long days.

Once home again I realised how much I had missed the hills and valleys. Norfolk was a very flat and watery landscape, beautiful in its own way, but nothing to compare, I thought, with my own county. As we turned in at the gates and made our way up the road to the house, I was in a fever of excitement, though I hid it from Mark, not wanting him to think me a mere child. But then the dogs began to bark, and the door opened, revealing not just my mother and brother but also my dog, who at my dismounting capered around me like a thing gone mad. How could I not show my pleasure at this greeting?

There was no reticence with my mother. She gave me a hearty embrace, as did my brother. It had been only months since I had seen them, but it felt like a decade. Hugh had grown, and it appeared I had not, for he was now near to my own height. Our mother could not keep the smile from her face, and both Hugh and I were the same.

There was no talk of letters or commands; indeed, we none of us mentioned my father until I had bathed and eaten. It was a great luxury to immerse myself in warm, fragrant water, and I was most grateful to my mother for thinking of it. It was no small business to fill the bath, and so it usually came out no more than twice a year. I lay within, relaxing my joints and muscles after several days of hard riding, while Hugh sat beside me on a stool, chafing me to hurry up and finish my lounging so he could avail himself of the water before it was too cold. At first we were giddy with jokes and hilarity, renewing our happiness at seeing one another, while he told me how dull he had been here while I was away. Then I talked of Oxford, and then of Norfolk, and the family I had stayed with. At last, when his eager catching up with my life was done, I raised the subject that had followed me all the way home.

'Do you have any news of Catherine? Is she married?'

Hugh kept his voice low. 'She is no longer in the village, and I dared not ask direct questions of any. Mother, thinking no doubt that you would ask me, told me yesterday that she is married to a farmer and living at some distance, mistress of her own home. I do not think Mother to be telling me an untruth. I'm sorry, but I'm sure it is so.'

Was I sorry? Part of me was. Our love had been so exciting, and so tender, but time and new experiences had gone some way to cool it. I was sorry I had caused both of us anguish, and prayed with all my heart for her to have made a good match with a kind man, and to be happy. But a goodly part of me was content at how things were. Staying with the family in Norfolk had shown me that there was more than one comely, intelligent girl in the world. Indeed, my parting from both Aurelia and Aphra had been bittersweet. I would miss them both, in very different ways. But there was one thing that still plagued me and I must ask my brother about it.

'And is there talk in the village? About a babe, I mean?'

Hugh looked at me sharply. 'If there is, I have not heard it, but then I don't frequent the low inns hereabouts.' And then, more quietly, 'Did she tell you she was with child?'

I shook my head. It was too complicated to explain. If she was with child or sick, had women's complaints or was beginning a natural process, I simply didn't know. I did want to, but I had better let it go.

There was much else to think about, since letters from my father to us all demanded our full attention. In mine he expressed his pleasure in knowing I had left *that hotbed of parliamentarian displeasure, the county of Norfolk*, and hoped the Earl had made arrangements for the defence of his home and family against *all and sundry who might wish them ill, from whatever quarter*. That alarmed me. Did he not trust the Earl's many servants to do their duty? My father commanded me and my brother to take charge of organising the defence of our own home, taking advice from our mother and the steward, who he trusted completely. Our father did not expect any trouble, *but it behoves us to make sensible preparations in these uncertain times*.

'The unrest is due to arguments between the King and his parliament,' said Hugh. 'How should that affect us? We have nothing to do with those matters here.'

'But your father is with the King, and everyone knows it,' said Mother.

'Unless things have changed over the past year, our father is not a member of the privy council,' I said. 'If he is so worried for our home, why does he not come back and live quietly until the arguments are done? It will not go on for ever.'

Our mother looked angry. 'Your father has two sons,' she said. 'It is a son's duty to support his parent, and you, Thomas, are the eldest. This estate will be yours in time to come and you are more than old enough to order things while he does his duty to the King. He may not be a member of the council, but the King likes him to be at court, and so he will be there until His Majesty wishes it no more. Furthermore, you must realise that not all hereabouts are for the King. Do you not know that where money goes out, resentment comes in?'

'It's the clothiers,' said Hugh, who was much better informed than me. 'Their trade is in great difficulties it seems, and so there is poverty, and hunger roundabout with the weavers falling into penury, being not so needed by their masters.'

'I have been away, and am somewhat ignorant of the situation,' I said, feeling ashamed that our mother's scolding had been well justified. Dislike for my father had also coloured my obvious duty. 'I am sorry,' I said. 'You are right. I will speak to the steward directly. Hugh and I will look to the defence of the house, and more than anything else, your safety. And,' I added, 'I will learn more of the local situation.'

She smiled at me then, and I could tell I was forgiven.

Perhaps it does not set us in a particularly good light, but Hugh and I had tremendous fun over the next two weeks, playing at soldiers. I was assiduous in examining the house and its environs, taking a count of every able-bodied villager and servant who could be relied upon, and assembling an armoury of sorts for their use. We were not badly off for swords, pikes and poleaxes; we also had a variety of armour, much of it too old and heavy for us or our horses to carry with any comfort. None of it was new-made, nor was any well maintained, so we set some boys to clean everything and told the blacksmith to sharpen and repair all he could. We also ordered a little-used room to be set aside to store the weapons. The carpenter, blacksmith and leather worker were all kept busy, making a rack for the pikes and poleaxes, hanging the armour once it was cleaned and repaired, and generally ensuring everything was to hand and in good order. There were a few guns on the estate, so I commanded the steward to organise instruction and practice. In addition, I set my mind to munitions, obtaining powder and shot. The existing trained band was hardly more than a few men who paraded once around the village green every month, before beating their retreat to the inn. Hugh and I felt ourselves very successful in creating a band much more worthy to be called at least partially trained, although we ourselves were hardly experts.

It was not an easy time of year to set all this in motion, for spring is of course a time of great busyness in the country, when seeds must be sown and animals must be bred. However, the young boys in particular were keen to leave the plough and parade in their grandfathers' iron helmets with the sticks they had cut in the hedge. Hugh and I were at pains to encourage them, and we enjoyed marshalling them into some kind of order and discipline. At the same time I had to make sure enough work was done on the land to ensure that the crops were sown and cared for, so hunger would not be our companion in time to come. There would be little advantage to marching about in the spring if the winter brought famine. We were lucky that our family was well liked in the area. Any concern I had that Catherine's family might take against me, and cause trouble, was unfounded. I think my father had been astute in smoothing that eventuality by judicious use of coin. Certainly, when I met her father at church on the first Sunday he was all compliment and politeness. The incident, it seemed, lay all in the past, and I was much relieved at that.

After all was ordered and in place, Hugh and I took to riding around the countryside in our most martial attire. Our mother, seeing all was done well, praised our work and smiled at our wearing of a newly cleaned breast- and backplate apiece while we rode. She made no comment about our armour, and we thought ourselves the very epitome of soldiery. Only time, that great stealer of youth, would show us how, like children, we played at battle in the spring sunshine, knowing nothing of the reality of war.

By the time April arrived I had another letter from my father, praising my diligence as conveyed to him by my mother, and telling me that he was much reassured by the measures I had taken. He informed me that he had confidence in Hugh to continue the good work, and told me I could return to Oxford. *It is not just for your studies that I urge you to return*, his letter said. *But also, in these troubling times it is good for our family to take advantage for ourselves and our loyalties. While the King and his court is now in York, I do not expect it for ever to be this way. I would not advise you to visit London, but being at Oxford places you well in the country for wherever you may be needed. God knows what the future will bring, but I trust you will make good connections at the university, and be ready at all times to serve the King.*

I was fired with pleasure at the praise in the letter, and found within myself a hitherto dormant respect for my father. Our relationship had always been awkward, but perhaps I could hope that in future there would be more understanding between us. Certainly I had always craved his approval, while becoming convinced I would never have it. Maybe I had been wrong.

I had also received not one, but two letters from Aphra. In the first she informed me of her family news, and in the second described her eagerness to debate with me on various topics we had touched upon in Norfolk. She seemed unimpressed at my martial activities, and urged me to resume my studies at the earliest opportunity. *For how can I learn*, she chided me, *except you relate to me what you have been taught?* Her words went some way to mitigate my pleasure at my boyish games with Hugh. I wanted to please her. She was no meek girl, but one with fire and intelligence, chafing at the restraints her womanhood forced upon her. She was lucky enough to have access to her father's extensive library, but insisted that discourse and debate was vital to help her fully master what she read. Added to Aphra's demands, I had latterly also received a letter from Richard, telling me how he missed my company. Both letters reminded me of the things I was missing at the university and I resolved to obey my father willingly, even though it meant abandoning my play-soldiering with Hugh. Indeed, if I had been Hugh I would have chafed at being expected to continue at home, but he was not a fellow for university life and protested himself heartily pleased that I was to go back to Oxford, so he could make our trained band his own.

I found the city awash with febrile debate. There had always been animosity between the students and the city apprentices, but now things were a lot worse. Richard and I decided to not risk a broken head and kept away from the most violent inns. Even so, to go about the town was to invite attack. I had never been interested in politics, but now it seemed everyone had an opinion on the King, the parliament and everything to do with both. It was no longer possible to tread a neutral path. Not having been much exercised by lack of resources, tax had never been a subject of interest to me, but it was to Richard's family and to every other who suffered when having to pay it. Those poor students who knew my father was at court in York sought to harangue me in the hope I could influence the King through my father. It was sometimes hard to keep an even temper when so much foolishness was bandied about. However, I had a deal of sympathy with Richard and others like him. There was much the King had done that I realised I did not agree with, but at the same time it was no answer to be rebellious. I was all for reasoned argument and patience.

I had decided to wear my breast- and backplate, and ride my horse armed to Oxford. Perhaps there was an element of showing off in my decision. In fact, I know there was, but I was glad I had done it. The students had formed a militia and I was able to take a useful role, being well mounted and armed, and in addition having recently drilled my own company at home. Richard fared less well, having no horse and being unable to easily afford one. For a while he forbore from taking part, but eventually he had to make his decision and came across for the King, in spite of his arguments with His Majesty. He undertook exercises with a pike, which to me looked both alarming and fiendishly difficult. There was much talk of war, but it seemed to me that most of the heat was stirred up and increased by the old animosity between city and university. There had been unrest in the country before, and would be again. Marching about in a military manner didn't mean it would come to war. War was for other countries, not England, for our nation had been at peace for a great many years, used to resolving difficulties with words, not swords. That was my callow opinion, and I was not the only one who could not believe that political argument would translate into anything more than a few intemperate, drunken brawls and broken heads. I, alongside many of my fellows, was still playing at war and thought it a very fine game.

Having been taken to task by Aphra for that very activity, I also spent much time in study. Through Richard I fell in with a student who had been at the university much longer than I, but who was not much older. He had been intent on joining the church, but had decided there was little chance of a good living that way, and had fallen upon on medicine in its stead. For a little while, Richard and I attended the same lectures as Thomas Willis, my new acquaintance, but Richard soon tired of learning about the teachings of Galen and Hippocrates. He was still determined to take his philosophy to court and educate the Crown how better to rule. I, however, was fascinated by these studies, and so Master Willis and I were often in conversation. There was, in spite of my determination to forget it, still a needling of my mind about Catherine and the possibility of a child of mine in existence. For a while I searched in books and debated with others, more informed than I, about the early stages of pregnancy. As always, there were many opinions; the only thing perhaps agreed upon was that until the mother felt a child quicken in her womb it could be assumed that there was no child there. I had not known of a woman's courses, so had not known how they usually ceased when carrying a child. But there were other reasons they could cease, so in spite of my work I found I was none the wiser. I abandoned the study of women's health and turned to the way a man is made. There was the promise of a dissection, when a criminal's corpse could be obtained. That intrigued me and drew me in, though at the same time I wondered if seeing a man's flesh opened and his interior displayed might be repugnant to me. It proved to be the contrary, once I had mastered the odour of the cadaver. Examining God's work this way enthralled me. The complexities of the body are extraordinary. It would take a lifetime to understand it all but I was determined to undertake the challenge. I wrote to Aphra, *I would I were a painter, and able to send you a portrait of the interior. Seeing meat hanging in the kitchen had not prepared me for the beauty and variety of the colours God has chosen to use for the parts of a man we do not usually see.*

*If this is unsuitable to write, pray let me know and I will cease, but I am filling with wonder and excitement, and want to know how it all works!*

She replied to my letter with great speed. *By no means is what you write unsuitable, or if it is, I reject that, and wish you to continue. Have you seen the fire within that gives our bodies heat? I have often wondered where our source of warmth is situated. It must, surely, be contained deep within us? I sometimes suffer a burning of the throat after I have eaten, and wonder if I have stoked that internal fire too high?*

I resolved to take particular note the next time I had a chance to see a dissection. I also consulted books and engaged in discourse with learned men about that subject, but our fire within was another subject about which natural philosophy could only make conjectures. There was so much to discover! Aphra urged me to continue my work. *For who knows what discoveries you may make?* she wrote. *And what salving of men's hurts you may undertake as a result? Surely that is of the highest calling, to soothe men's pain with philosophy and physick? I wish I were a man, and could be with you in your endeavours.*

I wrote back to her that night. *I too wish you with me to share in my work, but I confess I do not wish you a man under any circumstances, as you are to me all perfection within the body you inhabit.*

I read over what I had written and the words leapt off the paper and into my heart. What a partner she would make! She was a little above me in station, but was a second daughter, and I an eldest son with a good estate to inherit. Should I speak to my father about her, requesting he speak to his friend, her father? But he might think me fickle, so lately having entered into an unwise liaison. And they were both much taken up with the King's concerns. It would be politic to wait, until the unrest in the country had settled down, but I thought about how it would be to share my life with Aphra, and the prospect didn't displease me.

As spring gave way to summer, the news from all around continued in violence and disarray. I was shocked when I heard the fleet had declared for parliament, and later in July that parliament had resolved to raise an army of its own. Suddenly, our world was become more dangerous, and for the first time I began to feel more than a little disquiet. I thought of the brief tussle I had endured with the men in the barn, and recognised anew how slim the distance between the world of life and that of death. I was not at all certain how willing I would be if commanded to put myself in the way of a naked sword. Wielding one and receiving a cut were two very different things, and my flesh shrank from such a possibility. However, I felt glad my father had told me to see to the defence of our home. I was sure all had been done to protect my mother from any disaffected people who might come to alarm her, and Aphra had assured me similar precautions had taken place on her estate. It seemed there were quite serious clashes in the north, but that was far away. No army threatened us here. It was beyond belief that war could happen in England, and it certainly *would* not when the King acted decisively to put down the threatened violence, and then addressed all the honestly felt woes as a father to his subjects.

It was while I was in this frame of mind that a letter arrived from my father, informing me that the King had raised his standard in Nottingham. His two sons were with him, as well as his nephews, the Princes Rupert and Maurice, lately come to join him. It is hard to explain the mixture of emotions I felt at the news. It felt as if a momentous and sobering thing had come to pass. I had wanted the King to be decisive, but did he feel that so many were against him that he needed to rally men to his side? Why Nottingham? Had it been a mistake to leave his capital as he had? He was our king!

Stilling the disquiet swirling within me was the feeling that now all but the most rebellious must come to their senses. At the same time, an undeniable excitement ran somewhere in my veins. I felt I was living through extraordinary times, never seen before, certainly not in my lifetime or that of my parents. Of course wars raged in Europe. That was their fate, with kings who quarrelled and fought. But we, happy on our blessed island, we were better than those warring factions over the sea. We had no need of war to settle our domestic differences. Since the time of his father, James, our king's line was secure with sons to follow him. In his wisdom, and that of his advisors including my own father, he must have decided a show of strength was needed. Indeed, had I not been asking for that very thing? Perhaps now he would march with banners flying to London, gathering thousands of loyal followers along the way. I could be part of that happy conclusion to this present unrest. I too could ride to meet him and follow him safely to his great city of London, where its citizens would see their error and fall on their knees to beg forgiveness. It would be a heroic occasion, and I wanted to be part of it! Where London rebels would lead in apology, so the rest of the country would follow.

'All will now be well!' I said to Richard as we sat that evening at our leisure. 'People will flock to support him and we will see how hollow cowardly parliamentarians are. For no one wants war, and no one will be ready to promote it, not when it truly comes to it. Raising his standard does not mean war, it means peace!'

From that moment we were all mad for news, and more news came, from many quarters. It was not all good. A troop of horse arrived in Oxford, after having lost a skirmish, but I decided that it was a small setback, and simply showed how important it was to be well drilled. I was not even too concerned when Portsmouth fell to parliament. The fleet, after all, had already proved traitorous. It could be safely brought to heel once the rest was settled. However, when the Earl of Essex marched against the King I was outraged.

'How dare he?' I demanded of Richard. 'For the son of such a great family to be a traitor. He will pay with his head for this.'

Richard was amused. 'Perhaps he finds his king just as infuriating as do some of the apprentices in London,' he said.

I glared at him and he raised his hands as if in surrender to a foe. 'Yes, I am for the King,' he reminded me. 'But all the same, I can understand that others, from wherever they belong, may have genuine grievances that we can little understand. It is beyond my wit to know what troubles that great earl so much that he has come out against the King. I can guess, however, that something has not been resolved between them, for unlike most, he must have had the ear of the King. Perhaps your father would know.'

'Perhaps,' I agreed. 'But I doubt he would tell me. Or he would tell me at such length I would be obliged to stop up my ears.'

At the beginning of October we heard that Prince Rupert had routed the Earl in the county of Worcester, and I had something to cheer about. There was even more drilling and exercising as the threat of violence drew nearer. I was proud to be given command over a small number of horse. Our numbers were few, not above ten, but we made much play of patrolling the outlying areas, watching for any enemies we might discover, though we saw none. I still wanted to be one of those who would follow a victorious king into his capital, and of course lead my men to that position, but it was clear at the moment that my university men and I were wanted here in Oxford. Besides, my father had commanded me to be in the city and I was not ready to disobey him again, however much I fretted at being on the sidelines during what I considered a historic time. Would I be obliged to tell my children that their grandfather had been with the King as he rode into London while I languished at the university, more of a student than a soldier?

Master Willis had returned to his family's farm near Abingdon, so I no longer had him to engage in conversation. Richard and I continued good friends, but his lack of horse kept us somewhat separate in our martial pursuits, and there was less opportunity to study, with command of my troop taking much time.

I can remember exactly where I was and what I was doing when I heard of that great coming together at Edgehill. I was leading Arthur along Broad Street, back to his stable. He had seemed a little lame, and I wanted to rest him so I would be able to go out on patrol the following day. At the same time I was in something of a hurry, because there was a lecture to be given very soon that I didn't want to miss. Some fellow was selling bulletin sheets, and was shouting their headlines to attract buyers. I was usually hungry for news, but this day I was thinking of my horse and the lecture. It was only as I drew near that the words drilled like an awl into my brain.

'Terrible battle fought between two great armies!' he was shouting. 'Many killed on both sides!'

I can remember coming to a dead halt in front of the man, with my horse chewing his bit, knowing where he was going and eager for a feed. Other people were standing nearby, listening to what the news seller had to say.

'Who won?' asked one man who was a master at one of the colleges. The bulletin seller didn't seem to know.

'Many dead and wounded!' he shouted, as if that was the most newsworthy information.

I bought a sheet from him but there was no mention of any battle, although much conjecture about who had the greatest number of men in their armies. I set off with all speed to the stable. As soon as I had someone attend to Arthur's foot, which was not thought badly bruised, I made my way back to the centre of the city. The news was being shouted now by every bulletin seller. Two had the story in print, still wet and smudged, such was the haste to sell the story, but there was still little known. I met another student, who told me our lecture had been cancelled, so I made my way to my lodgings, stopping to buy every sheet on offer. Shortly afterwards Richard arrived and we fell to reading them all.

The next day we heard that the King had won, and so we expected him to advance with all speed to London, there to rout his enemies and regain his capital. I determined I would be with him, for surely all risk was now gone for this city? But on the heels of that intelligence came word that the King's army was much depleted. There were alarms everywhere. I was in a fever to know the truth, but all was awry, with each piece of news contradicting the other. Then the following day a letter came from Hugh, at home.

*Do you have word of our father?* he wrote. *We have heard nothing from him since before the coming together at Edgehill, but we know a companion of his was killed at that terrible place. Please let us know if you have any news.*

Why had I not considered my own parent's situation or my family's concern? I cannot explain or excuse myself. I had been too carried away by the general to think of the particular. I suppose if I had given it any consideration I had assumed that because the King was well, his advisors would be also. The King had soldiers to give him and his advisors safety. They would not have been engaged in the distasteful matter of slaughter. I had to reply to Hugh's letter.

*I regret, no news*, I wrote.

# CHAPTER EIGHT

What young man does not, however much he loves his parent, long for dominion over his own life? I did in no way wish my father dead. I had, surely, only recently been shown that we could perhaps come to an understanding, now I was grown. Even so, I found my mind thinking of the house, which would be mine, the lands, mine, and the money, paintings and plate. Mine. I would, of course, have my mother live in the house until she died, but the estate would be mine to order, with the aid of my brother, Hugh. Of course those thoughts sailed heedless into my mind, but no. I did not wish him dead, however much I had bridled under his treatment in the past.

Two of my troop disappeared, to swell the ranks of the King's glorious army. A few days earlier I would have also been tempted to slip away with them, but now I was not so sure. I was the eldest son. I should keep within a day's ride of home in case I was needed, so I stayed in the city, chafing at my inaction. News came in drips as if from a leaking gutter. And how could we tell if it was true or false? There was so much confusion. The King's army was marching on London, or no, it was not. Accurate intelligence was not to be come by, for only the King knew the King's mind. All I knew from my mother and Hugh was that until she heard otherwise, her husband must still be with the King. But in that case why had he not written?

A few lightly wounded men appeared in the city, but their news was old and partial. Weeks went by and it seemed that the King did indeed march his army ever closer to London. Richard had word from his parents, who were concerned for their safety and for that of their business. They were not for either side and feared war reaching their streets, when all they wanted was to make their living and do no harm to any. I thought they must be in the minority, for as far as I could tell, London was a veritable hotbed of parliamentarianism, and had been so for a long time, but Richard told me that in his opinion, in spite of hothead apprentices the majority wanted nothing more than to avoid these violent tangles.

In late November we heard that the King had been rebuffed by his capital. I could not decide whether to rail at the traitorous dogs who had refused him, or his soldiers who had allowed themselves to be stopped. I assumed he would travel north again, but almost at once preparations were being made by the university to receive him here, at Christ Church College!

I watched the army march in from an upper window, and although I looked as hard as I could I did not see my father's distinctive black horse with the burly shape of his owner astride him, or his colours anywhere. It seemed for whatever reason my father was no longer in the King's company. The army seemed very great, but I suppose it was much depleted. They said there were fourteen thousand at Edgehill, but if that many had entered our city, I think there would not have been an inch of street to stand upon! Even so, we were very crowded everywhere. I wondered if I would be able to carry on any of my studies. Chaos was our master now, not education. But in spite of the anti-royalist feeling in the city, we at the university made the whole company very welcome. Colleges were given over as residences for the King and his party. Almost every house in the city was obliged to rent rooms to those who could afford them, and tents were pitched on every green space, heedless of the danger of flooding.

I daresay there were rewards aplenty for the men of business in the city. Quantities of bread must be baked and other food provided for the masses of men. Harness needed mending, swords sharpening and horses shoeing. The cacophony was deafening. I doubt many merchants suffered, at least in the early days. My most urgent task, however, was to find word of my father. I owed it to my mother to discover his whereabouts, and now surely I could. I went to Christ Church, where the King lay, but there were hordes of people equally determined to find answers to a myriad questions. I was directed from place to place across the city, eventually being directed back to Christ Church, but at least with the name of someone who should be able to help. By this time the best of the day had gone. I began to despair of ever finding what had happened to my father, but going in again at Christ Church I was fortunate enough to speak to one who had the answer.

'I am enquiring into the whereabouts of Sir Thomas Chayne,' I said to him, without expecting a useful answer.

'I saw him not long ago,' said the man, who looked exhausted with care. 'May I ask your business? You will understand that not all in this city are enamoured of our presence.'

'I am his son, also Thomas,' I said, feeling a smile of relief breaking out on my face. 'I have had no news since Edgehill, and was much alarmed at his silence.'

'Well, we have been busy about our work,' said the man. 'And your father has been wounded not once, but twice. However' – he held up his hand to stop my voice – 'he does well enough. He is determined to stay with the King, but would better serve him by returning home to heal. Is it your plan to recover him, now you see he lives?'

'Until I see him I cannot say.'

'Well, you will find your father at his lodgings in the High Street.'

He took me outside and directed me, as if I did not live here, which of course he did not understand. I thanked him for his trouble and hurried towards the place where he lay, my mind a jumble of emotions.

Because of his injuries, my father could not walk. But he could talk. He did so at some length, before he wearied and fell silent.

'Have you seen the surgeon, sir?' I enquired after he had related his recent experiences to me and demanded to know if I had kept my behaviour more becoming to my station than before.

He did not mask his irritation. 'Do you not see my wound bandaged?'

I did, but it looked more like a hasty dressing made in the field than the considered plaster of a physician who had time to be careful. I thought of what Master Willis had told me, that if oil was not applied to a cut in the flesh it might go bad, causing a person to sicken and die. I did not want to anger my father. It was obvious he was troubled much with pain, both from the cut on his leg and the one on his temple. But it was surely my duty to advise him what I knew, for the sake of his life. How to do so, while keeping him calm? I was sure he would have little respect for my opinion. As I wondered how to speak I observed his condition. His head wound was perhaps the older, for he had no bandage on it, and although there was much bruising there was no fresh blood, and it looked to be healing well enough. I knew little enough about the practicalities of medicine, but had, with Master Willis, been able to practise the skill of stitching the skin and flesh on a cadaver after it had been dissected. We had thought the knowledge might be useful, if war came to Oxford. I did not imagine my father would need or allow me to perform on him what I had so lately learnt on the body of a criminal, but I hoped he might at least consider my advice about seeing a physician while he was here.

'I wonder, sir, if the surgeon who attended you poured oil onto your wound?'

He looked at me as if I were an idiot. 'Do you think a surgeon on the field has enough leisure or materials to treat every man as if he were at his own home? If you had come to fight you would know it.'

I felt this to be cruelly unjust, for I had been obeying his command in staying here at Oxford. If he had wanted me to join him surely he would have given me further instructions?

'Since you told me to return here I have been making a study of medicine, and I understand—'

'You would do better to make a study of the way this country is going, and understand your place in it. Now leave me be. Go and physick others if you are so inclined and return to me when you are ready to fight, rather than play a surgeon.'

Try though I might to excuse his temper because of his pain,

I left him in anger, although I did not express it to him. I fumed my way back to my lodging, and recounted my frustration to Richard, who was now sharing my room due to the squeeze on places to live.

'Perhaps he will be sent a physician tomorrow,' said Richard, always logical and soothing to my moods. 'He is a commander of men, is he not? The army will want him well again as soon as possible. And at least you have found him alive.'

'The King's man told me he would best serve the King by returning home,' I said. 'And from what I could tell by the bandage on his leg his wound looks large, and perhaps more serious than he will admit.'

'Well then, why not send a physician yourself in the morning? He need not know he has been sent by you.'

'That is an excellent idea, Richard! Thank you!'

It was well nigh impossible to find any qualified person to attend my father. There were so many wounded that needed care, and indeed I did what I could to assist. There was much suffering, especially in the tents, where men were cold as well as injured. Some lay so close to each other for shelter it was difficult to examine them. Several times I came upon a poor dead soldier, still crammed between his wounded companions because there was no organisation by the able-bodied to extract and see to his burying. I bought materials, and was able to clean and stitch several sword cuts, but wished I had Master Willis with me, who had a better eye than I, and more experience. Still, experience is what I was getting, and that was all to the good.

In the end, as dusk fell, and it was too dark to attend the men camped out, I spoke to a surgeon who I had watched and admired while I was working near him.

'My father, Sir Thomas Chayne, is lying wounded not far

from here in good lodgings,' I said. 'He does not wish me to attend to him, but I fear his wound is in need of inspection. Would you be prepared to visit him on my behalf, while not letting him know it is I who fears for him?'

The good surgeon asked me a few questions, and I told him what I could, which was little enough. He offered to go at once, before he took his meal, and would send word to me at my lodgings afterwards.

'You have done good work here today,' he told me to my surprise. 'As I noticed you watch me, so I paid attention to you. I do not say all your patients will live, but you are steady, intelligent and practical. It may not be your calling to be a physician, but in these days anyone who can work as you did is of credit to an army. I congratulate you.'

I returned to my lodgings tired, dirty, but proud of his words to me and grateful that it would be him who attended my father.

No more than an hour later a note arrived for me from the surgeon. *Your father assumed I had come as a matter of course, and I did not mention your name. His wound is deep, and his knee as well as the bone of his lower leg are both damaged. I told him he would not walk again and would likely die of a fever if his leg was not removed. He resisted, and so I told him that if he will not have it off, he must go away from this place. I do not know what he will decide, but I have treated his wound as you requested.*

I sent a note back, thanking him and enclosing money for his fee. In the morning, even before I had eaten, a message came from my father, urging me to hasten to him that instant. I was much alarmed. I took a piece of bread in my hand and set out. It was not far, but the throng of people on the street, even at this early hour, made my progress slow. Had he tried to get out of bed and made his wound worse? Had he a sudden fever? But no!

When I arrived he was sitting up in bed and with no preamble started at once to order me about.

'I have decided to go home today. You will accompany me.'

I could not help myself. I was so put out by him. 'Why me?'

He stared at me. 'You ask your father why you? Because I command it is why.'

'You got here without me, Father. Surely you can travel a little further without my company? I spent all day yesterday working with the surgeons and today I must do likewise, as well as having a care for my troop. There is more than enough to do here to serve the King. I am glad you have decided to return home, where you will have Mother and Hugh to assist you, but I really am needed here.'

I think it was the first time I had so openly defied him. It was also the first time I had felt a real duty elsewhere. He did not need me, except for his own satisfaction. He had servants to accompany him, and could call on men from his company to make his journey safe. I was not needed by him, but I knew that my abilities, limited though they were, were badly needed by the wounded in the city.

It was not so long ago that he had given me a whipping, but he could not do so that day. His helplessness must have been a severe trial to him, but apart from his heightened colour he didn't betray his frustration with his condition. Instead he simply stared at me, his dark brown eyes firing sparks of anger into mine. 'Have a care,' was all he said, in an icily measured tone. 'Have a care.'

For a few moments we simply looked at each other. At last I gave him a bow. 'I will,' I said, as if it was friendly advice, rather than a threat. 'If it pleases you to do so, give my greetings to my mother and my brother. I wish you well on your journey, sir, and a good recovery.'

He made no reply, but simply continued his silence. I felt unable to leave without saying more.

'I will keep doing all I can to relieve the suffering of the wounded soldiers, and continue to drill the troop of horse under my command. When this present conflict is over and all is peace again I will go to Leiden to further my studies, for you should know I mean to become a physician.'

I looked for some surprise and pleasure in his face that I, too, had a command of my own, but none appeared. Instead, he showed only disgust.

'You wish to squander your brain and your breeding to waste time collecting herbs and pulling teeth. You show yourself, though eighteen years old, still a child. You want to marry beneath you and practise a trade? You would, I think, mislike the reality of such a life when up to now you have only experienced higher things.'

I could not help telling him proudly, 'The Lady Aphra encourages me in my studies.'

He looked amused.

'Well, well. So maybe the bee has found fresh nectar.'

It was my turn to look surprised.

'You think her father and I would all unthinking have allowed you to meet? Or that she would have written to you without his approval?' He shook his head. 'I fear that setting bones may indeed be the only trade of which you are capable. In any high estate you would very soon find yourself led by the nose.' He yawned and rested his head back on his pillows with a wince. 'Now go. If you are not going to accompany me, you are no use to me here.'

His tone at the last was so dismissive I made my way back into the street with my thoughts all awry.

Had Aphra played me for a fool? Had my fondness for her been deliberately managed, while I, all innocence, thought my affections hidden from my parent? I had hoped to conduct an interview about marriage with clear purpose and dignity, but I felt humiliated. I tried to tell myself that it mattered not. I wanted her. It seemed I could have her, and should be content, but did I want a girl who had tricked me into feeling more than I might otherwise have done? Was her intense interest in my studies nothing more than flattery with a purpose, and a sham? Her debates with me had seemed so heartfelt. I had admired her fine intellect. It had been much of why I liked and admired her so much. Now I didn't know what to think.

I pushed my way, all unheeding, through the crush of people. Just when I was beginning to believe that I had some autonomy from him, my father showed how little I ruled myself. I would have to write to Aphra and demand she told me the truth. But could I believe what she said? Would it be possible? Meanwhile, I had at least stood my ground about not going home with my father. I would not be his puppy any more. I owed him duty as his son, but surely a higher duty was to the King? His army needed surgeons and I would work at that, whatever my father said. I wished I had thought to use the argument of a higher duty with him, but I had not thought of it in time.

Judging that my father must travel slowly, I sent a letter to my mother post haste, telling her of the condition of his wound according to the surgeon who had examined him. I explained that my father did not know it was I who had engaged the surgeon, and she would oblige me by not volunteering the information. However, I thought it politic to let her know the opinion so she could nurse him in knowledge, rather than innocence. I sent my heartfelt hopes for his recovery, and my affection to her and Hugh.

I told her what I was doing in Oxford, and hoped for peace to come as soon as possible, to save any more suffering. *I am well, and believe I am easing the suffering of some of the poor soldiers, who have few to attend them. If it comes to more fighting I may be involved with my small troop of university men, but I will take every care with my person. I live in the hope and expectation of seeing you before the year is out, and in any case, when this dreadful war is done.*

My days grew into a rhythm, so that I soon had little memory of any different beat. I was always tired, and always had more men to attend to, for camp fever soon had the city and its environs in its grip. I don't know if the miasma arrived with the army, or if it followed the men here, but it was a sorry business. I wrote to Master Willis, telling of our plight and asking if he would not return from his farm to help, but he refused. The fever had struck all around, even onto his farm, leaving his siblings without any parent. He had no option but to stay and run the farm lest they all starve.

I wonder I did not succumb, but thank God I did not. Richard also stayed well. He was still drilling and ready to swell the King's army, which still lay close by. I, concerned for his person, obtained his permission to find him a horse so he could join my troop. I bought one and all equipment from a wounded trooper, who had no further use of it.

'I need more men,' I told Richard when he at first had demurred. 'And you are a rider without a horse. Accept this partly as a Christmas gift if you must, but also as duty to the King, for pikemen are many and troopers few. Besides, I will feel safer if you are with me.'

He turned all his energies to learning what my troopers had achieved. We practised the commands, especially 'Present and give fire', pistol practice being much needed by us all. I managed at the last to have eighteen in my troop, and was very proud of every man. We were honoured when Prince Maurice took an interest in us. He and his brother, Prince Rupert, had been bred to tactics and the command of men, while we were for the most part untried. Prince Maurice told me one afternoon that we should look to accompanying him to Cornwall after the start of the new year, but as the year turned he was given a task much nearer to home.

'We are needed,' he told me, 'to put down the enemy in the county of Gloucestershire, and you come from there, I believe.' I liked the way he spoke to me, so easily, almost as if I were his equal. It was not difficult to admire him, and want to be one of his company, but he told me his regiment being in good order, I should join his brother's. 'For Rupert's Life Guards have been much engaged, and are somewhat depleted,' he said. 'Come with me. I will introduce you. You will be useful where we are going as you know the country.'

It is a salutary thing, to go from playing at soldiering to being part of a regiment of horse. I was pleased to see that by now we had more discipline than some, but we still lacked tactics, and had not engaged in formal battle. I thank God we had enough time to learn a little before being thrown into it. Except in the melee there is need to act as one, and we had much more to do to learn that. I had thought we would engage in a large battle, like the one at Edgehill, but in that I was wrong. In fact, to begin with we got more practice at moving through the country than anything else, and when we did finally engage, we were set on to attack a town, not an army.

From Oxford to Cirencester, where we demanded the surrender of the town and were refused. I had thought we would straight away attack, but Prince Rupert told us we would not waste our efforts but give our horses a good feed at the town's expense before returning to Oxford. Towards the end of January we set out again, and after meandering through the countryside arrived at Sudeley Castle, which had been taken by the enemy. We lay that night near the castle, in great misery because of the snow that fell upon us in the open. There were several thousand of us, or so they said, but we were spread about, and besides, I was never very good at estimating numbers in the field. There was nothing heroic about shivering through the snowy night and I think we were all relieved when told to mount and move swiftly on. The country was ideal for good progress of men and horses, and the exertion brought warmth into our bones. Soon we were near to the town, and set our bivouacs to the north-west, taking what rest we could in the cold.

When the grey daylight came I could see the stone rooftops, with much smoke from morning fires trickling from chimneys, and the great tower of the ancient church dominating the view. The people living in the town would for the most part be warm, while we were numb with cold. I stared at the smoke as it curled into the sky. I knew Cirencester. It was no further than a dozen miles from the place of my birth, and yet here I stood, making my breakfast in the field instead of freely walking the familiar streets and buying a hot pie. How could it be that soon I would sit my horse in readiness to attack this place, where I had come as a boy with my mother to choose cloth for a suit, and for her to select the silk to be made into a fine gown? Why had they stubbornly refused to send anyone to join the King's army, when to have agreed would have avoided this attack to come? Would we be falling on a sleeping town, or were they ready for us?

Before we even began our assault we had reinforcements from Oxford arrive, with men, cannon and a mortar, which sounded to be a terrible machine.

'It will send fire into the town,' said Richard, who had been talking to a man who had seen such a piece in action. 'And it will cause panic and dismay. All will be well for us, my friend. Do not fret, or be afeared.'

Perhaps he had seen me shiver. It was due to the cold, but I am sure we were both afraid. His expression, designed to encourage me, showed me bravado on his lips and fear in his eyes. Perhaps it is always like this before men throw themselves knowingly into mortal danger. I stroked Arthur's neck, feeling the place where he had been struck by the villain's knife on my way home from Norfolk. It had healed well, but the hair would never grow there again. I felt grateful to have this horse. He had so much more experience than I. I trusted him totally after the experience in the barn. In addition, although I knew that Aphra had never ridden him, I could imagine her perched up high on his huge back, that bold girl I had decided to marry, a valiant Boudicca.

We were commanded to mount, and move forwards, and soon it became clear to me how we were to enter the town.

'Let me explain a little of the place,' I said to my troop. 'At the bottom of the hill before us we will need to turn to the right to gain the centre of the town. But there is a high wall along the right of that street, and I fear there may be men on top trying to frustrate our progress.'

'What lies on the other side of the street?' asked Richard.

'It is all buildings,' I said. 'Fine townhouses for the most part.'

'So we will no doubt be assailed on both sides,' he said. 'I hope we will be commanded to move speedily through that place. And,' he added quickly, 'I am sure we shall.'

After a few minutes a message came for me to attend our commander. I dismounted, and did my best to hasten to him through the churned-up mud and snow.

'I hear you know this town,' he said as I approached him.

'Yes, sir.'

'You know your way to the church from here?'

'Yes, sir.'

'Good. The more who can guide us, the better. When the command is given you will lead us as swiftly as may be to the church. Our job is to take and hold the Market Place. Go now and bring your troop to the fore.'

We moved up and took our place somewhat diffidently at the head of the troop. It was by then almost midday and still no shot had been fired. We saw some musketeers drawn up and sent, as a forlorn hope, marching forward through the snow to attack the house and buildings to the left, which responded with much fire and confusion. It was my first sight of battle, and I pitied our poor fellows taking on that well-defended position with no possibility of winning it alone. The shouts and screams of our injured and dying were horrible to hear and it was awful to see them struggling against the well-defended buildings while we sat on our horses and did nothing. After a little while it was judged safe to take our cannon closer, and they fired upon the town. All this while we waited in good order, soothing our impatient horses. Arthur stood quietly enough. He had seen action abroad, and must know what would come better than I, and yet he remained calm, in spite of the noise. Pikemen were sent forward and the confusion increased until at last we saw that the houses and buildings had been fired and were burning fiercely.

'Queen Mary!' They were the words we had all been waiting for. A part of me wanted more than anything to turn and ride away from what might come, but I could not. I would not. I had my university men to think of. I must lead them bravely or what would they think of me? Together, with Richard at my side, we advanced in good order slowly down the hill. We were in the fringes of the town now, and expected resistance at any time, although the street was empty. A great explosion came suddenly from our right and in front of us the slushy mud spurted up with a violence that sent small stones, snow and stinking mud over us. My steady horse shook his head and neatly stepped over the ball that now lay half hidden in the mire. Another ball came, and another. I could not help flinching at each explosion. The whine and thud of the balls falling about us was most alarming. Prince Rupert was unperturbed, urging on the foot soldiers, and once even dismounting to command where best to deploy our ordinance. Then, close behind me, I heard one of my men scream. I looked back to see him clutching his shoulder and likely to fall.

'I will help him,' shouted Richard. 'You go on.'

The Prince came back up towards me at a canter, almost riding into Arthur, who snorted, but held steady. The Prince hastily drew up, and his horse slithered in the mire. 'One barrier against us is broken!' he shouted into my face. 'Now our horse can get in. Go to the Market Place and clear the streets.' He went on past, urging others to follow me.

Without waiting, I spurred Arthur on. The church was not far away, but there was musket fire coming from the houses on either side of the street I was in. It was a miracle I was not shot. I saw a man with a musket leave a house nearby and run into Black Jack Street. I shot at him but missed. Riding up to him, I shot my other pistol at his back and he fell. I didn't wait to see if he lived but rode on up the street towards the church. It was then that I realised I was alone. Had the others not seen which way I went?

I reloaded my pistols with all speed, fearing that at any moment the enemy would find me. Before I had quite done, two more of our company appeared to my left, much muddied, both horses and men. One I knew to be the Earl of Cleveland, the other I did not recognise.

'Which way to the Market Place? Which way in these damned streets?'

I gathered my reins after holstering my second pistol and beckoned them on. I set my horse to a swift trot, but around the corner to the left, partly blocking our way, was another barrier, a cart piled high with furze and wicked bramble and rose. I think my brave horse would have tried to leap it all, but fearing disaster I pulled him up so hard he almost sat back upon his haunches. Several enemy musketeers were hidden there, and they shot as one towards us. My horse screamed and staggered, but rose swiftly. After returning fire and killing one of the enemy we managed to make our way safely past while they were employed in reloading their pieces. We left the foot to clear the cart away while we went on.

Now we were in the narrow alleys by the church. I fired at a fellow's face that I spied in an upper window, but could not tell if I had shot him. Coming out of the alley into the open space where the market was usually held, I could see many enemies at the further end. As I made to ride towards them, Lord Cleveland fired his gun by my left shoulder. His enemy fell, and my horse rode over the man while he screamed most horribly. And then another man rose up and raised his musket to me. I pistoled him at close range and he collapsed, shouting 'Dogs! Dogs! Dogs!' before falling into the mud.

More of our company of horse were arriving every moment, to my very great relief, and behind them, many additional foot.

I heard that a great barrier and chains that had defended the turnpike were now clear, enabling more of our force to enter the town that way. The top end of the Market Place would surely soon be secured. But more of the enemy were discovered every minute, far too many for me and the few gentlemen originally with me. Then some of our foot gained access to the houses hereabouts. They made short work of the men within, very soon appearing at the windows to fire upon the enemy, as the enemy had done to us. There was great confusion everywhere, with some running, some trying to hide and others turning to fire upon us, determined to sell their lives bravely. Having fired both pistols again I drew my sword, and along with a good number of our horse now with me, rode at speed towards their cavalry, which immediately fled. We pursued them along Dyer Street until we were met by another defended barricade or turnpike. By this time our commander had caught up with us and ordered us to retreat. It was well he did, because several hundred of the enemy were grouped together in a walled close on the left-hand side. We were too few to win against them, and he cautioned that they might have a way of getting behind us into the Market Place and so trapping us. We would have been slaughtered if that had happened.

While we waited for our foot to reinforce us we had much work to do, for a great quantity of the enemy were hidden thereabouts. We drove many to the close where their fellows stood, in this way and others taking many prisoners, which were eventually shut up in the great church of St John. Any who resisted we pistoled or slashed and many soon lay dead or dying in the streets round about.

I, along with some others, was sent back to the top of the Market Place in case my knowledge of the town could be useful there. As I rode past the inn called the King's Head, where I had in happier times stopped to eat, a Spanish cannonier ran out in an attempt to reach his piece, which stood nearby. If a gentleman had not ridden with swift courage between him and it, denying him his shot and his life, much damage could have been done to us. I had slowed my horse, but not thought quickly enough to do it myself, and I much admired the gentleman for his speedy action. However, as I called my admiration to him, the Market Place now being a scene of veritable peace after the battle, a flurry of musket shots came from a window high in the inn. My good horse Arthur stumbled again. I thought he would regain his feet, but he did not. I only just had time to scramble free of him before he fell. I also stumbled and went to my knees, only managing by the grace of God not to be trapped by his body where it lay on the ground. I could not believe it. That faithful horse, who had carried me about in Norfolk and safely home to Gloucestershire, lay dying before me.

There came a fury upon me. I ran at once into the inn and leapt up the stairs. I knew my way about the place and soon threw open the door to expose the men who had shot poor Arthur. Before they could bring their muskets in from the window and defend themselves, I slashed at them. I cut them again and again, mad with a fury I had not known I possessed. When I came to myself I felt badly shamed. I think the men must have been dead almost at the first cut, but I had been blind to the result of my actions. I felt exhausted, and leant heavily on the casement to regain my breath. There below me lay my fine horse, his blood turning the snowy mud to red. Beyond him was the body of the Spaniard and his cannon, all mute.

I made my way back down on shaking legs, weary beyond mention. Back in the street were many of our men, both foot and horse. I spied Richard, watering his horse at the trough in the centre of Market Place and went over to him. He viewed me with alarm.

'You are hurt!'

I shook my head, rubbing at my face and bringing away my hands covered in the blood of my horse's killers. 'It is not my blood. I am not hurt.' I sat on the edge of the trough. 'I am not wounded, but my poor horse is dead.'

It was not until that night, when I tried to remove my shirt, that I realised a bullet had grazed my upper arm, the blood sticking my linen to me like another skin.

# CHAPTER NINE

The storming of Cirencester was my first experience of attacking a town in concert with many others, and the first time I had killed men. It was also the first time I had taken arms against my own neighbourhood, for the town of Cirencester lay less than an hour's gentle ride from my home, and many of the inhabitants were known to me by sight. My part took only an hour and a half, but the lessons I learnt about myself have lasted my whole lifetime. It was a shock for someone of my sunny nature to discover that the death of a horse could send me into such a killing fury. But I discovered that others had entered similar states during the fray. Even so, I could not countenance such behaviour for myself. I felt shame, and resolved never to allow myself to exhibit such unhinged fury again. I am pleased to relate that in this I succeeded, though it took a while to subdue the feelings that prompted such wild behaviour. Speaking of myself, I think much of it stemmed from fear. Fear at having my horse shot from under me, rendering me more vulnerable, and fear of my inability to kill by the sword, in spite of being taught the theory of using it.

To my great shame I killed those two unfortunate musketeers at the window in the inn not once but several times over. It was not until their horribly mutilated and gory bodies lay at my feet that I understood they were dead, and no longer a threat to my own life. I truly believe that my behaviour was detrimental not just to my physical self, which was exhausted by it, but also my spiritual being. Those men were my enemy, but might they not have wives, mothers or sweethearts to mourn them? It was not a noble deed, to leave the men not simply dead, but also so brutally mutilated that their loved ones would find it hard to recognise them. The corpses of those men haunted my sleep for a long while. Some might boast of their killing frenzy, but I could not. And so I took my lesson from others, greater and more experienced than I, who displayed economy in battle. I saw that they killed quickly and cleanly when possible, and took prisoners rather than killing, when that was advisable.

The Princes Rupert and Maurice were known for their bold tactics in battle. Now I saw that it was not just the studying of maps and the geography of the land that was important. As well as outwitting and outfighting the enemy, it is important to manage one's own men to inspire the greatest loyalty. I saw first-hand how Prince Rupert's personal bravery encouraged both his horse and the common foot soldier. Also, when he saw that some of the enemy against us in Cirencester had engaged at

Burford with some of ours, he allowed our men to take revenge for their earlier hurts by slaughtering them. As for the rest, he took over one thousand prisoners at Cirencester, showing mercy to many who cried for it. For is not every man's life precious? And how can we have hope of turning a man back to loyalty if we have killed him? So, by courage and self-control, a prince of men, whether noble or not, can afford to show compassion for the enemy, as well as revenge.

That afternoon, after our fighting was over there was no time to rest, for there remained much to do. At Barton Mill, a chain barricade still held some of our horse back for a while, until the foot arrived to overcome the defenders and break down the chain. After that, the town was completely overwhelmed. We rode about, finding many enemies skulking secretly in gardens and alleys. Some were content to surrender without a fight, knowing it was the best way to preserve their lives. They were taken at once to the church to be kept under guard. Others, still surly and rebellious, must be routed out at no small risk to our persons. In an alley near Castle Street I was fired upon, being lucky to avoid being severely wounded or killed. I cut the man down while he was reloading his pistol. Only then when he lay bleeding before me on the ground did I see that he was the baker who made the best lard cakes I had ever tasted. He was not dead, but faint with his wound. It would not have been wise of me to dismount, for other enemies might have been nearby, but I sent two soldiers to him, commanding them to bind his wound before taking him to the church.

Eventually there were few still prepared to resist. However, several thousand of our foot soldiers were to be left as a garrison against any further rebellion and so they must be found safe quarters, as well as meat and drink. Every building in the town was entered and made secure. Even late into the evening a few men were still being found, hiding in cupboards or under beds, being sheltered by their women. There was more trouble from women who took pains to break the church windows to throw their men food and medicine for their hurts but the town was at last secure.

Richard and I, along with several of our troop, found quarters for the night in a fine house in the Market Place. As part of Prince Rupert's forces we remained close to him, which gave us excellent lodgings.

The King had ordered that as much cloth as could be found was to be taken and sent to Oxford to be made into uniforms, so once the town was safe, forays were made to nearby towns and villages, to take what was needed. As a person with some local knowledge I was able to direct men to Minchinhampton, Malmesbury and Stroud, where a great quantity of that excellent Cotswold cloth was recovered. I also knew of two warehouses in Cirencester, and so I guided some men to break the locks. I admit I suffered a pang at seeing some bolts of good imported silk also taken and loaded onto a cart. I could not conceive that they would be needed for uniforms, but maybe they would be sold for the exchequer. Mr Simons the clothier would be much inconvenienced, as would the gentry, like my own family, who would have to look elsewhere for such lustrous fabric. Maybe Mr Simons would be ruined, but I hardened my heart, for that was the payment for rebellion. Mr Simons himself was locked in the church with others, and I hoped he now regretted his town's disobedience.

We spent a much more comfortable night than the prisoners. It continued cold, but we were inside with a warm fire and hot food in our bellies. We drank the owners' wine with an easy conscience, but I insisted my men were courteous to the women in the house. Women, after all, must follow where their menfolk lead, and they had plenty of reason to be sorry. One young servant's sweetheart was slain, and another's son was wounded and a prisoner. The mistress' husband too was thought to be in the church, though she had no word of him.

The following day, our work done there, we were to return to Oxford. We saw the prisoners taken out of the church and tied with cord to prevent them from escaping. It was difficult for me to see these men, some in great difficulty with their wounds and all cold and hungry, brought so low. But they were the enemy, and must be taught their error. Even so, it pained me to recognise several: a boy who used to take our horses at the inn in happier times, the man who sold us ribbons and other small goods, a cobbler whose shop I had visited on several occasions as my feet grew through childhood. The baker was there too, looking somewhat recovered with his wound bound up as I had commanded. He nodded to me as I passed. If I could have released all those I recognised I would have done so in a moment, asking only for their word to take arms no more against the King's interests. But such a thing was not in my gift. And Prince Rupert had a different purpose. Every man, including two members of the clergy, were stripped of shoes and stockings, and the poor horse boy had no more than a shirt to keep him from the cold.

'Where are they being taken?' I asked the captain of our company.

'Why, to Oxford of course,' was his reply.

I did not say it, but *poor fellows* was what I thought. As a woman must follow her husband, so a man must follow his master. I did not doubt that some of these men would have been content to lead quiet lives, but were led on by those in authority over them. Others, though, stood defiant, uttering curses at ourselves and the King. Not a few clods of mud were thrown at them by some of the soldiers, while many women wept to see their menfolk taken away. On our way we passed them, shuffling along, up to their knees in the icy mud. I heard later that they lay for one night in the church at Witney, and were received in Oxford the following day, being greeted by catcalls and much more throwing of mud and garbage. I later saw some of them working on the defences at Oxford, and I heard that they were soon pardoned by His Majesty, some returning to their town, while others entered the King's army, whether by choice or being pressed I could not say. I never again saw the horse boy, the cobbler or Mr Simons and sadly cannot tell what became of them. The baker, I heard later, had died of his wound, although it had not been so very great. I wished I had been able to go into the church to minister to all the wounded there, as well as the few hurts to my own side, but had not the authority or the confidence to request it. I was sorry to hear of the baker's death, which I was sure could have been avoided with proper care, though such lack of care was, I suppose, simply part of the punishment for rising up. I found his death more difficult to deal with than it should have been, and it made me wish never to return to that town, where I had as a boy happily spent my pennies in the shops. I remembered walking down the Market Place with Hugh to meet our mother, both of us taking great bites out of those sweet, fruity lard cakes. No. I did not wish to return. It would be too painful to do so.

Back in Oxford, I wrote to Aphra. My experience in Cirencester had taught me not to be tardy with matters that were important to me, so I told her I was going to ask for her hand. I no longer had Arthur, the fine horse she had named, to remind me of her each time I mounted with my troop. Since his death I had felt cut further adrift from Aphra, and ever more anxious at the distance between us.

So I also wrote to my mother, asking her advice. I did not want to spoil my chances with Aphra by giving my father any reason to forbid the union, but I felt a great need to press it urgently. She was able to reassure me. *Do write to ask your father's wisdom on the match. I can tell you he and Aphra's father are in agreement about it. There will be no difficulty, but I caution you, my dear son, to be ever humble and grateful to him. You are both so full of determination, as were he and his father, but when a son shows strength of character it can be taken as wilfulness. Question him not at all, and if all goes well I think you may be fortunate enough to make a love match as well as a dynastic one.*

When my father's reply to my enquiry came it did promise eventual good news, but he spent so much of the letter making slights at my part in the taking of Cirencester, noting the inconvenience to him at that town's reduction, and how much better he would have done things than Prince Rupert, that I was at the end gnawing my fist at his ungenerous words. Could he never praise me or my efforts? He had scoffed at me for not being at Edgehill, only to rail against me for injudicious fighting at Cirencester, which I found disloyal of him, not just to me but also to the King through the Prince. He misliked that I had allowed some good men in Cirencester to suffer, when I should not, though it was not up to me who was sent to Oxford at the end of a rope. I allowed my anger to run its course and then tried to put all thoughts of him aside, and to dwell only on being joined to Aphra. We were both very happy to know that at some time in the future we would be wed.

Our marriage could not be soon enough for me, but there was much to do in Oxford, and I was in no position to marry just yet. To my great pleasure, Prince Rupert suggested that I should stay in the city for a while. Soldiers and citizens still needed doctoring, my studies beckoned me and I must also spend time with my small troop. He suggested I should build up the numbers under my command, and indeed my little troop did grow as people heard of our experience at Cirencester. Somewhat to my surprise I discovered I was a popular captain. Recruits wanted to follow me because the word had gone out how enjoyable it was to ride with me. Several told me they felt safe because I brought back every man I took. It was pleasant to be thought a good captain, and soon I found myself commanding twenty-five men. It was still a small number, but was a useful addition to the defence of the city.

The court was well established in Oxford with the King in Christ Church and the Queen at Merton. The various offices of government were now so spread amongst the university colleges that the students remaining must needs be crammed into one crowded space. Defence of the city was also being attended to, with a great earth wall being dug and thrown up, with many prisoners being forced to labour on it. There was talk of parley with the enemy, as if all this preparation for war coming to the city might prove to be unnecessary. But talk is easy, agreement not so simple. By April it was clear negotiations were not going well, and by the middle of the month they were abandoned. The parliamentarians were not far away, but so far they held back from attacking the city, contenting themselves with other towns roundabout.

I worried about Master Willis, vulnerable at his farm.

To live in the country was dangerous, and to ride around it without protection was to invite attack. My troop and others went out regularly on patrol, dividing up the outlying areas between us so we could protect as many farms as possible. It was not just the farmers we wished to protect. For how can a crowded city such as Oxford be fed without the crops and animals thereabouts to feed its people? Horses were taken by both sides too, and more than once I saw old men, women and young children drag a plough through a field, having no other means of cultivating their land. We couldn't protect everyone and plunder could be indiscriminate. I know that some of our army took cattle, bringing them into the city as ransom, and they weren't always punishing those who supported parliament. It was a chaotic time. When war comes in, morality becomes a poor relation.

When on patrol, we joined in several skirmishes, which usefully increased our knowledge of combat. My troop was given the area in which Master Willis's farm lay, which pleased me, although his was only one of many properties we tried to protect. We also gathered information about any enemy forces we saw, and harried them if they were few enough in number for us to attack. We knew they had taken Abingdon, and so any intelligence about their further plans in the area could be valuable for the defence of our city. For the first week I rode out every day. We did not always engage, but even when we did not, our presence made several small enemy bands flee, and the local inhabitants were much cheered by us. Sometimes we split the troop, half going on patrol while the others attended to their harness and weapons, and the well-being of our horses. I was pleased by the results we were getting, and the men's discipline improved. We had suffered no more than at worst a ball grazing the side of Richard's helmet and several slight sword cuts.

Perhaps some thought us charmed, but it was luck more than magic that kept us safe, and even luck doesn't last for ever. Ours ran out one day when I had chosen not to go on patrol, a decision I later regretted. It had rained heavily a couple of days before and as a result I had a slight chill, with my nose dripping and a cough disturbing my sleep. In addition, I very much wanted to attend a lecture that day to be given by the King's physician, one William Harvey. I had long wished to engage him in conversation, as I greatly admired his knowledge. He had revolutionised our understanding of the way blood flows in the body of a man, and I had marvelled at reading how he had shown that valves in the veins send blood strictly towards the heart and not away from it. I considered him a veritable genius in the field of natural philosophy. Having him in our midst in the city and not managing to hear him speak was unthinkable. More, there was a rumour that he might demonstrate some of his experiments. I could in no way consider missing this event.

My whole troop went out at nine in the morning, on a beautiful day that belied the rain that had fallen the night before. I saw them go, my lieutenant leading them proudly, with Richard close behind him. Not for the first time I wished my father could see my troop, and show a little pride in what I had achieved. I shrugged the feeling away and went about my business. I would never please him. Even if I brought him an elephant it would not be enough! My foolish thought saved me from too much sadness about a father who could not, or would not, be the father I wished for. I thought of his ire if I arrived with a veritable menagerie of exotic animals as a gift for him, and knew I was wise to smile away the hurt.

At the lecture there was an experiment on a living dog, as well as Master Harvey's famous experiment on the arm of a living man, to show how the valves allowed blood to flow only one way. There was also the excitement of speaking briefly to the man himself. I told him I purposed to replicate his experiment on my arm and he warned me about it.

'Do not keep the arm bound for too long,' he said. 'A limb needs a constant flow of blood to all extremities. It may be damaged if you starve it for an excessive time.'

'I will be careful, sir.' I paused. 'And I wonder, can you recommend the best place to further my studies? I was thinking perhaps of Leiden.'

He nodded. 'I hear Leiden is a good place. My own studies were undertaken at Cambridge and Padua, but it is not so much the place but the people and the availability of good books that are important. If you will take my advice,' he said, 'read Galen. But follow Aristotle.'

He gave me another nod and passed on to speak to others. If only Master Willis had been there! He would have enjoyed the occasion at least as much as me.

I ate my midday meal in an inn close by, thinking I might see my troop return from their patrol if I sat in the window. I was not to be disappointed, but to my great distress they were in a sorry condition when they arrived. I went out at once to greet them, my heart leaping in my throat at the sight in front of me. My brave lieutenant was slumped against his horse's neck, a trooper riding close beside to aid him. Richard, unharmed, was leading them, but as I counted I could see that instead of twenty-five, they were only twenty-three.

I ran out and caught hold of my lieutenant's bridle. 'Get him down!' And then I saw how badly injured he was. 'Bring him in and lay him down.'

Even as we lifted him from his horse the life went out of his eyes, and his soul flew away. But I would not have his body lie in the street. We brought him into the inn and laid him gently on the floor.

'Stay with him,' I ordered the white-faced trooper who had helped me. 'I will come back as soon as I have spoken with Richard.'

'What of the other two?' I asked my friend.

'We didn't see the enemy hiding behind a hedge until they opened fire. Gregory and John fell almost immediately. We had no chance to recover them, being pursued for some distance by their horsemen, but will go out again to do so as soon as we can.'

'The trooper here with the body is in no state to go out again,' I said, thinking of the trembling of his limbs and his white face. 'Are you?' I looked at his fierce face and saw that he was. 'I will send the trooper back out to you. Take the men to the stables. Make sure they have some beer, then choose half a dozen who are steady and prepared to risk more action. Get my horse saddled and I will come to you as soon as I have dealt with the body. You are my lieutenant now.'

He nodded and led the troop away. I went into the inn and arranged for my fallen lieutenant's body to be taken to his lodgings and prepared for burial, but the commotion had caused agitation in the crowded inn. People wanted to know what had happened.

'It was an ambush,' I said.

'Will they attack the city?' asked one foolish fellow.

I left him to his fear and hurried to my men.

To do them credit, all my men wished to go out to recover the fallen, but I thought it better to risk only a few. To my surprise we met both riderless horses near to the city wall.

'We scattered to throw off the pursuit,' said Richard. 'And our fallen men's horses must have galloped away with us. I admit I was more concerned about our men than the horses, and didn't think to look for them.'

'No matter,' I said as we caught them without difficulty. 'They knew their way home, and are happy to be reunited with their fellows.'

After scouting carefully all around we discovered our men, both killed. One had taken a ball in his throat, and had doubtless been dead before he hit the ground. The other had been pistoled and then finished with a sword. Both had been stripped of their breast- and backplates, and their helmets were also gone, along with their pistols and swords.

'Take some comfort,' I said to my men. 'You could have done nothing for them. Now let us get them back with all speed in case the enemy returns.'

It was a bad business, loading them onto their horses. We were all much affected by it. We had by then become like family, and several troopers wept when we brought the bodies in.

After all had eaten, drunk and rested, I spoke to the men, expecting some of the gentlemen students to think twice about continuing under my command, but the contrary was true. Several more came to join us, having heard of our misfortune. I was much moved by their confidence in me, and determined to do my very best for them all.

So it was, in the height of summer that year 1643, with Richard by my side I rode out from Oxford again, with a troop of thirty men, to aid Prince Rupert in his siege of Bristol. We arrived in time to see that city fall. Almost immediately, the King's army marched to besiege the city of Gloucester, and we rode with them. Unfortunately, the Earl of Essex, a man I hated although we had never met, brought his army to relieve the siege and we were beaten off, which was a bitter disappointment.

With Prince Rupert's agreement I brought my troop to rest for a little while at my parents' house, it being close by. The house, lying as it did at the bottom of a secluded, wooded valley, felt immune to the war, even though several of the farms thereabouts had suffered, having soldiers of both sides take food and pay nothing for it.

I found my mother and Hugh as ever, but my father was much reduced in health. He had eventually succumbed to the surgeon's saw and had his leg off above the knee, the pain being too much to bear in the injured limb.

'His stump is recovering well,' said my mother when I asked her. 'And his pain is much relieved, but his mood is not so good.'

'He is angry about it?'

'I think it is more that he feels defeated.'

I could see what she meant. He didn't berate me, or goad me, although he was not particularly friendly or interested in me. He seemed turned in upon himself, as though life held little interest for him now he had no hope of setting his own two feet upon the ground.

I told him that Aphra had written to me, telling me how pleased she was that we should be wed.

'Have you decided with the Earl when that should be?' I asked him.

'When things are more settled,' was all he said. Whether he meant the war or some discussion between the two families that must be decided, I had no idea, and he did not enlighten me.

I could see that he was eating and drinking well enough,

but taking away his leg seemed to have also taken away his spirit. I was sorry for it, because although he no longer goaded me, he had not had a change of heart towards me. He had simply lost what little interest he had ever had in his eldest son.

# CHAPTER TEN

The next two years were a mixed time of huge effort and also tedious waiting. The waiting was for our marriage, which Aphra and I were both fidgeting for. But with the country in so much upheaval the families felt it sensible to wait until the war ended. We two were of the opposite mind. With life uncertain, surely all the more reason to marry and get an heir? But her family and mine knew we wished to live together in Oxford, and that was not thought a suitable place for a young wife, even though the Queen kept court there. So Aphra was stuck at her home in Norfolk, and I had my responsibilities in Oxford, with no way of providing a suitable home for her. I might dream of her sharing my lodgings, but we both knew it was impossible. She longed to attend debates at the university and engage with some of the great men there, but it was never going to be anything but a desire. That being so, I would not wish for her to marry me and be stranded in my parents' house with my difficult father to make her situation unhappy. And so we waited. Not for the first time, I wished I had wings and could fly over all the violence and confusion to land at her feet. I had long got over my concern about her true feelings. She continued to encourage me in all things to do with natural science, and thrilled, as I did, to have William Harvey in the city. What other woman could have said what she did so convincingly? Her words, both on natural philosophy and her feelings for me, had gone far beyond the instruction of a parent. They came, I felt sure, from her heart.

I felt my ardour grow with every letter I received. Once we were united I was sure our marriage would be one of strength and love, with children we both would cherish. I longed for children, a longing that echoed the maybe child I might have fathered and still hankered after. Sometimes I dreamt of it, the babe laid in my arms, perfectly made, a thing of wonder. But maybe it was a dream of children to come in the future, for I never saw the mother's face. I don't know what it was in me that cried out for them. Perhaps it was a yearning to be a much better father than my own, and maybe, with the death and injury I had seen and tended to, I longed to have something wholesome in my life. But we had to wait, and for now our vows were written privately to one another, not spoken in church. We told each other they were none the less binding for that. Our souls sang together, she wrote, and ever would. There would come a time, pray God soon, when we would be together.

There were few full-time students at the university now, but there were some, and I joined them whenever my other duties allowed. Together, we watched in awe as William Harvey demonstrated his experiments on living dogs, chickens, snakes and, of course, criminal cadavers. My good friend Master Willis returned at last, answering the call of the King, who had asked for more local men to defend the city so the army could go out and fight elsewhere. Master Willis, too, when he could, attended the lectures. He and I spent many a night in discussion about what we had learnt from William Harvey.

But Oxford was become an unpleasant place to live. Overcrowding brought many more vermin, along with much dirt and squalor. One day there was a bad fire. It did, I suppose, go some way to cleanse by burning, but it also destroyed many houses, as well as much of the cloth from Cirencester and Stroud, stored in an Oxford warehouse since the storming of the town. Some, I assume, must have been used to make uniforms, but I couldn't help remembering Mr Simons' warehouse being plundered due to my knowledge of it. The loss was only a small thing, especially compared to men's lives, but it made me consider anew the futility of war. We might as well have left that town their woollens and silks for all the good they had done our cause.

Then came plague.

Master Willis urged me to abandon doctoring and save myself, but he refused to do the same.

'I am not much of a soldier,' he said. 'I can watch on the walls, but would be of little use in a fight. I am best occupied with treating my patients. But you,' he went on, stopping my objections, 'you have a troop of horse relying on you. The cause needs you. Go and fight! Leave me to these poor souls.'

He was right. My troop of horse was now over thirty strong, and proved in many skirmishes. With people like Master Willis to defend our walls, we should ride out and join our prince again, wherever we were needed. So it was that in high summer 1644, with news of a catastrophic battle having been fought at Marston Moor, we rode out to replace some of the slain, after saying fond farewells to our friends remaining to defend the city.

I embraced Master Willis like a brother, sorrowful that I would likely never see him again. With battles to come for me, and the sick and dying for him, how could we expect to both survive?

The morning we left Oxford I had another letter from Aphra. I had told her of what I was going to do, and she enclosed a daisy from her garden and a slender ribbon from her dress. I had much to do before we rode out, but had already composed what I considered, if things went ill, my last letter to her. In the past we had sent each other poems and discussed them. She was above me in her understanding, but in the letter I now sent her was a poem clear enough, even for me. *It is, I believe, not a great piece,* I wrote. *I think Mr Carew borrows from Mr Shakespeare, and does not always do him justice. Can you see what I mean? Let us by all means dispute it when we are able. But oh! If only you could send me wings, and a wind to blow me to you. Without them, I send you this poem, in love. Thinking of you, always, and praying that I may reach your safe embrace before too long.*

*To Her in Absence; A Ship*

*Toss'd in a troubled sea of griefs, I float*
*Far from the shore, in a storm-beaten boat;*
*Where my sad thoughts do, like the compass, show*
*The several points from which cross-winds do blow.*
*My heart doth, like the needle, touch'd with love,*
*Still fix'd on you, point which way I would move;*
*You are the bright pole-star, which, in the dark*
*Of this long absence, guides my wand'ring bark;*

*Love is the pilot: but o'ercome with fear*
*Of your displeasure, dares not homewards steer.*
*My fearful hope hands on my trembling sail,*
*Nothing is wanting but a gentle gale,*
*Which pleasant breath must blow from your sweet lip:*
*Bid it but move, and quick as thought this ship*
*Into your arms, which are my port, will fly,*
*Where it for ever shall at anchor lie.*

In years to come, later generations will doubtless learn from others much about the battles won and lost in this terrible war, but I have no stomach for the telling of it. This is an account of my own life, made so that my heir, and his, might know something of the man I was. It is not a boastful telling of deeds in battle that I wish to convey, but more how I felt, seeing our fair country pulling itself in two. All I will say is that by the time another Christmas had come and gone, and another spring had tried to promise renewal, only to be followed by a despondent summer, I was tired. We all were. The whole country was tired, and yet like heedless beetles we still ran from one dispute to another, fighting, advancing or in retreat. It began to seem all one, for there was no end to it. There were calls for the King to make his peace with parliament, and for parliament to end the slaughter, but that rising star Cromwell was in steady ascendancy, building with careful skill his Model Army, giving even our own Prince Rupert cause for hesitancy.

Eventually, in September, Prince Rupert lost Bristol to the enemy. He was then in disgrace with the King, who would have him leave his army. Some said that even Prince Rupert would sue for peace with parliament now, but that the King would not listen. Others could not believe that this great warrior would ever be tired of fighting. For myself, I did not know what to think, only that I was exhausted, and that we were outnumbered by increasingly well-trained and disciplined men, while our troops were depleted. For the second time, and after a long while in the field, I led my ragged troop home for a rest.

I found my brother completely grown, with a manly beard and moustache, my mother pale and as tired-looking as I felt. As for my father, to my utter surprise he was walking again after much struggle, a false leg having been made for him. He seemed much recovered, even hearty, and greeted me with what almost seemed pleasure.

I saw first to my troopers' hurts, and then to my own. We were reduced by now to fifteen unhurt or lightly wounded, and three with serious wounds, one of whom died that night. My remaining men greatly benefitted from being able to take their ease in a place that had somehow escaped serious damage to the house and buildings, although crops, animals and stored food had suffered several raids by hungry soldiers from both the King's and parliament's armies. Hugh told me that they had taken to storing food in small caches, in order to preserve what they could, lest the family and tenants starve.

'I am sorry to have brought my men,' I said. 'I should have thought you would be short of food, but to my shame it had not occurred to me. This place has always felt to me to have a charmed existence.'

Hugh looked embarrassed. 'No matter,' he said with an awkward catch in his voice. 'If they are not fussy, we can feed them for a day or two.'

I could see that the defence of the house now fell to the very old and the very young, all others having gone to the war. Indoors, my family home looked the same, but there was a heaviness of heart about my mother and brother, although my father continued unseasonably cheerful. I very soon took to my bed. I was dog-weary, and yet my bones had become unaccustomed to a soft bed. After falling into a deep slumber almost as soon as I lay down, I woke with a jerk, as if we were under attack. I had reached for my sword before I was properly awake, then I lay for some minutes, listening keenly to the sounds of the house. All was well, and yet it was a while before I could get back to sleep. In this way I spent the night, sleeping and waking, until shortly before dawn I fell into another deep sleep, emerging from it somewhat bewildered, as if I had drunk too much wine.

I went to see my men before I broke my fast. They were well served, having eaten good bread with plenty of small beer. I had suggested to Richard that as my lieutenant he should rest like me in a chamber in the house, but he had insisted on staying with our men.

'For,' he said, smiling at me through his grimed face and straggled beard, 'some of the troop are more gentlemen than I, and I would not want any resentment. Besides, we do very well here at the stables.'

'I will see if we can provide beds for all in the house,' I said. 'I would like us to do that if I can, but I must speak to my family first.'

When I went back to the house they were all waiting for me with bread and some cheese for my breakfast. My father still looked cheerful but I took little notice, being so hungry that I fell on my meal with no ceremony.

'Now you are here I will tell you what is to happen from now on.'

I glanced at my brother for a clue as to our father's meaning, but he would not return my gaze.

'You have, I think, been long in the field, and oftentimes that results in having only a partial understanding of the whole situation.'

I looked at him sharply. 'I have been doing my duty as always.'

He let out a grunt, which could have been agreement or displeasure, or perhaps a simple acknowledgement of my words.

'While you have been following the Crown, perchance bravely, I have, due to the difficulties of my leg, been forced to take a more thoughtful role in the fortunes of our nation. There has been much correspondence between myself and others, and we have come to an inevitable conclusion.'

I wasn't interested in his verbal machinations, but he obviously wanted me to ask, so I did, not missing the opportunity first to respond to his gibe about my courage. 'It is not for me to say how brave I have been, or not,' I said. 'All I can say to you is that I bear all my hurts before, and none on my back. But tell me, Father, of your deliberations.' I poured myself some more of the best small beer I had had for over a year. The flavour, even though it was thinner than I remembered, spoke strongly to me of home.

My father looked pleased with himself. 'I have studied the progress of this war, and can see, with the King's waywardness and the advance of parliament's great army, that your cause is not only lost, but also misguided.'

I had the tankard to my lips, and had just taken a mouthful. For a moment I wanted to spew it back into the vessel, but with an effort I swallowed. Slowly I lowered the tankard and placed it carefully on the table, regarding it closely. My experience as captain of my troop had taught me many things over the past three years, but how to deal with my father had not been one of them. Even so, my voice, when I found it, was quiet.

'What of loyalty?'

'Oh, loyalty!' He said it as if he had rehearsed this moment. 'The King is hardly being loyal to his people, dragging them hither and thither to fight one another, while bleeding them dry with taxes, and inviting Catholics from overseas to join him and his French queen to overthrow our good English men.'

I could not find more than a continuing low voice. 'I think you will find that parliament, just as much as the King, has welcomed many mercenaries into their army during this war.'

'So do not boast to me of loyalty,' he said, as if I had not spoken. 'Your loyalty, and mine, is to our family. How do you think I have kept our house and estate for the most part untouched? Politics is more than bowing to the King or arguing in parliament. It is also keeping hold of what is important to us.'

I looked at Hugh, but spoke to my father. 'It is not you who has kept the house safe, but Hugh. He has drilled his men and boys, and patrolled the land. Give him some credit for your safety while you cannot fight.'

'You have no idea what you say,' he said in reply.

'I say what I see, which is Hugh come into manhood with dignity and purpose. He has risen to the need, so give him some credit for it!'

'Thomas.'

'It's true, Hugh. You know it is.'

Our father shifted in his seat. 'It is time you listened to reason. I have been too lenient with you in the past. I blame myself for that.'

'Too lenient!' I looked to my mother for the first time, but she was staring at the table.

'Yes, too lenient. And perhaps you are not too old for a whipping, even yet.'

'I am twenty-one, and captain of a troop of horse in His Majesty's army, while you are an incomplete man. Do you propose to be the one to administer this whipping?' I stood up and pushed back my stool.

My mother spoke a warning as my brother had. 'Thomas.'

I stared at my father, but he refused to look me in the eye although he spoke haughtily to me.

'Sir Thomas Fairfax is pleased to accept Hugh into his army. He is ready to go. There is also a place for you and any of your troops prepared to stay loyal to their captain. You will not lose your command. I have assured Sir Thomas of your qualities.'

I completely lost my temper, I admit it, but am not sorry for it.

'Do my qualities include being a traitor to my king?' I glared at him. 'Does your disappointment at not being a member of the privy council lead you to this?' His face darkened, and I knew I had struck a painful blow. But I was not ready to stop.

'Do you imagine I will command my ensign to trample on my own banner?' My blood was raging, and I forgot he was my father. Indeed, he did not deserve the title. 'What do you think *Pro rege et regno* means? Are you telling me that these past years of strife, and the numbers of dead and wounded are as nothing? *You* may be able to abandon your duty to your king at a whim, but I cannot, and I will not. Furthermore, I condemn you for commanding Hugh so ill. I will never believe he is a willing traitor, unlike you!'

# CHAPTER ELEVEN

I thrust back from the table, sending my stool flying. I almost believe that, had I been wearing the hanger he had given me, I would have slashed him with it. But I was not, and so saved from parricide. Instead, I turned away from him in disgust and left the room. Indeed, I left the house, my blood racing and my mind in turmoil. I very nearly commanded my men straight away to make ready to leave, but two things prevented me. First, my two sorely wounded men. They had managed to arrive here on horseback, but were in no state to go on. I had to decide what to do for them. The second was my family. I had no more to say to my father, but I could not go without speaking to my mother and Hugh. In consequence, I changed direction, turning away from the stables and instead went into my mother's garden.

Her garden had ever been a place of solace for me when a child. Here, I had always been reminded that I had the love of at least one parent, even if that love was not able to be expressed as I wished it. In her garden there had always been something to soothe me. That day, her autumn pleasure ground was full of colour. I was never a gardener, and knew few names. All these bronze and yellow flowers looked to me like daisies, and so I thought them, nodding as they were in the breeze. They had no care for man's disputes, but would likely carry on flowering for a thousand years after we were all done. And yet, our strife had affected even this gentle garden. Much of it had been given over to cabbages and other vegetables. No doubt she reasoned that here, out of sight of casual plunder in the fields, such food would sustain the family, should hungry soldiers take everything else.

I sat on my mother's favourite bench and leant my hands on my knees. I must calm myself, so I could make the best decisions. Would my wounded men be safe and cared for if I left them here? I could by no means guarantee it. I should take a cart, and carry them with us. I must write to their families, and to that of the dead trooper. They might want to recover their sons, but I knew that one of the wounded had a family of split loyalties. I had pitied that man, that his father and uncle were on opposite sides, and that he was of his uncle's persuasion. Was I now to be pitied, as I had pitied him?

The sound of gravel turning underfoot made me look up. It was not my mother, but Hugh. Without a word he sat beside me and gave a great sigh. I put my arm about his shoulders and hugged him. He turned to me with anguish in his face.

'Don't do this, Thomas,' he begged. 'Don't defy our father.

Please. The war is lost for the King and we must continue our lives as best we can.'

His face was close to mine, and we were both grown adults now, but beneath his wispy beard and moustache he still had a boy's face.

'And you think this is a good way to go about it? To abandon the King when he most needs us?'

'To fight the King's army is to bring the King to proper negotiations,' said Hugh.

I removed my arm from about his shoulders. 'That is our father speaking, not you. Did you see our father's expression when I mentioned the privy council?' I said. 'He has burned about that ever since I was a child. I remember it from when he took me to court. He could not accept then that the King held him in any less than the highest regard, although he was undoubtably in his favour! That is why he has turned against him.'

'That is not the reason,' said Hugh. 'He has been watching the politicking, while you have been fighting. It is time to bring things to an end. Even your Prince Rupert thinks so.'

'He does not!'

Hugh regarded me with a heartbreaking yearning in his voice. 'Oh, Thomas. I have longed to join you in your endeavours. For three years I have dreamt of us riding out together, you as my captain, I as your trooper. You are my elder brother! I love and honour you. Please make it so I can do this.'

'Hugh. You are asking me to go against everything I believe in.'

'But for me! For family.'

It was my turn to sigh. Although he had not suffered so much as I with our father's wrath, he had always taken my part and been entirely loyal to me. Had he not even been whipped for supporting my foolishness with Catherine? From little boys we had been as one. Was he now asking so very much? Would it be the right thing to do for the King and country, to bring an end to this long, lamented war? And if so, was it right to change sides to bring about that end?

'What you ask is very hard.'

'But not impossible. Others have done it. Round about, more and more are coming to feel this way.'

'I am not others, Hugh.'

We both fell silent. And then he spoke again. 'It would be sad if you were prevented from marrying.'

'What?'

He had that sheepish look upon his face, as if he knew he had said something he should not, while having decided to say it anyway. 'Our father, and hers, the Lady Aphra. He told me, Father I mean, that he and the Earl were of the same mind.'

I stared at him. 'What are you saying, in your tangled way?'

'Simply that both families have the same opinion regarding the war, and Father says the Earl will not allow the marriage if you continue in a different persuasion.'

'And he told you this?'

'No! But I overheard him and our mother speak of it.'

I got to my feet, my heart thumping in my breast as if it might set itself free and fly away. 'I'm sorry, Hugh. I cannot speak to you any more.'

'Where are you going?'

I could not bring myself to reply.

I ran back to the house and threw open the front door. It flew against the wall with a crash, bringing the dogs barking. A servant carrying an armful of linen hurried to see what the commotion was.

'Where is the master?'

She shrank under my anger, even though it was not for her.

'He is in my lady's room, I believe, sir.'

I took a few large breaths in an attempt to steady myself and then opened the door. He was indeed within, sitting with his good leg on a stool, near to my mother, who was sewing. They both turned to look at me, my mother with anxiety and my father with belligerence.

'So now you look to block my marriage to Aphra!'

He laughed. 'No one blocks it but yourself, if you adhere to your foolishness in the King's army.'

My mother sought to soothe matters by speaking. 'Her parents have come to the conclusion that we, and other families, have,' she said. 'There is no need or reason for further slaughter. We need healing now.'

'Aphra has always supported me!'

My father spoke again. 'But she will obey her father, as you must.'

'Must? *Must?* I am no longer a child, I . . .'

'Then stop behaving like one.'

He could always bring me to lose my temper at the end. 'I will not, now, or ever again allow you to bully me. Not for anything!'

He had a slight smile about his mouth that enraged me even more, and his voice was infuriatingly calm.

'So you are willing to have your inheritance sequestered when parliament wins, your family thrown out of their home, to abandon your supposed love, and even allow your mother to be shamed in public, all for your pride?' He did not wait for an answer, nor did I have one for him. Instead, he went on in his falsely reasonable tone. 'I say to you, you unnatural child who is set on ruining my family, that if you persist in fighting on for the misguided royalist cause I will disown you as my son, knowing as I do that you are no child of mine, but the result of an illicit liaison between your mother and another, while she was betrothed to me.'

I stared at him. His words hit me like a great blow to my helm, stopping my mouth and sending my senses reeling. I don't know how long I stood there, dumb and deaf, with a rushing in my head as by degrees his meaning dripped like burning oil into my brain. How could he even hint at so dishonouring my mother? He was speaking thus about his wife, simply in order to bring his son to heel? I would not look at him. Not for anything would I give him the satisfaction of seeing my face. Nor would I rage, as he expected me to rage. Instead, I made a deep bow to my mother and turned my back on him. Then I left the room with as much dignity as I could find within myself and went out into the air.

I didn't know where I was going when Hugh came upon me. I think I might have had some idea of hanging myself from a tree. I was blinded with tears that ran heedless from my eyes, and I felt so trapped I wanted no more than to die. It was, by a great measure, the worst moment of my life. I felt as if I were cast adrift, with no safe harbour anywhere, nor was there any man to cast me a line to save my life. But then Hugh found me. He found me, and became for that time my elder. Not knowing why I was so distressed he treated me with the utmost loving kindness. He asked nothing, but took me by the arm and led me into a copse that had been our favourite hiding place when young. He sat me down upon the now-weathered trunk we had sat upon all those years ago, before the war.

For a while I could do nothing other than rage and weep. It was as if I were a child of five again.

I had seen men die in horrible ways, I had even killed outright, to my certain knowledge, at least five men. I had tended to plague victims and in battle once or twice thought my hour had come, but nothing, none of it, had distressed me as much as that man's words. Why? They were just words. Should I not be happy, after all, that perhaps he was not my father? But his words struck at the very core of me. He had undone in one sentence all I had ever thought I was.

'He has cost me everything,' I said, still weeping. 'He has taken it all away and I am without hope. My Aphra, my mother, my father who is not, even you. There is no one and nothing for me now.'

'Am I not here, comforting you?' said Hugh.

Indeed he was, and I was glad of it, but for how much longer could we be each other's comforter?

At last, when I was somewhat calmer, I told Hugh what the man who I had thought my father had said.

'Don't for one moment believe him,' he said stoutly, trying to hide his shock. 'You are my full brother. I would die before I believed anything different. He simply tries to bring you to heel. Besides, you would not think that behaviour capable of our mother, any more than I would. Isn't that so?'

I could not say yay or nay. I could remember how Catherine and I had dallied so unwisely. Desire is a very dangerous playfellow. Only my mother knew the truth, and how could I ask her? But speak to her I would, if I could manage it without that man's knowledge.

'I ask only one thing of you,' I said at last, my tears all spent.

'Anything.' I knew he could not mean that but I was done with arguing.

'Bring our mother to me somehow, without his knowledge. I would speak to her briefly, before I go.'

'You don't need to go anywhere, brother. This will always be your home!'

I loved him for that. I loved him then and ever shall, in spite of everything. I blame the person he was then for none of it. Not a thing. He had been schooled by his father, and there is no more to be said about it.

I spent the day caring for my wounded and making ready for our departure. I spied the cart I would use, along with a horse to pull it, and made sure the animal was fed, as well as a quantity of good, fresh straw laid in the cart to cushion the jolts as much as possible. I set the rest of the men to check all was ready and made sure they and their horses were well fed and watered. Then, in the afternoon, I sat in my mother's garden and composed the letters I had to write. To the family of the dead man I said how bravely he had acquitted himself. To the families of the wounded I said the same. It was no more than the truth.

I knew my mother would come, so I sat on, well into the twilight, when the bats came out to swoop about my head, and the birds had done their evensong. When I heard the gravel being tumbled underfoot again I quickly turned to greet her, and saw instead my brother.

'He keeps her too close,' he said. 'And now he has taken her to his bedchamber. I have no chance to speak to her tonight. And too . . .' His eyes seemed to swim in unshed tears. 'He said privily to me that he is decided utterly to make public his disowning of you, by reason of your paternity, unless you submit to his will by this month's end. Thomas! Consider our mother. Think of her.'

I gazed at the flowers, all turned to grey in the growing dark.

'Thomas? Please . . .'

'I do think of her. But none of this is of my making. To hold my mother's honour to ransom in order to bend me to his will? That is so evil I cannot describe my feelings to you. What man loving his wife would dream of making such an accusation? He is become a monster, Hugh. He cannot love her, or respect her, or himself. And if I fought against my friends to save our mother, what would be his next demand? There is no end to it, Hugh. He has no respect for loyalty or conscience. My loyalty to the King is a matter of my conscience. It cannot be given away like alms to the poor, not for me anyway. It's all very well for him, sitting in his chair. What of my situation? In changing his colours he will not have to meet his erstwhile companions and strive to kill them. That would undo me utterly. I cannot do it. I know what you are asking, Hugh, and I cannot do it.'

'But surely . . .'

'Listen. I have had men follow me, and come to lose their lives, their everything, for the cause under my orders. Now how can I say stop, lest my family lose their house?'

'Not that, but to stop more slaughter! And most of all to save our mother from shame.'

'Hugh, in a perfect world the people would have spoken of their hurts to the King and he would have listened and changed his policies to make things right. But we do not live in a perfect world. In this world there will always be men who do not agree. And in the end it will still come down to negotiation, however many men die before that happens.'

'So stop it now!'

'But I have faith in the King and his ministers to make the changes needed when the time is right. He is a king! If he is forced, and humiliated, any change will not be heartfelt.

When kings fall, chaos rages. Witness all the pamphlets and newspapers now being published every day! Even the Church is not immune. How do we know what to believe without some sort of authority? Every faction has its own philosophy. Some say there is no God, or he dwells in all things. Others have it that we are God. There are men who now say there should be no clergy, no government, and no man should own his property, but it must be shared with the meanest vagabond. How would that fill our bellies? Every person it seems has a different view, and there are more and more factions rising who would try to force us into their way. We already have war; we do not need utter chaos to follow. We need proper government, and for that we must have a rightful king.'

Hugh shook his head. 'Where you see chaos I see opportunity. We will still have the King! But only when he loses the war will he truly understand the need for change. When that happens all will have their chance to speak, and when the King has wise advisers from every part of our country there will be peace and fairness everywhere.'

'I cannot agree, but will not argue with you, Hugh. I have more immediate concerns.' I looked at my young brother. 'Your father has given me to the end of this month. I will wrestle every day to find a way to save our mother from his hateful threat, but at this moment I have to tell you that I can see nothing to help her, unless he comes to see what a laughing stock he would make of himself.'

For a moment Hugh was still, his head bowed. When he spoke his very soul sounded in it, and I could feel him tremble with emotion. 'Tom. I am to join the army next week. I had thought I would ride to join it with you. I wanted to fight alongside you to give me courage . . .'

'Hugh . . .'

'I wanted to ride under your banner.'

'The only way you could do that would be to follow its motto, but the army you propose to join is not for the King.'

I took my last piece of paper and wrote upon it before giving it to Hugh.

'Here. This is the place where my friend Richard's parents live in London. You, and our mother if she wishes, can write to me there. I will get the letters eventually.'

'But where are you going?'

'I cannot tell you. We are, it seems, on opposite sides.'

I could see his mouth twist with the agony of denying tears, and my heart went out to him.

'Hugh. I will make you a solemn promise.'

'What?'

'I promise that I will never stand in the field against you. You will never have to fire your pistol at me, nor will you ever feel my sword at your neck. I cannot be on the same side as you. I will never be a parliamentarian, but that does not mean I will fight you. Have no fear of meeting me in battle. You may face others you recognise, but you will never face me. And know that you *will* find courage when it is needed. I also promise you that.'

I stood up. 'Come here.'

I embraced him, and he hugged me back, so fiercely I thought he would never let me go. I wanted to tell him he was much too young to fight, but I could not. I would not have listened if anyone had said that to me at his age.

'Keep yourself safe,' I told him. 'Don't be heroic. Rather stay alive, so I can see you again. And give my greetings and love to our mother, when you see her.'

He could not reply for tears, but simply nodded and turned away. There was no moon, but I could see his shape well enough as he went along the path, up the steps, and to the corner. Then he was gone.

# CHAPTER TWELVE

Until I had decided what to do about my wounded men I could not move my troop, but nor could I lie in the house that night. I had no stomach to enter the place again. Instead, I went to my men in the stables. I first checked that all was well with them, and then drew Richard aside.

'I need to speak with you.'

We sat outside in the warm end-of-summer dark, discussing quietly what to do.

'I had thought we would engage with Fairfax,' said Richard. 'Surely, Prince Rupert will lead us to fight him? But if you want to keep away from his army that is obviously impossible.'

'For me,' I said. 'But not for you.'

'You mean to give up your post?'

'You are more than capable of leading them.'

'They would rather have you, as would I.'

I couldn't avoid making a sigh. 'I'm sorry. But I am not going to relinquish the cause. I will still fight for the King, just not here in the south.'

'I understand. And I think they will also. So . . .' He hesitated. 'Will you return to Oxford?'

I thought about it. In some ways it was an appealing prospect. I supposed Master Willis, if he lived, still resided there, and I could return in some way to my medical studies. But that held a huge risk.

'I think it very likely that Oxford will be besieged before too long,' I said. 'The enemy grows stronger every month. What if I am caught there by Hugh's army and unable to escape? I would rather cast my weapons away on the field than face my brother in battle, so I think I can be of more use elsewhere.'

'In the north?'

I shrugged. 'In truth, Richard, I have not yet decided exactly what to do, but yes, I suppose I must ride north. My only plan so far is to load our poor injured fellows onto the cart I have prepared, and take them to a farm I believe will still be for the King, unless every man hereabouts has turned his allegiance. Plenty of the towns are for parliament, but in the country I believe some are still for the King. The farm is not too far distant, and I hope they will be able to bear the move. The cart and horse can be in payment for their care. I think the farmer will agree. After that, I do not know, other than to keep away from here, and most of all from Fairfax.'

'Why not leave England entirely?'

I stared at him. 'What do you mean?'

'England is not the only nation involved in this strife,' he said.

'There are also Ireland and Scotland too. They have their parts to play. And Scotland is the King's own country. Surely Fairfax will not march his army so far when he has much to occupy him in the south?'

'Perhaps not.' I strained to see his expression but it was too dark. 'Are you serious? I know nothing of either country.'

'No more do I, but it would be something wonderful to see them before we die.'

I so wished I could see his face. 'What do you mean?'

'Only that Mark Compit has the ear of the men, and their loyalty. They would be well served by him.'

'Do you mean we should make our ensign into a captain, and that you would wish to come with me?'

'Would you rather be on your own?'

He asked it diffidently. I could tell he did not want to presume I would need his company, but I thought of how earlier I had so needed the quiet care of my brother. If I knew anything about myself, I recognised that fellowship of one kind or another was vital to my well-being, especially now, with the private hell I had been cast into by the man I had thought my father. I had barely begun to wrestle with the question of how my life would be in future. All I knew was that I did not expect that man to row back on what he had said if I continued to defy him. It was a terrible thing, to suddenly lose the identity I had thought was mine, but in a way, the truth or otherwise of what he had said mattered not at all. Truth could come later, perhaps; for now it was all about power, and he had it all, every drop.

I did not know what I could do about that, but I was very moved at Richard's quiet, unassuming friendship. If he was willing to come with me then I would not refuse him. Perhaps together we could discover a way of me protecting my mother's honour while I still stayed loyal to the King, but now was not the moment to speak of that.

'What of your family, Richard?'

He laughed. 'They have always known of my desire to wander. If it had not been the war, it would have been something else. You know of my ambition to be of influence at court. I longed to eventually be sent as ambassador to the furthest land I could imagine, but Scotland will do for now. Or Ireland if you prefer it.'

'I am more moved than I can say. I had thought to give you a letter for Prince Rupert, informing him of my situation, and for you to take my place, but if you wish to take your chance with me I would welcome it. If you are really sure.'

In reply he simply gripped my arm and said, 'Of course. We are good friends, are we not?'

'We must speak to the men.'

'Then let us do that now.'

The discussion didn't take long. I'm sure that having another among us who was from a divided family made a great difference to their understanding. There was no hothead in our troop, only seasoned men who had been greatly sobered through conflict. Their vote was to rejoin Prince Rupert's regiment immediately, under the command of Mark Compit, who, by the light of the lamp in their quarters, was obviously very keen to take hold of the command. And so it was agreed. I gave to Mark all the badges of my office, and he took them with a seriousness that became him. He pledged to beg the Prince's pardon for our absence, and to explain our purpose to join the fight further north. Then we all settled to sleep.

I do not know how the others fared, but my rest was unsettled. So much filled my mind. Talking to Richard had cheered me, but had chased away not a jot of the sadness about my family, and I had only told him of my brother's decision to fight for parliament, not about my paternity, or of my hopes of marrying Aphra drifting away. I would tell him those things when we were alone on the road, though how I would get the words out I did not know. Lying quietly in the straw, surrounded by the breaths of men and horses, all my troubles assailed me. I wanted nothing more than to get up and hurry into the house, to embrace my mother, and ask her for the truth, but I could not do it. The man I had called my father floated before my eyes, and would not let me pass. He had shamed my mother in front of me, and threatened more. I could never forgive him. Round and around these poisonous thoughts kept me sleepless. In the end I got up, wide awake, as the first glimmer of dawn came in at the window.

I harnessed the farm horse myself, and gave her some oats. Then I began to saddle my own animal, a pale gelding that had replaced my much-lamented Arthur at Cirencester. As I reached to lift down his bridle, I almost struck Hugh with my outstretched arm.

'Hugh!'

He said nothing, but thrust a bundle into my arms, mumbling incoherently. Then he backed through the door and hastened away. For a second I had stupidly imagined that he had come to ride with us, but of course, dutiful son that he was, he had not. Instead, he had brought the belongings from my room. It was thoughtful of him, but I wished he had not. His brief appearance had made my departure that much harder. I thrust the bundle into my pack and finished making my horse ready. Richard tethered his mount to the rear of the cart so he could drive it. We lifted our wounded men in, as gently as we were able, and Richard got up to take the reins. The troop that had been mine was ready, and soon mounted. Together, we all moved off. I was not going to look back at the house, but found I was quite unable to resist. There, in the increasing light, clear at her window, stood my mother in the green gown she had always loved best. It was, I expect, out of fashion now, but was the one that gave me the deepest memories of being a little child. She raised her hand to me behind the glass. After a heartbeat I did the same. I cannot be ashamed to admit that I felt tears behind my eyes. I do not regret them, except that they blurred the last view I had of her.

Below, standing at the door, was my brother. He waved vigorously, but I did not have it in my heart to reply in kind to him. I was too sad for such demonstration. Instead I briefly saluted him as I had done our mother, and then turned my face to the road ahead.

On the high road we parted company. Richard and I watched the troop trot away in good order east towards Oxford. A large part of me went with them. Had I not raised them to a fighting force, brought them, and myself, discipline and courage in the field? I was proud of them all, and would have given much to stay with them but we turned west, to deliver our fragile cargo.

'I think it might be wise to keep this mare if we can,' said Richard from the cart after some minutes of silence between us. 'We may be glad of a pack animal on our travels.'

'I was thinking more of a spare horse to ride, should one of ours become lame,' I said. 'She has been ridden in the past.'

'Then we are thinking similarly.'

He looked across and smiled as if to encourage me. I might no longer know who I was, but Richard seemed to see no difference in me.

We delivered our two wounded men without mishap. The farmer was very pleased to be given a cart, his own having been taken some while ago by a band of soldiers.

'They said they were for the King,' he said. 'But it little matters, because neither King's nor parliament's men pay for what they take these days.'

I thought it wise to give him coin in lieu of the horse we kept, so I did, and he was happy enough at that.

We had divested ourselves of our last responsibilities, and I could see the pleasure in Richard's face. I resolved to put my personal difficulties from me for a while, lest I spoil his enjoyment of our sudden freedom. Our simple plan was to put as much distance as possible between ourselves and Fairfax's army before joining another troop, so I led the way across country until we reached the road north. But Wales lay to our west, and Richard professed a desire to see that country too. As far as we knew, the port of Milford was controlled by the King. Perhaps we would be able to find a boat from there to take us to Ireland, or up the coast to Scotland? Fighting men must surely be needed everywhere, with the whole country aflame? Getting to the Welsh port, however, meant us crossing the Severn, which would not be easy. We did not dare risk parliament-held Gloucester, so we kept going north in search of a crossing in royalist hands. Richard became merry at our freedom to roam, and I too felt a lifting of my spirits, although I still had much on my mind. We set an easy pace, as if on a holiday, and took pains to avoid any confrontation. The war had ravaged some places with fire and slaughter, while other parts seemed to have escaped conflict entirely. And yet, even in the most bucolic of places there was evidence that the villages had not been spared. Even if every building stood unscathed, we saw women and old men at work in the fields, but few young men. I could see, coming from a landed family as Richard had not, that the people would struggle to gather in the harvest this year.

We stopped in a shady spot by a stream in the middle of the day. We ate some of the rations I had been given at home, and every bite reminded me of what I had been told I no longer was. Neither of us were inclined to talk. The day was too warm, and the stream did enough chattering for us both. I lay back under a tree and closed my eyes. I must have slept almost immediately, and deeply, because when I woke Richard was attending to the horses, and the day was far gone.

'I was beginning to think I would have to lift your sleeping form into the saddle!'

I struggled to my feet. My throat was dry, and I felt drugged with sleep. 'No need for that, but I see we have lost much of the afternoon.'

Richard tightened his horse's girth, and then attended to my mount. 'No matter. I slept too. I think we are tireder than we know. But we should perhaps go a little further today, and find a safer place to sleep.'

'You're right, of course.'

He looked at me. 'I have been thinking . . . having no letter of permission, we could be accused of desertion.'

I knelt by the stream. I drank deeply and splashed my face with water before replying. 'I have been thinking the same thing, Richard, and it troubles me to think I may put you at risk. We should have sought a letter from our commander before we did this.'

He had already tied our spare horse's lead rein to his saddle, and now he mounted. 'That would have meant going to Oxford, and we decided against that. You have decided to avoid facing your brother in battle, and I support your decision. It doesn't mean we are deserting the King, just searching for another way to help him.'

For the next few minutes we were quiet, as we listened for any other horses on the road. Hearing nothing, we turned north again and rode at a steady trot. 'There's many a captain in need of men and horses that wouldn't be interested in my concerns, nor our loyalties,' I said. 'We could be pressed into service by either side.'

'Then,' said Richard, 'we had better make sure we are not caught. And consider this: no letter of introduction from our commander would be of use if we were pressed by the enemy. I feel sure that if we are careful we will eventually reach some of our own kind who will welcome our swords. But, Thomas?'

He rarely called me by my full name.

'Yes?'

'You made an honourable decision. In normal life you would be praised for it.'

'It's kind of you to say so, but in truth I know I would make a very poor soldier if I came to the field against Hugh. It would be enough to even suspect he was in the army to make me fearful and distracted. That is no way to lead men, nor even to defend oneself. If that makes me a deserter in the eyes of others, then so be it. But I gave him my promise, and can do nothing more or less than I am doing now.'

'I have no such honourable reason. But our lost afternoon shows me how very tired we have become. If we ride gently, we will restore our energy for our future, whatever it may hold. And I know I fight better with you by my side.'

'And I you.'

He offered me his fist. '*Rege et regno.*'

I met his with mine. 'King and kingdom!'

We were still young, and Richard became ever more festive as we travelled. He began to sing the old drinking songs from the Oxford inns, and I joined in. A man observing us might have considered we were students again, except that we were at pains to keep our wits about us. For a while I forgot about my family, but then my father's words came back into my mind and my singing faltered.

'Come on, Tom! Did you not study that pamphlet I gave you?'

'Of course I did. I would never spurn any gift you gave me, but that was an age ago, and I am terrible at remembering songs. And there is no help, for I have no idea where it is now!'

'Then I shall make up some new songs and school you myself. There's no escaping me.'

His mood had infected his horse, which began to fidget, so Richard gave him his head. They cantered away from me along the road, Richard waving his arm at me as he went. It took a little while to catch them up because I did not want to tire my horse for no good reason. Riding alone also gave me an opportunity to let drop the mask of happiness and brood on my troubles again, to which I still had no answer. Eventually I saw them. He had dismounted, was off the road, and allowing his animal to graze. I think he had not a care in the world. Something about the scene made tears prick at my eyes. I willed them away, put on an expression of pleasure and joined him.

When we reached Upton, we found the bridge too damaged to cross. In the end we went on to Worcester, and took a room in an inn near the cathedral. I had been trying to remain cheerful for Richard's sake, but once we were settled in our room, without anything to attend to excepting ourselves, he quickly saw the truth.

'Are you thinking about your brother?'

'No, at least not entirely. I'm sorry to be so dull.'

'Then spill all to me, or whatever it is will eat you like rot in timber. Are you having second thoughts about what we are doing?'

'No. But I do need to speak of what troubles me, if you are willing to listen.'

He immediately poured us a little wine, handed me mine and took his seat nearby. 'I am more than willing.'

How well his expression showed me the truth that lay behind his words. A little exasperation, yes, but only that I had hesitated to speak. The tears that had been so close behind my eyes all day swelled until I could hardly see. He filled the silence I was forced to leave by resting his hand briefly upon my shoulder.

'Are we not the best of friends, and have been through much together? Whatever it is, I will support you. You know I will.'

I could only nod, but it was so hard to form the words. It was not just tears I fought. There was shame as well. In the end, what I said surprised even me. 'I think I have decided to change my name.'

His expression was so comical it even made me smile through my tears.

'Why ever so? Are you *mad*?'

'You said you would support me!'

This gentle sparring was such a good way to begin. It went some way to chase the tears from my eyes, and helped me concentrate on the facts of the situation, rather than the feelings that had threatened to overwhelm me. As I spoke, anger at that man held sorrow away, at least for a while.

I told him everything I had not shared before, of losing Aphra, and of my father's words disowning his paternity, while shaming his own wife.

'So,' I said at last. 'You see me now, not knowing who I am, or where I belong, with no certainty about the name I have. If I could have spoken to my mother before we left I could have asked her account of it, but he kept her away from me.'

'Don't you think your father's assertion, vile though it was, was simply to rein you in?'

I shrugged. 'Hugh said that too, but I simply don't know. I have thought it all ways around and cannot come to any judgement on the matter without speaking to the only person who would know.'

'Your mother.'

'Yes.'

Richard looked at me carefully. 'I have, as you know, met the lady, and found her most charming and friendly, but what makes you think she would tell you the truth, if it was to her and your disadvantage to do so?'

'She would not lie to me!'

'She would almost certainly feel she had to, if what your father said is true. Maybe I am wrong, but I hardly think a court would allow you to be disowned after over twenty years of him naming you as his heir. But your mother's reputation would be ruined, whether she were guilty of a liaison or no. If you were there now, she would say the accusation was not true. Of course she would.'

I felt even more despondent. 'So I will spend the rest of my life not knowing who I am? I had hoped she would write, to reassure me, or if not that to tell me who I really am. It is extremely burdensome, to have all I knew to be whisked away in a moment.'

'And yet . . .' Richard paused. 'You have never felt an affinity to him . . .'

I shook my head in despair. 'I am not the only person to have had a difficult parent, but now it feels almost as if I have wished this upon myself. And yet I never thought him to be harbouring such a reason to dislike me! And I cannot see that my mother would have had the opportunity to behave as foolishly as did I with my Catherine, even if she had wanted to. Girls of that status are kept very close until married. Her family is not of the middling sort.'

'Indeed not. And yet you doubt . . .'

'Richard, I doubt everything about myself now! Where I am going, where I came from, whether I will ever now find a suitable wife, who my parents are, if I even have a brother at all . . .'

'You have a half-brother at the least, Tom. And I have seen how he loves you. And I would be another if it were possible. For I have no brother of my own, and would dearly love to be yours.' He reached out, as was his way when moved, and put his hand on my shoulder again.

I covered it with my own, feeling the watering of my eyes once more.

'You are as good as any brother.'

There was silence between us again, and then he got up and refilled my glass.

'I will go down and ask that we should be served our meal up here. Then we can make our plans without any overhearing us. Does that meet with your approval?'

He took my nod for assent and left the room. I listened to the sound of his feet on the stairs and breathed a deep sigh to steady myself. By the time he returned I was looking out of our window onto the yard below, and had rubbed my eyes to banish all threat of tears. He spoke heartily, and I was glad of it.

'They say our meal will not be long in coming.' He picked up his glass. 'So, Tom. You purpose to change your name.'

I nodded. 'That, and if you would oblige me, I would ask you to inform my family that I am dead.'

To do him credit his expression did not alter. 'Ah.'

'You see,' I said. 'If I am to stop that man from shaming my mother I have to convince him I no longer support the King. If I am dead, he has no need or ability to bend me to his wishes.'

'While being alive, you can keep fighting for the King under a new name.'

'Exactly!'

'It is, I think, a good plan. But to allow your mother to believe you are dead . . . Is there no way of avoiding that?'

'If you can think of a way to do that without jeopardising the secret truth, I would be more than pleased to hear it.'

'Surely there would be a way to get a letter to her . . .'

'And if he read it? I dare not risk it. He has me trapped, Richard. He gave me until the end of the month to cease my support for the King. After that, if I don't, he will destroy my mother's reputation, and publicly disown me.'

'You really believe he would do that, and that this is the only way?'

'I do believe it. He must be unhinged, because he will make himself into a laughing stock for all the years he presented me as his son, but I am sure he is capable of carrying out his threat. I tell you, he is poison. Better for me to be thought dead than for my poor mother to be brought down so low.'

'I wish I could think of an alternative. It is very hard for you, and will be for her too.'

I walked about, unable to be still a moment longer. 'It is very

149

hard for us all! But if I am dead to my family, Hugh will be able to inherit with no impediment, I will no longer have to bear that man's company, and Aphra's father will straight away be able to look for another betrothal for her. No doubt,' I added bitterly, 'some parliamentarian idiot will take her, one who will not have the brain or wit to appreciate her.'

'We must save her from that! Go to her and marry in secret. I would be your witness.'

'Believe me, I have thought of that often over the past few years, but she loves and honours her father. I think for her, duty would reign over desire. And, they already keep her close. Furthermore, I am not going to revisit the disaster of my attempt to lure a girl away from her family. I have learnt from my youthful mistake. Besides, she would not change her name and come along with me as a vagabond.'

He looked at me with compassion. 'Of course you are right. But what of *your* desire?'

'I have not seen her for so long I hardly know, Richard, if I love her or not, but I am very fond of her, and hugely admire her mind. We would have made an excellent match.'

'It sounds as if you have already given her up.'

It was so like Richard to get to the very nub of that matter. He was right. I had decided she was lost to me. All I wanted now was to try and make the situation as clear and simple as I could. 'If she thinks me dead she will be able to turn her attention elsewhere, but I cannot help but be sad. It feels as if I am losing two families. So, Richard, I need you to write to my mother and that man, advising them of my death.'

'What would you have me write?'

'I care not, except you must make it quite certain in their minds that I am no more.'

'Then I will give you a hero's death, that they will be proud of.'

I found a smile. 'Don't overdo the gloriousness of my demise. I know how much you like to spin stories.'

He went to his pack at once and spent a while attending to his nib. Then, taking up a scrap of paper that held a past list of provisions required for our troop, he turned it over and began to write. I waited with an odd feeling of unreality. There cannot be many men who wait while their friend manufactures his death. At length he stopped, and read silently to himself. Then he looked up at me. 'See if you approve of this.'

*I regret very much having the dolorous task of informing you of your son's death. We engaged on the road and it was a furious skirmish. Thomas, having already taken severe sword cuts to his shoulder and right leg, refused to withdraw, seeing me in difficulty. He rode alone, straight at my tormentors and pistoled one. That enabled me to throw off the other, and in a short time we had the enemy routed. I was a little ahead of him as we made to ride on. I had not known the severity of his wounds until he called to me. I pulled up my horse, and went to him. He was faint with the loss of so much blood, but I think he might have survived if a further shot had not wounded his horse. I could not prevent Thomas's heavy fall, and he died later that day, commending his soul to God and requesting me to write to you at once. We buried him on the moor, and I fashioned a hasty cross to mark the spot, it being a wild and empty place.*

'It is no more than you have done already, several times,' he said, passing the paper to me.

It was strange to read his words. Richard had indeed described an incident that had happened very much as he wrote, except for the injuries and the ending of it. It made me shiver to think how easily this account might have been the truest, and me cold on the ground. It was near real enough to be believed by any who knew about skirmishing. I could not fault his account.

I gave him a crooked smile. 'Thank you. I am already in pain from the sword cuts, but see it will soon all be over with me. You have even mentioned my grave, but neglected to say what moor holds it.'

'We do not want them searching for the cross!'

'But they are bound to ask you, Richard. What will you say when they do?'

He spread his hands and grinned. 'I don't suppose I would admit to receiving the letter. But if I did, it would be a simple matter not to be able to identify where you lay. Someone could easily have taken the cross for another place.'

My back prickled, and I felt as if my real grave was not far away. I handed him back the paper, trying to suppress a shiver that threatened to run up my spine. 'Thank you again, Richard. It is excellently done. I am sorry that I will cause some of my family grief, but better for them, I think, to put an end to speculation. When someone is missing it must be a very torture to those who have a longing to know.'

Richard shook his head. 'I understand your reasons for doing this. Of course I do, and if I could wish it all away I would. But I cannot pretend to be comfortable with the letter. It feels to me rather as if I am tempting the fates. But do you wish me also to write to your betrothed?'

I didn't think I could bear to stand by while he wrote lies to that honest girl. 'No. My mother is sure to write to the family, so better to let them attend to such things.'

'Then we are done.' He folded the letter, and hesitated before putting it on the table. He kept his hand upon it and tapped it with his finger. 'Now are you *sure* you want this to be sent? Think about it one more time, to please me. In fact, think about it tonight, and make a final decision in the morning. The month is young. You have time to discover if a night's sleep alters your mind.'

'It will not,' I said. 'But if it will please you, I am content to wait until tomorrow to send it. I am most grateful for your help. There is no other who could do it.'

'It is not a matter of pleasing me,' he said. 'Just that I worry about you. What if you hear in a month that your father is dead? Consider, if you were then to change your mind, and appear alive, you would be thought at best a cruel fool to those who will mourn you. But if you did not you would lose your inheritance for nothing.'

I sat in silence for a few moments, and when I spoke it was with new resolution. 'I think those who love me would understand why I had been driven to such extremities. But I am content for Hugh to be master of the estate. There is a certain freedom in knowing that there is no going back. He will do well for it, and all under his care, while I can set my face in a direction of my own choosing. And that is what I shall do.'

I could tell by his set expression that he didn't agree with me. 'You are giving away a great deal, Tom. A very great deal. From wealth and position to penury.'

He was right, if the war left my family all their wealth and influence intact. But what if it did not? What if those who argued for communally held property had their day? Or what if that man could not correctly judge the winner of this great conflict? What then, for all I thought I was giving up in the way of land and riches?

'Not such a great deal,' I said. 'Considering that I have not yet had it. And better men than I have had to make their own way in life. You are also set on the same path, are you not?'

He simply gave me a steady look, before leaving the letter upon the table.

# CHAPTER THIRTEEN

We had hoped to cross the River Severn at Powick, but the next morning when the keeper of the inn heard of our plans he looked doubtful.

'Did you not hear that the parliamentarians have again taken control of the south coast of Wales?'

The innkeeper had fought at both Edgehill and Marston Moor, receiving a wound to his hand that had sent him home again, and made his fetching and carrying a difficult business. If he had been a labourer, instead of the owner of an inn, he would doubtless have become destitute. As it was, he had become a conduit of news from any traveller prepared to speak.

'They say that many soldiers were coming from Ireland to swell our armies,' said the innkeeper. 'But now that must be in doubt.'

We looked at each other. 'What of the coast further north?' I asked. 'Could soldiers come from Ireland that way?'

'They could, if the ports have not yet fallen.'

'What of Chester?' said Richard. 'I remember my cousin in London speaking of that city as a good trading port.'

The innkeeper shook his head. 'I have no recent news from there, although some time past there was talk of it being attacked. I know no more.'

'Then let us carry on north,' I said to Richard, 'if you are agreeable. It sounds as if there will be plenty of work for us to do at a good distance from Fairfax's army.'

'If even one port were retaken it would help the soldiers get back from Ireland,' the innkeeper offered.

'Thank you for your advice,' said Richard. 'And I am content to continue north,' he added to me. 'I would be glad to help Chester or any other city to withstand the enemy so that we can have the troops we need.'

'Have you heard of the King's whereabouts?' I said. 'Is he still at Oxford?'

The innkeeper shook his head. 'He's safe, I pray. I hear news from all directions, but these last few months, since Naseby battle, there has been so much confusion. The cursed Covenanters from Scotland, the New Army, foreign mercenaries . . . our king is much beset, and would be best to stay where he is well defended, wherever that may be. I hear the Covenanters are somewhere to the north of here, so beware meeting them. I hope the Scots do not come to Worcester. Of all the enemies I have fought, they unsettle me the most.'

We warily took the north road out of Worcester, but before that, we sent the letter to my family, having been assured that the post boy would take it directly. I had thought a weight would fall from my mind when it was done, but felt little relief, in spite of my protestations to Richard. It is no small matter to abandon those who one loves, nor to tear up the history of one's life. To have to make my way entirely without inheritance or family influence was a more frightening prospect than I had admitted. I was resolute, but I felt the fear. From the other end of life it does not look so bad, and I have of course written another history for myself, but at that moment I felt like a ghost, cursed to wander without substance for the remainder of my days. I had done what I thought best, but it sorely hurt. Most of all I deeply regretted not being able to speak to my mother. I would have given almost anything to be able to reassure her. If it had been possible I would have sent a private note to save her from thinking me truly dead. But I did not dare. Maybe it would have been easier if I had come to hate her for her supposed betrayal, but I wasn't made that way. Instead I grieved that we were lost from one another, and feared she might think I had left in disgust at her. Nothing could have been further from the truth. I had the memory of my time with Catherine to remind me that youth is rarely steady when it comes to love. No. If she were guilty I could not censor her, if innocent I was outraged for her. As to the matter of my real father, real or imaginary, I had experienced the care of one and did not wish to know another.

While deep in these thoughts, I should have remembered how perceptive my good friend Richard was. Riding in silence for a while, he eventually spoke in a cheerful tone.

'So, Tom. Today we must find you a new name. I think you will feel the better for it.'

He was right. In thinking of names I liked, I was soon deflected from brooding. I have seldom been proof against

Richard's determination to counsel cheerfulness in almost all circumstances. He could take serious account when it was needed, but saw golden fringes even behind the darkest cloud. In spite of the need to be on our guard at all times, and the parlous state of our nation's fortunes, he determined to set me with equanimity on a new life. That somehow made me feel that it was at least as much of an opportunity as a loss. Throughout that day, as we rode ever northwards, at pains to avoid being engaged, questioned or pressed, he regaled me with names, some sensible and some preposterous.

'First, your last! What family name are you going to bestow on the dozen children I wish for your future?'

'I cannot think . . .'

'Mr Think, then?'

'Don't be ridiculous!'

'Mr Hill . . .' He waved his hand at the handsome countryside around us. 'Or how about Cloud, Rivers, Tree . . . ?'

'I'd rather not be known as part of the landscape.'

'Why not? In fact, if you want a name of substance, how about Mr Landscape? That takes in the whole world.'

'You are teasing me.'

'I? Tease you?'

He went on in this way for a while, until we decided to stop by a stream and eat a little of the bread we had in our saddlebags. The horses drank at the stream, but Richard had bought beer to wash down the bread.

'Would you like some more?' I asked Richard, offering him the flagon. He took a long draught and set the flagon down upon the grass. Then he picked it up again and looked at me.

'More.'

I shook my head.

'I mean More, as a name for you. It is a positive name.'

'Not if it refers to my supposed resting place.'

He folded his arms. 'I mean more as in having more.'

I picked up the flagon and took a small sip although I had just declined it. 'I don't know. I'm not sure . . .'

'Spell it how you like, you will do More things in your life to come than you can possibly dream of. Take that new life and make More of it than you ever have before, Mr Moore.'

He fell quiet, but regarded me still. I stopped the flagon, taking deliberate care while I considered. Would I in the future have more than the solitary life I had reduced myself to, disallowed from my betrothed because I could not abandon my king? Not quite solitary, for I was with Richard at present, but that would not be for ever. What of that shadowy future? But none save soothsayers can draw that curtain aside.

Richard cleared his throat and spoke quietly. 'Do you want Moore?'

'More than I now have? You know I do . . .'

'Then start as you mean to progress. This is just the first step.'

We both felt the seriousness that had crept over our conversation. 'Few are given the opportunity to make their own name,' I said, feeling the burden of it.

He was about to say something to me but I held up my hand to stop him. I had to decide some time, and here, in this sheltered, grassy spot, was as good a place and time as ever. 'I do want more,' I said. 'More in my life and a life with the name Moore. It suits very well, so thank you.'

Richard looked ridiculously happy. 'Congratulations, Mr Moore!' He took me in a firm embrace. 'Now, should I toss you in the stream to baptise you?'

'By no means!'

Our afternoon ride followed the same pattern of trying out names. My spirits rose now I had decided at least on one. Moore seemed cheerful compared to Chayne, which had always felt like a burden to me. I wondered privately if that feeling had come from some part of myself knowing that the name was not truly mine. Would I ever know the truth? A little part of me hankered after knowledge, while another shrank from it. Better to leave it alone, lest I discover a story I liked even less than the one I had.

'Henry?' Richard was intent on not letting me brood, however often I fell into silence.

'John?'

'Humphrey!'

I shook my head. 'Not that. Simon,' I mused. 'George, Arthur . . .'

'Wat?'

I began to feel like laughing. 'Wat Moore? That's a terrible name! It would always be a question.'

'Roland, then.'

'I quite like that. Roland Moore.'

Richard wrinkled his nose. 'I think you had better not adopt it. While not a question, it makes a foolish phrase. You would sound like a trencherman.'

'Hmm . . . so no names ending in "and" . . . How about Ptolemy?'

'Ptolemy? Where did you find that?' He turned in his saddle, looking about him with a mystified expression until I couldn't help laughing aloud.

'I don't know. It is an ancient name, though heathen, not Christian.'

'No matter. Your real given name is, and although it sleeps it will still remind God that you are his creature.'

'I think I have seen too many good men with solid Christian names die these past years to think their names to be any sort of talisman.'

Richard frowned. 'I admit I am also of that mind. And I like the name Ptolemy. It is not too common, but it is a good, solid name. It suits you, and works well with Moore. To me there is a slight echo of Tom to the sound, and yet the word is nothing like.'

'So I am Ptolemy Moore,' I said, savouring the names as I said them. 'I doubt there is another so called in these isles.'

'In which case,' said Richard, 'it is entirely yours to make splendid.'


By the time we had ridden about twenty more miles we saw a small town ahead of us. 'Shall we find a barn to lie in, or some other building?' I said to Richard. 'I don't like the idea of meeting trouble in a town, and the situation seems to change so rapidly these days that we cannot be sure which side is in charge of any place.'

'It would also serve to save our store of coin,' he said.

I agreed. I had more money than my friend, but we had not been paid by the army for some time. Even added together, our two purses would not last long if we continued to pay for our beds.

We were lucky that night. The building we settled upon was away from any habitation, on the lee of a small hill. We should not have found it if I hadn't heard horses approaching, causing us to veer off the road and make for the shelter of the far side of the hill. We had seen several foraging parties, and had heard talk of many sieges being planned by our enemies. Vulnerable towns and cities were bound to gather supplies where they could, as well as hungry soldiers being obliged to feed themselves. If any of these had known what they had missed in our hiding place they would have been angry, for many bundles of oats and barley were neatly stacked inside the barn, ready for the flail, and a clamp full of roots lay outside.

'Our horses are happy, but I could have wished for something more tasty than swede and raw barley.' Even so, we were glad enough to chew the barley, thinking it unwise to start a fire to cook it.

At first, every creak and rattle of the barn alarmed us, but as darkness fell and the wind and rain began to beat harder upon the door, we decided we were safe enough. Surely only a fool would be out on such a night? We were still weary, and did our best to be comfortable, along with our horses.

'What is your plan now?' said Richard, having laid several bundles of barley together to make a rough bed.

'If we continue north and then west we will come to the northern English ports. It would be a splendid thing to keep a way open for reinforcements from Ireland, don't you think?'

'Essential, I would say.'

'Then, for want of a better idea, in the morning, let us take the road for Chester.'


As we rode ever further north-west, the weather fought us. The rain fell heavily and the wind blew chill. It was autumn, but each day it felt as if we were riding into winter. With our heads bowed against the spite of the weather, we stopped remarking on the beauty of the countryside, or singing Richard's bawdy songs. All we wanted by the end of the day was shelter. We regretfully skirted Shrewsbury, it having fallen to the enemy earlier in the year, and as far as we knew was still held against us. We also looked longingly at several country inns along the way, but thought better of them too. One night we lay in a leaking shepherd's hut, a thing of little more than piled stones and a hurdle roof. We fared little better the next night, but had a fortunate conversation in the morning with a girl watching over her geese as they came to graze nearby. She must have become used to meeting dishevelled soldiers, for she didn't look askance, but simply asked outright if we were for the King.

'For the King,' I said. At once she offered us some bread and cheese, which I admit we fell upon. She told us that the whole country hereabouts was patrolled by the enemy and that Chester was not far, but she had heard it was still under heavy attack.

'What about the coast roundabouts?' asked Richard.

'If you go that way,' she said, pointing to a muddy strip crossing the turf, 'you will come to Hawarden Castle. It is taken, but if you pass it and go on carefully there are two others, near the sea. I think Flint is still for the King, and Mostyn too.'

We gave her thanks and took her advice. 'How fortunate to meet such a kind and helpful young girl,' said I. Richard gave me a stern look.

'If we had said we were for parliament I do not doubt she would just as readily given us victuals, and the same news but with a different slant.'

'I'm sure you are right.' I felt a little ashamed as I ate the last of the cheese she had given us. 'You know, I think she also maybe offers up her meal to soldiers to try and avoid them taking her geese.'

Richard gave me a wry smile. 'Such is war, Ptolemy. The poor starve and die, while the soldiers continue their quarrel. It is a dirty, discordant business, however you play the tune.'

We spied what must have been Hawarden Castle from a distance, and so were easily able to avoid it. The weather became a little kinder, but our clothes had been wet for several days and we remained chilled and somewhat disconsolate. Eventually, after taking pains to avoid several patrols, we reached a wide estuary. The tide was in, boats floated upon the water, and I would like to say that for my first view of the sea the clouds parted, the sun shone and the water looked like a spread of blue cloth, but it was not so. The spiteful rain came again, spattering into our faces, the wide river looked like so much liquid mud and the sea in the distance was grey as a helm.

'Chester must lie that way,' said Richard, pointing upriver. 'I wonder that the enemy has not blockaded it, but it looks as if boats are freely moving up and down.'

We hurried on along the estuary shore, away from the city, in the hope of finding shelter. In the distance we could see another castle, close to the shore and in a commanding position.

'This must be one of the castles she told us was still held for the King,' said Richard. 'Flint, perhaps.'

'We must be careful. Even if she told us truth, her knowledge may be out of date.' We stared into the rain, trying to make out if any banner flew on the tower, but if there was one, it was sulking in the rain, and we could not see it.

'What is it like, riding away from land in a boat?' I asked, idly watching one sailing effortlessly along in the centre of the estuary.

'It is very similar to riding in the back of a cart, and watching your home recede,' said Richard.

'But unlike a road, there are no ridges and hollows to jar one's teeth,' I observed.

Richard laughed. 'Oh, the sea has plenty of ridges and hollows,' he said, 'when it cares to make them.'

There was a small copse between us and the castle, and a narrow track leading through it. But to our dismay, as we almost reached the welcome shelter, out of it rode a troop of a dozen men in double file, blocking our way. Richard immediately tried to turn his horse, but the track was narrow, with the muddy estuary to one side and a steep ditch on the other. Besides that, it was too late to run. Our horses were tired, and the troop would soon have outridden us.

'We are too close,' I muttered to him. 'We have no option but to face them, and hope they are of our persuasion.' Being strangers in this part of the world, we did not know the banner their ensign carried. It hung limply, and could have been a lion, but it was impossible to tell.

We reined in our horses and waited. Their captain halted his troop and hailed us immediately.

'Who are you, and what is your business?'

'Whatever we can do to help the cause.' I felt Richard stiffen beside me, but what else could I say?

'Who sent you?'

I hesitated. 'We were split from our troop and decided ourselves to come to join another.'

The captain urged his mount forwards, until our horses' noses were almost touching. He was not a young man, but well built, and did not look a fool.

'Were you lately at Rowton?'

I had no idea where that might be, nor what may have happened there. Richard filled the silence. 'No. We have come from further south.' He paused. 'To help.'

The ensign behind the captain checked his fidgeting horse and grumbled aloud. 'There are people starving not ten miles hence. Will you help by swimming that fat pack horse in for them to eat?'

'Silence!'

But the captain spoke too late, for Richard and I had what information we needed. Royal Chester nearby was under a long siege, and this soldier's bitterness had betrayed his loyalty. I saluted the captain and Richard did the same. 'We are loyal servants of the King,' I said. 'Come to do what we can.'

That night we lay on straw pallets, within the walls of the ancient castle of Flint, while an autumn storm raged on outside. We had been taken by the still-suspicious captain and his troop under close guard into the castle. We were required to hand over our weapons, and our horses were led away. We spent an anxious night, but it was clear that we had reached a royalist garrison. The old castle of Flint had been recently repaired, but the thick walls kept the interior cold, and there was not much light through the slender windows. Although useful as a garrison, I could not imagine being comfortable here, even hundreds of years ago when it must have been built, and perhaps thought the very latest thing.

'When we are taken before the colonel in the morning he will soon realise where our loyalties lie,' I said to cheer Richard, who was feeling more apprehensive than I. 'We can tell him much about our time in Oxford, and mention my problem with my brother, without having to reveal who I am. I have never heard of the Mostyn name, and am sure he won't have heard of Ptolemy Moore or of his mythical family.'

In the morning we were examined by Colonel Roger Mostyn, who was the governor of the castle, although he lived further off. He was young, I would guess very close to my own age. His father had apparently died only a couple of years before, leaving him with a large estate and county responsibilities at a time of war. I couldn't help reflecting on my own situation, and how, if that man I had known as my father had died from his wounds, how different my life would have been. As it was, I introduced myself for the first time as Ptolemy Moore. The name felt strange on my tongue, and I had to school myself not to look at Richard as I said it, but the colonel seemed to see nothing amiss.

Colonel Mostyn made it plain that he liked us, and I certainly took to him, but he was no fool, and questioned us closely. With Chester besieged nearby, and both Mostyn and Flint Castles holding the Welsh side of the River Dee, his control hereabouts must be vital to the royalist cause, and no doubt he was at all times alert to the possibility of spies. He had taken his men to fight at Edgehill, and wanted to know if we had been there.

'No,' I admitted, keeping as close to the truth as possible. 'We were then in Oxford, but my father fought, and took a bad wound there.'

'Indeed. I am sorry. Who is your father? I do not know the name.'

'My father no more,' I said, cursing myself for having mentioned him. 'He died of his wounds. Since then,' I added, having made a lie out of wishful thinking, 'I have been captain of the troop of thirty I raised in Oxford, and seen battle with them under Prince Rupert. I then sent them back to defend Oxford for the King under a new captain from their ranks. We had heard that men were needed to defend the ports and so we two rode here to help where we can.'

My account of our experience seemed to have deflected his interest in my father and, to my great relief, he asked no more. Indeed, he was persuaded that we were indeed for the King, and told us so.

'I will command that you and your horses are made use of. I am recruiting at the moment, and will be pleased to have you with us. Flint has already been besieged once,' he said. 'The garrison was reduced to eating the horses, and in the end it was forced to surrender.'

'And yet here you are,' I said. 'How fortunate that you were able to retake such a vital place.'

'Indeed. If we had not been relieved by a contingent of Irish soldiers, things might have been very different. As it was, they turned matters around for us. With the Irish added to the Welshmen I recruited, I was able to capture Hawarden before going on to Chester, but that was two years ago. Hawarden is back in enemy hands again and Chester is in a very bad way. Matters have not been going our way.'

'I'm sorry to hear it. But you are right. The war has not gone well this year for us.'

'Well, we are still doing what we can to relieve Chester, but the siege has been renewed with fury, and the city is hard-pressed. Come with me, I'll show you just how important this place is to poor, besieged Chester.'

He took us up a tower, and we could see that the water came right up to the castle walls. 'What we really need is more men willing to protect our ships and sailors,' he said. 'Out at sea, in the mouth of the estuary and in the river, there are ships that harry ours. The pinnace you see moored below is being repaired after almost being sunk. We lost several men and need to replace them, but it is a dangerous business, and most of my men prefer to keep their feet on the ground or astride their horses.'

'When will the pinnace be ready?' asked Richard.

'In a few days, I hope.'

'Well, we have put ourselves under your command,' I said to him. 'So, whatever you require us to do, we will do it to the best of our ability. Richard has some knowledge of boats, though I do not.'

The colonel gave me a nod. 'Thank you. You can be assured that in one way or another we will make good use of you both.'

We preceded him down the stone steps. At the bottom, Richard paused. 'I think we forgot to mention that Ptolemy has some knowledge of medicine,' he said to Colonel Mostyn.

'You know about fever, and wounds?' said the colonel to me.

'I do. Enough to have been useful when the army came to Oxford after Edgehill.'

'That is good to know. I won't forget.' He led the way into the castle yard. 'I am required at a meeting in Denbigh later, and will take a few men with me as escort. It is not far, and I would like you both to accompany me. It will give you a bit more knowledge of the country. You never know when that knowledge might be needed. Meet me here, mounted and ready in an hour.'

In the stables, our horses looked rested and pleased to see us.

'I will be happier when they see fit to return our weapons,' said Richard as we saddled our beasts.

'Me too,' I agreed. 'Though I too would take my time to totally trust newcomers such as us.'

Six others were to ride with us as escort for the colonel. When he joined us in the castle yard I asked Colonel Mostyn about our weapons.

'Oh yes . . .' He considered for a moment. 'Well, you won't need them now, but never fear, they will be returned to you later.'

We lined up with the other troopers. I felt vulnerable without my sword and pistol, and I know Richard did too. However, the company felt relaxed, and so we made the best of it. We rode inland, crossing hills and valleys and an ancient earthwork, which Colonel Mostyn told us had been built by someone called

Offa. 'His dyke stretches a long way,' he said. 'It is said it was to keep the barbarian out, but who is the barbarian now?'

A little way further on we saw the castle of Denbigh, which is where Colonel Mostyn had been summoned. It was a striking place, built high on a rock, and with its tall towers keeping guard over the town below. The gate was opened for us and we rode in, in good order. Colonel Mostyn disappeared inside for his meeting, and we dismounted. There were several dozen horses here, but space was found for ours, and water brought for them. We were invited into a room containing little more than a table and a few benches. After a while, we were given some thin beer to drink and a little bread.

Our fellow troopers were interested in any news we might have, and also wanted to tell us their own.

'My sister is in Chester with her husband,' one said to me. 'I wanted her to try to come out by boat, but she will not leave her husband.'

'I'm sorry,' said Richard. 'Have they children?'

The trooper spat. 'She is with child, and how will she ever deliver a healthy brat when the whole city starves?'

I realised he was the trooper who had made the remark about eating horses when we first came upon them. 'I have a brother who is fighting in the south,' I volunteered, not mentioning which side he favoured. 'And I worry about him too.'

'This war is hard on families,' agreed another of Colonel Mostyn's men.

Richard and I sat down, the better to enjoy our beer. We were facing an internal door that stood wide open, revealing a passageway and another room opposite. It seemed empty, but then a couple of men appeared. One was our colonel, but the other had his hat so low over his face I could not tell what kind of man he might be, except he was slightly built. For a while the two men conversed, the colonel with his back to us and the other facing our room. They spoke too low for us to hear their voices as more than a murmur. I looked down at my mug, not wanting to seem impertinent by gazing at the men. When I looked up again, they had gone.

'It seems, Richard,' I said, 'we have arrived in a country of castles. I have seen or heard of more here than I ever saw in our own country.'

Before Richard could reply, one of the troopers spoke. 'We are famous for our castles,' he said proudly. I think he was about to say more, but at that moment Colonel Mostyn appeared at the exterior door.

'Come with me,' he said. 'No, not you,' he added to Richard, who had risen to his feet as well.

I could tell that Richard did not like us being separated, any more than he did being unarmed. I admit I was somewhat alarmed as well, but there was nothing to be done about it. Colonel Mostyn was armed, and he had six troopers here, to order as he wished. I had no option but to obey.

# CHAPTER FOURTEEN

The colonel's manner was still friendly as he led me to a small upper room. There was a fire burning brightly, and a man seated by it with another standing nearby.

'Yes,' said the man by the fire in a testy voice. 'It is him. Sit him down, for God's sake, and stay with us, Mostyn.'

I had heard that voice before, and had seen him going about in Oxford, though he had never spoken to me. He had been in the habit from time to time of watching his troops exercise, and had several times been nearby when we rode past, but he was the last person I could have expected to see here. I started to bow, but Colonel Mostyn shoved me towards a low stool and leant on me to sit. I stumbled, staggered and fell onto the creepie stool, my knees nearly as high as my chin on this diminutive seat.

The King looked irritated. 'You are Thomas Chayne's boy. Why did you give Colonel Mostyn a different name? What are you doing so far from your troop? Are you playing the spy against me?'

Even just before going into battle I had never felt as frightened as now, before my king. Was my new life to end almost before it was begun? My fuddled brain stumbled over astonishment at seeing the King here, and surprise that he had recognised me. All I could do was to be honest.

'No, sire. I am your honest supporter, but I have renounced my family name because it shames me.'

He sighed. 'What nonsense is this? Have a care. We are at war, and I will have you hanged if you do not satisfy me.'

How could I tell him? But I must, or I would lose my life, and maybe Richard's too. I took a deep breath. Nothing mattered but the truth, the truth told briefly, and to the point. 'It grieves me to say that Sir Thomas is turned traitor to Your Majesty, and sends my younger brother to fight with Fairfax. I fear to meet him on the field and so came north to fight for you here.'

Someone came and put a goblet by the King's hand. He took it up and drank. 'Look at me.'

I raised my eyes.

'No. Look at me properly, boy.'

I looked at him, looked at his tired eyes with my own, and he looked back at me with a hard stare. 'Why change your name? What need for that ridiculous step, unless you mean ill?'

'He told me that if I refused to also turn traitor he would disown me, and accuse my mother of . . .'

'Well?'

'He would say I was not his son because my mother had lain with another man.'

He looked startled. 'What man?'

'I don't know, sire. But I believe he would carry out his threat so I changed my name and asked the friend I am with, Richard, to write, informing him I had died in a skirmish. I hope if he thinks me dead he will spare my mother.'

The King sighed. 'I have no time for this. Listen to me. I know something of loyalty between brothers. That is all well and good, but to wilfully reject your inheritance? Well . . . you are young, and your father was ever a fool, though a useful one. You are the eldest, aren't you? Where would the world be if we all gave up our responsibilities when in difficulty?'

'My brother will make a good heir, sire.'

'I think that's hardly the point.' I could feel him still looking at me, but I could not raise my head. 'Oh for God's sake. Don't weep. Give him some wine, someone.'

A fine goblet was put into my hand. I sipped the wine, half afraid I might drop the vessel, and cursed myself for letting my tears fall. After a few moments the King spoke again. 'Colonel Mostyn says you have offered him your sword.'

I could only nod.

'Then I thank you for your loyalty. He has need of more good men.' He paused, and when he spoke again he sounded weary. 'Your father was in my service a long time, and was wounded, I seem to recall?'

'Yes, sire.'

'And now, when I need loyalty the most he chooses to turn his back. Well, I will have your father's head, if your words prove true. And if in time to come you decide to resurrect yourself and claim what should belong to you, I will defend your claim, if you prove to have been steadfast in my service. No son should hear his mother shamed without reason. But you must know you are

174

the very spit of your father. The least of it is that he is a fool. Now, I have important matters to discuss. Go.'

I got up from my lowly position and bowed. Someone took the glass from my hand and led me to the stairs. Colonel Mostyn caught hold of my sleeve before I could descend. 'You will understand I had to be sure of you,' he said in a low voice. 'Being not entirely convinced. I am glad His Majesty recognised you, but it would be foolish of you to speak to *any* of seeing him here. Besides, he will be gone before the night.'

'I understand.'

I tried to compose myself as I returned to Richard, but his expression of alarm told me he realised something unexpected had happened.

'All is well,' I muttered. 'Is there any more beer?' I asked in a louder voice. A trooper passed me the jug and I poured some.

'You were gone a while,' he said.

'The more I know about the area, the more use I may be,' I replied. 'Tell me of this castle. It is a very fine place.'

I could feel Richard chafing beside me as we rode back to Flint but he curbed his impatience. Once back and our horses fed and watered, it was a different matter.

'Speak to me,' he hissed.

It was the hour when men could take their ease. With guards set, the garrison felt secure. We, too, were secured. Our arms had still not been returned, and before he left us, Colonel Mostyn made it plain they would not be, nor would we be allowed to wander freely for another day or so.

'You will understand why,' he told me privately. 'I am convinced of your story now, but I do not mean even the slightest chance of anything I do to put the King in danger. You will sleep under guard tonight, and perhaps the night after. By then the

King will be far from here. And when the pinnace is ready, I warrant you will be able to join her.'

We were therefore locked into the small room we had slept in before, by one of the troopers who we had ridden with earlier. 'I do not believe you intend to signal to the enemy,' he said. 'But our colonel is become cautious these past few weeks. No doubt you will be earning your bread soon enough.'

Once we were alone, Richard naturally wanted to know all that had transpired. I had been examined by Mostyn's superior, I said, which was the truth, and that eventually they were both satisfied.

'And yet here we are!' he said. 'Contained again.'

'There are rumours flying everywhere,' I said. 'Spies are assumed to be behind every hedge, and at the meeting today, perhaps new plans were being discussed. I too would be cautious if I commanded this place. He has told me we will be free once the pinnace is ready, and I believe that to be true. Rest easy, Richard. I intend to.'

He gave me a long, steady look. 'I am not entirely comfortable at believing all you say,' he said at last. 'But I have never had any reason not to trust you in the past, and so I will continue to do so, even though I am somewhat uneasy.'

I thought a long moment before replying. 'I am not at liberty to say all that is in my mind just now. However, I can say that I am heartily glad you know me so well.'

He favoured me with a wry smile.

It was obvious I had not said enough to reassure him. 'Richard,' I said. 'I swear to you that we are in no danger here. In fact, we are safer locked in this room tonight than we would be if allowed to stroll about at our pleasure.' I had only just understood the truth of this before I spoke, and I could see that he understood this of me.

'Then I am entirely content,' he said with a proper smile.

Richard slept long before me, and I was happy that I had been able to reassure him. I, however, had much to dwell on. For the first time in my life I had spoken directly to the man I had given up so much to follow. Physically, he was much as I remembered, but his exhausted face didn't make me feel confident that he would prevail. Had my supposed father been right? For the first time I wondered if abandoning that tired-eyed king would be the right thing to do. I tried to think of what my country would be like with the King defeated, but I could not imagine it. Would he retreat to Scotland, leaving his young heir to rule the rest of his dominions? But history taught us that young kings were often ruled by their advisers, who squabbled over their power, furthering strife in a nation. What if some factions supported the King while others wanted one or other of his young sons to rule? Would peace ever come that way? But to have no king was impossible, for a people must be ruled, and how else could it be done? The various ideas being written about would surely bring chaos. For how could one radical idea out of so many disagreements possibly prevail?

I was grateful that the King had recognised me, and had treated me kindly. And he had thanked me for my loyalty. I thought hard about that. To whom was I being loyal? Was it the man, the anointed King? I had to admit, lying there within the ancient walls of Flint Castle, far away from all I knew, that it was not the man. I had thought it was, but it was not. It was more that I was loyal to the idea of being ruled by a king, to the status quo. I asked myself: why? The answer was instantly there. Because I could imagine no other way. Surely there *was* no other good way? I felt sure that, when all the fighting was done, the King and his advisers would steer our country back to peace, putting right all the wrongs that had led to this terrible war. They would have to. And if he lost? Then parliament would become a many-headed serpent, with no one to tell them nay. How could they rule our land, if they could not rule themselves?

I wished Aphra were here to dispute with me. We had not discussed the right of kings. It had not been a question between us, but I was sure I could have relied on her to think her way clearly through the tangle. Would she say that loyalty should go to the person best fitted to rule? But how could all agree who it should be? So many for this man and so many for another. We would be in chaos again. Surely better a bad king than none at all? And if a bad king would not listen to his advisors? I realised I was suddenly angry with my king. Was he not bad to allow this terrible war? Or had he received bad council? Aphra was not with me, and Richard was a plain man, not given to anguish over such matters. My temple throbbed and I ached to be asleep. It would be morning before I had stilled my mind, and yet morning light came through the narrow window and I realised I had slept, though badly. And to my surprise, my mind was easier. I would remain true to the Crown, because that way I saw a lasting peace most likely to be restored, and that was what mattered most.

While we rose at the start of day I allowed myself to wallow in how it could be. A land at peace again, good harvests, no hunger. Our king ruling a country of contentment at last, and me, magically lord of my estate, with my brother and our wives and children at our sides, and our mother enjoying her grandchildren. It was a pleasing dream, and so of course Aphra came flooding into my mind. My mother and brother would surely love her almost as much as did I. With me, she could read and study as she liked. Together, we would travel to Oxford, Cambridge, even Leiden, to hear the great men dispute, while at home our children, and there would be many, thrived.

It was a pretty scenario, but an unlikely one. As it flew away I sent up a silent prayer for my mother, brother and Aphra, that they might come to no harm. Aphra had lost one betrothed to illness and another through a family change of loyalties. She might now be seen as unlucky, tainted. Was it wrong to hope she might yet be unwed after the war, when things might be more favourable for us?

Later that day we were allowed to go down to the quay, to look at the pinnace. We gazed out over the river, and saw a similar size vessel, which the trooper who accompanied us said was an enemy ship. It was mid channel, and it seemed clear that it was observing us.

'They dare not come too close, or our cannon would blow them out of the water,' said the trooper who accompanied us, no doubt as he had been instructed to do. He laughed. 'They think they are so clever, but we have a spar and sail hanging over the side of the pinnace to confuse them. They will think our repairs some way off finished, so with luck we will be able to evade them, and get it back out to sea very soon.'

In the afternoon our pistols were returned to us, but not our hangers. The armourer gave us each a shorter blade, which he explained would be much better onboard, where there was not space to swing a long sword. I had hoped to see Colonel Mostyn again, to make our farewells, but he was on business elsewhere.

That night, when it was full dark, we embarked, leaving our horses, our hangers, our buff coats and the rest of our belongings in the castle, exchanging them for the hats and rugg coats of the sailors. So, quietly and without formality, we began our new lives. As we slipped away, the tide taking us out towards the open sea, I couldn't help wondering if we would ever see our belongings again. We had been told that the woollen ruggs and thrum caps were more practical, and warmer out on the water. Also, it was thought advisable to hide our martial selves, making it seem to the casual observer that the pinnace was unarmed and unthreatening. I am sure that was all true, but I felt a great loss, and it was painful. I had now given up everything that belonged to my old life. From clothing to sword, horse, troop and even my name and family. Unlike Richard, I had no knowledge of sailing, and yet here I was abandoning horsemanship and taking to the water. I tried to think on it as the adventure it was, but that dark night, when we embarked and slid out onto the ink-black, pitch-like water, it felt as though I had taken a wrong turn, and one that might be my utter undoing.

I was, however, glad to discover that the motion of the ship gave me no qualms. I felt neither sick, nor found it difficult to get my balance, though Richard warned me not to take our gentle motion to be constant. 'More men have been lost through misunderstanding and carelessness on the water than any other reason,' he said. 'At all times keep one hand upon some part of the ship, in case a sudden jolt sends you overboard. You would be swiftly carried away in this current, and likely never found again.'

That was enough for me to keep a tight grip, at least to begin with, and his wise advice did save me on several occasions. It seemed a pinnace could be as unpredictable as a wayward horse, but I got used to it, and soon felt easier in my mind. It was a matter of respect for both vessel and water, and how they spoke to each other, with the captain as intermediary, coaxing both as far as possible to temperance. I had thought myself a good horseman, but I would never make a proper sailor, in spite of all the times I have been at sea. Let those who can do it, for I could never sail a vessel. I concentrated on my work defending the sailors, who went about their business with a will.

We had been commanded to discover if any ships of soldiers were coming from Ireland, and if so, to guard their approach and landing. Every now and then we would return to Flint to report, and re-provision with the scanty supplies our garrison could spare for us. We sailed several times towards Ireland, but didn't land, trying to lure enemy ships away from the ports so the promised soldiers could safely set sail. We patrolled up and down the narrow, choppy sea between the two countries, and our enemy did the same. It was a veritable game of cat and mouse, and to my surprise not one shot was fired. All the while, Chester suffered the siege, with little food, coals and arms getting in to them.

Autumn turned to winter, and our routine was unaltered. Then, one day towards evening, some snow fell. I was intrigued to watch the flakes drift down and dissolve silently into the dark water, but in a few minutes it ceased. All the same, winter was truly upon us, and the seamen grumbled warnings of winter storms ahead. We dropped anchor in the lee of a small promontory and shivered through the night.

The next morning, there was snow on the tops of the hills. When we returned to Flint the next evening, Colonel Mostyn was at the garrison, and commanded our presence.

'I am resolved to wait no longer but go to Ireland myself, to gather more support and, God willing, bring the soldiers I have been promised. You will land me, and immediately return to the estuary. Give me ten days and then come back for me. If I am not there, wait another ten days, and so on. We will obtain those men if it is the last thing I live to see. Meanwhile, you can make life difficult for our enemy in the estuary. And if you could manage to capture some of their boats it would be all the better when the troops come.'

I had been feeling that we were on some kind of miserable, inactive holiday. I had fired no shot, nor drawn my cutlass, but had simply bobbed up and down, itching to fight, while no enemy seemed inclined to engage with us. But now, with the prospect of capturing other vessels, I became more cheerful. We slipped our moorings just before dawn and drifted down to sea, as we had done numerous times before. At the mouth of the estuary we met a stiff wind, and the waves were high. It took us a long time to reach the Irish coast, and for a while we were unable to land Colonel Mostyn where he wanted. At last, taking advantage of a brief lull in the wind, we shot into the harbour with no mishap.

I had thought we might stay for a while, until the gale blew out, but the master of the pinnace was anxious to get back out to sea as soon as the colonel had gone ashore. 'If the enemy got wind of us being here they would keep us cooped up, and attack if we ventured out. I'm not going to allow them that pleasure,' he said.

Without delay we headed back out to sea. It is relatively narrow, the stretch of water between Wales and Ireland, and it has a reputation for being stormy. In spite of what the seamen said, I believed I had ridden all its ill-tempered waters. But I was a landsman. I had never seen a proper winter storm at sea. I had never even stood on the shore and watched mighty waves crashing onto the rocks below, or hurling the shingle high up until it broke windows in houses, and lay in the street as if a builder's cart had overturned, spilling stones all around. I had not been in a trough of water at the bottom of the tall waves as they towered over me, threatening to swamp my boat. I had listened to these stories, knowing how seamen are said to be fantasists, and thought them playful, exaggerated tales for children. I did not for one moment consider them real.

I did, at least, remember Richard's wise words on the day we sailed from Flint for the first time, and that advice surely saved my life. As we came out of the small harbour and hit the wind again, the pinnace was struck almost broadsides by the speeding waves and I was so nearly thrown into the sea. I was sure we were lost in those first few seconds, but the vessel, shuddering all the while, was brought round until the wind caught the tiny scrap of sail the captain had set. My admiration for him grew tenfold as he brought her under control, but he was working at the very edge of her capabilities. His helmsman did his best to hold the course, and for a while I thought we would reach shelter off Anglesey, but suddenly all was awry.

'We have lost the rudder!' shouted Richard to me above the sound of the storm.

The captain called for oars, but the seamen were already getting them out. Even as they attempted to control the ship the storm blew even harder. They struggled to keep her steady as the wind and waves drove us ever on. We took our turns at the oars as the storm redoubled its attempts to make us flounder. All that night the storm raged, and all that night we were driven ever north. Disaster struck before dawn. In spite of the noise of the wind, our seamen detected a different sound to the waves. The lookout strained to see ahead, while every effort was made to slow our pace. The wind had dropped somewhat, but the sea was very high, and still drove us on. All of a sudden even I was aware of waves breaking, and at that moment we were thrown upon a shore. At once, several seamen jumped into the surf. Richard dragged me with him.

'We must lighten her,' he yelled into my ear above the roar of the sea. I followed into the icy surf, slipping on rocks and then, gratefully, finding sand underfoot. Together we hauled the pinnace further up the beach, working with the waves as they drove her in.

It was then that Richard fell. I saw it happen, right next to me in the eerie light of the storm-blown dawn. He lost his footing, and was instantly under the foam. I thought he would surface immediately, but he did not. I felt for him, and found his limbs loose in the sea, like weed about my legs. I grabbed him, and pulled him up, lest he be ground under the keel. Blood was dissolving into the sea from a great gash on his head, and that was not his only injury. His arm was badly broken too. Worst of all, it was not until I had him laid on the shore that I knew he breathed no more.

# CHAPTER FIFTEEN

All the sounds of waves crashing, the wind still screaming, men cursing, and the sand and stone grinding under the keel of the pinnace were filling my head with such a cacophony that I could not think. At the same time, a circle of quiet seemed to lie over the still form of my friend. Some part of me thought if I could only break that circle he would wake. If I shouted loudly enough would he not hear, open his eyes and sit up, reassuring me that he was perfectly well? I did shout then, but my words were whipped away by the freezing wind and he lay there as before, the watery gash on his head still leaking blood, and his arm at an impossible angle.

But if his head still bled, did not that mean his heart continued to beat? I could not allow myself to behave like any ignorant fellow. Was I not trained in some aspects of medicine? Should I not believe him alive until I proved to myself that he was indeed beyond life?

In spite of my learning I had never needed to know how to save a drowned man. All I could think was to copy the shepherd at home, who used to breathe into a stillborn lamb's mouth. Sometimes it gave them life, sometimes not, but it was all I had. First, I turned my friend's lifeless body onto its uninjured side, to see if I could drain water from its lungs. A little trickled from his slack mouth. Returning him onto his back I breathed into his mouth, pinching his nostrils shut, as I had seen the shepherd do. His lips were cold as metal, and as unresponsive. I tried to remain calm, but my mind screamed panic at me.

*He is dead, dead. This is futile. He is dead. Leave him in peace!*

Then, as I tried once more to give him life I remembered his heart. Had it now stopped? No more blood ran from his head. A blow to his chest might start a silent heart, but if it did still beat, a blow could stop it. With the screaming wind and the rattle and pound of the pebbles and waves on the shore I could not tell. He was wearing too many clothes. I had to get them open so I could put my ear to his chest, and I must breathe for him too. But my fingers were stupid with the cold, and too clumsy to do it. I abandoned his soaking clothes and breathed into him again. A sudden gout of foul water shot from him into my mouth and I spat it out. I looked at him and saw water dribbling from his nose. Then he gave a small cough. I turned him onto his side again and beat his back with the flat of my hand. He lived! He lived. Now all I had to do was to keep him alive.

\* \* \*

Full daylight showed us how lucky we had been in the manner of our beaching, but in truth, we were all in such misery at being wrecked in such a storm-ridden place it was hard to feel thankful. We had, due to the sharp eyes and ears of the crew, managed to run up a narrow strip of sandy shingle. How we had not hit the rocks that lay all around was extraordinary to me. Even so, the pinnace was damaged. The rudder, of course, was gone, and one part of the keel must have hit rocks, for the next day, when it was turned for inspection, I could see it was damaged, as well as other parts of the boat. Our future seemed hopeless, for I could not think what we could do to fix it in this deserted place.

But that I left entirely to the men who knew what to do, for all my care was for Richard. Every one of us was wet, cold and shivering, but we at least could move around. Once he had come to himself he could not stand, and should have been laid in bed, with a fire to warm him and his injuries attended. On this bleak beach there was nowhere to shelter that I could see, and anyway, moving him without his arm being splinted would cause him agony and exacerbate the injury. In addition, because I had no knowledge of boat repair I must set myself to do my best in other ways for us all, not just my friend. The first thing was fire. Discovering that we still had the means to make a spark was a great relief. I at once set off in the driving rain, without hope, to find some material that would burn. Knowing that the cold would fast kill my friend if his injuries did not, I was desperate to somehow make fire.

I had walked around a small headland, my head lowered against the rain, before I came upon the cave. At first, it looked as if all the debris inside would be as wet as us, but then on a ledge I found much that was dry. I marvelled that a storm even greater than the one just past must have tossed the sticks and seaweed this high, otherwise all would have been sodden from the night past. I hastened back to the others. As soon as I had roughly bound Richard's arm to his body we carried him to the cave, out of the foul weather. We laid him on dry sand, well into the cave where the wind could not reach him. He had swooned as soon as we picked him up, but now his eyelids fluttered and for a moment he opened his eyes. He looked at me, and I am almost sure he knew me. His mouth moved but I could not tell what he said.

'What is it?' I said. 'You are safe now.' I laid my ear close by so I could hear what he said.

'Be not afeared,' was all he managed before he became senseless once more. He should not have felt he needed to reassure me, but I was indeed very afraid. I feared he would die, and I thought I would not be able to bear it. He was all the family I now had. How could I countenance facing the enemy without him by my side? I remonstrated with myself. I should not be thinking of myself, but of him. I needed to concentrate only on his welfare. That way he would have the best chance to survive, though another fear was that I had nothing to help him with.

That the sun came out later that morning seemed more like an insult than a bounty. It was a thin, liquid thing, with no heat in it, but we at last sat reasonably snug in our cave, with the flames burning blue and yellow as we added more dry material. Richard woke from his long swoon, and definitely knew us. His head wound was not deep, but he was in much pain both from his head and the break in his arm. Once I had the fire going, and we were beginning to feel a little warmer I attended better to his arm, with the help of a seaman to hold him still while I put the bones back more exactly where they belonged, and bound his arm securely to his body. His bones had, thank God, not broken through his skin, which would have been a matter for even greater concern. For while unbroken skin acts as a good bandage, ill vapours from the air can reach the inner parts of a body should they become exposed, and that can often end in death.

For several hours all lay exhausted in the cave, while I tended the fire and our clothes gradually steamed dry. At length, the captain roused his crew and set them to various tasks. The waves were still rolling angrily upon the shore, and so the men made great efforts to make sure of the pinnace. They also brought into the cave everything that could possibly be useful. We had carried enough food for a few days, but much of it was ruined. The captain rationed what was left, our immediate future being so uncertain. I was at pains to dry the charges for my pistol, and Richard's too, setting them on a ledge, well away from the risk of fire. In the afternoon, two seamen were set to fishing by the headland, in a sheltered spot, and brought the sea's bounty for our evening meal. I felt it was a small recompense for the damage the sea had done to us, but a very welcome one, for all that.

Over the next two days the seamen worked on repairing the pinnace, while I did my best to make our enforced stay as comfortable as possible. Fortunately, the weather improved every day. A cold November wind still blew, but not as strongly, and it remained dry. To my great relief, Richard went on well enough, though he had little appetite, suffering as he did from terrible headaches, and his vision was blurred. I was concerned that his head wound had caused more damage than at first I had hoped. He, wishing to spare me anxiety, continually insisted that he was well enough, though it was obvious to me that he was far from right.

On the third day, the captain came to speak privily to me.

'We have done our best with the vessel, and think we now have a good chance of making our way back to Flint. However, I am uneasy about one of the repairs. With all of us aboard it may be under too great a stress and so risk coming away as we sail.'

'What are you saying?'

'Only that seeing as your friend is injured, and needs your care, I am persuaded to leave you both here, first because of the state of the ship and your lack of skill as a sailor, but also because I can see it would go hard with Richard if he were forced to sail in the condition he finds himself.'

I was confounded. And into my mind slipped the unworthy thought that if I had not brought Richard back to life I would most likely have a place in the boat. Instead, my care of him was leading to me being marooned with a man who might yet succumb to his injuries. The thought shamed me, and I thrust it away, furious with the treachery of fear. 'I hardly know what to say,' I muttered. 'Except that you are right about his wounds causing him much distress. At the same time, he needs care that I cannot give him until we return to Flint.' I looked at the captain and put as much force as I could into my words. 'It is urgent to get him back with all haste.'

The captain looked most sorry. 'I am sure you are right, but I am captain here, and all must obey my orders. My decision is that you will both stay here until we can return for you.'

My heart beat loudly in my chest as if it wished to escape me. 'And when would that be?'

He shrugged, looking awkward at what he must say. 'As speedily as possible, but I cannot put a day upon it.'

I looked bitterly towards the cave, where Richard lay. 'I see I can do no more than bear what must be.'

The captain looked relieved, as well as sorry. 'We will leave you with as much as we can spare in the way of fish hooks, the small water barrel and some rum. There is little else, but the fish are plentiful. I do not think you will starve while we are gone.'

There was a part of me that wished to take up my pistol and force the captain to take us with him, but I knew that would be futile. I had been a captain myself, and knew what it was to command men. He was a thoughtful, incisive commander, and I had no doubt he was making the best decision he could, taking all into consideration. My role was to obey and make the best of what I was commanded to do.

It was hard work, getting the pinnace back down the beach and afloat. I helped with a heavy heart, but would not been seen as sulky. As soon as the sea took her the seamen were kept busy, fending her away from the rocks and eventually rowing her out to safer water. I watched as they put up the sail, which soon picked up the favourable breeze. They did not wave a farewell, as I had half expected them to do, but set their faces entirely away from the shore. Perhaps there was awkwardness in their hearts at leaving us this way, but I will never know for sure.

I took great pains to make light of our situation to Richard, but he was not to be fooled. He might be forced to mostly lie prone, silently battling the pains in his head, but he was very aware that every soul but me was absent.

'Where have they gone?' he asked when I returned to the cave.

'Home,' I said, 'the ship being too damaged to take us all. They will return as soon as possible. It will likely only be a few days.'

He closed his eyes for a few moments before speaking. 'Or a few weeks, or months, or never,' he said.

'We have not been deserted!' I said, in as cheerful a voice as could be. 'And we will do well enough until they return.'

'I had thought they had maybe gone to discover if we had landed on an island, or the mainland, and if any other souls inhabited this place.'

'They managed the repairs with what they had,' I said. 'But I could see that where it had been stove in under the bow they had been unable to make a perfect fix.'

'They should have gone to seek help with tools and materials,' he insisted. 'It is not impossible for people to be living not far off.'

I had not considered that, and wondered if the captain had thought about it. It was too late to ask him now. 'We will do well enough,' I said again.

'I suggest you should explore this place,' he said. 'Do not rely on their return. What if they founder before getting back to Flint? None then would know to come and find us. We must help ourselves, Tom . . .' He smiled slightly. 'Ptolemy. I think neither of us can endure a diet of fish for very long.'

That afternoon I went to the usual rock and fished. I also found two crabs and brought them back, uncertain if they were edible or not. They made a passable meal baked in the fire, but we were getting low on fuel, and so I went out again foraging for material to dry by the fire. When I eventually returned, Richard was standing, looking out of the cave's mouth. 'I thought you were gone,' was all he said before making his way unsteadily back to his place by the fire.

That night it snowed. It didn't settle on the rocks or beach, but a little way inland it covered the short grass and heather. Higher up, the hills were completely white. I was relieved I had dragged several washed-up branches into the cave for burning. The fishing was bad that day, and so we had to eat some of our poor store of rations. It got dark very early, and so we both lay by the fire, Richard mostly sleeping, while I kept the flames alight. The more I thought about it, the more I knew Richard was right. I should rove further, and explore this place properly. We needed better shelter, because I trembled to think how we would fare if a storm from another quarter drove the sea into our cave. We would surely die, if not of drowning, then of cold, hunger or injury.

In the morning I put a store of wood within reach of Richard's good arm, along with the small water barrel and the remains of our rations. 'I am going to do as you suggest, and explore this place,' I said.

He watched me as I put on my belt, along with the short sword. 'Take your pistol. You might meet a rabbit.'

I did my best to grin at him. 'Or even several!'

The likelihood of killing anything was remote. I was not even sure if the powder was completely dry, but to humour him I stuck the pistol in my belt, and took some powder and shot. I tried to cover him with my burr coat, but he would have none of it.

'I have the fire. Your need is the greater.'

'I don't know how long I will be, but don't expect me before dark. I will make an exhaustive search.'

'I will be patient,' he said. 'But please take care not to fall and injure yourself. I doubt I would be able to find you.'

'I will be careful. Just make sure you tend the fire.'

I could feel him watching me as I left. I turned at the cave's entrance to give him an encouraging smile, but his pinched face, his eyes huge in the light of the fire, and the shadow of fear passing over him froze my expression. All I could do was to raise my hand in a salute to him. And so we parted.

# CHAPTER SIXTEEN

I decided to go inland, to climb the nearest hill. I hoped that way to settle if we were on an island or not. No further snow fell, and there was no frost, so I soon became warm, climbing in my thick wool coat. Once away from the coast the ground was covered in wiry grass, and then heather and gorse. There were no trees to be seen, and the gorse was carved into extraordinary sloping bushes, due it must be to the wild winds hereabouts. As I climbed, the wind grew stronger, and I became glad of my coat again. The sea was as silver grey as my sword, with white tops to the waves here and there. After climbing for a good while I stopped to catch my breath. Looking back, I realised it would be very easy to lose where the cave was. The coast was broken with rocky edges and low cliffs. It looked as if a giant infant had tossed his wooden bricks about in a fit of temper. All was dull, and sullen, with no other land to be seen out to sea. I set my mind to remember the particular tumbled cliff under which the cave, and Richard, lay hidden.

Turning my face again to the summit, I continued to climb. The hill was higher than I had thought, and it was tiring work, trudging through the snow, which lay thicker the higher I went. As the view opened out behind me, every time I stopped to take breath I saw more of our prison, stretched out below. Around to one side lay much wider beaches, the sand gleaming almost as white as the snow. The country all over was the same heather and gorse, although far down I saw what seemed to be a couple of stunted trees. I was becoming concerned about the short amount of daylight left when I finally reached the top of the hill. I had expected to have a vision of the entire land, but ahead of me was another summit, and I still could not tell if we were on an island or no. If we were, it was much larger than I had imagined, but there was no smoke rising in the landscape below me to betray any sign of human life. Under the hill to one side, and not far off, a wide valley sheltered some more trees, and a stream ran, a dark thread in the colourless landscape. It looked as if it tumbled over rocks on its way to the sea. The day was more than half over, and I could not risk going on, or I would be benighted before I reached any sort of shelter. Indeed, there was no relief that I could see in the whole valley, apart from those few stunted trees. It was dismal to countenance returning to my friend without any cheerful news, but I had no choice. It looked as if the cave, our precarious toehold on life, was the best the island had to offer. That being so, we were desperately vulnerable.

By the time I managed to find our cave again it was almost full dark. Richard did not chide me, but I could tell he had been anxious. Indeed, it would have been very easy for me to have fallen and twisted or broken an ankle while clambering over the tumbled rocks. The dusk had tricked me into thinking the cave lay further west than it did, and I had wasted time and risked injury clambering over rocks when I could have made an easier path. I had returned safely, but other than that I had no cheer for him, and so we were both in low spirits.

'Ah well,' he said at last, after I had described the lack of any better shelter or habitation. 'I never did believe in unicorns.'

'I will spend tomorrow fishing, and collecting fuel,' I said at last. 'I will also fill the water barrel for you. The following day I will leave at first light and explore further. If I can find shelter I will stay overnight if there is more to explore. I think it unlikely a boat will arrive for us in the next couple of days, but if it does, they know where the cave is, and you will be able to tell them what I am doing.' It was not much of a plan, and it would be hard on Richard being deserted again without any means of knowing how I did, but it was the best we could do to attempt to help ourselves.

I slept heavily after my day's exertions, but when I awoke Richard was well astir, sitting on the far side of the fire, which he had blown back into flame. He was still in a lot of pain, it not being eased by lying or sitting, while standing made his head spin as well as ache. I was more anxious about him than I had ever been, but as always he made light of his suffering. Indeed, he worked as a one-handed quartermaster, stowing the fuel I brought, cooking the fish and generally making the cave as shipshape as was possible. I think the activity helped to distract him from the pain, but only a little. There was nothing to be done about it. He refused to take any of the rum, saying he would rather save it, for what additional disaster I could only imagine.

It was low tide at daybreak, and I decided to try my luck at walking along the coastline. From my earlier climb I had seen there were not so very many tumbled rocks between our tiny islet and the large, white beaches to the east. So, leaving Richard as well provisioned as possible, I set off. I found the going much easier than the day before. The large expanses of sand had been hidden from us by a large outcrop of rock, but at low tide I could get around it by wading no more than up to my ankles in the sea. In this way I went from one beach to another in relative ease, though as the tide turned and the sea rose I was forced to wade deeper, or climb over more rocks. At last I came to the place where a stream ran into the sea. I followed it up the beach, hoping it was the stream I had seen in the distance two days earlier. I slaked my thirst and sat beside it for a few minutes, trying to decide on my next move. Should I continue along the coast? What if I got overtaken by the rising tide? Should I not try following the stream instead? It must be nearly midday, and there was little shelter here, with no cliffs to offer the possibility of a cave. If I was to explore further I would need some sort of cover for the night, even if it were no more than under some gorse to keep away the worst of the prevailing wind. I would go inland.

I struck gold almost immediately! As I followed the stream back from the beach I could see a distinct path beside it, worn in the thin soil. It might be no more than some sort of animal track, but it was the first sign I had seen of any living thing, and I could not help my spirits rising. I trod the path up the gentle incline, happy to have the company of the trickling stream. It became noisier as we climbed, having cut a narrow, tumbling way through the tough grass and stones. A little higher and I was out of sight of the beach, sheltered in a narrow valley running ever upwards. Here, bushes and small birch and rowan trees grew along the stream, their fallen leaves littering the path and caught in the little pools between stones in the water. The snow was melting as I walked, and that too raised my spirits. I paused for a moment, very happy to be amongst trees, although they were naked, and poor, stunted things compared to the rich oaks, elms and beeches of my childhood home. There were nut bushes here, but sadly no nuts left upon the hazel wands. Perhaps there were squirrels, or mice had taken every one.

I was so busy with my own thoughts, I came upon the little plateau almost without noticing it. I had been thinking of my brother, and our childhood escapades in the woods, and wondering how it went with him now. When I happened to look up it took me a moment to see what lay before my eyes. There, not a hundred paces ahead of me, was a tiny cottage. There was a closed door, a shuttered window and what looked like a good roof, though much greened with mosses. It was set back against one rising side of the valley, while in front of it the unseasonably retreating snow revealed the remains of a small vegetable plot. Attached to the cottage was a shed, built of the same stone. Its roof was higher than that of the cottage, with two doors, one above the other. I could not think it a hay loft, for where would hay be found here? It little mattered. I looked eagerly for signs of life, but there was none. It was, I thought, most probably deserted, through famine, disease or war I could not tell, but it was certain shelter, and that was a thing most wonderful to me.

I wanted to return immediately to Richard and bring him here with all speed, but I tempered my excitement with caution. There were a few hours' daylight left, but not enough to reach him without risk of getting caught on the rocks, or having to swim the cold sea in the dark, which would be foolish in the extreme. Instead, I should use the time to discover if the cottage was indeed deserted, or simply unoccupied for the day. I would not want to help myself to this place if its owner was nearby, but would ask for shelter. Surely there would be a place for us in the shed, if not the cottage itself?

I kept to the path and carried on past the buildings, having first knocked at the door and received no answer. As I continued to climb the zigzag path, the trees and bushes disappeared as the stream ran steeply through a section of broken rocks. After that, the path flattened out, and the stream meandered on its way through a patch of tough grass, dotted liberally with reeds. It was difficult to be certain, but I thought I could roughly identify where I had stood up high, looking over this wild, windy plateau between two steep hills. The cottage had been totally hidden from that vantage point; indeed, it was hidden from me now, only a few hundred paces from its door.

I took some time to scan the landscape, near and far. It still looked totally deserted. I kept gazing, hoping for some other sign of humanity, but there was nothing. Then something in the distance caught my eye. It was a deer, with a magnificent antlered head. I knew there was no way for me to get close enough to shoot it, but maybe, if the land could support deer, it would also hold smaller animals that I might be able to trap. Hugh and I had enjoyed making snares and catching rabbits when we were boys. Perhaps I could do the same here? But surely we would be rescued in a few days. This cottage would be useful while we waited, but I mustn't begin to think like a resident of this inhospitable place or I might cease to think of escape. I shivered. I should return to the cottage, see if I could get in and decide how to bring Richard here. It would not be easy, with him so unsteady on his feet, but if I were to save his life it was essential to get him to more reliable warmth, which only a small space would provide.

There was no lock on the door, and although it was a little stiff and swollen in its frame, it opened easily enough with a bit of encouragement. Within was a simple room, with two cots and a fireplace with a pot hanging over it. There was of course nothing as grand as glass in the window, so it would have to remain shuttered. In the summer, however, I could see that it would be a pleasant thing to have the shutters back to let extra light within, and to see the small trees waving their leaves in the breeze.

Soon, sitting next to the lit fire and eating the last of the fish I had carried with me, I thought of the siege at Chester. Had the Irish troops managed to embark and land at Flint? Were they even now relieving the siege, while I sat here at my ease in some peasant's cot? Whatever was happening in the war was of no consequence here. It seemed like a dream, a half-forgotten fantasy that could not possibly be true. It was so quiet here. Only the stream made any sound, apart from the occasional thump of snow falling from the trees. I was sure there would be no storm this night. Richard would be safe in his cave, and I would somehow bring him here on the morrow.

The cot I slept in was in truth a poor apology for a bed, but after the gravelly floor of the cave it was a kind of bliss. I sent up a silent thanks to whoever owned this place, and a prayer to God to protect Richard until I could go to him in the morning. In spite of my feet overhanging the end of the narrow cot, the warm little room made me more comfortable than I had been for a long while, and I slept deeply after my exertions. Although our situation was difficult, and I was particularly worried about my friend, I felt that once here, he might mend more quickly. That was, at least, my fervent hope.

# CHAPTER SEVENTEEN

The sun was not in evidence when I woke, but it was full morning and I had slept late. A damp mist hung about the trees, and when I went outside I couldn't see far ahead. I pulled the door closed and drank from the stream. I was anxious to get back to Richard, to give him some good cheer about this place of shelter I had found. After some thought I went back in and left the pistols on the little table. I would not need them, and I preferred to keep them dry, as well as making myself as unencumbered as possible, for I would need to carry all our belongings, as well as to support Richard on the way back here.

I could not tell what hour it might be, but I feared it was late, and I had the tide to beat. I bounded down the path as quickly as I was able, and soon emerged onto the beach. The mist was as white as the sand and swirled all about me. It felt as if I was entering a land of clouds, which teased by almost clearing, only to become in the next moment a thick blanket of vapour, deadening the sound of the gentle waves on this still morning. The mist drifted myriad drops of water about my wool jacket, which set it glistening like so many diamonds. In spite of its mysterious beauty the mist promised to chill me right through, so I quickly followed the stream across the sand and down to the water's edge. All I had to do now was to follow the coastline west and I would soon come to the tiny cove where Richard lay in our cave.

I splashed, ankle deep in the sea, being careful to keep shallow water on my right side. Soon, I was wading past the first of the piled rocks to reach the next beach. As I went I thought how the cottage had been built of similar stones, some of them quite huge. How the builder had managed to carry them up the path I could not imagine. Had they been carried, or rolled, like poor Sisyphus was obliged to do? Maybe there had been some kind of cunning hoist constructed, so they could be hauled, and maybe many friends had helped, though it seemed unlikely in this isolated spot.

By the time I reached the next pile of rocks I was forced to wade out up to my knees to get past them, but by now I was not too far from our cove. The problem occurred at the large outcrop that had hidden the big beaches from our cove. The tide was racing in, and even though I waded up to my thighs in the icy water I was still faced with a difficult climb unless I went even further out. It didn't help that I couldn't pick out a useful route over the rocks because of the ever-thickening mist. I had clambered over a few of them when going the other way, so perhaps I should do the same now, but the tide having covered the low rocks, these were much more difficult. Maybe I would be better advised to retrace my steps and climb the hill, regaining our cove that way, instead of risking the sea? I looked in the direction of the hill, but there was nothing of it that I could see. I might as well be in a totally featureless place, for all the landmarks were hidden. I would almost certainly become lost inland. There was nothing for it but to wade further out.

I kept one hand on the rocks, but suddenly the sand shifted under my feet and I was plunged in over my head. I came up spluttering and gasping with the sudden immersion in the icy sea. I reached out, but could feel nothing, nor could I see anything apart from the water closest to me, slopping saltily into my mouth. I twisted around, but could still see nothing. Which way was the shore? The water was suddenly too deep for me to regain my feet. I was in the middle of a cloud of misty nothingness, with no idea of which way to go, and no means of rescue at hand. Besides that, my thick coat had become saturated and, with my boots, dragged me ever down.

I struggled to keep treading water, and began to divest myself of my coat, trying not to panic. A wavelet splashed into my face and I swallowed a quantity of water. Down I went, down until my feet hit sand. I pushed off from the bottom and emerged again into the shining mist, one arm out of my coat. I couldn't be far away from shore, unless a current was taking me out. If I could just keep my head above water, surely the incoming tide would help me? I turned again to look about me and my knee hit something. Now I could see a bit of glistening black rock above the surface, and reached out thankfully for it, divesting myself of the coat as I did. The waves slammed me into the rocks and I held onto the slippery, weed-covered surface as they sucked back out again.

Fear remained my companion as I slowly scraped my way past the outcrop. As soon as I was past I struck out for the shore. I was cold to the very bone, and already being exhausted from my exertions found it difficult to drag myself up the beach. As soon as I was half out of the sea, the wind sent a blast of ice at my skin. I wanted no more than to lie prone in the sand, but I would soon die of cold if I did that. Wearily gaining my feet at last in our little cove, I must have made a pitiful example of my race. My stockings and breeches were both torn, and scarlet blood ran unheeding down my lower legs. My body was too chilled to feel any pain, and in truth my injuries were not serious, but when I staggered back to the cave Richard's expression of alarm told me that he feared I was in a bad way.

'I am well enough,' I told him untruthfully, my teeth chattering noisily in my skull. 'I just need to get warm.'

He made to build up the fire, but I took the wood from him. 'I must keep moving.'

'And you must remove your clothes,' he said. 'And put on my burr coat.'

By degrees the fire warmed me, and I began to feel more alive. We exchanged our news and even became cheerful. Richard had managed to take himself out to the fishing rocks while I had been away, and had managed to catch a fish, which was excellent to hear.

'I only had one bad headache,' he told me, 'and I believe I am less unsteady too, when I stand and walk.'

That was good news indeed. It seemed entirely possible that I would be able to guide him safely to the cottage, as long as we made sure to leave early enough in the day. I did not intend to risk either of us needing to swim again. Richard wrote a note in the cave sand for our rescuers. It had an arrow, and the words 'stream' and 'follow inland' which was admirably succinct. Meanwhile, I laid out some stones in the pattern of a larger arrow in plain sight on the beach, pointing the direction in which we would go. While doing so, I found my discarded burr coat, still sodden, but fortuitously given back to me by the tide.

'If when they come there is a mist like today, they may not see my arrow,' I said on my return to the cave with my coat, 'but your note will certainly direct them well.'

'I am good at taking note,' said Richard with a quiet smile. 'But our efforts will only be useful if they do come.'

'We have enough to consider without worrying about that,' I said, anxious to deflect both of us from such dolorous thinking. 'For one thing, the cottage certainly offers much better shelter, and a good store of fuel, but the fishing might not be so good on the sandy beach.'

'In that case let us spend some time fishing here, while it is still light.'

So the rest of the short day found us perched on the fishing rocks, casting and recasting for as many fish as we could catch. In addition, I kept a watchful eye on my companion. Richard was still not as well as he insisted, at times wavering eccentrically during our walk over to the rocks. What might help a bit was a stout stick for his good arm to lean upon, but there was nothing suitable here. I wished I had thought to look for something on my journeying but tried to excuse my lack of thought. I at least was in a parlous state so far as my mind was concerned, with the fear of losing Richard eating away at me. I could not afford to descend into despair, although the thought of managing to get him all the way to the cottage in one day was of great concern to me. But I had no choice. It was winter, and another storm might finish us. So, with the remains of the light we made a bundle out of everything we had that might be useful, which in truth was little enough, and lay down to sleep our last in this salty place.

In the morning the mist had gone as mysteriously as it had come, and we made haste to leave. I was in agony to get past the outcrop safely, which was our first and most challenging obstacle. Richard, however much he wanted to hurry, was not capable of it, and we made heavy weather of the crossing. Fortunately, we had judged the tide well, and although it was not as low as when I had first crossed three days earlier, I did not have to wade too far out. I was at pains to give Richard the easier way, and he did manage to get no wetter than up to his knees. However, he stumbled and jarred his arm badly a couple of times, and his grey pallor betrayed the agony he refused to own. By the time we reached the beach with the stream he was utterly done.

We both drank our fill, and lay for a while beside the stream. At length Richard sat up. 'Shall we go on?' I said, thinking him recovered.

'I fear I am unwell,' he said before vomiting violently.

'Has this happened since you were injured?' I asked.

'Only a few times,' he said, lying back down carefully.

I was greatly troubled by this revelation because until now he had denied any such thing. 'You should have told me,' I said.

His eyes were closed against the obvious pain he felt. 'What use would that have been,' he said weakly, 'other than to alarm you further.'

I could not deny that. I had no medicines with me, or ability to procure any, but there was one thing at least I could do. 'There is no rush,' I said to him. 'The weather is being kind to us. You rest while I fetch something that might help you at least a little.'

I set off straight away to climb the path. As soon as I reached the small trees I searched until I found a branch that would hold at least some of his weight. It was not tall enough to go under his arm, but would work well enough to at least help him balance. The path by the stream was narrow, and it would be easier for him to use the stick in places where I was not able to walk beside and support him that way. I soon returned, and with my help he struggled to his feet.

'It will be worth it,' I tried to cheer him. 'For when we arrive you shall lie upon a proper bed, while I make a decent fire. Meanwhile, as your physician, I insist you take a mouthful of rum.'

He did so for the first time without demurring, and so we went on. At last, when I was beginning to fear that he would never make it, we reached the little place where the cottage and shed lay.

Like a child, I would have loved Richard to show some excitement at seeing the cottage, but he was far too exhausted to do more than stand, swaying on his feet as I pushed open the door. To give us light, I left the door wide while I helped him to a cot, and covered him up with the meagre blankets available. He let out a great sigh and closed his eyes again. 'Are you like to vomit again?' I enquired. His 'no' was faint but decisive, and so I left him to his rest. He passed almost immediately into a deep sleep, while I lit the fire, and a lantern I had not noticed before. I closed the door and eventually the cold stones of the cottage began to warm. I had not searched the place before, thinking it hardly polite if the owners were near. Now, however, seeing that the pistols lay exactly as I had left them, and all else being as before, I decided that if the owner still lived, he was far from this place. On holding the lantern up I saw in one corner a small wooden barrel. To my great delight, when I removed the lid I found a quantity of oatmeal. It looked and smelt good so I at once put some into the iron pot and added water. In a small pot on the only shelf, I found salt, and added a little to the mixture. Several wooden spoons were also on the shelf so I took one up and began to stir. It was not long before the scent of warm oatmeal filled the air. It seemed like a lifetime since I had tasted anything like it. Fish was all well and good, but a man must have more than fish in his belly. I made so bold as to wake Richard when it was done. 'I have something that will help you,' I said as he opened his eyes.

'More sleep will help,' he said. Then he smelt the gruel. 'Are you a cook now?' He turned his head and watched as I ladled some of the mess into one of the bowls I had found. 'No. No, I can do it,' he said as I made to help him to eat. He struggled to sit up and took the bowl and spoon from me, wedging the bowl amongst the blankets covering him. At the first taste he frowned. At the second he hurried it down.

'Take it steadily,' I said. 'I hope it will help to settle your stomach, but if you eat too quickly it might have the opposite effect.'

When it was done he looked for more, but I refused him. 'One bowl each is enough to start. If it proves good I will make more, but for now rest again, as I soon shall.'

I took the pot, bowls and spoons to the stream and washed them. Then I put water into the pot and set it back on the low fire. My whole body was sticky with salt, and I ached to clean my skin. While the water heated, I took my linen and stockings to the stream and washed all vigorously in the icy water. I felt quite the housewife as I hung the dripping garments around the fire. Richard had fallen back to sleep, and his colour looked better than it had in days. I felt better too. It was so excellent to have something of substance in my stomach.

While I was astir and Richard still slept, I took the lantern and went to investigate the barn. I don't quite know what I had expected, but stored there were various nets, which must surely be for fishing. There was also a barrel similar to the one in the cottage, but much larger. This was full of unground oats. I desired to look further at the winter garden, but the short day was fading and it was too dusky to see well. I went back into the cottage and rested the lantern on the table. The candle was much burnt, and regretfully I decided that it should be saved. So it was, after checking again on my friend, that I blew out the candle and took myself to bed by the light of the fire. To one such as I, used to light whenever I fancied it, it was strange to behave like an animal and obey the rhythm of the day. But Richard was not the only one to be fatigued. I think we had both been at pains to shield the other from our concerns, but worry is exhausting, besides which, even I, being able-bodied, had exerted myself enough on the meagre food we had been eating until now.

For the next few days I stayed nearby, at pains to keep Richard as rested, warm and well fed as possible. I watched him closely, but there was no further vomiting, and his skin began to lose its grey tinge, becoming altogether more healthy. The porridge did us both good, filling our bellies in a satisfying way. The garden yielded some greens of various sorts, and even a few roots that had been missed in the digging. It was little enough, but we were both glad of the fish stew I made with a bit of everything I found, and with a sprinkling of oatmeal to thicken it. I made a much better splint for Richard's arm, which brought him more comfort. His headaches grew less as he was better rested, having nothing to do but eat and sleep. All progressed very well, except that we were cast away in this forsaken place, with no means of telling when, if ever, we might be rescued.

As Richard's health improved we took to sitting either side of the fire at night, talking over our situation. We both fretted that when the pinnace returned the men might miss our note and pebble arrow. It also worried us that the boat might have floundered on the way home, with no one left alive to know where we were. I had wanted to slough off my old life and take another, but had not for one moment thought of such a dramatic change in circumstances. It felt as if we were in a nutshell, shut off from the rest of the world. All was silence with us, while beyond our reach our country fought and argued, with blood, hunger and dismay. The war had been going badly for us. What was happening now? I told Richard of my extraordinary meeting with the King, which I had been unable to speak of before. Where was he now, our monarch? His presence had not relieved Chester. Was he still in Wales, or had he gone north into the land of his birth, looking for more soldiers there? We did not know if we ourselves lay yet in England or had crossed into Scotland. There was no line in the ground to tell us.

We also thought much about our families. What of Hugh? Did he lie injured or dead somewhere, or was he becoming known for his valour in Fairfax's army? Had his troop met mine? Had he killed some of my men, or been killed by them? These were bitter thoughts, and it did me no good in thinking them.

We discussed making a signal fire to alert any passing vessels to our distress. 'But what if we attract a parliamentarian vessel?' said Richard. 'We know they are about in these waters.'

I was also plagued by still not knowing if we lay on an island or not. 'For,' I said, 'what if around the next corner a fishing port lies, with shops and inns and all kinds of help for us?'

'It is hardly likely,' said Richard. 'While you were away finding this place I spent many hours watching the sea from my cave. Never once did I see a sail. Surely, if we were close to habitation, I would have seen some signs of life?'

'I still think I should at least go a little further, and try to discover if we are surrounded by water or not.'

'And if help comes while you are away?'

'I would hope they would be prepared to wait for a day. Maybe a signal fire would be useful for that purpose, to alert me if help arrived and I was away.'

'Maybe. But there is not a great deal of timber about this place.'

We did not get around to building a fire, neither being convinced of its merits compared to its possible dangers. And I agreed to be gone no longer than a day and a night. If help arrived, they would surely be happy to wait overnight for me to return? It was a risk, whatever we did, and sitting here without shifting for ourselves did not seem to be a useful plan. We were, however, alive to the possibility that with every passing day, and with good weather prevailing, help was either likely soon or would not come at all. With that in mind I set out as dawn was hardly breaking.

I was not minded to risk the sea again, so crossed the stream and headed uphill, looking to gain the further hill I had seen from my last venture inland. It was a much steeper climb, with some scrambling needed. I followed what might have been a deer track, which took me past some almost sheer outcrops of bare rock. As far as possible I continued north. It was a beautiful day, with a sky as pale as my mother's eyes. In several places the gorse was in flower, shining golden splashes of light in the dull landscape. I saw more deer, one very close, it starting away as I came upon it all of a sudden. I wished I had brought my pistol after all, though it would have been a sorry thing to see a wounded deer run, and me with my pistol unlikely to make a clean kill. As I climbed higher the heather ceased, and only poor, small, tough plants grew. I saw a hare, and various birds I could not identify. There was game aplenty on this hillside, but it would take lying in wait, rather than striding along, to have a good chance of getting any.

Eventually the foundation of the earth was laid bare. Nothing grew but stones and distant bird calls, while the wind blew as if from the beginning of the world. It was not easy climbing through this desolate landscape. The loose stones gave me no purchase, and several times I slid back as much as I went forward. When eventually I reached the top I was exhausted, and rested on my hands and knees before being able to stand and look about me. It was like standing on the shoulder of a giant! I had never been so high. From here I could see quite certainly that we did indeed inhabit an island. To the north and east at some distance other lands lay; some were obviously islands, while it was difficult to tell if others were joined onto the land or not. To the west I could see no land at all. I wondered if we had been blown north of Ireland. If so, was there any land in this direction nearer than the Americas?

This bleak beauty, revealing God's majestic work, was entirely indifferent to my tiny life. I felt a mere speck upon the earth, insignificant and without meaning. I turned to look south, from where we had been blown, and saw another small, rather flat island beyond ours, and then open sea. Somewhere beyond my eyes' sight were soldiers in Ireland, and my comrades at Flint. Was there a smudge of smoke far in the distance? Was that Chester burning? Further south inland lay my family home. What was happening there? And on to Bristol and Gloucester. Were they yet in Cromwell's hands? I was remote from men's endeavours, and I did not know how I felt about that.

I sat down upon the naked hide of the earth, upon the ancient rock that had surely been here longer than any man. I felt its marks and contours under my hands and looked upon it. Why had God made this part high and another low? He was surely the supreme artist. The beauty of His work lay all around to inspire us, yet we men toiled like beetles upon its grandeur, hardly looking at anything apart from our own little concerns. It seemed arrogant to believe that He would spend even a moment concerning himself with our desire to be rescued from such a magnificent example of His work. Indeed, was God, who made all this, troubling Himself at all about England's squabbles? Kings came and went. Whether they knew they were God's chosen or not, whatever they thought they commanded, the land they ruled was in truth never theirs. It belonged to God, and men would never despoil it. Whatever they did scratched only tiny marks upon it; yes, even London's tower and all the other castles I had seen. Compared to this, men's works were as nothing.

I spent a while looking out to sea but could see no ships upon it. It was late in the year for sailing, but I had hoped for something. Still, I had discovered what we wanted to know. There was no need for me to spend a night away from Richard. If I made a good pace I would reach the cottage before dark, so I stood up and spent a last few minutes carefully gazing at every part of our island. I was looking for smoke that would betray some other hearth fire. I could see ours, trickling up into the sky, but no other. We were utterly alone.

# CHAPTER EIGHTEEN

I wish we had thought to number the days. When more than two weeks must have passed we tried to retrace them in our conversation, wanting to have some idea of how long we had truly been in this place. The best estimate we could make was seventeen days, or maybe sixteen. It is astonishing how the mind forgets such things as days passing, but in truth, one ran into another with little to tell them apart.

We were slow to think that we might be here for the duration of the winter. Every dawn that broke invited us to think that this day would see us rescued, but it never did. As the days grew ever shorter, and the weather grew more often stormy, we knew we had to shift to make sure of our survival until the year turned. The fishing was good here, if we went to a particular set of rocks at one end of our long beach. We also found a quern in the shed, so our supply of oatmeal was secure, so long as the store of oats lasted. Not knowing how long we would be there, we rationed it, and to make breaking our fast a little more interesting we ground some to as fine a powder as we could make it, and tried to make a sort of flat bread with it. We were at the extremity of our knowledge, but that itself kept our minds busy, while we scrambled for other ways to vary our diet. Richard had more idea of the domestic than I, but I outdid him in hunting. I made and set many snares across the smaller of animal trails I found in the grass, and further up amongst the heather. It took a while to recall the skill, and I had many failures, but one day, while Richard was toasting one-handed his apology for bread, I found two rabbits, snared cleanly and quite dead, while some bird I did not know flapped in another, caught by one leg. I killed it at once, and returned triumphant to our den.

As the days turned into weeks, we attempted as far as we could to give up fretting, but I for one found it difficult to sleep unless my body was worn out with effort. For how long did we need to make the oats last? What would happen to us if no one ever came? Could we ever construct a boat or raft with few materials or tools and almost no knowledge? Those dismal thoughts I kept to myself, but we both often wondered aloud how the war was progressing, as well as how our loved ones were faring. We both had sunny natures, and both were inclined to make the best we could of whatsoever our situation brought us, but it was impossible for me to view our plight with equanimity.

When the weather was bad, and during every long, dark afternoon on into the night, we distracted each other by telling stories by the light of the fire, sipping hot water in the absence of wine, beer or any herbs for tea. When we both had told as much about our family histories as we could recall we turned to other tales. My mother having had an Irish parent, I knew some of the legends of that race, and so was able to regale Richard with the salmon of knowledge, the tale of Oisin and my favourite, the white wolfhound. Because of this story I had always yearned to own a wolfhound, but my father would never allow it.

By mutual consent we avoided the Odyssey, not wanting to remind ourselves how long it might be before we got home. Instead, Richard told me of a magical performance of *A Midsummer Night's Dream* that he had seen as a young boy. I responded by telling him of the Queen's masque in which I had almost performed. One evening between us we made up a fantastical story to go with the three nymphs I had met. It owed something to Spenser as well as Mr Shakespeare, and contained a little of Troy, as well as a magical dog.

We rationed food, heat and light to make all last, so almost always were a little hungry, sometimes chilly, and lived like moles in those dark, stormy evenings, but that particular night will live long in my memory. For we managed to create a little of our own magic, which took us away from our troubles long enough to ensure that our sleep was full of pleasant thoughts. We both remarked on it the following day, and admitted to each other for the first time that in spite of trying to remain jolly for the other, our true thoughts were often much more dismal. But there was nothing to be done, other than to bear it, and so we did.

Eventually, I determined that enough time had passed for Richard's bone to have knitted, and so it proved. I was anxious, once his arm was no longer protected by the splint, that he would overuse it, but he took commendable care, suffering my anxiety with wry good humour. At last I was persuaded that he was entirely well, with his headaches gone too. This was a great relief to us both.

We had no books or paper, but we recalled games of our youth and with some ingenuity created others from the materials we had to hand. It was simple enough to use stones for draughts and nine men's morris, but the difficulty was having light in which to play. We felt such a great need to husband our candles and firewood, and with the door closed the cottage was lit by no more than a glow. But as the winter deepened we were forced to stay indoors ever more as storms increasingly swept our island. Whenever we could, we ground oats, fished and fossicked in the muddy garden for the greens we came to yearn for. There were further discoveries in the shed, and in the cottage. A small supply of candles in a little box we had overlooked, stowed far under one of the cots, felt like a great prize. We celebrated that by playing three games of draughts, of which Richard narrowly won two and was declared champion for the night. In the same place we discovered a crock with a wooden lid, half full of flour. Why had we not thought to reach under the cots before? The flour excited Richard so much I fell to teasing him. He insisted on putting a little into a bowl and adding water, then leaving it near the fire for a few days. He fretted about the lack of honey, but in spite of that he succeeded in making a softer flat bread on the iron griddle this way, and if we had come across a tub of honey and a pat of butter I think his life would have been complete. That evening we feasted well on hare stew, thickened with oats with bread to dip into it and thought ourselves kings.

With the dark days came thoughts of Christmas. We both, I know, turned more inward at this time. For my part I thought even more about my family, and Richard I am sure dwelt also on his. I thought a lot about Aphra and her family too.

All were lost to me now. I had dark days and dark thoughts. Were we going to die here, and never be discovered, except as a collection of bones? To try and make a balm against these dismal feelings, we came up with a new game that didn't need light. Each lying on our cot, we took it in turns to speak of a chosen subject. The game was to persuade the other that what we said was either true or false, against the real truth of the matter. I tended to believe more easily than Richard, and had to counsel myself to be suspicious. Richard's immediate reaction after I had laid out an argument for something I thought he would surely fall for was invariably his usual dismissive phrase. *Ha! I don't believe in unicorns, Ptolemy!* I asked him once where he had come by the phrase. He said he thought it was by Mr Shakespeare, but could not recall which play. That set me off in a fever for a volume of the plays, so I could discover it, but of course books had we none.

One thing of which neither of us knew the veracity was the correct date. Amongst all else that troubled us it should have been of small importance, but we both worried away at it. Was it foolishness to fret so much at not knowing which day was Christmas? It felt as if it mattered a lot. In the end we designated a day, and looked forward to it as best we could. We fashioned each other Christmas gifts. Richard gave me a peg to hang my snares upon, and a long wooden spear for killing deer. How he had fashioned it without me guessing I do not know. He kept what he was up to very well hidden. For killing it was not useful, but I used it to carry my game home, and so could reward his efforts with my pleasure. For him I contrived a series of wooden runnels at the stream, that caused water to spill conveniently onto a saucer of rock where he could stand his pot to collect water for his cooking experiments. It worked moderately well, though was more fragile than I would have liked, and needed almost constant repair.

We decided we should do something different on our feast of Christmas, and so it being a clear day we went for a long walk up to the top of the hill to sing carols as loudly as we could manage. It was one of those cold, sparkling days that occurred sometimes through the winter, and the walk did us good.

'Perhaps this is not a real Christmas Day,' said Richard as we reached the summit, panting hard. 'But up here we are doubtless closer to God, and can hurl our hymns even higher than usual, so He hears them in heaven, and knows we are doing our best to keep His son's nativity.'

So we managed to keep good cheer on that day, but on the day we decided should be kept as the beginning of the new year we both fell into the deepest despondency that we had done since being abandoned. Our lives seemed a hopeless endeavour. The regular visits to the cave to check on the sand note and pebble arrow brought nothing but continuing disappointment. We had written directions in pebbles too, thinking the other might be missed. That was much of a day's work by the time we had collected enough pebbles of the correct size, and our efforts were for nothing. Our thoughts turned often to making our own way off the island, but the nearest land was much too far to swim, and the sea far too cold at this time of year. We came to think that our shipmates must have been almost certainly killed by the enemy. We could not believe they would have willingly left us to our fate here, but then even that became less certain in our despondent mood. The day was a brooding, discontented animal, and towards evening we fell out seriously with one another, something we had always been at pains not to do. I cannot even remember what sparked our argument, but it was bitter, and ended up with Richard stalking out of the cottage.

I was certain he would return by the time our meal was ready. Besides, it was a bitter, cold day, and not long until dark. He was far from being a foolish fellow, and would know that I would apologise profusely for whatever had angered him beyond words. But as time passed, and it became full night, I was anxious. I lit the lantern and went out to the barn, thinking he would be skulking there, but there was no sign of him. I walked a little up the path and down. It was icy, and the path was very slippery. After nearly falling twice I decided that I would do no good if I broke a leg, and so carefully regained the cottage. I did not see him at first on my return. He was huddled on his cot, and when I did notice him I at first thought he was asleep. When I spoke to him gently he didn't reply, but then I realised he was weeping. I went to him, uncertain if he would throw me off, but he did not. We were both at such a low ebb. All we could do was cling to one another for some small comfort and both weep.

Our falling-out did have one good result. It brought home to us how much we relied on the other, and feared being alone. Our lives here were only somewhat bearable because we had each other's company. Our friendship was vital not only to our physical health, but also that of our minds. Eventually we dried our tears and ate our food, feeling unaccountably fragile. We became awkward with one another, as if we had only just met, and were uncertain of friendship. At last we both slept, and in the morning were painfully polite to one another. It wasn't until we agreed to go out for a walk that we became easier, and things were gradually settled between us. There is something about walking, something to do with being together and yet not regarding the other that makes difficult conversation easier. At any rate, by degrees we returned to how we had been before we fell out, except that our friendship felt renewed, and stronger and more serious than before. When I look back on that time I can see all the inexperience of our youth, and how we matured through that difficult winter.

I would soon be two and twenty years of age, whenever my birthday happened to be. I would not have mentioned it, but Richard had remembered, and determined that we would celebrate it by choosing some new endeavour. He had never given up thinking of venison, believing that we must be able to find some way of killing a deer without spending hours in the freezing cold, lying in wait. Now he proposed using some of the nets in the barn to construct a way to catch one. With no boat to take the nets out to sea there was no other use to which we could put them. So somewhere around the day of my birth we struggled up onto the moorland with the nets, and argued in a good-natured way about how and where to set our trap. By the time we had strung them into a V shape across one of the deer paths, and staked them as firmly as we could, needles of sleet were sweeping across the moor. There was not one animal to be seen and so we retired to our cottage, well pleased with our fun. I was convinced nothing would come of it, but the next day, when we went to look, a doe was lying in it, horribly tangled. At once Richard shot her, and we carried her with some difficulty off the moor, being very glad of the spear he had fashioned, which made the work easier. The net was quite ruined, and we never got another deer, but my designated birthday was remembered as the day we set a most excellent trap. I think the doe must have been frightened by something to have run at such a pace into the net to get tangled in it. I do not think there were wolves there, or we would have seen some sign of them, so it was a mystery, but one we were most cheerful about.

\* \* \*

By slow, reluctant degrees did the year turn. Winter seemed unending. The biting frosts, which sometimes made the heather crackle underfoot like a newly lit fire, were easier to manage than the horizontal rain and sleet. One day I got caught in a powerful hailstorm when I was out on the hill, checking my snares. It came suddenly, the sky looking at first like rain, and then turning to something much worse. It hurtled huge gobbets of ice at me, the size of a child's fist. All I could do was put my arms over my head and offer my back to the storm, which pounded me unmercifully for several minutes. As suddenly as it had come, it went, leaving the hillside strewn with these round rocks of ice. I took a couple back to Richard, who was amazed, not having had any raining down on the cottage roof. That made me feel rather as if it had been a personal attack on me by the bad-tempered weather, though what I had done to deserve it I could not imagine.

One night I went out for a piss late on in the evening and saw something I simply could not fathom. It was a clear night, but there was no moon. Suddenly, as I gazed up at the stars a strange curtain of colours appeared, and began to waver in the sky like a living thing. I wanted to call Richard, to share it with him, but I could not speak, or look away. Dread crept over me as the curtain, or creature, or whatever it was continued to snake about, in the most chilling, utter silence. Was it a dragon? Or truly a curtain, waving in some celestial wind? And if it opened entirely would heaven be revealed to me? If it was, I would be sure to die, for I think no man living has seen into God's country unless he be dead, or about to die. The vision lasted but a few moments, then shrank to fragments, and did not come again. I felt a terrible dread, fearing that it was a sign of death to come. I would not share my fears with Richard, and so I did not tell him of it, but the dread image stayed with me, haunting my dreams for a long time.

Eventually, the days grew longer. We still took turns visiting the cave to check on our communications, and on this particular day it was Richard's turn. There had been a thaw, so he bounded swiftly down the path, while I attended to my makeshift waterspout, which had come adrift yet again. As I worked, the stream tumbled at my feet, keeping me company with its noisy chattering over the stones. A slant of sun came down onto my head and I almost fancied there was a little heat in it.

Richard came back much sooner than I had expected, panting hard.

'We have company,' he said.

I glared at him. I was angry that he should think it acceptable to jest about a subject so close to our hearts, but did not want us to argue. I thought to use his unicorn phrase against him in a gently chiding manner but had not got further than 'I do not believe—' when he shook his head violently and put his finger to his lips.

I listened. At first I could hear nothing amiss, but then the unmistakable sound of human voices came to my ears. I looked at Richard in astonishment, hope and disquiet all rolled into one.

'Who are they?' I whispered, but it was too late for that.

# CHAPTER NINETEEN

'Where's Douglas?'

Two men appeared on the path. Both carried knives and looked warily from me to Richard.

Richard spoke. 'If Douglas is the man who owns this place, I know not.'

'Then what are you doing here?' The second man was more belligerent than the first.

'We were wrecked on this island last autumn, and if it had not been for finding this place we would have surely died.'

Both looked sceptical. 'We saw no evidence of a boat, wrecked or otherwise. Nor do you look much like shipwrecked mariners.'

'Our fellows repaired her as best she could,' I said. 'But not well enough to carry all, and Richard here was injured too badly to travel, so it was thought expedient for us to remain here until they could come back for us.'

The belligerent man still looked unconvinced. 'He looks well enough to me.'

Richard nodded. 'Indeed I am, but were it not for the knowledgeable care of my friend I fear you would not find me in such good health, for my arm had been broken, and my head was injured.' He raised the hair on his forehead where a scar remained.

Things were difficult between us for a while, but eventually both the men seemed to decide that we spoke truth. To our great relief, they were from a royalist vessel, and had anchored to fill their water barrels from our stream. These two officers had left others of the crew to do the work down near the beach, and had thought to come and give the owner, Douglas, a greeting, as they had met him several times in the past.

'It is perhaps a little early in the year,' one said. 'But around this time he comes with his daughter for the better part of the year.'

'I will be sorry not to meet and thank them,' I said. 'But we are needed back at the garrison at Flint. We had been engaged in watching for the promised Irish soldiers to aid Chester, but our pinnace foundered in a storm. We would be most grateful if your captain would be able to take us at least part of the way there, or to drop us somewhere on the mainland, from where we can make our way back.'

The more friendly of the two men shrugged. 'We can take you onboard once the men have filled the barrels. You can speak to the captain then. But if you were looking to help relieve the siege of Chester you are too late.'

To hear of the fall of Chester was doleful news. And the privation of the inhabitants was awful to hear, more terrible by far than the months we had spent marooned on our island.

With the agreement to take us off the island, Richard and I were thrust into an excess of energy, rushing to gather together our few belongings, and making the cottage tidy as well as safe from the fire inside and any storm without. We were beset with the awful thought that if we did not make all haste the men would change their minds and set sail without us. I daresay our fears were foolish and without cause, but the more minutes that passed, the more anxious we were. However, all was well. I left what few coins I had on the table and before we had properly come to terms with our rescue we were being rowed to the ship, lying at anchor offshore.

The captain of the frigate was interested to hear of our plight, and the pinnace that had been promised for our relief, but could tell us nothing of it.

'The enemy has been much in evidence at sea as well as on land,' he told us. 'Your pinnace may of course have foundered on its way back to Flint, or been captured or sunk by the enemy, but I do not know any particulars of it. Our business is in the plundering of such enemy vessels as we can find, to raise money for the cause. I think the lack of money to procure ordinance, and to pay the army and navy, not to mention feeding them, is most detrimental to us. What's more, most every vessel has difficulty in finding enough men, so if you wanted to join us freely you would be most welcome.'

It was a tempting offer, but both Richard and I felt our duty lay back at Flint, where our few belongings had been left. We were fortunate that the frigate was heading south, in search of colliers that had sold their cargoes and were returning north with their coffers full of coin, ripe to be taken. The captain kindly put us ashore just down the coast from the River Dee, from where we could make our way back to the ancient castle.

It was only after we had scrambled ashore, and were making our careful way to Flint, that we had a chance to speak privately about how very generous the captain had been. Being undermanned, as he had said, it was a miracle he had not simply refused to set us down.

'If we had been common seamen, no doubt he would have kept us,' said I. 'Because it was sailors he needed. I think he could tell that I would have been of little practical use.'

'I wonder if he was concerned that our abandonment by the pinnace might have been because we were troublemakers,' ventured Richard. 'No captain wants discontent sown onboard. He might have also decided that to press us would be to invite trouble.'

Whatever the truth of the matter we were grateful to him for allowing us to return to where we had pledged to serve. We found the garrison at Flint much the same, except for a new atmosphere of anger and dismay. By all accounts the siege at Chester had been a terrible thing, leading to many deaths. The trooper who had been so bitter about his pregnant sister's situation had further disaster to report. He had his sister with him now, and was sharing his rations with her to try and bring her back to health, but she had lost her baby, and her husband too.

We had fared better on our poor island than the garrison at Chester, but we were glad to find a barber to shave us, and we discovered we were mad for bread, cabbage and cheese, which amused our fellows. Our horses had been ridden, and not well, but were in reasonable health. We had need of them now, for all thought of harrying the enemy by river and sea had gone when Chester had fallen. The pinnace had indeed returned, but was lost with all hands shortly afterwards. The garrison had known of our survival and abandonment, but what were they to do? There were no willing men to send, nor a vessel to spare. No one knew exactly where we had been left and so our rescue was set aside in the urgent need to aid Chester. The city had fallen but three weeks before, and we arrived back at Flint the day before my birthday. We had been a great deal out in our reckoning.

I did not feel like any sort of second celebration, but there was a surprise awaiting me at the castle. Thrust into Richard's bag of belongings was a packet of letters, sent to him from his parents. He owed the colonel for its payment, an unexpected kindness from him, given that we might well have been lost for ever. It was wonder enough in these times that Richard's letter had reached London, and equally that a reply had safely arrived back to Flint. Richard was much encouraged to have the packet. I would have left him alone to his reading but he called me back.

'Ptolemy! Come here. There is a message for you too!'

I found a smile for him. 'Does your mother ask me to keep you from all foolishness?'

He held out a paper. 'No. I mean a letter. There is a letter for you within my own.'

Three short steps and I had it in my hand. It was from my mother! Who had told her that I still lived? I broke the seal and read the letter. It was full of family news, her concern that the stored fruit would not last the winter, two rams had fought and both had to be killed. The farm would doubtless send some meat up to the house, but she feared it would be tainted. There was news of Hugh too. He had written to our mother about army life, and how his horse must needs be trained more in warfare by the firing of guns and beating of drums while he was at his oats, for he, like his master, was as yet untried in battle, or at least they had been many months ago.

I paused in my reading and thought about Hugh. I could thank God that he had been well prepared, but I hated to think of him facing the cannon, and maybe even my own well-trained troopers, in battle.

It was clear my parents had not received Richard's letter informing them of my death. I was glad of it, because it was a joy to receive so much news. At the same time it made me fear for my mother. While we had been cast away, time had run out for me to write that I had put aside my loyalty to the King. I scrutinised the letter closely, looking in vain for any hint that that man had indeed cast her off. Had he truly been bluffing when he had threatened to shame his wife on my account? My mother made no mention of the war or politics, nor did she say much about her husband, except to mention him obliquely, so I knew he still lived when the letter was written. I wished at once to take pen and paper to reply to her, and assure her that I went on very well, sending her my love, as she did to me, but I did not do it. I was still afraid of risking my mother's honour. Far better for them to think me dead. I would ask Richard to write again with that untrue news.

I was young. Would maturity have brought me to a different decision? But during our winter exile on the island I had come to terms with being reborn as a new person. I was Ptolemy, not Thomas, and was free from the father who had always seemed to despise me. And there were the questions of honour and principle. Setting all that against an inheritance that might well

231

be denied me by parent or by war . . . It was not a difficult decision to make, and so I pushed into a secret part of my mind the grief my death would cause my mother. I suppose I was not the first young person to feel that principle outweighs grief. And so I prevailed on Richard to write again, and he kindly did so, giving no return address, and this time his letter was delivered, for soon afterwards he had a reply from Hugh via Richard's family address.

*As you might expect*, he wrote, *we are much dismayed at your news, but most grateful that you should have taken the time to write it. My mother is distraught, and insists that she will continue to write, although I have tried to dissuade her with every argument I can bring to bear. I think there is a small part of her that refuses to believe him dead. Indeed, I can hardly believe it myself. Thomas was so very full of life and laughter. I have lost my dear brother, and my finest example. As you will doubtless know, I am little at home these days, but where possible I will attempt to intercept my mother's letters, so your family does not have the bother of them, but if any should arrive please do not concern yourself with them, and certainly do not be persuaded by the post boy to pay for them. Perhaps if one is returned to her it will finally convince her of the truth of your doleful news.*

Although I was sad to read of my mother's grief I think now that I did not have the maturity to fully understand it. She still had Hugh. I am ashamed to admit that my greatest feeling at reading the letter was that I was free.

So we did our duty at Flint. We had successes, and the castle held prisoners from time to time, but food was short, so we did our best to extract promises from them that they would return home, and not take arms against the King any more. With that oath we released them, to honour their promises or not, which was the best we could do. We never captured any worthy of a ransom, they were for the most part ordinary men, some of which we could tell would be happy if they had to fight no more.

I had further letters from my mother. In beginning each one she wrote that she had been told I was dead, but could not resist writing to her dead son as she did to her live one, wishing to treat them both equally, in life and in death. Perhaps pouring out her heart in this way was a solace to her. She was not gone mad with grief, but sensible of what she did, and why she did it. Indeed, her tone was quite measured for the most part, almost like a journal of her days. She wrote of how hungry soldiers had broken several times into our small valley and taken much that could not be spared. At this hungry time of year there was little in the garden. Due to the soldiers trampling over it almost all was now spoiled, and every animal from the farm driven away, saving a few hens the men had not be able to catch. She was calm in her telling of it, but I felt sure she must have been most fearful. Her husband, she wrote, had sores on his stump that would not heal, due she thought to his persistence in overusing it, and his only recourse from the pain was to take as many spirits as he could get, until he fell into a blessed stupor. Blessed perhaps to her as much as to him. My heart was full of pain for her troubles, but I still felt sure that soon I would be no more than a memory of the son she had lost. It was melancholy, but for the best.

We had news of the war from other sources, very little of it good, until the worst of all flew on evil wings from Newark to our garrison. For His Majesty had surrendered to a Covenanter army. At the same time, we heard Oxford was besieged, and that a while ago Fairfax had beaten our army in the west, while other reverses made it clear all was almost up with our endeavours. The mood at Flint was sober and uneasy. The weather improved but we were not minded to notice or enjoy it. And then, one day, with the wild roses in the hedge beginning to bloom, all went totally awry for us, for we were suddenly besieged by land and water. In the confusion, upwards of about fifty of our men managed to ride away, escaping before they could be shut up. With our cause all but lost, what point was there in defending this poor garrison, when all around was falling to the enemy? But defend it we did, for we hoped against hope that we might be relieved. The enemy did not seem to be in any hurry to take the castle, and surely we would be able to receive troops and supplies by river, if not from the land?

The truth proved very different. A little got through in the way of food, but not enough to sustain us, and of troops to raise the siege there were none. We were restrained, as we had been on our Scottish island, but without the opportunity to procure any food for ourselves. As well as that, we were bombarded both from the river and from the land. I was kept busy tending to all who were injured, many by great flying chips of fractured stone from the walls, as well as wounds from bullets, and cuts from enemy swords whenever we tried to ride out to protect our village from harm. In spite of our best efforts, the village was much mutilated, with blood running in the streets from both our soldiers and the local inhabitants. The pounding of the ordinance caused us all much fear and more than a few deaths, as our situation became ever worse. War is terrible in all its guises, but I do think that to siege and destroy a habitation is a particular abomination. At least in skirmishing, and also in a full battle, there is soon an end to it. But the attrition of a siege, killing by slow degrees is evil, and does no one any credit at all.

Both sides in this war were guilty of the practice and I hope to never experience it again.

At length we had to slaughter and eat our horses. We had no hay or oats for them, nor any other means of feeding ourselves. We were often on watch at the river side of the castle, but could do nothing to drive off the ships that fired upon us whenever they chose. Only at night was there some relief, except that then we all became ever more conscious of how hungry we were.

One evening, after the river had become quiet, Richard pointed towards the sea, at a ship that had just arrived and was sitting in the estuary.

'Is that not the frigate that rescued us from the island, returned again?'

I squinted towards it. The sun was very low, turning the ship into a black shape. 'I cannot tell in this light. And even if it is, our enemies know it cannot sail up to us at low tide. Remember that it carries money, not bread for a starving garrison.'

For a while we looked at it, as the light faded along with any hope of filling our bellies. It was the second time the ship had appeared, to pause in the estuary for a short while before going on her way. I regarded Richard. Even in this dusky evening it was obvious how much he had been reduced by our privations. 'Of course,' I said slowly, 'it cannot sail up to us, but we might float down to it.'

He stared at me. 'We could, if we did so before the tide turned, and if we had a boat.' He hesitated. 'If we had the means to float we might very well not drift close enough to hail them, and might be swept out to sea.'

'But you are a good sailor, are you not?'

He gave me a wry smile in the gloom. 'Only if I have a boat to sail. Besides, what if it is not the ship I thought it was?'

'Is it better to drown or to starve? And if we arrive at an enemy ship and are pressed, then we at least have our lives, which are likely to be snuffed out here before long.'

'Have we done our duty here?'

It did not take me more than a second to have an answer for him. 'Of course we have. It can be no more than a matter of days before we die in yet another bombardment, or of hunger or disease. There is no army coming to relieve us, of that I am persuaded. We are abandoned. I am convinced that with the way the war is going there will be no rescue for us this time.'

For several long moments Richard gazed out at the last rays of the sun casting pale yellow stripes into the darkening sky. There was a light breeze, sending us the rotten smell of river mud as the tide continued to fall. 'Come, Ptolemy,' he said at last. 'I cannot trust you to the river without my help. You are not yet enough of a sailor to achieve what you desire.'

My heart lifted. I could not ask him to accompany me on such a desperate task, but oh, how much I longed for him to come. 'You could advise me before I go,' I said.

He had a wry smile on his face. 'Do you not recall that I have long wanted to travel?'

So with the moon rising and hunger chewing at our bellies we planned our escape. The river was wide here, tidal, being so close to the sea, and the enemy held the far bank. We had managed to prevent them from gaining access to the castle, but our armaments by now were few, and we had to husband what we had most carefully. In truth I think our enemy was in no mind to risk themselves, but preferred to starve us, all the sooner to bring our utter defeat. In addition to blocking all food and arms coming in by boat, they had shot and holed our moored vessels, but Richard, since seeing the frigate and hearing my suggestion, was hopeful that we could find some means of transport, however damaged.

He scowled at the moon. 'We dare not set off by this light, or they will see us.'

'It is still a few hours until the tide turns,' I said, looking out over the water to where our adversaries lay with fuller bellies than us.

'Indeed. But the nearer to the turn, the less to our advantage the flow will be. Well, let us at least look at these poor vessels. It may be best to choose one now, if there be any suitable, and then to wait until a cloudier night to leave.'

'But for how much longer will we have the strength to attempt it?'

We looked at one another. We did indeed make a very sorry sight, with our clothes hanging on our diminished bodies. 'Very true, Ptolemy. So we must do all we can with the time we have.' In a few minutes he had found a small boat he thought might do. It was half full of water, but yet it floated, and appeared sturdy enough. 'Maybe this . . .'

'We will need to bail it.'

'Better not,' he cautioned. 'We will need to appear more as wreckage than a manned vessel, and us in it looking as dead as possible.'

'Will it carry us both?'

He smiled, but his eyes were sad. 'I do not know, but we can hope, my friend. We can hope.'

In the end we did bail it a little, in that hope. We took nothing with us other than our short swords. It would be impossible to keep powder dry, and our small store of powder and shot would be more useful to our fellow soldiers than to us. I felt little unease at deserting them. They would have our rations as well as our arms, although I hoped our stubborn captain would be persuaded to surrender before the inevitable end.

We quietly furnished our chosen vessel with two oars, and the pot for bailing. Then we sat in the shadow of the wall, waiting with diminishing hope for a cloud to cover the moon. We were both silent, intent on our own thoughts. We had been dying a slow death at the castle. What chance did we have of saving our lives with this desperate enterprise? I thought of what the sailors in the lost pinnace had said to me when I boasted of being a strong swimmer.

'Then hope not to be wrecked,' said one with no humour in his voice. 'For swimming just prolongs the agony of drowning.'

'Come.'

Richard was getting cautiously to his feet. He pointed to the sky and I saw what he had noticed. A cloud was tantalisingly close to the moon. As we watched, it dallied, teasing the moon with its pale fingers. Then, as if to draw a curtain on the night, it lay entirely over it.

'Now!'

I stepped in and lay as still as a corpse, instantly wet through, my head resting on the thwart just above the slopping water. Richard pushed us gently away from the quay and followed me into the boat. It floated heavily, agonisingly low in the water. We dared do nothing to help it on but lie still, as the river slowly, slowly began to take hold of us. For a few minutes I thought we should drift onto the mud and be stuck, like so much driftwood. Twirling slowly, we touched the bottom, and I felt Richard tense as he made ready to fend us off. But the tide was still ebbing, and with the river's current it was stronger than the mud. Painfully slowly, our little boat began to turn again, and the river took us close to the middle of the stream.

We were close now to where our enemy lay, too close. All was quiet. On, on we inched, with Richard trailing his arm silently over the side, to act as a rudder. The water was getting deeper in the boat, but Richard bade me in a whisper not to bail. 'Lie still, for your life. We are not past them yet.'

I took my breaths when I could, the water slopping into my mouth and nose and covering my eyes. And then it came. A single shot, fired from over the water. There was a sudden pain in my shoulder. It burned, like a branding must. I bit down on my lips to stifle my groan. Another shot came, and I heard the ball fall into the water next to my head. A laugh floated over the river, and then all was quiet once more.

'We're almost clear of their target practice. In a few minutes more you can bail while I sit up and row.'

I cannot recall if I replied.

Soon after he spoke to me again. 'Come, Ptolemy,' he hissed. 'We are safe. Take the pot now, and bail while I row.'

I tried to obey him, though it wasn't only hunger that made my senses fog.

'Faster! Or we will entirely founder.'

I did my best, but I was no match for the river invading the boat.

'Hey! Ahoy there! Help!'

His voice, full of desperation, carried over the water. I raised my head, and saw the frigate close by, but in spite of all Richard's efforts the current was taking us slowly past her. Our brave vessel was become impossible to row, and for every pot I agonisingly emptied, more than one flowed in. Then we were quite undone, for the river came right into her, and our little craft was entirely swamped. I wanted to add my voice to Richard's, but I had no power in my lungs, and I heard no reply from the frigate.

'We must stay together,' gasped Richard as we floundered in the water.

'Save yourself,' I whispered. 'For I am shot.'

I did my best to stay with him, but the struggle and the pain was too much. I gave way to what must be and turned onto my back. I would float if I could not swim, and let the sea take my lifeless body wherever it wished.

# CHAPTER TWENTY

I saw above me the kindly moon, out again from behind the veil of cloud. The heavens were full of stars. It was a beautiful night. Strange to relate, although my shoulder burned as if afire, I felt entirely at peace.

My arms floated gently from my body and I felt my soul make ready to fly away. It was a better death than the squalor of starvation amongst the ancient stones of Flint. There was a kind of freedom to being taken by the water. I welcomed it. The stars above blurred, swimming high above me, and I knew the moment of my death was near. And then Richard was there, his arm around my neck, pulling me with him.

But after a few minutes he stopped swimming and I felt sure he would have to let me go. *I am too much for him*, I thought.

*Hunger and ill luck have us both beaten.* I felt little sadness for my own death, but an unutterable melancholy for his. *Leave me and swim,* I urged him, though the words were in my head, not my mouth. Salt from my silent tears mingled with that of the water all around me. I wanted to be angry with him for not making more effort to save himself, but all I had left was pity, for myself, for him, for the waste of so many lives in this interminable war. Slowly, as if in a dream the sound of the water as it lapped about me became my whole world. It was the sound of beer splashing into our tankards in the inn at Oxford. And it was boyish splashing in the lake at home. Hugh was there, reaching out his little hand for me to take, uncertain of his footing on the weedy stones beneath our feet. I wanted to help him, but I could not. I drifted away, feeling overwhelmed with grief, and then there were voices, and oars, and the sudden sharp agony of being hauled into a boat. And then my senses entirely deserted me.

I came to myself on the deck of the frigate, to see my friend's face hovering above me. A lantern swayed gently nearby and the captain was there.

'Well,' he said, his voice coming from far away. 'So you have decided to join us after all.'

It is a wonder I did not die, and that is due entirely to Richard, though he would not have it so. Not only did he steer us to safety, he kept me afloat when our vessel sank. Once onboard the frigate, he would let no man touch my wound until he had received instruction from me about what to do. It being in the back of my shoulder I could not see the place, but I could imagine, and requested he should look deep into it, and remove every scrap of linen as well as the ball. If we had been closer to the enemy I feel sure the shot would have broken my shoulder; if any higher it could have severed the great artery in my neck, but the shot must have been at the very extremity of the musket's reach. The ball had buried far within the muscle, and until it healed there was no strength in the limb, but our captain, John Down, was patient. Having no surgeon aboard he had hopes of me. Richard, meanwhile, was soon made a useful officer, so Captain Down was well pleased at having rescued us.

There was no question of being set down anywhere this time. We straight away became members of royalist frigate the *Lord Henry*, and were grateful for it. We learnt how to be privateers along the west coast of England and up into Scotland, taking what we could, and paying in to His Majesty's account. Every merchant vessel taken for the King was one less for parliament, and a little more coin for the cause. It was not often a comfortable existence, but Richard and I had become well used to hardship. We were not as ill-served as the pressed men and boys who laboured long, suffered harsh treatment and, except for having the incentive of a little prize money to goad them on, must often have regretted their lives.

The news, when we had it, was increasingly bad, and fragmentary. The King was captured, or no he was not, rumours said. He was a guest. Next he had escaped his hosts and then was reported truly captured. We had neither horse nor armour, and could do nothing with our swords to help the King in person, even if we had known where he lay. At sea, in one of his few remaining vessels, we strove to replenish his capital until the day would come when his friends could gather a great force, rescue him and vanquish Oliver Cromwell's well-schooled army.

For two long years we sailed those waters, until parliament became so perturbed at the losses that it ordered convoys to protect the commerce. Our work became ever more hazardous. Prizes were harder to come by, and twice we were almost sunk. It was time, said our captain in the autumn of 1648, to think of other places to ply our trade.

There were safe harbours for us, where we had friends, but we must be circumspect about our sailing. Our thirty guns were more than adequate to take most merchant vessels, but increasingly we had needed to use our superior manoeuvrability to outrun parliament's ships, not being able to outgun them. As the summer of 1648 turned to a stormy autumn, Captain Down decided we would be best to winter in a small inlet near an island in the far north of Scotland. We had been safe there before, and hoped we would be again. It was a useful place to overwinter. Although the weather could be harsh, the mooring was sheltered, and we could careen and re-provision ourselves with some beef, and the goats our sailors liked for their skins, if not their meat.

I had no need of post offices, but Richard as always chafed until he could send word to his family. In one small coastal town on the way north, our captain had a contact who was part of a network of those still loyal to the cause. We could rely on his information, and his ability to transfer funds where they were needed. He also acted as our private post office, at no small risk to himself. Richard, who with his friendly demeanour and open face was become our post boy, rowed himself ashore at night and exchanged coin for letters, conversation and any items we had requested him to procure for us. His role was usually without danger, but I always fretted a little while he was gone. It was well known that spies from both sides were everywhere. If unknown to us our network had been broken, Richard might walk into a trap. I would have liked to accompany him on these trips, but our captain had determined that being at least part way to a surgeon

I should be preserved for the duties that only I could perform.

On this occasion all was well. Richard returned safely, with his boat well laden. Leaving the sailors to unload his cargo of flour, peas, rum and a few bottles of French wine, the officers met with the captain and Richard, to hear the latest news.

'I believe the King still resides on the Isle of Wight,' said Richard. 'There is no news of what he will decide to do, but the Prince of Wales is back in Holland, so he is safe.'

'Is there no more good news?' asked one of our fellow officers.

Richard pulled a small package out of his wallet and handed it to me. It was heavier than it looked. 'We can perhaps be grateful that the network is yet sound, the flour looks to be of fair quality and Ptolemy now has the instruments he requested.'

'Thank you,' I said to him. I was slowly building a very useful collection of medical instruments, and books too when I could get them.

There were letters to distribute, and then Richard and I were both at leisure for a few hours. Loath to go below, we took the package of letters that had arrived for Richard to the stern, out of the way of the sailors, who were making haste to set sail with the wind blowing to our advantage. I watched as he broke the seal. Over the past year or so, letters from my mother had become much less frequent, but there was one that day. Richard handed it to me and began reading his own. I hesitated, wondering if I really wanted to read it. The last had arrived about six months ago, the shortest letter so far, with little news, and a tone that betrayed sadness and anger. She had communicated that all went on at home as it always had, and that she was glad to hear that her second son was not dead or injured. That was about the extent of her letter, except at the end she had written, *I may not write again. It no longer brings me solace, nor can it do anything for you.*

But she *had* written again. Why? Was it only to confide that Hugh was now dead or injured, that her husband yet lived to torment her, and that the harvest had been terrible, there was little to buy, and a new fever was sweeping the village? I could not think of any other disasters she might want to torment me with, not knowing I would be tormented. Perhaps the ill news about the situation in the country had brought down my mood. I did not want to rehearse old unhappinesses; I chided myself for stupidity. There was no way my mother would rake over painful memories with a son she had no doubt was dead. Where would be the ease for her in that?

I undid the letter and began to read. There were no related disasters. At the time of writing Hugh was well, as were she and her husband, except he was less confident when he walked, and had fallen several times. *I think,* she wrote, *that as well as drinking too much wine to be steady, his sight is becoming bad, although he will not admit to it. He requires me to read all his business to him, and I must reassure him where the place is for him to sign documents. He knocks over glasses and breaks them unless I put them into his hand. However, he eats well, is hearty enough and seems set to live longer than me, though I am in robust health too, and without the blindness, drinking and lack of leg.*

I thought her mood better than in her last letter, in spite of her husband's tribulations. It sounded that with his need to rely on her so much, she was feeling more in command of the small things in her life, even though his failing sight was an obvious trial to her. But she had not signed the letter. I turned it over in my hand, and there, on the back, in small writing was a sentence dated much later, indeed just a few weeks ago.

*He is gone quite blind,* it read. *But I still have eyes to see you if only you were alive.*

'What is wrong?' said Richard, seeing me throw the letter down.

'Only what I never thought. That man! He is not dead, but is recently blind! I could have gone to see my poor mother secretly if only I had known, but we are now to sail for the north and then who knows where. My opportunity is lost!'

'How could you have gone? We have not been near the West Country for years.'

I stood up. 'You are right of course. I am a fool. A homesick, mother-sick fool.' I kicked at the timbers of the ship, feeling like a petulant child. But I could not help it. 'Why could he not just die, like any . . .'

'Like any decent person?'

I could not help a brief snort of laughter escaping. 'Well, yes! But he is not a decent person in any respect. Not in my estimation anyway.' I sat down again, feeling tears nearer than laughter now. 'Forgive me, Richard. It was the last sentence of her letter. It made me want to leap into action. It made me want to jump overboard, swim to shore, take horse and ride without stopping until I reached her, just to reassure her that I am alive, well and content with my life.'

He gave me such a look of compassion it almost undid me. 'Do you wish to read it to me, Ptolemy?'

'Do you wish to hear it?'

'Of course. If you wish it too.'

I picked up the letter again and turned it over. 'She writes, *He is gone quite blind. But I . . . I still . . .*' I found my voice faltering. My throat was quite closed up, and the paper blurred before me. '*I still have . . . eyes . . .* Forgive me. Just a second.' I put my hand to my mouth to stop a wail from bursting from me. In a few moments I mastered my emotion, took a deep breath and a run at the words before I was quite undone. '*I still have eyes . . . to see*

247

*you if only you were alive.*' I could not help lowering my head so Richard could not see the tears dripping from my eyes.

After a few moments he put his hand upon my shoulder. 'Tom . . . Ptolemy . . . My dear friend. Do you consider that after the past two years or more of grieving, your mother would want to be informed of the truth?'

I spoke low. 'What would *your* mother wish in the same circumstances?'

'I think . . . perhaps any mother who loves her children would forgive any disinformation if at last she were permitted to know the happy truth.'

I wiped my eyes and raised my head to look up to where our great sails were being unfurled and beginning to catch the wind. 'I fear I have made many mistakes in my life, Richard, and this may be greater than any other.'

'Do you mean you regret not following your father's command to abandon the cause of the King?'

'No. Not that, although things are going so ill for us that he may yet save his fortune by siding with parliament. But I do regret not having been able to speak to my mother before leaving for ever, and I regret bitterly that she still grieves while I live. I had never thought it would take her so long to forget me.'

Richard's hand gripped my shoulder tightly for a moment before he released me. 'I had not thought so either. I must admit it. But do not flog yourself with regret, Ptolemy. I think perhaps it is a rare man who understands what drives the mind of a woman, particularly his own mother.'

The creaks and groans of our vessel as she embraced the wind reminded me that every moment I was moving even further away from my home. I had not been able to help myself, but

I had hurt my mother more than I had thought. How could I begin to call myself a gentleman if I could not admit my mistake and make amends? But how? I could not address any letter in my own hand for at least some servants might recognise it. No. Richard must write the address, and perhaps even the contents too. Would it be safe for me to write directly to her, or should we devise some method of conveying the truth in a manner she would understand but any casual reader would not? I must consider carefully what I did, but I had considered before. Perhaps I should simply write and hang the consequences. My thoughts swung wildly to and fro while the ship gathered pace and settled to her rhythm. I did not know what to do for the best, but it seemed clear to me that neither I nor my mother would have peace while the truth was in thrall to lies.

'Do you have paper?'

Richard looked startled. His thoughts must have been elsewhere while I conducted my internal battle. 'I do. I bought some today, knowing it would be difficult to obtain more over the winter.'

'Then for God's sake may I have some, if you can spare it?'

'Of course you may.'

He looked as if he wished to say more, but did not. 'I am going to try and put things right between my mother and I,' I said, 'but I will need to ask you to write the address for me.'

'Anything. But I don't know when our next opportunity to send post might occur.'

'I am well aware of that,' I said, not being able to keep the bitterness from my voice. 'If only I had read the letter earlier, and had been able to reply before we set sail.'

He looked concerned. 'And yet that would have taken much haste, and without consideration of the wisdom of your action.'

'Well, I will have plenty of time for consideration now, will I not?' His expression of hurt shamed me. 'I am sorry, Richard. That was unkind. You have always been a wise and careful friend. You do not deserve my anger to any degree.'

'Perhaps not always wise,' he replied, 'but let that pass. And maybe when we make our last stop for stores there will be an opportunity to send what you are going to write.'

'Maybe,' I agreed.

I wrote that letter over and over in my mind, wavering from certainty that she would have total dominion over the letter, so that it would remain utterly private to us, to panic that she would not be able to keep her feelings to herself when she read it, or that some other would get to see it and so destroy my secret. I also pondered why the last few words of her last letter had moved me so very much. In the end I decided it was because I had so nearly lost my life during our escape from Flint, and for the first time understood just how precious life was. She had given me that life after losing her first infant. Of course she would find it hard to be consoled after thinking her second child too was dead. What a fool I had been. With all my heart I wanted her to know that I lived and regretted my grave error. That being so, every day that took me further from a post office was a kind of torture, but I bore it as well as I could, knowing that my anguish was as nothing compared to what I had caused her to endure.

It was November, and the weather turned stormy. We were not looking for prizes now, but running north as quickly as we could, hurrying to reach our safe harbour before seriously bad weather could destroy us. We made one last stop for stores and water, and with our captain's permission, for he professed himself satisfied as to my loyalty, and the village safe enough, I took the opportunity

250

of going ashore in search of a post office. There was none, but at the inn I was told a post boy called there once a week to take any letters for the official post. I did not feel confident that the letter would ever leave the village, but it was the best I could do before winter came. I put it into the innkeeper's hand, which was as hard as wood, and thanked him.

A man nearby said something to me, but his accent was so thick I could not understand what he said. Seeing my confusion, the innkeeper took pity on me.

'He says not to fret.'

Stupidly, I felt tears in my eyes, and blinked them away. 'Thank you,' I said to the innkeeper. 'And please thank this fellow for his kind words.'

# CHAPTER TWENTY-ONE

We were glad of our stores, for the wind changed and gave us much trouble. For three days we had to shelter in the lee of a headland before resuming our battle to move forward. It was further into the winter than we had hoped when at last we arrived at our destination, an island in the far north of Scotland. The sea loch we entered made a dogleg away from the open sea, and sheltering hills kept off the worst of the prevailing wind. Some thought it bleak there, but in spite of having been cast away on a similar island during an earlier winter I did not dislike this place. For this island was inhabited, and I found the villagers both welcoming and kind.

There was much work at first for the sailors. Our ship must be careened, while the carpenter checked over every inch of her planks for damage. I continued to treat injuries when I was needed, although I could not save one poor fellow, who was crushed beyond help due to his own and others' carelessness. I read much, particularly the latest books I had managed to obtain on all aspects of medicine. However, I did not neglect to also study *The Surgeon's Mate*, a volume that had been onboard when we first joined the ship. It was in truth an old text, much weathered and with some pages missing, but for all that it was very useful to me in my present work. I might wish I had a mate to help me, but there was no one I could entirely rely on. It would not do for Richard to take on the lowly task. I needed someone hardened to injury and deaf to the suffering of the patient, while also astute and educated well enough to anticipate or at least identify which instruments I would ask for. But I must be my own mate, except when it was imperative to hold a man down, when several of his friends would usually rally to help.

I also attended a birth during this winter; it was one of the sailors' women. They would insist on having them onboard, and the captain cursed them as being more trouble than they were worth, but I think in spite of the fights and jealousies it was mostly a good thing for the men. The infant died. In spite of all I could do it was over-young to be born. It was just as well because our vessel was no place for children. After several days the woman died too. I didn't know enough to save her, or maybe it would not have been possible in any case. I was called close to her end and she had a very high fever. I wish I had not agreed to be there. Usually the women attended to their own affairs, but her man had asked me very humbly for my assistance. I was more affected than I had expected, both at the infant's death and the real distress of the father, but I was not entirely comfortable at treating women. Give me a bullet wound or a leg threatening to go bad any day. I know where I am with those!

I do not want to give the impression that all was death, misery and hardship through the winter. The sailors made their own entertainment as they always did. It was pleasant to be onshore and to hear their merrymaking, their music floating to us over the water. There was music in the village too, and Richard and I were made welcome, as were most of the officers, whether gentlemen or tarpaulins. There is something very piercing and sweet about the music in this place, indeed in most of the country. They say it is similar in Ireland and Wales too, but I would not know that. All I know is that whenever I heard it I tended to become wistful about love. The letter I had sent my mother was of course often in my thoughts, its thread being reworked constantly through my mind, whatever else I was doing. I thought of Aphra too, wondering what, if anything, my mother would write to her of me. I hoped nothing, although I had not mentioned it. I had asked my mother to burn the letter, but that was out of my hands as well. I had asked her forgiveness for deceiving her, explaining why I had done so. I hoped she could find it in her heart to do so, though thought it entirely possible that she would rant against my deceit.

*I can command nothing*, I had written. *But I swear, when the time comes I am content for Hugh to inherit all, for I am quite comfortable, and well set up. More, if there is even a slight chance that I do not deserve the name and title I am even more happy for him, while being entirely your loving son. Let him not feel any guilt at taking something that should be mine, knowing me alive, but let him enjoy it fully, believing I am dead.*

I was neither well set up nor particularly comfortable, but when I examined my situation, in spite of everything I found I was most often happy enough. I was saving much of the prize money I earned, which, being surgeon, was generous. At not quite twenty-five, I had my life ahead of me, and I had tried to put right a wrong I had done my mother. So I settled to enjoy our winter sojourn with my good friend Richard, my fellow shipmates and the local inhabitants of this windswept but beautiful place. And yes, there was a girl I liked, a girl I had met the year before, the eldest of her six siblings, four sisters and two brothers. I had thought she would be wed by now, but she was not. She was needed by her mother and stepfather to care for her little half-sisters and -brothers who were much younger than her. Her sense of duty was strong, but I could tell she was pleased when our ship returned, and me still on it.

There was much between Abigall and I. She was very different to both Catherine and Aphra. Catherine had been romantic and frivolous, Aphra serious and with a prodigious intellect. Abigall had little formal education, but could read and write, both in her own language and a little in English too. More, she fitted perfectly into her place, being expert on all manner of things pertaining to her life on the island. When her father had died falling from the cliff when collecting gulls' eggs, she and her mother had been hard put to survive. Her mother had for a while almost lost her mind with grief, and so it fell to the village and Abigall herself to care for her. As a result, Abigall could climb a cliff, fish, spin and knit, prepare herbs, milk a cow, take the wool from a sheep, ride or drive the pony, salt the beef and much else besides. Beyond this, she also had the sweetest singing voice, much called upon during the winter dances that filled the darkest evenings with frivolity and light.

I had no wish to remove her from her life on the island, but there were many times during that winter when I wished I could exchange my shipboard existence for one by her side. I dreamt often of the children we would breed together, and the idyll of a life on a far island, away from care and duty, but I said nothing of it to her. My mistake with Catherine had been to imagine that desire could make all right. I had learnt that for me desire was not something to embrace with abandon, but something to be managed, lest it damage the very people it brought together. I admit I was much out of step with many of my sex and generation, but I had no wish to leave Abigall with a swelling belly and no prospect of sharing her life with me. There was plenty of time in the future, I reasoned, to find a proper wife in due course. For now, I still was in the service of His Majesty, and would not abandon his cause, even though he languished a prisoner on another island far to the south.

So I spent the winter as her shadow, helping with her tasks when I could, walking the hills with her when the weather allowed, and getting her to teach me something of her native language. For all the smiles and glances between us we resisted any declaration, and it wasn't until my birthday at the end of February that our unspoken passion became acknowledged between us. The rain that swept so frequently over the island had given way to a day with watery sunshine. Both released from our duties, we walked together up to the top of the hill that sheltered our ship. It was one of our favourite walks. From there we could see over to other islands, all topped with snow on the highest peaks. The salty sea kept most snow from lingering on the shore, so the dark seaweed was visible on the margins of the pale grey ocean below, but up here the frost crackled underfoot. At the foot of our hill, smoke, like goose down in a draught, curled up from all the chimneys into the lightest of light blue-grey skies. Most people were indoors for it would not be long before dusk fell. From our spy point we could see the sun sinking towards the dark clouds on the horizon. This landscape, so unlike my own, was a thing of little colour. Only the few gorse flowers, like bunches of unseasonable buttercups, brightened it. And yet it was to me such a place of peace and beauty. Tomorrow, no doubt, there would be horizontal sleet again, but today we could breathe the cold, clear air and see far into the distance.

Suddenly I recalled that fearsome night on a different island, where I saw colours lit up in the sky that had frightened me so that I had never dared to mention them to another soul. Now I asked Abigall anxiously if she had seen them. She laughed, but kindly, and took my arm.

'We have them here sometimes. They come and go. Some years they do not appear at all. Perhaps you might read about them in all your books, and be able to teach me what they are? I think of them like rainbows, sent by God to tell us that he loves us. But they are beyond my knowing.'

One of life's fears fell away from me then, and I vowed to remind myself in future that I was a philosopher. Whatever the phenomenon, it was not peculiar to me, which was a great comfort. For some minutes we stood in silence, still recovering our breath after the steep climb, then she surprised me with a gift that she had kept hidden under her shawl. It was a pair of gloves she had knitted, and a scarf, which she hung about my neck. Both made from the waterproof yarn spun by her from the grey and white sheep her family kept. How could I not kiss her, with her arms around me and her eyes full of love? She had not taught me the way to say 'I love you' in her language, but the way she murmured in my ear and kissed my neck made me sure of her meaning. I said it back to her in my own tongue, which she understood very well. I could not do otherwise, for it was true. My heart was entirely hers.

I was so close at that moment of throwing aside all my high-flown ideals. I think if a soft rain had not begun to fall and then an icy breeze begun to blow, we would have been entirely lost to our desire. But it was too cold to ignore the weather, in spite of our heated blood. I took my mouth from her lips and drew her cold hand into mine. We started our descent from the hill and soon we were sheltered from the worst of the wind. But the rain came on harder, and she drew her shawl over her fiery hair. I kissed her again, our faces wet with rain, and then we took the path down again, still hand in hand into the dusky end of day.

'There is the byre.'

But I had come somewhat to my senses. It is true that cold eventually cools even the hottest ardour. If I had followed her to the byre I would have had her, and begun the awful wait to discover if I was to leave her with a child. Others do it all the time and think nothing of it. She was not of my class or culture and many of my station might have thought her beyond consideration. But I resisted, on the anniversary of my birth. That evening I danced the wild country dances with her and with some of the other girls. And I sat with her mother while her eldest daughter sang. Abigall's last song was of love, as so many of their songs are of either love or war, often the two being intertwined with loss. As she sang she looked at me, holding me with her eyes. It was, I know, clear to all in the room with eyes to see that our friendship was not a simple thing.

Her mother turned to me. 'You'll not take her from me?'

Her husband, who I did not much like, laughed. 'Then you'll need to learn to climb the cliffs for eggs, and to fish for to feed the bairns.'

I did not reply, but when it came time to return to my ship that night I took Abigall's hand in mine and kissed it formally lest she throw her arms around me once more.

Richard and I were rowed back to the vessel along with several others. He said nothing until we were going to our berths.

'I thought you might not return to the ship this night.'

He said it mildly, with neither admiration nor disapproval, unlike some of the comments that others had made during the short journey. I laid down the gloves she had given me, and took the scarf from around my neck, although I would have preferred to keep it there.

'It is impossible. And I do not want to break her heart.'

He looked at me kindly. 'And yet I think you will, she is so far gone in love for you.'

'Then my own will be broken too when we leave.'

'Oh, Ptolemy. Do not be like the maid who spills the master's milk. I do not like to see you in such difficulty over a girl.'

I sighed. 'I blame myself for it. But I am determined to marry in time, when things are more settled. When I do, I wish to have a home, and live in it, not be a visitor, seldom seen. And I would not leave bastards behind me. It is not my way. Not now.'

'And yet you could stay if our captain would allow it, and make your life with her people here. It has something to recommend it.'

I looked towards him in the dark. 'Indeed, it has, but I know he would not. And I also know that although I would be very happy to begin with, the next time a ship came in and, after, made ready to leave, something of me would leave with it. It seems I have caught your wanderlust.'

'So there is nothing to be done?'

'Nothing. Except I must speak to her about it tomorrow.'

\* \* \*

259

So the last few weeks passed with difficulty before we loaded our salt beef and goat meat, baskets of hens and twelve live goats for the luxury of milk for a while, as well as more skins for the sailors when the animals' time came for them to die. For she did all she could to make me have her, knowing still that I was going to leave.

'Give me something of yours to keep when you are gone,' she said to me. 'If I cannot have you then give me your child to love instead. And when you come again he will be here for you, to dandle on your knee, as shall I.'

It was the most beguiling of suggestions. I am sure her mother fully expected her daughter's skirt to grow short over the coming year, but I could not do it, even at the pitch of desire for her. I would rather spill my seed upon the ground than leave a fatherless child. In the end she called me selfish, and unkind, while still twining herself about me. She knew I loved her, as she loved me, and to her, congress was the only and best expression of our ardour. She was right. I was selfish, for I did not want to be an absent lover and father. Besides, this overwintering would not last for ever. One year I would not come again, and that would be an end of it.

The last night before we sailed, I gave her a gift. It was not the one she wanted, and indeed, apart from myself I had nothing that was suitable to give a girl such as she. In desperation I took my shirt from my back and gave it into her hands. I had another onboard, though it was not so fine. She held it to her face, inhaling my scent.

'I will wear it always,' she said, kissing me. 'Until you come to claim it again.'

I could quite believe she would indeed wear it until it became rags, but maybe I flatter myself. For her sake I hope I do.

As the devil would have it, overnight the wind changed and we were obliged to stay at our mooring for another four days. On the second day she rowed out to our ship. I was below, reading, when Richard found me.

'Your siren with the flame-red hair is calling you,' he said. I looked at him. 'She has rowed out to us and is asking for you.'

It was too much. I would be a laughing stock. For the first time I became angry at her. 'I cannot see her,' I said. 'Please tell her begone. We have made our farewells.'

I was quite wrong to be angry. Was she not only trying all she could to retain me? I would have done the same if it had been the other way around. And although I was teased for it, I think there was more than one on the ship who envied me my beautiful girl.

# CHAPTER TWENTY-TWO

At dawn on the fifth day the wind changed. I was woken by the sound of sailors' feet drumming on the planks and our anchor being raised. Richard and I went on deck to look our last on that beautiful place. The sun was still hidden behind the hills to the east, but its promise sent rays of pale light into the sky. Behind us the little village lay sleeping, and ahead of us lay the tricky angles of the loch to navigate. I thought of Abigall, wrapped in my shirt, sleeping, her hair about her on the pillow. That is how I would have liked to have had her: in a great bed, with white linen in a warm room, loving at our leisure and sleeping together afterwards; not in a byre, or a haystack, nor against a cottage wall in the rain. I would think of her often, and many times with regret, but I hoped she, like me, would also think of our time together with less pain as time passed, and more pleasure. For memories, as time gathers pace, do become easier to remember with fondness.

As for us, we exited the loch and went at first full south, in search of news. It was not long in coming. On the third day of sailing we came across one of Prince Rupert's ships. He had been wont to do as we had, taking prizes from the enemy, but had not often sailed as far north as us.

A boat was soon rowed over, bringing an officer with their latest news. We were told that Prince Rupert was using Kinsale in Ireland as his port, and had gathered several ships to his flag. As we already knew, Cromwell was organising his fleet to protect commerce better, so if we were to continue our actions we would need more strength. Indeed, the captain of Prince Rupert's vessel sent an invitation to join the Prince's fleet and follow him to Kinsale.

'Have you heard of the fate of the King?' said the officer after delivering the invitation.

'No,' said our captain. 'The last we knew he was still on the Isle of Wight. Has he then been moved?'

The officer bringing us the news was younger than I. His face was heavy with seriousness, but even so, a light danced in his eyes. He seemed excited at his role of newsman.

'Aye,' he said. 'Moved, yes. Taken to London. But that is not the half of it, for the King, gentlemen, is dead.'

I, along with others, could not forbear from letting out astonished groans of horror and dismay. The King I had last seen in Wales, exhausted and harassed, petulant while also remembering to thank me for my duty, was dead? How could he die now, when his loyal subjects needed him so badly? He had not always been wise, but he was our king! I had been waiting to hear that he had negotiated an honourable peace, and that our country could return to farming and commerce and start to rebuild all that had been lost. How could his son achieve any of that, being as he was hardly more than a boy?

'Dead how?' I said. 'He was not an old man!' That was a foolish thing to say, for there were many ways a man could die. Even a king could die of a fever, or an accident. Was there plague in London? If there was, they should not have taken him there!

The young officer looked almost embarrassed. 'I regret,' he said, 'that he was put on trial and found guilty.' He paused. 'He was,' he said, 'beheaded at Whitehall.'

There was a shocked silence. It seemed to fill my head with wool. It cannot have been more than a few seconds but it felt as if no one would utter words ever again. Then everyone spoke at once, voicing outrage as if it was the officer's fault, demanding details. Anger, distress, bewilderment. I and everyone else expressed it all.

'When was this?' our captain demanded at last.

'On the thirtieth of January.'

The knowledge took every vestige of hope from us all. Our king not just dead, but months cold in the earth. Done while we had over-wintered in Scotland, with me thinking of love, rather than duty. I could hate myself for that. Him dead, not in battle, but beheaded at his own palace. How could they have done that to him? And how could he have ever prepared himself for such an act upon his person? My own flesh shrank at the very thought of it. Others were plying the officer with more questions but I was thrown back entirely upon my own thoughts. What use was my life now? Which direction should I go with our cause entirely lost? One prince fled abroad, another kept captive by the enemy and their father dead. At least my mother would not be turned out of her house, her husband arrested and his estate confiscated, as the King had once threatened. Hugh would be safe as the inheritor of the estate, and able to return home, for there would be no more fighting now.

I struggled to take in what else the young officer was saying. That Prince Charles, now the second king of that name, had been proclaimed so in Edinburgh. He had appointed the Marquis of Montrose his captain-general in Scotland.

'But what of England?' said someone. 'Is he content to be King of the Scots, leaving England alone?'

'I fear Cromwell will not be content to allow him even that kingdom,' said another.

'Parliament is going to rule with a House of Commons,' said the officer. 'Or so they proclaim. And I do not think they will be minded to give up Scotland either, nor Ireland. They will want it all.'

After the young officer had gone there was much debate about what to do. There were no orders, the captain of the other ship having no command over ours. There was just the invitation to join Prince Rupert, but it was by no means clear to us if that would be what the new King would want. Some were for joining the fleet at Kinsale, others to resume our work alone, in spite of parliament's efforts to stop us. Others suggested we should make our way to Edinburgh, to offer the new young king our fealty, but no one knew if he was still there, or where else he might reside. Our captain took all into consideration, eventually commanded all his offers to attend him and issued us our orders.

'We will continue south to pick up our letters with all speed, and in hopes of not being engaged. Then we will sail west, gentlemen. I do not propose to join Prince Rupert, for all that I admire him. As a frigate within a fleet our share of prizes will certainly be far less. Why should we divide our prize money, when I feel sure we can do better elsewhere, and still support the cause? To make the greatest use of our vessel and our skills we will sail to the Americas, and set about our plundering there. God save the King!'

'Long to reign over us,' we replied in the best naval fashion, though I for one felt that I was hardly ready to replace one king with another. Next, the whole ship's company was assembled. The captain announced the murder of King Charles to gasps and muttered curses. We said prayers for his soul, then the captain said the loyal words again and we bellowed the reply, the better to encourage the common sailors to take heart. Our eventual destination was not told at this time to the men. In spite of our best efforts the mood in the ship turned inward, with much muttering and ill humour. It was likely, I considered, that there would be desertions before we set our faces to the west. Some of the pressed men would doubtless try to go home, and hang the new, absent king. For what use is a king if he rules from afar in name only?

Richard and I discussed the situation together, as we had each time our fortunes had altered, since almost the first day we had met in Oxford. I had thought he might now decide to leave the navy as was my thinking, but his desire for travel had not been satisfied. It seemed he was far from done with making new journeys.

'There are three things that persuade me,' he said. 'The chance to make such an expedition at not my but the navy's expense, the small but real comfort that we shall still be harrying parliament's exchequer, however far we are from England, and also the lure of prize money. I am not yet well enough set up to live how I would wish, nor do I have a trade, excepting university philosophy, as well as being a fair sailor. They say that prizes are far more valuable in the Americas. We would not be taking coin from dusty colliers, but furs, sugar, spices and all other manner of exotic goods obtainable there. Neither of us should give up this opportunity to gain wealth for ourselves!'

He spoke much truth, but I was not persuaded. 'I find I am wearying of this life,' I said. 'I would like to settle somewhere, put away my sword and seek to preserve life, rather than take it.'

'So do you purpose to live out your life with Abigall after all?' he asked, sounding a little peeved.

How sorely I was tempted! But having made my break with Abigall, I knew returning to her was not the answer. I took a long, honest look into my heart. I did love her. Yes, I did, but not enough for my love to withstand a life of hard living in a distant place. And when I thought of how it would be if I attempted to take her into society, I saw that it would be a downright cruelty. If I had her it would mean rejecting everything else. But I was fairly sure I could make a good life in some city as a physician. If I went back to that island I would only ever be a small farmer and fisherman. I knew that would not, eventually, be enough.

As our conversation went back and forth, Richard became ever more agitated.

'Who *do* you want to be with if it is neither your girl in Scotland nor me?'

I looked at him in surprise. 'I would like to be with both of you,' I said. 'But I have come to realise that the life of a crofter is not for me, and as I have no desire to journey to the Americas, while you do, I think I must decide to strike out on my own.'

'So you mean to throw away both girl and friend, to instead moulder away in some witless English town, where minds are as small as tennis balls? I am surprised and dismayed at your lack of courage.'

Now he had me angry. I spoke to him coldly. 'It is not courage I lack, Richard, but simply the desire to go to the Americas.'

'I had not thought you to be the kind of man to let a friend down.'

Without another word he walked away. I looked after him in both anger and dismay. Why could he not understand my point of view? I was not trying to stop him from doing what he wanted. I would miss him badly when we came to part, of course I would, but I wanted a more settled life. The murder of the King had shocked me and the fight had gone out of me. It pained me to think it, but that man who had been my supposed father had been on the winning side after all.

In a few hours we would reach the small port where we would pick up those necessaries we needed, and any letters that might be awaiting us. I went to Captain Down and offered to be the one to collect the post. 'I am in great need of new linen,' I told him. 'And hope to find a shirt to be a change for my only other.'

Captain Down favoured me with an amused smile. I think my gift to Abigall had not gone unremarked by any onboard. Indeed, my only remaining shirt was in great need of washing and mending. 'Pray bring back any newspapers and broadsheets you see,' he said. 'For I think there will be much of interest to read.'

'I will.'

I went below in search of Richard, but he was playing cards with some of the other officers and did not look at me. I went to my bunk and opened my box. My coin was in a small bag, which after some hesitation I picked up and weighed in my hand. I had a large leather wallet, which would be useful for bringing the letters back to the ship. Being irresolute I lay both back down and returned to the card players.

'Richard?'

He looked up with some irritation. 'What is it?'

'I need to speak with you.'

He gave a heavy sigh and stood up. 'Deal me in,' he said to the others. 'I will return in a moment. What is it?' he asked, before we were hardly alone.

'I am going to collect the post,' I told him.

'And so . . . ?'

'And so . . . do you want to come with me? We could enjoy a meal at the inn . . .'

He looked away from me. 'I think you can see I am busy,' he said.

I put out my hand to touch his sleeve and he pulled away. 'I have no appetite to sit in an inn with you today,' he said. 'I feel no need to be in your pocket.'

'Richard . . .' But he was already walking away. A few seconds later I heard him say something to the others, and laughter followed his words.

I returned to my bunk. I was burning from his hard words, and hurt by them too. We so rarely quarrelled, but the dreadful news of the King's death had put everyone out of sorts. Swiftly, I opened the wallet and placed the coin bag and my roll of medical instruments into it. By the time we anchored I was ready, with the strap of the wallet over my shoulder. Before I climbed over the side I looked for Richard on deck, but he was not there. I got into the boat and sat with the wallet on my knees as I was rowed to shore.

# CHAPTER TWENTY-THREE

I asked a fisherman landing his catch where I might be able to find me a shirt. The one I eventually found was not new-made, but better than my own, and fitted me well enough. I hoped it had not come from a dead man but probably the best I could hope for was that the previous owner had not died while wearing it.

There was a good quantity of mail. I stowed it all in my wallet after ordering a pie and some wine at the inn. Amongst it there was a packet for Richard. After a few moments' thought I extracted it from the wallet and gazed at it. If I had not been out of sorts with him I would not have broken the seal, but I did not intend to do more than look to see if there was a letter enclosed for me. To my great delight there was! I extracted it, immediately refolded Richard's packet and returned it to the wallet.

I had not dared to think too hopefully of receiving a letter of my own, so my heart was leaping within me as I unfolded it. I reminded myself that my mother might not have received mine before sending this, and so nothing new might be said. On the other hand, she might have received it and be angry with me for creating within her a quite needless grief.

Richard, on seeing me hesitate, would have said, 'Just read it,' so I did.

*My dear son. If it had not been for the fact that your letter was written in your own hand I could not have allowed myself to believe it. Alive! It is a miraculous word, sending me at one moment from grief to joy. I have so many questions to ask, and so wish I could see you to reassure myself that your words so written are indeed the truth, but I must not be a doubting Thomas. Indeed, I am not, but I long, from a surfeit of a mother's love, to hold you to me and kiss your cheek, seeing for myself that you are well. I do not know where you are or what you are doing, but you are alive, which is the most important thing. Thank you for taking pity on this woman your mother, and sparing her any more sadness. I will say no more, other than that your brother goes on well, but your father suffers much through his lack of sight. It has made him very melancholy, and I do not know how long he will be able to keep body and spirit together. I go on well enough, and send you all the love I hold for my very dear son. Pray God there will come a time when I will see you again on this earth.*

I read the letter, and then read it again. She did not seem angry. Indeed, it was clear how delighted she was! In addition, all seemed well between her and her husband. No mention was made of being put from him and she referred to him still as my father. I could not forgive him for the words he had spoken to me, but I was filled with an enormous excitement. I longed to see my mother! I could hardly prevent myself from getting to my feet and walking about the room. Indeed, I had to do something to settle myself. While I waited for my food I would take a stroll. I told the serving girl I would be back in a few minutes and left the smoky room.

It was market day, which is how I had found my shirt. Even more stalls were there now, and hawkers were calling their wares. To one side, tethered to a line, were several horses and a couple of donkeys, every one splattered with mud. Nearby were baskets of shiny silver fish. Perhaps I should have asked for fish at the inn. They would almost certainly be fresher than the meat in a pie. Still, I had had a notion for a beef pie, rich with hot gravy.

Remembering my promise to the captain, I bought both the newspapers on offer and then, taken by a moss green coat draped at the end of another stall, I took it up and tried it on. I was in the mood to spend, and I had money in my wallet. It was a shame Richard had been in such a bad mood. We could have had fun there that day. I looked again at the coat. It had been fine once, though was worn at the cuffs, and rather dirty about the skirt. Still, it was a colour I liked, and I had not worn such a coat since the green velvet at Aphra's house. Where was it now, that coat? I had no idea. So much had happened since then. I could not recall where my box lay. In Oxford? Or had it somehow been returned to my home in Gloucestershire? Perhaps more likely it had been purloined by some rogue, and my garments even now lay scattered on similar stalls in similar towns to this. My belongings in Flint were gone too. No doubt my fine sword was being brandished by some fellow who thought a lot of himself. Well, I hoped he had joy of it. I had my short sword still, and that was enough to dissuade any casual thief in a town such as this.

In any case, I would have this coat. If my eventual plan was to return to gentlemanly pursuits, I could not wear the salty clothes I now owned. This would be a start. I felt well pleased with myself as I bargained with the woman who was selling it. There was no one else there, I ventured, who would want such a coat as this. She agreed, and I got it for a good price. On my way back to the inn, I wandered along the line of animals. There were three cobs, all sturdy, being well-formed animals. One was rather old, but looked an honest sort. I hoped he would go to someone who would ride him quietly, and excuse his years.

Between the donkeys and the cobs was a pale, well-bred mare. She was the dirtiest of the lot and yet had the finest bearing. She was taller than the cobs, and her legs were slim, though her hindquarters were strongly built. As I approached her she nosed at me for some treat, but I had nothing to give her. It had been a mistake to show interest. A hopeful man approached, and began to speak of the many advantageous reasons why I should buy her.

'That is all very well, my friend,' I said to him. 'But I fear she would be wasted onboard a ship.'

He laughed. 'Ah! I see. But it is a pity. She is a good animal, too good for these parts. I will have to take her to a larger town than this if I'm going to make the price she deserves.'

I gave her a pat and she put her head into the crook of my arm.

'Good luck to you,' I said, to the man and his horse.

Back at the inn they had forgotten my order, or someone else had eaten it. The innkeeper was apologetic.

'It's market day, as you see. And we're run nearly off our feet. But I will bring your food and wine at once, sir.'

I found a corner and sat, eating the pie while I tried to read the news, but found I did not want to know of the many reverses of the old king's fortunes, or about where the new King might or might not be.

'Do you have something I can put these papers in?' I asked the innkeeper when he brought me more wine.

'I can find you something.'

He returned with an old flour sack that had been patched several times, and was wearing into more holes, but it would do for my purpose. I stuffed the sheets into the sack and put it on the floor while I finished the pie. It was very good. The best food I had eaten for a while.

In spite of my stomach being pleasantly full, I was out of sorts with the day. I didn't want to return to the ship quite yet, but neither could I settle to anything else. What I really wanted was to ride that horse for an hour or two, to take some exercise on this sunny day. I had not been on the back of a horse for a long while, and she had tempted me far more than had those honest cobs.

I folded the letter from my mother that had so excited and unsettled me and opened my wallet. There lay all the rest of the post for the ship. I transferred it all to the flour sack so I would have room in the wallet for my new shirt. I finished my wine. At the quay, the ship's boat was there, with a seaman guarding a couple of sacks of supplies.

He told me the quartermaster still had items on his list, and would most likely be another hour or so.

'Then take this for the captain,' I said. 'And stow it somewhere dry. I also have more to do. I will hire a man to row me over to the ship if you have departed before I get back.'

The horse line was still there, although both the donkeys had gone, along with the best cob. The man was still there too, giving his remaining animals a few wisps of hay. He greeted me eagerly.

'Will you hire me that mare for a short while?' I asked him. 'I have a mind to take a ride.'

'And if you lame her, what then?' he said. 'I would be even more out of pocket, with her eating her head off until she was sound again.'

'I will not lame her.'

'No, you will not,' he said mildly. 'Not while I own her, at any rate.'

There was no heat in her legs, and she was well mannered, lifting her feet for me to look at them. There was a long, thin scar on her side, which looked to me like the passage of a bullet that had grazed her belly. Her owner watched me run my hand along the scar.

'She has a history, like so many of us,' he offered. 'But I do not know what it is.'

'You don't know anything about her?'

'Only that her owner was in debt.' He reached into a bag and gave her a bare handful of oats. She took them politely, blowing husks from his palm. She was a little too lean for my liking, but did not seem desperate for food. 'I'll tell you what I'll do. You obviously like her, and I got her for a good price. You buy her from me, and if you bring her back in good order in a couple of hours, I'll return your money with a deduction for her hire. That way she will have at least earned her keep for another day or two.'

I laughed. 'No doubt in a couple of hours you will be gone!'

He looked at me seriously. 'I take no offence, but I am a man of my word. I will be here until four o'clock, and I am well known in the town. I live nearby. Any would direct you to my dwelling.'

We bargained to and fro and eventually shook on the deal. He brought a bucket of water for her, but she was not overly thirsty. She stood easily while I mounted, and she moved off well. My spirits lifted. One never forgets how to ride a horse. I felt so much pleasure in this jaunt. It had been the best decision I had made in a long while. I took the coast road. The sun-sparkling sea on one hand, and the bright, polished gorse blooms on the other was exactly what I needed.

Four days later I was still heading south.

# CHAPTER TWENTY-FOUR

How life's journey is so often a matter of small decisions! I did not always take my instruments with me when I went ashore, but sometimes I did. Why had I done so that day? Why take all my money, when a little would have sufficed for what I had thought to spend?

I truly believe that I had not intended leaving the ship that day, but those two small decisions certainly made it possible. Was there a little part of my mind that wished to make it so? I do not know, but my irritation at Richard, seeing the coat that reminded me of my earlier life, the pretty mare and most of all that letter from my mother . . . all together those things drew me on. Of course, more than anything I wanted to see my parent, but even with my new coat and shirt I deemed myself far too much in tatters. I carried on south, past my county, and ended up at last in Bristol, well pleased with my willing mare. I straight away, after finding good lodgings, engaged a tailor to make me a new suit in a dark blue serviceable cloth. It was of the latest Bristol fashion, but sober enough to suit my profession. I could do nothing about my weathered face, but had my tangled hair washed and trimmed. I topped my sartorial turnaround with a handsome beaver hat, and for my feet I bought both riding boots and a pair of buckled shoes. Then I turned my attention to my mount.

Apart from the long, thin scar on her belly, I found a small one above her right eye, running up toward her ear. Both had healed well, a long time before. After a lot of work, some done myself and more by the boy where I stabled her, she turned out to have a luminous grey coat, dappled on her hindquarters. I called her Luna. Her saddle and bridle were, like her, of good quality but had been neglected. Once cleaned and repaired we made, I think, a handsome enough sight in the city, and would, I was sure, reassure my parent that I was at ease in my life. As soon as I was presentable as a gentleman I made enquiries about the need for physicians in the city, and was almost immediately introduced to a Mr Bevoirs, who was a member of the Merchant Venturers, charged to retain a physician to care for the distressed seamen inhabiting their almshouses. It did not pay me much, but was a toehold into the city that I was liking more each day. Moreover, Mr Bevoirs turned out to be a beneficial advocate for me with those of influence. I was delighted to discover that many people there felt the way I did about war and politics; that it was better now to get on with our lives, and leave such things to others.

Thoughts of the privations and uncertainty of a voyage to

the Americas made me very well pleased with my decision to turn from a seafaring life. I was glad too that I had avoided informing the captain of my decision, by making it after I had ridden away. At the least he would have tried to dissuade me, and most likely would have detained me, surgeons being in short supply. But I had no experience of the diseases of the Americas. He would surely do better to recruit a man there, instead of retaining me. I knew very well that thought was but a sop to ease my conscience. But however others viewed my sudden alteration, I was sure I had made the correct decision for me. It was astonishing to realise how few days it had taken to change my life entirely.

The only thing that gave me pause was that I had opened the letter to Richard from his parents in search of one for myself. I felt he deserved an explanation, and so I wrote to him. As well as explaining about the letter I told him I regretted that we had not parted on better terms, and assured him that I held him in the same high regard that ever I had. Wishing him well in his new adventure, I gave my address in the city so he could reply. After half a year I heard nothing from him, which was a cause for some sadness, but letters to ships were always a chancy matter, particularly at a great distance. I schooled myself that no disaster had come to him. Most likely the letter had never reached him, or perhaps it was simply that our friendship had run its natural course.

As soon as I was settled and had secured my post at the almshouses, I made plans to visit my mother. I could not bear to write and wait for a reply, so I set off as soon as I could. Throughout the ride from Bristol the whole country was quiet, as if exhausted after the late war. The fields were being worked, and some buildings that had suffered in the war were being rebuilt but I knew it was not simply my imagination that showed me fewer hearty men to do the work. I had found the same during my ride from the north of England. The dead had left holes like rotting teeth. The whole country was aching, and holding its breath, waiting for parliament to tell us all how it would be from now on.

Instead of riding up to the main entrance of the house, I took the path through the woodland my brother and I had often used when rampaging boys, playing at our youthful games. I hoped to avoid my so-called father knowing I had arrived, preferring to see my mother alone if I could. The path took me close to the high wall that hid my mother's privy garden beyond, but the door in the wall was locked. Tying Luna to an elder wand nearby, I stood on her back to climb up on to the top of the wall. Fortune was smiling upon me, because there with a basket of flowers stood my mother, quite alone. I hailed her in a low voice and she looked up from her cutting of the blooms, but could not see where my voice had come from. I made haste to climb down, but on the garden side of the wall I did not have Luna to help me. There had been a large plum tree, with a useful branch to aid boyish climbing, but to my dismay the branch had gone, to storm, or rot, or whatever reason I did not know. There was nothing to do but to let myself down as carefully as I could. It was not a tidy climb down, more, I admit, a straight fall. As I tumbled, bringing leaves, twigs and loose pieces of the wall with me, my mother gave a cry of alarm.

I think each appearance shocked the other. For myself, my skin was more weathered than it had ever been before, and I was a grown and broadened man. My mother, although it had not been many years since I had seen her, appeared much aged, with a slight stoop, careworn face and hands thin and veined. After that first moment of shock we were both full of emotion. We clung together in a long embrace. I could feel the thinness of her, but for all her seeming frailty she had a greater steeliness in her than I had seen before.

'Why did you come unannounced, and creeping into the garden?' she asked at length, making to brush the twigs and green marks from my new clothes.

'I am no longer a soldier,' I said. 'But I did not know what reception I might get from a parliamentarian household, nor did I want your husband knowing I was here.'

There was a long moment before she replied, and when she did it was not to speak directly. 'I had a letter from Hugh last week,' she said. 'He is still with the army, and is now a captain. He says that the war is *not* over. He thinks that the young King has many adherents in England and abroad. Charles will not, he feels, give up his throne without a fight, and will bring more slaughter to his people before all is done.'

'Well, I have no stomach for it,' I said. 'When the old king was murdered, my war ended.'

She embraced me again and I could tell that her heart rejoiced to hear it. 'Stay quietly here,' she said at last. 'You are quite safe, but I understand your reluctance for your father to know you are here. I will make the way clear for you. Do you have a horse with you?'

'Yes,' I said. 'You'll love her. She's a beauty.'

'Then bring her in and water her at the tank over there. You can tether her to the old apple tree. She will not do too much damage, I think, and will save us the bother of taking her to the stable, where people will speculate. They do like to gossip.'

She took the key to the door in the wall from her waist and gave it to me. 'I will go back to the house to arrange things for us to be private,' she said, giving me another hug. 'I will be back very soon.'

We went to her sunny chamber, where her sewing basket, brimming with threads just as I remembered it, lay on the side table.

'We will not be disturbed here,' she said. 'Your father sleeps for much of the day and he has a servant to look after him, so if he wakes, I will not be called to go to him.'

She was, I fear, much worn down by her husband, who was now both blind and almost deaf, but rather than tell me of her life she wanted to know why Richard had written with the lie of my death, and all that had happened afterwards. When I had related all, she sat quietly for a few moments, gazing at her hands in her lap. Then she looked at me. 'I must tell you, Thomas, with all sincerity, that you are indeed my husband's son. There is and can be no doubt about it. I was a virgin girl when first I went to his bed as a bride, and I have known no other man.'

I found it impossible to look at her. 'It grieves me that you have found it needful to tell me this.'

'Tom. If I had not, you would still believe a lie, in spite of any glass telling you otherwise, for you must know how alike you are to your father in the face.' She paused, and then took a breath that came deep from within her slight body. 'I would not be disloyal to my husband. But he was wrong to lie to you. All I can say to excuse him is that since he was wounded his moods have become much more extreme. And you and he have always had a difficult relationship.'

I would have spoken, but she stopped me.

'So you see there is no reason to spurn your inheritance, which is legally and honourably yours. And have no fear of Hugh's reaction when he too hears that you live. He will be content.'

'Oh no!' I said at once. 'I am quite happy for him to have all. I am well set up in Bristol, and doing what I love. I would not have let him believe he will inherit just to later deny him.'

My mother said nothing more, but she looked sad, and more than a little doubtful. We spoke much of other things, and shortly before I left I asked about Aphra.

'I heard tell she was married last year to someone in Somersetshire,' said my mother. 'I am sorry.'

'I expected nothing else,' said I. 'I hope she is happy.'

I rode home after promising to return before too long. My spirits were high, in spite of Aphra being married. I had not really expected that she would still be a girl, though it was a pity. But there were plenty of good families in Bristol. I might not aspire again after the second daughter of an earl, but there would be a wife for me when I was ready. As for my inheritance, perhaps it had not been entirely wise to throw it away so freely, but our father might live for another ten years or more, and I was not prepared to be an heir-in-waiting. Instead, I got on with my new life in Bristol and found it agreeable in every way.

As soon as my mother had word that Hugh was coming home on leave she wrote to me. At once I made plans to be there. She had not told Hugh that I lived, preferring to let my presence speak for her, so it was in high excitement that I rode Luna to Gloucestershire again. This time I took her to the stable. I was a regular visitor now, and no longer excited gossip amongst the servants. I was Ptolemy Moore in Bristol, because that was how I had begun, and would not alter now, but my mother would always call me Tom, and I was content with that. First of all, I went to greet her.

'Go and give greetings to your father,' she said. 'Then come and take some refreshment. We expect your brother late this afternoon.'

I would not say I had become reconciled to my father, but his condition, keeping him entirely now to his rooms, made it possible for me to be civil to him for a few minutes at every visit. His lie to me about my paternity had been countered by my lie to him about my death, and so we counted ourselves equal. At least I could walk away from him, he being powerless to follow. This day I was so happy at the thought of being reunited with my brother that I managed to be quite friendly toward the old man.

'If I can,' I shouted to his deaf ears, 'I will see you again before I leave tomorrow.'

I am not sure if he understood me or not. His clouded eyes looked in my direction, but it is certain that I was no more than a misty shadow to him. I was sorry to see him brought so low, but still I could not like him.

Hugh finally came with the dusk. He arrived with little ceremony, but looked every inch the successful captain, on a fine bay horse and with his orange sash bright in the dwindling light. Seeing him at a distance as I did from my chamber window, my guts began to churn, before my head reminded me that I was no longer a soldier and that I had sworn never to use my sword against this parliamentarian.

I watched as he dismounted and was greeted by my mother at the door. I gave them a few minutes together before I hurried down the stairs. I found my mother alone.

'He has gone as you did, to greet his father,' she said.

I sat beside her and took her hand. 'I confess I am nervous,' I said. 'He has thought me dead for this long while. How will he take this news?'

'With great joy, as I did,' she said, putting up her hand to fondly stroke my hair.

Suddenly he was there in the doorway, glaring at us both. I felt a terrible guilt, as if Mother and I had been caught in some compromising situation. She must have felt a similar unease because she pulled her hand quickly away from my hair and folded both hands in a more seemly manner in her lap.

Hugh showed no inclination to come into the room and so I stood, and spoke.

'Hugh? Do you not know me?'

He looked to his mother and back to me. Suddenly his face paled as he realised what he was seeing. It must have seemed impossible to him that I was standing, undeniably flesh and blood, in his mother's room.

He said it slowly, bewilderment in his voice. 'Tom?'

I wondered if he might faint at the sight of this ghost in front of him, and for the first time wished our mother had taken him into her confidence as soon as she had learnt that I lived. I stood up and went toward him. 'Hugh! It is me, your brother, Tom. Take my hand. See how real I am!'

Tom sat awkwardly upon my tongue, being known as Ptolemy elsewhere, so I said it again. 'Hugh, it really is I, Tom, your brother. Please take my hand.'

Instead of that he took a faltering step before bounding towards me, taking me into an excited and wholehearted embrace. Then he shook me by my shoulders, like a terrier with a rat. There were tears on both our cheeks when he finally put me from him.

'We were told you had died! *Years* ago. And now you suddenly appear without warning, as dark as a Spaniard and twice the man you were! Where have you *been*?'

Our mother spoke then. 'There is much to say, much to catch up on for all of us. You must not be angry with your brother, Hugh. He has always tried to do the best for us all.'

He looked at her in astonishment. 'Angry? I am not angry, Mother. Simply amazed!'

Yet I could detect a thread of anger in him, and I felt sure more would arise as he discovered how the truth had been kept from him. Surely, though, his anger would fade as he understood the reasons for it?

We spoke long into the night, and when our mother eventually left us for her rest we continued our conversation. We spoke little of our opposite loyalties. He was, I think, a very professional soldier. I imagine he did at all times most capably what he was commanded. He was at pains to inform me that his duty and the duty of all was to continue the peace, and to put down any attempts, from wherever they came, to take our nation back to civil war. He feared war would come again, but hoped against it. We could both wholeheartedly agree on that.

Hugh's greatest difficulty lay in my return from the grave. It was natural for him to feel along with joy a measure of anger at having been kept from the truth. Any brother would have felt the same, but more troublesome for him was what to do about my return. It meant little to him that I was content to renounce my inheritance.

'Having been told you were dead I thought I would be Sir Hugh when our father died,' he said. 'Now all of a sudden I am no longer that man, although I am betrothed, at least partly on my expectations.'

This was news to me. 'Nothing need change,' I said. 'Except that I must congratulate you, and wish you well!'

He shook his head. 'You can say whatever you like, Tom, but the fact remains that you are the eldest son and you live. The inheritance will be yours, whether you want it or not. Your children will inherit this place, not mine. And I believe no father would want his daughter to marry a man who says he is entitled to something when he is not. He will deny Elizabeth to me when he finds out.'

'But you did not know!'

'Our mother knew, did she not? And yet she kept quiet.'

His voice was quiet, but the tone betrayed his bitterness.

'Hugh. She has only known for these past few weeks, and she thought it better to tell you in person instead of in a letter.'

I stood up and refilled my glass and his. 'Listen to me, Hugh. I will do whatever it takes to help your marriage happen. I will write to your Elizabeth's father if you like, swearing that I do not intend to take ownership of the house and lands. They will be yours. Apart from here I do not even use my given name. I am rather Ptolemy Moore, and have been almost since we parted in the stable when you were about to join Fairfax's army. You know now why I chose to kill Tom Chayne. It was to save our mother from our father's threat to her honour. I could not risk him carrying it out, could I?'

The expression on his face told me exactly what he was thinking. He had no sympathy, but thought I should have obeyed our father and abandoned the King. We stared at each other, neither quite daring to speak what was in our minds. For me, Hugh's revelation that he was betrothed had been like a punch to my belly. I did not want to take away his future happiness, but creeping into my mind came the thought that if he could not appreciate my difficulty between loyalty to the King and obedience to a man I had thought was not my father, why should I give away what was rightfully mine? I tried to ignore the clamouring in my mind, but it was insistent, crying out that Hugh did not deserve my inheritance.

We went to our beds without giving voice to our discontent, but the warmth that had at first been between us had dissolved into an uneasy truce. The next day he was gone before I rose, without giving me the chance to say farewell. I broke my fast with our mother, who also had not known that Hugh had left without warning.

'I can understand that your brother is bewildered and confused by your sudden reappearance,' she said. 'But his sudden departure without making his farewells does not become him.'

'He fears his marriage will not now go ahead,' I said. 'Because he is no longer the heir.'

She shook her head. 'That is foolishness. He is being overdramatic. There will be no difficulty. Hugh is rising in the army and has the ear of important men, which appeals to Elizabeth's father.' She sighed. 'You are both my sons, and I love you equally, but never let Hugh suggest that you are other than a good man. Your attempt to protect me from your father's ire, while also being true to your own inclinations, was honourable. I will always admire you for that.' She turned in her chair and smoothed my hair with her hand. 'We can hope that the war is over, even if your brother does not believe it. You are no longer a soldier and I am no longer in peril from your father. Listen to me, Thomas. You have no need to forsake your inheritance. It is yours by right.'

'But to do that is to take away what I freely gave to Hugh! How can I do that to my own brother?'

'You cannot give your brother what you do not have. Your father yet lives. Hugh is to be wed next year, and because of that there will be a settlement coming to him from the estate. He will not be a pauper, and moreover, he shows every intention of making a career for himself in the army. Rather than worrying about him, think of yourself.'

* * *

The years fled and I prospered. It was fortunate I had fallen in with the Merchant Venturers in Bristol because they were a powerful force in the city. I became well known at their hall in King Street, near Broad Quay, and as my reputation as a good physician grew, I obtained some wealthy patients. I even grew accustomed to treating women, though I always found their soft, pillowy flesh more difficult to read than that of men. They were wonderful as objects of love, but their flesh kept hidden their ailments more than the thin stretching of skin over a man's frame. I fear I was less successful in treating them, although their husbands and fathers paid handsomely for my advice, and I did my best. As my reputation grew, so my fees increased. Soon I had money to speculate and, with advice, invested in a vessel sailing to the Carib sea. When it returned my investment several times over I was able to invest more, and eventually buy one of the fine houses that were being built in Bristol at this time.

Cromwell busied himself in slaughtering the Irish and Scots, while I was invited to join the voluntary company that would help protect the city if war came back to us. I was not minded to be an army man again, but nor was the city minded to revolt. I was only one of many who took the oath of loyalty to the Commonwealth, not because I wanted to, but to avoid persecution. Later that year the Treason Act passed, another good reason to eschew war. Hugh had been right: war was not entirely over, but it did not come to our walls. Young Charles eventually turned up in France, but his army had been routed at Worcester, and was no more. It was surely over, and the country gave out a long sigh. Mostly, its people then got on with living quietly. So, being an officer in the militia was more for social than martial reasons. It was a good way to meet many lords and gentlemen at our annual military feast, which did my prospects only good.

It was at one of those feasts that I heard of the death of Aphra's husband. She was not mentioned, but I knew her husband's name. He had been in Ireland, and was shot during a skirmish that should have been no more than a small incident, for the population was entirely and savagely conquered. I remember the year clearly. It was 1653, and I was twenty-nine years old.

I wrote a letter of condolence to her parents' address, hardly thinking to receive a reply. However, a month later Aphra wrote to thank me, telling me of her two children, and remembering our philosophical communications in the past. She made no mention of our thwarted betrothal, and neither did I, but I felt a kind of glee as we began to pick up the threads of our old friendship. Our parents had halted our marriage plans in the past, but they had not taken away our mutual regard.

# CHAPTER TWENTY-FIVE

My fortune grew ever larger, more quickly than I could ever have imagined. As well as my few wealthy patients I was become quite the merchant, and had recently begun investing in plantations in Jamaica. The demand for sugar was great, and only increasing. Thousands of indentured servants sailed from Bristol to supply the need for workers, and profits were good. Edward Bevoirs put me in touch with a good man in Jamaica, a Mr Chepstow, who dealt with my land there, advising me whenever more land adjoining mine was to be had. In the city I went more and more into society, and living not too far away, I was able to visit my mother regularly, restoring I hope a little of the hurt I had caused her.

My brother and I met seldom. Sadly, when we did our relations were cool. Our mother kept telling me that he would eventually understand me better, but he showed no sign of it. His career in the army prospered and he had travelled far from the uncertain boy who had wanted so badly to follow me into war. He had Cromwell's ear, or so he said, as if to point up my past misguided adherence to the Crown. I wanted to like Hugh, love him indeed as of old, but increasingly it felt as if he was turning into a young version of our father. He gave the impression that my adult life had been undertaken badly. It meant nothing to him; even my success in Bristol little impressed him. It angered me that I felt obliged to impress him. I strove not to. I had no need, but could not resist. The result was that I felt ever more like a failing, younger brother, and so liked him less and less. Even paltry things gnawed at me. Each time he visited his wife he seemed to father another child. At every birth he crowed to me about it, and teased me about my single state. I made no response, but his repeating fatherhood hurt me badly for I still had no child to my name. I knew if Aphra was to be the mother of my children I needed to be slow, gentle and circumspect with her. I knew she would not be rushed, however much I wished to carry her off to the nearest church. I knew too that I should count my fortune and discard the pointless irritation with my brother. Apart from my relations with him, all in my life was going well. Aphra and I continued to correspond frequently and fondly. I sent things to amuse her children when curious items arrived from abroad: a huge nut, a curious carving and a piece of cloth made from the bark of a tree. In reply she sent sketches she had made of the children, and amusing accounts of their reactions.

*I am so grateful to you for awakening an interest in the children for things beyond their own small world. More than anything, our country needs open minds and considered opinions*, she wrote. *The desire for knowledge was one of the things I appreciated about you,*

*almost as soon as we met. I am obliged to you for encouraging my*
*children to be thinkers too.*

I replied at once. *Thank you for your letter and latest delightful*
*sketch. I have just recovered from a long afternoon and evening*
*drinking with my friends. You might not think this behaviour*
*the mark of a philosopher, but keeping company with George and*
*Edward is nonetheless an education of sorts. They are the funniest*
*gentlemen you could ever wish to meet, and they are also full of*
*sound business ideas. George tells me he is investing in a new trade*
*with the Afric kings, who are willing to supply people to labour in*
*the sugar fields. They will, he tells me, fetch a good price, and be*
*excellent workers. Coming from that hot continent they will be better*
*than any number of indentured servants, particularly the Irish, who*
*being pale of skin, and underfed, having been treated most terribly*
*by Cromwell, soon wilt and fail in the Carib climate. Perhaps I will*
*invest in African labour for my lands too.*

Her reply surprised me.

*And what do these people think of their transplanting from one*
*continent to another?* she wrote. *Do they choose it?*

I could not fathom what she meant.

*Do you wish a philosophical discussion about the feelings of slaves?*
I enquired. *I understand from George that the people are captives*
*from late Afric wars, and would be killed if not sold to live elsewhere.*
*I propose that they would most likely prefer life in a strange land to*
*death at home at the hand of their enemies.*

*As a woman,* she wrote back to me, *I think I can understand*
*what it is for a person to have no control over their life. I do not*
*labour in the fields, but I have been no less a slave to the men who*
*have owned me. However, I have never desired death as an escape,*
*and perhaps neither have those poor souls. I feel I am arguing from a*
*weak position as I know little about the subject.*

*But,* I replied, *you have the advantage over me of more personal experience. I am sorry you have felt enslaved. I remember your desire to attend the university, and to study much that is denied to women. I would not have enslaved you, Aphra, nor would I now.*

She made no obvious encouraging response to my words, but neither did she chide me for them. I would not rush her. She still needed time, but I felt increasingly confident that Aphra would in the end agree to become my wife. While I gently wooed her I would increase my fortune until it was suitable for such a rare jewel as she.

I was thirty-six when Charles II came into his own, with bells ringing and a mood of celebration almost everywhere. In the end, rather than winning by force, he was invited to return as king, after the previous year had seen a troubling slide back towards war. I'm told that Fairfax was one of the heroes of the situation, urging General Monck to restore the monarchy, but I think there were many elements to it, perhaps the most decisive being the death of Cromwell a couple of years before. Like or loathe him, he was a formidable man with a tight and intelligent grip on the country. But I heard that his son was a shadow of the father, and did not have the support of parliament. Charles Stuart was likely to take care to keep his head upon his shoulders, and bow to the power of parliament. I doubted he would be allowed to, nor wish to make his father's mistakes, but time would tell. For myself, all I wanted was for peace and harmony in our country to prevail. There were plenty of wars on the continent, should any hanker after the martial life, but I had been done with it since the king had been murdered. A business life might be dull in some respects, but I was successful at it, and so, after skirmishes, killing, being besieged and cast away, my hopes for an eventual life with Aphra was excitement enough for me.

The feeling amongst my friends in Bristol was that more business opportunities might occur with the advent of a new king. Several of our members were well used to arguing for the city in parliament, which was often of advantage to we Merchant Venturers. I was asked if I too would stand for parliament. I thought about it quite carefully, but suddenly I had other things to manage, for at this time my mother fell ill.

I found out quite by chance, because three days after she took ill I rode all unknowing to visit her. It was early summer, and the breeze in the country was all sweet with the fragrance of woodbine. The fields were full of haycocks, and skylarks flew ever higher in the sky until they vanished, before drifting back down to sink into the ground. Just before I reached the house I reached up from my saddle and pulled down a long stem of woodbine flowers from a tree, thinking to give it to my mother. Luna looked very fine with it wound about her neck and it amused me to think of my mother's expression at her romantic finery. But when I arrived there was no laughing mother to receive me. Instead, the door was opened by a servant, who informed me of her mistress's indisposition. I was not overly alarmed because the servant did not seem to be, nor had I been summoned by any message, calling me to an emergency. When I hurried to her room I found her dressed, but wrapped warmly in spite of the warm day, and sitting in a chair by the window. I took her hand, and put my other on her forehead, which felt clammy to the touch.

'What have you been doing, to be having a fever this fine day?' I asked her.

'It is a mystery to me,' she said, squeezing my hand. 'And I am sorry for you to find me like this. If I had known, I would have written to advise you not to come for your own health's sake.'

'If I had known I would have come the sooner!'

I had not been going to spend the night, but did so. She was perhaps a little better, certainly no worse the following day, and so I left her to the capable ministrations of her maid and her housekeeper, after commanding the latter to send a message at once if her condition worsened. My father was fretting for her company so I tried to make him understand that his wife was unwell, but it was hard to communicate with the old man, and he had never been much inclined to listen to anything I might say.

I rode home in the twilight, with ghostly owls floating about us, making Luna toss her head and roll her eyes. Apart from the Bristol coach rattling past us, sending up clouds of dust and grit from the road, it was a quiet journey home. She was in my thoughts, of course she was, but I did not think to hear that my mother had worsened. She always had a very good constitution, so it was something of a shock the following week to receive a message to say she was finding it hard to breathe.

I immediately sent a message to the Merchant Venturers' Hall to say I had been called away, hurried home, called for Luna to be saddled and, pausing only to collect my medicine box, set out at once, thanking God that I lived less than a half-day's ride of the house. Even so, I drove Luna hard. As soon as I arrived I commanded the boy to take particular care of her, and hastened to my mother's bedchamber.

All the plasters, poultices and infusions I knew for her condition did very little for her, although she insisted they did. She had already been bled, but I did this again myself, knowing it to be the most efficacious treatment for infection. I also commanded all the windows be opened to allow the air more easily to reach her lungs, although the housekeeper, with her scant knowledge of simples, would be scandalised. I also called for more pillows, and did myself prop her into a more upright position. The kitchen made her good broth, which I did approve of, although my poor mother was unable to sip more than a few spoonfuls at a time. At night, when the air was more likely to contain a poisonous miasma, I had them close the windows and light a herb, the smoke of which I had heard was excellent for labouring lungs. It was fragrant, but her breathing was no better for it. I knew in my heart that no physician, however skilful, could cure this kind of drowning. It was in God's gift to either give her the strength to overcome the poison that caused it and live, or to let her succumb and die.

I gave up my entire time to her care, as she had done for me when I was born that snowy night over thirty-six years ago. I told my father's servant not to alarm the old man about her condition, for I feared he would make much noise and agitation, which would counter the calm and quiet I had imposed in my mother's chamber. I did, however, write to Hugh at his house in Oxfordshire, with the instruction to send it on urgently to wherever he might be. Since the return of the monarchy he had sworn his allegiance, doubtless relieved that only regicides would be punished, and remained in the army. He happened to be in London, from where he wrote to command that I should keep him informed, but said he could not come.

Each year that went by we drew further apart. I hardly recognised the authoritarian he had become, given to command not just his men but also to try the same behaviour on me and even our mother. It struck me as I read his tetchy reply to my urgent message that I might by ill fortune favour our father in looks, but Hugh was now become his very twin in behaviour. He listened to no one in the family but himself. It saddened me to think that of him, but there was nothing to be done about it. Then, as I sat quietly at the side of my struggling mother, I realised there was something I could do. It offended me so much to think of another tyrant owning this place, causing grief and alarm to its servants and tenants. My father had ruled his domain with a punishing grip. I remembered him storming through his wife's tranquil garden, scattering frightened servants as he went, all because some small thing had been done or not done to his liking. I would not allow another tyrant to own it. I looked at my mother, her face so pale but for the heightened colour of her cheeks. Her eyes were closed and her breathing was ragged. She had urged me to not relinquish my birthright, and I so wanted to do something to please her in her time of travail. It would anger Hugh dreadfully, but our relations were most likely irreparably broken anyway. Sitting there at her bedside I resolved that when our father died I would after all keep the house and land, and love it as our mother did. Its people would have little to fear from me. I would care for the estate for her sake, and I prayed she would wake well enough to hear what I had decided.

Much to my delight and relief she did wake a little better. Her eyes were disturbingly glassy, and her skin still clammy, but she had all her wits, and drank both some good wine and a little of her broth.

'I am so glad,' she said when I told her. 'I feel sure you will not regret it.'

Talking tired her, but she wanted conversation, so I fell to telling her much about my life in Bristol, and of that great city, which I had been told rivalled London for trade and splendour. Then I told her of my resumed relations with Aphra, and if she had been well enough to clap her hands in pleasure I am persuaded she would have done so.

'Happy conclusion,' was all she had breath to say. Her eyes continued for her, and it was obvious how pleased she was for me. After a while she found more breath for speaking. 'You will have children!'

'If all falls the way I wish,' I said. 'But we are the same two people, so I am sure it will.'

'When that little boy was born . . .' She tried to raise her head, but a fit of coughing defeated her. 'He so reminded me . . .'

'What little boy? You have not met Aphra's boy, I think? And I have not had that pleasure yet. But I will!'

She shook her head a fraction. 'The lost boy . . . I sent presents . . . his birthday.'

I stared at her.

'She called him Tom.'

She closed her eyes and concentrated on breathing. I waited as patiently as I could, but my heart beat overfast in my breast, and I felt sure I knew who she must mean.

'She called him Tom? Do you mean Catherine? She had a boy, and she gave him my name? Is that what you are saying?'

She opened her eyes again and looked steadily at me while struggling for breath. Her words came as a whisper.

'Best for all you did not know.'

'So why tell me now?' I hadn't meant to sound plaintive, but that's the way it came out.

'I'm sorry . . . Getting feeble . . .'

'No. No, of course you're not.' But illness didn't simply lower physical strength. I took her hand and stroked it. 'I wondered, but never knew. I'm glad you've told me. I always wanted to know. And you have met him?'

'Once . . . So sad when he died . . .'

'Oh.' It was inadequate.

Tears were spilling from her eyes. I took up a cloth and wiped them for her, but still they came. Her tears made me want to weep too, for myself, and for the boy . . . my son! 'When did he die?' I thought she would say in infancy, when so many are lost, but she did not.

'He was twelve.'

When I was near thirty! A child of mine had been in the world for twelve years, and I had never known it. But had I not felt it at least a little? Yearned for it, in some sense wanted it to be true? But it was as my mother had said. Better I had not known, to fret and interfere, and make Catherine's life so much harder. It was difficult though, so difficult to discover I had a well-grown son, and then to lose him in the next moment.

'I'm sorry . . .'

'Don't be. I'm sorry I gave you so much trouble when I was a boy.'

She squeezed my hand. 'You didn't.'

When she was sleeping again I left her in the care of her maid and went out into the garden to think over what she had told me. I felt pulled all awry. I had a son! He had been in the world for twelve years, and I could have known him, but did not. He had been born, lived and died without my knowledge. I could not celebrate his birth but only mourn his death. That was the unkindest thing. If I had known him I would have memories to sustain me in his loss, but he was no more than a shadow to me. I had never heard his voice, seen him at play. I did not even know where his grave lay. I would have to ask my mother when she woke. I had never discovered where Catherine lived, except to know that her husband had his farm at some way distant from here. Had my son been loved and cherished by his stepfather? Should I go, even after all this time, to give Catherine my condolences? But I shrank from it. There was nothing between us now. Just memory, and the bones of our poor boy, lying in a churchyard somewhere.

When she woke, my mother felt a little better, and she wanted to speak of the child, after keeping the secret for so many years. I was afraid she would become too tired, but she wanted to unburden herself.

'Catherine's mother spoke to me about it. She said, unknown to her, her daughter was misguided enough to take an infusion to stop a baby. Such a sinful thing to do! And then, when it didn't work and she became pregnant, she didn't realise, but feared God was punishing her with a deadly illness.'

Even after all the years that had passed I felt horror and sorrow in equal part. 'She told me none of this!'

My mother smiled sadly at me. 'You were both children, Tom. And if she had confided in you, what would you have done?'

'I . . .' I shook my head. 'Lust is a terrible master. I hope I would have counselled against such a sin, but . . . I think I might not. It is so sad that she bore all the responsibility when we were equally to blame.'

'It is ever thus for women, and always will be. That is the truth of it. But all turned out well. The babe was born easily, her husband is a good man, so I hear, and other children followed, a comfort for the loss of my grandson.'

I looked at her in surprise, but of course, he had not simply been my son.

'Catherine's mother and I became friends, Tom. It was an unexpected pleasure to come out of all the pain. And so, although we weren't able to see each other often, and only once was I able to dandle him on my knee, I heard all about him. He was much loved by his parents, and is mourned by them both. He had a good life. Though it was short, it was a merry one.'

She told me the place where he lay, which was not so very far. To my great relief she took no ill from her exertions, and so, as she continued to improve in health, I took some time to ride to the village and went into the churchyard to find where he lay. There was a wilted posy of flowers laid upon his grave. It felt strange to think that Catherine had probably put them there. I did not wish to meet her, should she come this way, so I put the flowers I had picked in the garden close to the faded posy, and pausing only to pray for his soul I went away. I thought I might have felt something, some closeness to this dead boy that was part of myself, but I felt nothing but sadness and regret. Still, he would be in my heart now for ever, where before all unknown he had not.

After a week, my mother was feeling so much better I thought it safe to leave her while I went back to Bristol. There were things I needed to do. I had documents to sign, for a ship was due to sail soon to Jamaica, and I meant to invest in her, as well as speculate on some land near the harbour in Bristol, which I was sure would attract builders. I had seen plans for a fine building of five gables, which would look very fine there, and would bring me a handsome rent.

It was a glorious morning when I set out, with the hint of a hot day to come with a mist that lay lightly in our valley. I made my farewell to my father, who looked most unwell. I advised his man to have him bled, thinking that he was surely not much longer for this life. My mother was up, though not dressed, and was sitting in her favourite chair by the window. She asked me to open it, but I chided her gently.

'Wait until the mist is gone,' I said. 'The sun will soon chase it away, and then you can listen to the birds sing to you.' I kissed her. 'I will be no longer than three or four days. Then I will return.'

'There is no need, Tom. I am so much better.'

'Indeed you are, but I will come anyway for I love to see you.'

She smiled at me then, took my hand and held it a moment before letting me go. 'In that case, I look forward already to seeing you again, and perhaps you will have a letter from Aphra?'

'I expect I shall!'

# CHAPTER TWENTY-SIX

Three days after my return, a letter from Aphra did arrive. As always, I opened it eagerly, settling down with a glass of wine at hand to enjoy her communication.

*My dear friend, I have been thinking for some time of how to write to you about my feelings on a certain matter, which has not been mentioned by either of us, but which, because of our past betrothal, I feel certain is in both our minds. I mean the question of my remarriage. Please forgive me, for this is too forward for a woman, but I think as you know I have always been outspoken in my views, and unafraid to express them, at least to a good friend!*

*The fact is, I had until recently been clear in my own mind, ever since my husband was killed, that I would never marry again. This was against the advice of my parents, my sisters and many of my* friends, who doubted I could survive without a man to guide me in all things. But I did not have an easy time with my husband, and I think I have proved to them now that I am quite capable of ordering my affairs well enough, and running the household that will eventually go to my son, Robert, as well as attending to the education of him and his sister. One of the things that has sustained me recently is the rekindling of our friendship, and our many cheerful letters on a wide variety of subjects. You must know how much your letters mean to me, but I reiterate it here.

Of late I have found myself considering my situation more and more, and wondering if I made a too hasty, incorrect decision as to my future. It seems to go against nature to deny a woman's natural purpose, to have children. But I am no longer so very young, and I worry that if we wed, I would be unable to provide you with the children I know you must desire. Moreover, I find I have a great dread of death this way, having been so ill after my second child was born. You are, however, as well as my dear friend, a physician, who would I know give me all the gentle care in your power. I would not fear death through childbed so much if you were with me. Knowing this, you have been in my mind so much these past months, so much so that I could not do otherwise but write my thoughts and feelings to you.

Please forgive me, dear Thomas, if you have no intention toward me, but you have no wife, and your letters are tender enough to be those from a lover too delicate to mention love. I make so bold, then, to take it upon myself to mention the subject.

Dear Thomas, please do not think ill of me for this letter, but it would break my heart to have to refuse you, should you make me an offer. This is why I have written, to tell you not to put your faith in an affirmative reply. You will see from the words I have written here that I have given the question long and exhaustive thought. It is not

*a decision I have made without considerable discussion with myself,*
*but it is one from which I know I shall now not waver. I hope we can*
*remain the loving friends by letter that we have become. I value your*
*friendship more than any other as you must know, but that is all I*
*can offer you. I hope so much that it will be enough. If I have hurt*
*you, forgive me. If I have spoken on a subject you have no interest in,*
*spare my blushes. More than all else, please write to let me know that*
*all is well between us.*

*Your best and very dearest friend, Aphra.*

# CHAPTER TWENTY-SEVEN

I read it, and then read it again. I was astonished at the subject, and bewildered at her vacillation. Her argument went one way and then the other. Did she have a fever? How had she thought it was suitable for her to refuse me, if that is what she had done, without having been asked the question? I could not understand her. Who could possibly understand such ramblings from a woman, other than perhaps another woman?

Suddenly I hated to see that paper, and the humiliating words upon it. I folded it roughly and thrust it into my pocket, thanking God that I had been at home, so that I had at least borne my humiliation alone. I drained the glass in one, and shouted for my servant.

'Order my mare saddled, and pack my bag. If any call, tell them I will return in a day or two.'

By the time Luna was brought to the door I had downed most of the bottle. I threw on my cloak against the drizzle that had just begun, mounted swiftly and kicked her on. I had not the heart to acknowledge my neighbour, who raised his hand to me as I galloped past. I daresay he looked after me thinking I was called to some medical emergency. Well, let all think what they would. The hammer of Luna's hooves acted as a counter-beat against the thudding of my heart. From disbelief to humiliation, from humiliation to anger and back to disbelief. I could not confide in any of my friends in Bristol and ask advice from them. I would be a laughing stock. But I needed to tell *someone*. There was only one person I could trust to give me measured, sensible advice. I needed a woman to read this letter, and to tell me how I should proceed. That woman, the only woman I could utterly trust, was my mother.

Both I and my horse were blown by the time we arrived at the house. I slid to the ground and looked with some unease at Luna as she was led away. She was a little lame, and I regretted that. I would not usually treat a horse so, but my feelings had driven me on. I did not give the servant who opened the door an opportunity to speak to me, but pushed past her with a muttered apology, and went at once to my mother's sitting room. She was not there so I turned to the servant, who hovered nearby.

'Where is she?'

'In her bedchamber, sir.'

'Very well. Get out of my way!' This to the servant, who still dithered in the doorway. And then more gently to her, 'Bring us some wine if you would. And some ale. I am very thirsty.'

'Yes, sir.'

I went quietly to my mother's chamber in case she was resting. When I opened the door, there, sitting at her bedside to my surprise and great discomfort was my brother.

'Hugh!'

He turned to look at me. His face was blotched, as if he had been weeping. 'So *now* you come,' he said.

It was only then that I fully took in the situation. Our mother was not propped up on her pillows as I had advised, but lying flat in her bed. It only needed a couple more steps towards her to know that she was dead. Even so, I took her wrist and felt in vain for the throb of her blood. None came. All the colour had drained from her face, but her wrist was still warm. She had been alive not so very long ago, but now she was dead, and would never speak with me again.

As a wolf howls, so that sound began to issue from my mouth, but I choked it back. I bent to cover her dear face, but Hugh took my arm in a painful grip. 'NO!'

Instead, I gently moved a wisp of hair from her forehead. Going to the other side of her bed I knelt, and prayed quietly for her soul's rest. My mind was in turmoil. There was too much filling it up. I could not settle to one thought, but raced from one to another while I tried to pray. A relapse and death after a patient had begun to recover was hardly unknown, but in this case it was so very hard to accept.

And then, from elsewhere in the house came that wolf howl that had so latterly been in my throat. Someone must have told my father. There was a great commotion, and it was impossible any longer to pray quietly by my mother's bed. I got up, sick at heart, feeling near to death myself and went to my father's chamber. It was as if a war had broken out. His chair was on its back, stools were on their sides and even his table was thrown over, spilling wine, food and his Bible onto the floor. My father had got himself out of bed and had fallen. His manservant was trying to lift him, but as well as his great weight he was thrashing his body from side to side, trying to evade capture, his fists knocking every way, looking for somewhere to land. I did not feel in the least part calm, but I must appear so if I was to be of any help to the household.

Between us, the servant and I managed to get him back into bed, although he threatened at once to leave it again. 'Tell him I will take him to pray for her when he is more calm,' I told the servant. 'It would not be seemly while he is so disturbed, but I will give him something to calm him down, and then he can go to her.'

It was fortunate that I had been in the habit of keeping a few medical necessaries at the house, since a while ago a stable boy had been kicked by a horse and had needed my help. I went to see the housekeeper, who held them for me, and took up the powder I used to bring sleep. A smaller measure should help to make him manageable, while allowing him to visit his dead wife's bedside.

Adding the powder to a glass of wine I managed to get him to take a mouthful after much protest.

'So now you look to kill my father!'

I looked to the doorway, where my brother stood, but did not reply, resolving to force my mind to stillness. Grief made people behave in different ways. I would excuse my brother's words, and not upbraid him for them. I gave my father another sip. This time he took it quietly.

'When he is entirely quiet we can take him to where she lies,' I said.

'Thank you, sir,' said the servant. 'Should he drink all of this?'

'I think it will not matter if he does not,' I said. 'He has exhausted himself with his roaring. I will return in a little while and help you.'

We lay the old man back on his pillows and I nodded to the servant. 'Well done. He is far from easy to care for.'

My brother was no longer at the door. I went back to our mother's room, but he was not there either. Her maid was there, tears streaking her cheeks.

'I thank you for your tears,' I said. 'My mother should not be alone, but I must go and find my brother. Would you be content to sit with her body for a while? You do not need to fear. She is entirely at peace.'

'I'm not afraid,' said the girl, bravely attempting to swallow her tears. 'We all loved her, sir. I am so sorry . . .'

I put my hand on her shoulder. 'Thank you, Lizzie. Know that she was so very fond of you, and appreciated all you did.' I wanted to weep with her but I could not allow myself to do it, although I felt sure my mother would have not disapproved such unseemly behaviour from those who loved her. Without another word the girl went to the chair by the bed and sat quietly gazing at my dead mother's face.

Hugh was in our mother's garden. The rain had stopped and the sun was out. All the garden was steaming. He had a stick, and every time he struck and wounded a plant it sent sparkling raindrops into the air.

'Hugh.' I went down the path to him. 'Hugh. Don't.' He made to strike me with the stick but I held it until he gave it up.

'Why were you not with her? You were not even here! And you say you are a physician? You killed her with your neglect!'

It was grief. Only that.

'I was with her a long while, Hugh. I left her but three days ago to attend to things in Bristol. She was so much better when I left. She said I was not to return, but I had promised I would, and she was happy to hear it . . .' I swallowed the sob. 'When did you come?'

'This morning. In time to sit and watch her die!'

'Did she know you?'

'No! She was sleeping and I could not wake her.' The misery on his face was painful to behold but a tiny part of my mind rejoiced at such fairness. If I had not been able to say my farewells, then neither had he. I chased the thought guiltily away. Grief can be a mean and treacherous master. I laid my hand on his shoulder but he shook it off.

'You *always* let me down, and leave me to deal with things alone.'

'Hugh. What . . .'

'You abandoned me when I was to join the army, and you left me to watch our mother die, all on my own.'

I took hold of him and he wept. For a while we both did, but eventually I had to put him from me. 'Hugh, listen. Our father needs to visit her. We should be there as well. We should all be together. And the servants too. I hope he will be calmer now, and so we should help him to be there while he is.'

While I read the prayers before all in the room, I marvelled that I was so calm, and that my voice did not waver. It felt a little like the way I had learnt to show a steady exterior when attacked during the war, or when a soldier was injured, and needed to be prevented from getting into a grave panic. I had learnt how to lock up my own feelings, and keep them away even from myself, while I had such need. I know that this day a part of myself had flown to the top of the hill on that island, where I had been cast away, years before. It was where I had felt closest to heaven, the day when Richard and I sang carols, thinking it Christmas. I forced myself to feel again the snapping cold of that winter's day. It kept my mind numb, while the bright, warm sunshine shone outside in the garden where bees visited the flowers. While I spoke the words before my dead mother I left it to God to raise her up to heaven, where surely her good and generous soul belonged.

Hugh and I both stayed until after she was buried. Hugh's wife came, leaving her brood behind, and the church was filled with local people from the estate and roundabout, and even our aunt and uncle came, who resided in Berkshire and who I had not seen for a great many years.

Our father not being fit, there were various things to attend. I wanted Lizzie to be found another good position, rather than being turned off without a word. There were our mother's clothes and personal belongings to be decided upon. Hugh's wife did not want any of her dresses, as she had plenty of her own. I felt a little shame as I packed her old green gown into a box. What I would do with it I did not know, but it was a thread that ran right through my childhood, and I could not quite let it go.

The morning both Hugh and I were to leave we sat early at our breakfast. We had taken to eating in our mother's sunny room, where she had sewn and written letters. Our father woke late and demanded food at all sorts of hours, so this was a kind of haven against the chaos of his life. It was still high summer, but this morning I could feel the first slight chill that warned of autumn. We were both fragile, I know, but at pains to remain if not friends, at least brothers while still together. Hugh had, I think, wept often, but since that time in the garden I had not been able to shed any tears. My heart felt permanently sore, as if like a badly broken bone that refused to heal.

We were eating new baked bread, with that good butter from the farm, and some of the confit from the fruit in our mother's garden. I can remember exactly that a blackbird was scolding our mother's favourite cat, which I had noticed outside, sitting all innocence on the bench outside the window. Hugh was telling me about the pony he was going to buy for his little son, and I was trying to pay attention, although my mind was on the confit, and the cat, and the scolding bird, none of which she would see or hear any more.

It was the housekeeper who came in to tell us, her voice hushed and apologetic. I remember her words exactly, although they seemed to come from a long way away.

'I'm sorry, sirs,' she said, as Hugh unwillingly paused in his peroration to allow her to speak. 'But when Edward went to wake your father just now he found he couldn't. Edward says he must have died in his sleep for he's quite cold. I am so sorry, sirs.'

It was too much. I felt a great rushing, as if a torrent was about to overwhelm the house. It crashed around me, filling up the room; changing the light to foggy darkness. The torrent spurted from my eyes, and I could no longer see. My whole body was taken by it, taken up and shaken until there was no strength in me and my head fell of its own volition onto the table amongst plates and knives, crumbs and smears of butter. All I could think was to wonder why the blackbird still scolded, and then I knew I was weeping.

# CHAPTER TWENTY-EIGHT

At length I was afraid of myself. I lifted my head and everything was still there: the table, the window and the view without. It was clear again, but skewed, as if pushed sideways. I felt such a terrible weakness, as if I would fall from the stool and melt into the floor. I had forgotten about Hugh until he spoke. I turned slowly and looked at him. It felt as if a week had passed since last we had spoken, and it was as if there were a closed window between us. He looked afraid, as if the storm that had swept over me had alarmed him too. Then he spoke again, and as he did so his expression changed, from one of alarm to one of disbelief, even disgust.

'I said why are you weeping? You did not even like him!'

He did not understand a thing. 'I'm sorry, Hugh,' I said, my mouth forming the words as if through lack of skill. 'I am not quite well. You will excuse me.'

I lay on my bed through that long, sunny day in a stupor. There were things I must do, urgent things that could not wait, but I could not have got up to save my life. At last I was aware of a great thirst but there was nothing to drink. No one had come near me all day. I raised myself and sat on the edge of the bed, afraid I might fall. I have never been so weary.

When I finally reached the kitchen my mother's maid was there. What Lizzie saw must have alarmed her for she quickly came to me and helped me to a bench.

'What can I get you, sir?'

'Ale,' I said. 'Small ale.'

She brought it to me and I drank deeply. It felt as if I had wept all the liquid from my body, and ale was a salve that was repairing it, even as I swallowed. She refilled the mug and I drank again. When I was done I sat on for a few minutes.

'Do you know where you will go when you leave here?' I said at last.

'No, sir. It is hard to find work these days.'

'Well if you want to come to Bristol I am sure I could find you a place with a good family.'

'Yes, sir! I would like that very much.'

'Then consider it done. I don't know how long I will need to remain here, but I will tell our housekeeper that you are to stay until I return to Bristol and send for you. Until then I am sure you will be able to make yourself useful here.'

At least I had done one good thing this day. So I told myself as I went to see what the day had brought.

Our father's body had been readied for burial, for which I thanked his servant, Edward. He was keeping a vigil by his side.

That was another servant who would soon need to be found different work. I left him and went to the library. I would have to send for Mr Slade, our father's lawyer in Cirencester, and I would need to see about another funeral, unless Hugh had taken any of that upon himself. He had not, but I found him in the library, with papers scattered across a table and our father's box open.

'What are you looking for?'

He looked belligerently at me. 'As you absented yourself I thought it wise to make a start on things.'

'Have you sent for Mr Slade?'

He shook his head. 'Not yet.'

'Well, he will have the will, Hugh. We can leave all that to him. We do need to call at the church though. And everyone will need to be informed of our father's death.'

Hugh shovelled all the papers together and thrust them hastily into the box. I did not have it in me to wonder what he had been looking for, but he gave me an indication anyway.

'You are very ready to call him your father now, when you used to refer to him as "that man". And you shed hardly a tear over our poor mother. Yet this time you proffered unseemly tears, more than any girl would be ashamed to admit to. What are you trying to prove?'

'I have no need to prove anything, Hugh. And I cannot explain my sudden distress, except to say that his death was the most recent of a piling up of things, and the one that pushed my multiple griefs to the fore. Please do not let us fight. We have had much to distress us these past days, and you are now all the close family I have. I would wish us to be friends as we were in years gone by.'

His eyes filled with tears then. He came over to me and put his arms around me. 'I wish we could go back to those days,' he said. 'We were happy then.'

I held him close, immeasurably moved by his words. 'We were,' I said. 'But I love you still. And you have a wife and children who love you too, and make you happy. Is it not so?'

'It is. But what about you, Tom? Is it not long past time you had a wife?'

He didn't know how much his words cut me. 'Ah well,' I said. 'It never quite seems to happen for me.'

'Then should you not settle your mind to it?'

I hugged him again and then put him from me. 'What I have a mind to do is to go and look at my horse. She was a bit lame on the journey here. If she has recovered well, we could take the long way around to the church to obtain a little exercise. But we should send a boy to Mr Slade first.'

But Luna was still lame and if anything, she was worse than before. The groom told me he feared that she would never be sound again, and I took the news quietly, along with all my other sadnesses. I could not even feel that it was unexpected or unreasonable that I should have yet another thing to regret. She was well on in years anyway, and had earned her retirement. I would not have her shot. I decided at once that she could live out her days here. So the boy was dispatched to the lawyer, Hugh rode his horse the long way round to the church, and I walked the short distance across the formal garden to the door in the churchyard wall that connected our house to our place of worship.

Through the following days I did all that was required in a calm manner. There were no more tears, but all I did felt removed from me, as if I was a bystander, watching with little interest all that I commanded to happen. First to leave was Hugh, straight after our father was laid beside our mother. He rode beside the coach that held his wife, who had made the second journey for a funeral in as many weeks. I waved them off and went back indoors. The house felt cold and empty, although all the servants still remained. Hugh had left dissatisfied with his inheritance from his parents, although their gifts had been generous. He did not say it, but I knew he wanted the estate, and wished to doubt that I was our father's son. Perhaps he had been looking for evidence of my bastardy when I found him in the library with our father's box. I confess I also looked, although our mother had convinced me I was true-born. There was nothing. Mr Slade told me that as the firstborn and surviving son I was now Sir Thomas Chayne, with the house, estate and all, my own.

The first thing I did on my own account was to order a new horse bought for me. I did not care to choose it myself. Any beast would do so long as it would take me safely back to Bristol. I could not call Bristol home, nor would I call this empty house home either. I was entirely set adrift, with only my old dog, who still lived here along with the others, to show me any love. He was aged, and would die soon, adding to the total. I was seized with a fear that it would happen almost at once so I made unseemly haste to leave, sleeping only one night after Hugh and Elizabeth had left. My father's manservant found a place on one of the farms, and was well satisfied with that. As for my mother's maid, I found Lizzie a place almost immediately with the wife of one of George's friends in Bristol. I had spoken to all the tenants, servants and all, commanding that the house should be kept ready for when I might return. I had done all my duty and intended to pick up the pieces of my life in Bristol, but I knew I was struggling. I was conscious that my mind was adrift, but this was not a sickness I knew how to cure.

When I got to my house, a letter waited from Aphra, begging for a reply to her last. I could not think what to say, so I said nothing. I went out and met my friends at the Merchant Venturers' Hall. When they learnt of the deaths of my parents, they showed sympathy, but business did not stop for grief, and I felt out of time with the city. More, it was not simply my parents I was grieving for. I had so much sadness to weep for, and I was alone to bear it. The son I'd had, and then lost, all in one conversation haunted me, awake and asleep. Would it have helped if I had been married to his mother? We could have clung to each other in our times of sorrow, but I had no one. All were gone. Indeed, it struck me that I did not know even if Catherine still lived. And my hopes for a life with Aphra, and children of my own to love? Gone. Swept away by a cruel nib. Last, not a death, but my continued estrangement from Hugh. He had his wife and children to sustain him. He did not need me, but I, I had fair-weather friends, their faces set entirely toward commerce. I had no one who knew all my woes, and none I would wish to tell. The years seemed to rise up before me like an impossible mountain I could not begin to climb.

I had no need of the money successful commerce brought. The imperative to earn a living had gone. I had no interest in gambling, or raucous parties, where all the talk was of women or trade. Should I return home, to run the estate? My mother would have liked that. But she was no longer there, and the day I had left, the house had felt hollowed out. I tried to interest myself in the purchase of a new horse. I could afford the very best, but could not be bothered with the search. Luna had been a thing of beauty in my life. If I had ruined her, then the honest cob I had ridden back from Gloucestershire would do for all the riding I intended.

I did not intend to become a hermit, but as I went out less, my house became my retreat. To begin with people missed me, and there was a parade of my friends, who came calling to see if I was ill. Finding I was not, or so they considered, other than at low spirits, they advised exercise, wine, company and any amount of dubious remedies. They came with books, sweetmeats, exhortations and, at last, much shaking of heads. Eventually I told my housekeeper to turn all away, but I think by then they had already decided I had turned surly, and was lost to them. I ate less, drank more and brooded over what I read. One day I picked up a volume of Mr Shakespeare's plays that I had taken on a whim from my mother's shelves after her death. There was a dried flower in the book and so I began to read there, part way through *The Tempest*. At length a line stood out above the others. It was the one Richard had quoted so often at me, 'I don't believe in unicorns'. But he had had it entirely wrong, for the line said the very opposite. I started up, as if to tell him so, or write it to him, I do not know which. But almost immediately I sank back into my chair, for he was long gone from me too. I threw the book down. It fell to the floor and there it must have stayed for I saw it no more.

Some days I tried berating myself for my weakness, and took to my books, to discover a regime to cure myself, but was too exhausted to follow the discipline for long. On other days I told myself that my sunny nature would return if I concentrated on cheerful memories, but they all led me back to loss. I ordered nourishing food, but found I could not eat it. I bled myself, which almost led to total disaster. Weakness of my mind brought weakness of my body, and too, I think, weakness of my soul. Eventually, I could not even settle to read without staring into space for hours on end. To add to my misery, if such a thing were possible, two more letters came from Aphra, the last accusing me of petulance, being willing to destroy a good friendship for the sake of sulking. Oh, Aphra! I was in such need of a good friend then, but even you deserted me, not knowing how ill I did. Every time I picked up a pen to tell you, my hand faltered. I needed you to fold me in your loving arms, and tell me that all would be well, but I could not ask for that, knowing you would not grant it. In the end I ceased to believe that anything would ever be well again.

I cannot tell how long I was in this state, wavering between fury and grief, but it must have been not much less than a year. Having failed to physic myself, I told myself that drink took away the pain, but of course it did not. At first it dulled me, but then I needed more and more to kill my thoughts. My spirits became so low I could not care if I recovered or not. I do not know what would have happened to me if things had stayed that way, but I fear I might eventually have found the will to walk to the gorge and commit a terrible sin by throwing myself from it. My mind was already considering such a thing, because I could not believe any worse hell existed than the one I was already in. As it happened, it was late spring, or perhaps early summer when something so extraordinary happened that I can hardly believe it, even now.

Someone came calling. It was a long time since anyone had, and this person would not be denied. At first I took no notice, but then I registered that the commotion was at my door, and not out in the street. I was not interested, and simply wished the arguing would stop, the person go away and leave me in peace. The person did not go away. If I had been well I would have gone out to my housekeeper's rescue, and thrown the intruder out myself, but I did nothing to help her, nor myself. I could hear the argument coming indoors, and the rapid opening and closing of doors along with the shock of hard shoes on boards. I shrank down into my chair, under my blanket. If I closed my eyes perhaps the noise would melt away, but it did not. The brisk footsteps, having inspected all other rooms, came unerringly towards the door of my library, where I read little and wrote nothing. I heard the door open, and an exclamation of disgust. Against my housekeeper's entreaties the intruder crossed the room, threw open the curtains, and then the window. A cool draught of sharp spring air immediately snatched at my blanket, and I shrank further beneath it. My eyes were dazzled by the unaccustomed brightness and so I squeezed them full shut. I cannot recall if I said anything. I think I did not, but simply cowered in my chair.

The voice was too loud in my quiet place. Much too loud. It was as if he shouted, but I think in truth he did not.

'Tom? Tom! Ptolemy! Damn it, you will answer me!'

He pulled savagely at my blanket and whisked it away. Shivering in the cold blast, I screwed up my face, opening my eyes into slits, through which I saw a tall tinker man, with a patch over one eye. He crouched down and glared into my face. 'Do you not know me? Where have your wits gone? I did not think to find you like this!'

'Leave me.' I looked for my blanket, but he had taken it from me and thrown it to the floor, out of my reach.

'You stink like a midden. Are you drunk?'

I tried to shake my head, but the light made me dizzy.

'Ptolemy. Look at me properly. I have come to you for help, but it seems I must help you. Your eyes must be used to the light now. Open them. *Open them!* And say you do not know me.'

There was *something* about his voice. I was not interested in his ill-mannered intrusion, but perhaps if I did as he said and looked at him properly it would shame him into going away. He *was* a tinker, with a weathered brown face and the black patch covering God knows what injury. A gouging like Gloucester perhaps, but I was not interested in physicking even my wealthy patients, if indeed I still had any. Why would I help a man like this? His face wavered before mine and I tried to focus on him properly.

'Richard?'

'At *last*.' His voice blasted my eyes shut again. I felt a hand take mine, and his voice became quieter. 'Ptolemy.' That was better. Quieter, less frightful. I opened my eyes again, a little wider now, and there he was, the friend I had parted from so abruptly, years before.

When I admitted that I could stand he got me up and walking. He walked me up the stairs and into my chamber, calling for hot water and soap as we went. He would have washed me with his own hands, while telling me how my stink had met him at the library door, but I found enough dignity to insist on doing it myself. I was too slow for him, and so he occupied himself by throwing open chests, boxes and cupboards, looking for, as he said, 'decent clothing' for my skinny frame. Indeed, I had not realised I had lost so much muscle. It was no wonder I felt weak, and preferred to sit in my chair. But Richard would not have it. He led me up and down the stairs half a dozen times, until I begged him to stop before I fell. At last he called again for the housekeeper, and demanded hot food and fortifying drink, after getting information from me about what I would command a patient to take for his health's sake.

I had become so turned in upon myself that it took a while for me to ask how he had come here, and what help did he need. To begin with I could only speak of myself, and he encouraged that. Richard alone knew most of my past story, and so to relate all my sorrows to him was a simple matter. The end of it was that I wept, and he held me in his arms as Aphra never had. When I tried to apologise for my unseemly emotion he took hold of my shoulders and shook me a little, gazing into my wet eyes.

'Do you not remember that day on our island, when I was so lost and broken? Did you not comfort me then, as I try to do now for you? Is this not the very meat of a true friendship?'

'And yet we did not part well.'

'I had your letter, and replied to it. Did it not arrive? I was sorry we had parted so awkwardly, most of it due to me being out of sorts. I did not feel any anger at you for taking your letter from within mine. It was yours to take and was nothing to fall out about. I apologised for being out of temper with you, simply because you wanted something different from me. I knew I had acted like a petulant boy.'

'I had no reply from you, Richard, but did not take it ill. And in spite of the terrible lack of welcome I gave you today, I am more happy than I can possibly say to see you after all this time.'

'Then that makes two of us.'

'But how did you find me?'

'I had your letter, my friend, and a little help. My eye had been troubling me for some time, and so, when I discovered we were to dock at Bristol I thought it wise to ask if any knew of you, this place not being so very far from your Gloucestershire home. Imagine my surprise and joy when I heard you were a man of substance in this very city, and then my horror when I found you in such a terrible state.'

'I am sorry to hear of your eye, but in truth, Richard, I am not sure how much help I could be to you. Do you not have a good surgeon onboard your ship?'

'He can splint a break well enough, but he has little finesse, and has been unable to help as much as I would wish.'

I regarded him anxiously. 'My hand is not as steady as it should be, and my knowledge is gone.'

'Your knowledge is only sleeping, my friend. As for your hand, time will heal that if you exercise it along with the rest of your body.'

'You sound more a physician than I.'

He laughed. 'You look like a scarecrow, but I see the old you still exists within, even though it is but a shadow yet.'

'And a shadow that might have gone entirely if you had not come when you did.' He looked most solemn at that.

We spoke long into the night. At one point he bent to pick up the book I had thrown down some weeks before. I was reminded of his erroneous quote, and took him to task about it.

'Is this what you have wasted your time brooding about?' he said, gently teasing. 'You should have read on further instead of abandoning the play. And there was I thinking you a very man of letters.' He put the volume down and said no more.

It was bracing to be in his company again. I had forgot how much I had missed it. But our evening was not all conversation. Every hour Richard would not be denied, but I must tread the stairs from the bottom to the top of the house, as many times as I could manage. His regime made my heart race, and afterwards I fell back into my chair, but he would not be denied. When, eventually, we went to our beds I slept deeply, and well, for the first time in months.

The following day he was up before me, whistling and in a high good mood. He had always been a cheerful fellow when circumstances deserved it, and I was willing to trail in his wake. He did not mention his eye again, and I admit I neglected to enquire, my hand still being in no state to examine it. I did suggest another physician I thought well of, but Richard shrugged, thanked me and did no more than note down the man's address.

We spoke a little of his past years. The ship he was on at the moment, one of the King's privateers, suited him well. He liked his captain, almost as well as the prize money he earned.

'Ptolemy,' he said, as we sat picking over our midday food. 'Tomorrow I will be gone, back to the Caribbean, and I would like to see you at least take the air outside before I go. Will you walk with me down to the harbour today? The sun is shining, the air is good, and I do think it would be of benefit for you to take the air.'

I smiled at him. 'Doctoring me again?' And then my smile faltered. 'I will be sorry to see you go. You have done me so much good in this short time. You have shown me that my decline might be reversed, and for that I am grateful beyond words.'

'So will you keep up your new regime of good food and exercise?'

'I will endeavour to do so, so as not to disappoint you next time you come.'

He looked touchingly pleased. 'I am very glad to hear it! Now, how about this walk down to the harbour, or elsewhere if you prefer? We would not go too far, and you can rest at an inn before we walk back.'

'How can I withstand your enthusiasm? Let us go to the harbour. You are right. It is not far.'

I cannot pay Richard a higher compliment than to say that I was eager to go with him. If I had been on my own, I know I would never have done it. He gave me my hat, and fastened my cloak about me as a mother might her child. Going down the hill I took his arm to steady me, but when we got to the bottom I walked unaided. The seagulls were screeching, and with barrels rolling, bales thumping and men calling it was a very cacophony. I had forgotten how the real world sounded. I had been as one asleep, and Richard had woken me up.

# CHAPTER TWENTY-NINE

'So which is your ship?'

Richard steered me, avoiding the leaking barrel that was spilling its contents in our way. 'She lies along here.' I looked to where he was pointing and saw a fine three-masted vessel, riding proudly in the water.

'Do you want to come aboard?' He looked at me diffidently, making me smile.

'It is obvious how much you want to show off your vessel,' I said to him. 'Of *course* I want to see all around her. I have never been on such a large ship, and she does look splendid. What happened to the privateer we both sailed on, before I abandoned you?' I asked.

'She succumbed to the teredo worm,' he said. 'Vessels don't

last long in the warm waters of the Caribbean unless they are frequently attended to, and our captain was unaccustomed to the needs of his vessel. I was not ready to come home, so I found another captain to serve. Captain Falcon is a good and fair man.'

After we had visited the upper gun deck I professed myself weary, and so Richard led me to his tiny cabin. I was grateful to sit a while on his bunk, after the exertion of both the walk and partial inspection of the ship. A shout came from above, and Richard listened.

'Will you excuse me?' he said. 'I think I should attend to that.'

'Of course,' said I. 'I am quite content to enjoy your bunk for a while!'

I was indeed weaker than I had supposed, so sat for a few minutes. As Richard did not return at once, and the bunk reminded me so of my past time onboard a ship, I made free and lay back. For the first time in a long while, pleasant thoughts filled my head. It felt as if this short walk had blown away most of the sad and lonely feelings I had long been prey to, replacing them with some of his cheerful, good-hearted remarks. I marvelled afresh that Richard had happened to have found me at the moment when I had needed him the most. I had tried to chide myself for mourning so deeply my poor mother, but of course I had more than her to grieve over. That young boy with my name and blood who, cruelly, I had never known. Aphra lost to me twice over. And whatever Hugh thought, I did also mourn our father. Not because I had loved him, but because I had not, and because he had never encouraged me by showing me any sign of parental affection. Hugh, too, I mourned, or at least the loss of our brotherly closeness. I think if I had felt able to speak to him about the way I felt so assailed, being sure of his loving kindness, I would not have dropped so low. And if I had been invited to be an uncle to my little nephews and nieces, well, that too would have helped fix me a place in the world.

But it was folly to think that way. I stretched out in the bunk and fell to remembering all the good and bad times Richard and I had shared. He was not my brother in blood, but we had experienced more than many true brothers did. And miraculously, when I really needed him, he had arrived, as if in answer to a prayer. I should ask him more of the injury to his eye. I had been selfish in my misery. I should at least offer to look at it for him because I might be able to suggest *something* to help him.

I closed my eyes, listening to the sounds of a ship and its company on the water, a totally different experience from being abed on land in a houseful of people. I had not slipped into peaceful sleep for so long I could hardly remember how it had ever happened for me. The previous night I had fallen unconscious with tiredness, which had at least been a welcome rest from my demon thoughts. That day, in that place, my body was tired and my mind was unusually calm, floating of its own right, as if drifting in a small boat, oars swaying in the gentle water. I let myself go, and floated to sleep in peace.

When I awoke it took me a few seconds to recall where I was. For a moment I half wondered if I were in a coach, splashing through a flooded road, but then recalled the pleasure of falling into such a refreshing, dreamless sleep. Of course, I was onboard Richard's ship. They were moving her for some reason; perhaps another vessel needed her berth. I swung my feet to the floor. I would go up on deck. Richard must be busy, or he would surely have woken me. It would be interesting to see the city from the water.

I went to open the door and found it too stiff to move. There must be a reason why I could not open it, but I had not thought I was so very weak. My peaceful mood threatened to evaporate and I counselled myself to be patient. I tried again, and failed. This was a ridiculous, embarrassing and alarming imprisonment. I told myself that Richard would never want to restrain my person, but I could not deny my unease. No longer did this feel a calm and restful cabin. I looked out of the small porthole and discovered that not only was the day far gone, but we were well into the channel, running down towards the open sea. I thought to shout for Richard, but felt foolish at such an idea. I should wait. He would come when he had time. But I grew ever-increasingly uneasy. Had he forgot me? This was no simple act of moving berth; we were leaving the city! I could make no sense of it, and did not wish to be constrained in this small space while I was taken ever further from my home. I tried the door again, still could not shift it and before I could stop myself I found that I was hitting the door with my fist and calling out angrily for my friend.

It was not so many minutes before he came, but in that time my anxiety grew so much that I considered myself pressed, as so many port-dwelling men were, to answer the constant call for crew. They left behind wives, children, sweethearts and parents, who little knew where they had gone. I had no loved ones to mourn me, and I was old, too old to be pressed! And yet, age did not always protect.

It was not so. Of course not! And yet, seeing Richard's shamed face when he arrived to open the door I felt sure he had done *something* he knew I most likely would not like.

'Where are we bound? Why did you not wake me, so I could go ashore before this happened?' I know I glared at him.

'You were sleeping so peacefully. I could not bear to wake you. And further . . . I thought . . .'

'Yes?' I was testy.

'I worried that if we parted so soon you might slip back into a dolorous condition, with all that risked. I only thought . . .'

'Well?' I believe I tapped my shoe upon the boards like some martinet. I am ashamed of that now.

He came into the cabin and sat upon the bunk. 'Oh, Ptolemy. Be not angry, or afeared. Listen to me. When I found you yesterday you were in a hellish condition. In your own words, like to turn to self-destruction. I could not see you damned for such an act against God! But I did not have the leisure to help you. I knew my ship would leave on the tide today, but you did not think to ask, so sunk as you were, and so I did not say.'

'So what? Am I kidnapped now? Pressed?'

'Of course not! I came back here to look upon you several times, intent on delivering you home when you woke, but you were in a deep sleep. Eventually I left it in the hands of God, and He saw fit to keep you here until after we set sail. Quite how, through all the shouted commands, running feet above your head and general commotion I do not know, but it is so.' For the first time he took his turn to look testy. 'There was no need to kick and shout as if you were locked in.'

'I could not open the door.'

'There is a knack to it.'

We were both silent at that.

'Ptolemy.'

I looked at him. 'I'm sorry I was so irritable, and hasty.'

'I too. It was understandable that you should have been a little alarmed. The fact is . . . in a few days we will make landfall again . . . perhaps near Lyme, I do not know exactly where . . . but we will stop to meet a courier, someone known to the captain, before we return to the Caribbean. Wherever it is I feel sure you will be able to take a coach, or hire a horse to get you home.'

'You make it sound so easy, but it may have escaped you that I have little coin in my purse, having thought the most I would need would be to buy us a drink at the inn. To my embarrassment I have neither coin, nor clean linen, nor anything other than the clothes you see me in. In one swoop, my friend, you have turned me from a wealthy man to a pauper, and one moreover who is not fit to ride all the way from Lyme to Bristol.'

Richard scratched his head. 'That is far from insurmountable. It would not be the first time we have shared our linen. I can repay you for the Christmas gift all those years ago in Oxford. And money is no problem. These days I have plenty and to spare. We can settle up eventually. We need not fall out about it.'

I found myself laughing. 'You have an answer to all, as ever you did. The next will be that you suggest I should go and visit my property in Jamaica for my health's sake!'

He stared at me. 'I did not know you had property in Jamaica.'

'No? I suppose we spoke little of my business interests. I am far from the only man in Bristol who grows sugar in the Caribbean. We have in Bristol been talking of building a sugar house, the demand for it is so great.'

'I suppose I should not be surprised. But I find I am! Well, perhaps you should consider it.' He smiled at me, a wide grin that so reminded me of our early days as students in Oxford.

I could do no other than reply to his smile with one of my own. 'Well, if I had no business to attend to in Bristol, and in truth I do urgently need to pick up the reins of my life again, I might consider it, but if I were mad enough to go, by the time I returned my friends and associates would have counted me dead, and out of all ventures. Even were I tempted it would be quite impossible at this juncture.'

'Of course.' He got to his feet. 'But I am enormously, if selfishly, pleased to have you my guest for a few days. I will clear my belongings from this second bunk, and make it comfortable for myself while you are here. It will be like in the old days, when we were cast away in that tiny cottage.'

'Indeed! Though there we were going nowhere, and here we are travelling, even while we put no foot in front of the other.'

I enjoyed myself enormously, being Richard's guest. I ate with the senior officers, met and enjoyed conversation with the captain, took the air on deck and thought about my life. Richard could very well have been correct in his concern for me slipping back into black thoughts, if he had abandoned me so soon. Onboard this fair vessel with excellent company, good air and ever-changing vistas to excite my senses I felt more alive each day. Richard did not mention that fair island of Jamaica again. Instead, he wisely left me to conjure it myself, contenting himself with describing the courier, who was always happy to take letters for the King's mail.

There were many small boats plying their trade along the coast, but we sailed well out from the shore, the better to keep away from the treachery of the rocks that lay in wait to destroy a great ship. I was on deck when we rounded the tip of Cornwall and headed towards the channel. The sea threw itself with fury against the broken cliffs, even when the weather was calm. I was glad our captain had such respect for this place, but it was an invigorating sight, both there, and later at what they told me was called The Lizard.

One day while Richard was at his duties, I sat in his cabin, thinking on what I should do. As the days had passed I had become ever more enamoured of visiting the mysterious and wondrous island that was making me a fortune. Why should I not visit it if I fancied such a trip? Did I not need a holiday? Moreover, it had been so good to renew my friendship with Richard. I thought he would not object if I asked the captain for passage, and Richard to share his cabin a while longer. Once in Jamaica I could meet my lawyer, Mr Chepstow, and arrange for funds. The venture would do me good, and when I returned home I would be refreshed. I could see no reason to deny myself, and many to recommend it. And so I took up paper and wrote several letters. One was to Hugh and another to my friend George in Bristol. I explained briefly that I would be away for a holiday, thinking it wise to follow my recent illness with some different air. I wrote also to my two housekeepers, the one in Gloucestershire and the other in my house at Bristol. I commanded both to close the properties, retaining only enough staff to keep the places sweet-smelling and aired, ready for my eventual return. I wrote to Aphra too, wishing her well, and telling her at last of my travails, being the reason why I had not been in touch the sooner. Also, I informed her that I was going away. All done, I sat on in his cabin, explaining to Richard later that afternoon what I had done. We were, I am glad to say, equally pleased at the decision I had made.

The following day, in late afternoon, we slipped quietly into a small, hidden bay, dropping our anchor well away from the beach.

'Look!' I said to Richard, holding out my hands to him. 'My hands are steady at last. If you wish me to look at your eye I will happily do so while we are moored and steady here. It is the very least I owe you, for you have saved me from myself. I was stuck in a mire of anger, fear and grief, and do not know that I would ever have got out of it without your help. I offer you my sincerest thanks, and will do my very best for your eye. I am just sorry that I have no instruments to help me.'

'Say no more about it,' said he. 'For I am so much better in your company than without it. Indeed, I think we are both better together than apart. As for instruments, I could ask the surgeon if he would lend some to you, or attend us himself. I feel sure he would do that. He is a pleasant fellow, and does not overestimate his skills. He became surgeon because there were no others when one was needed.'

'Then while the light is still good enough, let us do that.'

Richard had a lens, and the good sawbones a selection of tweezers of various sizes. I instructed my friend to lie down with his head well supported. I had expected to see a badly wounded eye, with no hope but for it to be extracted from the socket, but it was not so very bad. Once I had it clean, I used the lens to examine it all ways, while Richard looked up, down and to either side. I could see little other than a trace of pus coming from behind the eye.

'You have something stuck behind your eye,' I said, 'and it is infected.'

'I told him that,' said the sawbones, sounding well pleased with himself. 'I bled him, but the object is entirely stuck, hidden and unobtainable. Or at least,' he said modestly, 'it is so to my little skill.'

It was certainly not easy to find, and harder to gain purchase upon it. Poor Richard was at great pains not to groan, but he could not avoid giving voice a couple of times to his distress. Even so, eventually I had it. A ridiculously small item to have caused such pain. I cleaned his eye again and washed as much of the pus away as I could.

'I cannot be certain what damage has been done,' I said. 'No doubt the rear of your eye is badly scratched. Can you see anything?'

'Very little,' he said. 'But I feel sure that once it heals, the pain will be much better, and that is what I care about. But show the offending thing to my good eye,' he said. 'For I would curse it before it is thrown away.'

I laughed. 'Here then.' I took it up with the tweezers and put it into the palm of his hand.

He poked at it with his finger, and then looked at it through the lens. 'What is it? I thought it must be hard but it is very small, and soft to have caused me such trouble.'

'The waters of your eye have no doubt softened it while it lay there,' I said. 'As for what it is . . . can you remember what you were doing when it happened?'

'Not exactly. I spent a while watching the carpenter fashion a piece of wood to replace a little part that had broken from our figurehead. He is a very skilful fellow. Apart from that you know yourself how it is onboard ship, with ropes, sails and timber everywhere. I remember rubbing my eye at some point during the day, but do not remember anything obvious flying into it.'

'Well, perhaps most likely it was a splinter of wood from your carpenter's work,' I said. 'Splinters start off sharp and become soft when in the flesh, do they not?'

'Indeed so.' The sawbones was enthusiastic in his

agreement. 'I have pulled enough from men's hands to last me a lifetime. And even the smallest piece can cause pain if it is not removed.'

'Well then,' said Richard, getting to his feet. 'Let us agree on it being a splinter. It is the most troublesome one I have had the misfortune to suffer, so I will toss it over the side, and good riddance to it.'

He smiled at me. 'Thank you for relieving me of it.'

'You are welcome,' I said. 'I was glad to do it. Just keep away from carpenters while they work in future!'

The sawbones shook my hand. 'I will know in future where to send any man with a delicate injury,' he said. 'I am not jealous of my status. Indeed, I would be happy to share the responsibilities of surgeon with you while you are with us.'

I took Richard below and settled him onto his bunk to rest, ordering him to do little for a day or two, but he was fretting.

'It is my job to take the ship's boat ashore to meet the courier,' he said. 'If you insist on me resting, will you do that small job for me, though you be on a holiday? A sailor will row you, and all you have to do is put the packets of letters into the man's hands. You can give him yours also. He is a strange fellow,' he added. 'With a false hand that might be of professional interest to you, but I do not think he likes it remarked upon.'

I laughed. 'Then I will be sure not to mention it! I can see that between you and the surgeon sawbones, you mean to make use of me on this ship, and that I am not to be entirely a passenger. But with all my heart, I will be your postman.'

So it was that at dawn the following morning I stepped into the boat, and a sailor rowed me to the shore. In the grey light I could make out two horses and a man on the beach. I climbed out and splashed my way to shore. It was only then that I saw a poor boy, sagging with obvious exhaustion on the pack animal. He took no notice of me and I was at pains to conclude my business in a proper manner, without staring at something that did not concern me. However, since my late mother had told me of my young son's existence and untimely death, I had found myself taking extra notice of every lad I saw who might have a dozen years or so. Might he have looked thus? Might he have spoken thus? Had he been tall and slender like his mother, or brawny with broad shoulders and hair black as the night? Idle wondering does no man any good, but still it is hard to let off once one has begun to think this way.

I handed the fellow my bundle of letters from the ship and he held out to me his several packets.

'Make sure you only give them to the captain,' he said.

'Of course,' I said. 'I will give them to him straight away.'

I think I was already turning away to get back in the boat when he spoke again.

'You will oblige me by taking this boy.'

I was astonished. The boy's head still drooped, but I had the feeling he was watching me behind his hair. I was about to explain that I was simply a passenger on the ship and had no authority to take boys into the crew, but I doubted we were quite at our full complement, and no captain is likely to refuse to take an extra hand when it is offered. Besides, the man's words had not exactly been a question. I got the feeling that if I refused he would find some other way to divest himself of the lad, and it would likely not be to the boy's advantage.

'Should I know anything about him?' I said. He did not look a desperate murderer, but it is hard to tell the character of a person almost silhouetted against the rising sun.

The courier man shook his head and told me in curt terms not to bring him back. It was on the very tip of me to refuse, because I did not like his manner, but the boy was a person. I should not play with his future for the sake of not liking his master.

'Come on then,' I said gently to the boy.

Before he could begin to dismount, the man pulled him roughly from the pack horse. He tried to land on his feet, but his legs would not hold him and he stumbled to his knees. He had, I think, been on that animal for a long time, or was not accustomed to ride. He was not hurt, but he struggled to get up because his hands were tied. I did not like that. I did not intend to take a prisoner with me. Surely he deserved a little dignity, whatever he might have done. I could see him better now, and he was a comely boy, well-bred-looking, gently made, but with muscle on him. It was idle to wonder who he was, but I did wonder.

I told the man to untie him. He cut the rope from the boy's hands and immediately the lad let out a yelp. I had already got back in the boat but immediately went to him, being afraid that the man had carelessly cut his wrists. He had not, but the cord had been so tightly wrapped around him it had left deep marks and had almost severed the blood flow to his hands. I helped him into the boat. He was shaking from fear, so I sought to reassure him.

'Don't fret,' said I. 'We're going to the Americas, where there are fortunes to be made. You will make a new beginning. And don't worry about your hands. They will feel better soon.'

'Tell the captain he owes me for a cabin boy,' said the man.

I threw some offhand remark back at him, but we were already heading back to the ship and I was more concerned with comforting the boy, who began to weep, than speaking to the cruel man who had tied him so tight.

# CHAPTER THIRTY

When I first met young Abel, in that abject state on the shingle beach, he was twelve years old, and I had reached the age of fifty. I had never been one to believe in magic, though as a child, yearning for my father's love, I had often wished for it to help me, since it seemed that God could not command my father to love me. When I grew to be a man I looked for love in other places but always it slipped away from me. Perhaps, on the long journey that is a man's life, to search for love is a mistake. I had not looked for Richard, but there he was in Oxford, ready to be the best friend I ever had. Indeed I can see that he has been such a loyal, life-long friend that I can now say I have loved him without knowing it, though we do now admit each other to be as beloved as the best of brothers, as we continue to follow our destiny together.

That was slow magic, that crept up upon us during the fellowship of study, of war and of privation. That sort of love is a very precious thing, but it is not all. There are other loves to be had, if fortune or magic sends them. Love of a girl I had. Though brief, that love burned bright like an Icarus, whose flight was so glorious, and so brief. Love from my mother, of course. So utterly surrounding me I did not always feel it, because it was so much a part of me, and maybe the purest human love of all. But that pack animal upon the beach, that patient unicorn that carried that boy to me, it brought the love I thought I would never feel. But on that mysterious strand, when I took his poor hands in mine, I felt such a shock of love firing my heart, and from his eyes came the need of such a love. There is no explaining it, except that on the following day, when Abel sat close to me for comfort, afraid still of almost everything that moved, my friend Richard spoke quietly in my ear.

'That boy is in want of a father,' he said. 'While you are in need of a son.'

For most of my life I have had someone to speak to of things that troubled me. Mother, brother, friend. But motherless Abel, so recently having seen his father shot dead before him, had no one with whom to share his aching heart. My recent experience of lonely grief helped me to recognise that in him. As a consequence, in a few short days he came to trust me, and poured out his story to me like a river in spate. In return I swore to him that I would care for him as a father until my dying day, and so I shall.

Life on a privateer is no idyll, but it suits us both. Even before we had reached the Caribbean my past life in Bristol had retreated, as fast as the wind drove us on. If I had held any notion of taking Abel back to England, I lost it on that voyage. Sadness aplenty for us both lay in England, while new life in a different place beckoned us on. Why would I want to return when I had the two people I loved most with me on this ship? The good ship *Angel* was Abel's salvation, and mine too.

We were not many days out when the purser struck his head in a heavy sea and died soon after. Our sawbones, having as he did a greater skill and interest in accounting than medicine, took that man's work. And so it fell to me by the purser's misfortune to become the *Angel's* surgeon, ceasing entirely to be a passenger, and becoming a full member of the crew. As for young Abel, it took me no time at all to ask him if he would care to be instructed in the duties of a surgeon's mate. He had a most enquiring mind, and soaked up knowledge as flour does water.

All this was over a year ago. We have survived tempests, fever, cannon and cutlass, while taking many prizes. Richard and I speak of spending our last days on our estates in Jamaica if we are spared, but we are both still hearty, and see no reason to retire from this life awhile yet. He has a woman on his estate, and an ever-increasing clutch of children there. That life of partial domesticity would never have suited me, but he likes it well enough.

I have no need of the estate in Gloucestershire, but remembering my mother, I shall not will it to Hugh to be ruined by ill temper. Instead, I have left it to his second son, in the hope that he may be a gentler soul. The Bristol house is sold, and money invested. I have not yet told Abel I have left all remaining property and coin to him, but in time I shall. He is my heir just as much as if he had my blood.

What a strange life I have lived! To have been so stubborn for so many years, wanting only to have children with the right woman at the right time. And yet I end up with a boy who, for all I know, was born out of wedlock, who has none of my blood in him, but whom I love more dearly than my own flesh.

Sometimes I wonder about his lost family. His father had, it seems, been for the king and had fought during the wars, though Abel does not know where, or with what company he fought. I wonder if I might have met this father during those troubled times, but have said nothing of it, in case it upsets the boy.

I do often find myself thinking on those violent days past, when our nation was at war with itself, and after killing the king we tried another way of living. I have no answers to the difficulties of government, and this is not a history lesson, to be written down and taught to children yet unborn. But if only those in power had understood the danger of ill-tempered debate in a nation divided. Were they prepared for six years of war, an uneasy peace, and then, after all that strife, the monarchy invited back? Look at the fatherless children and lame men wherever your eyes roam. Burned houses like blackened teeth in a rotting head, and spoiled crops. That is how it was. Is it not the job of a king and parliament to work together to keep the nation safe? All say aye! But we were not in danger! Only from them.

I am still alive, when so many died, and I thank God for it. I have killed a few men, but in a life's accounting I would say that I have striven to heal far more than I have harmed. The sea is calm today, the wind just right, and no other sail is in view. Abel has brought Richard and I our evening wine, with a little for himself. We will drink it while watching the sun cast her last rays, and indulge ourselves in conversation. What will come tomorrow I cannot tell, but today I am entirely content. What more, I ask, should any man wish for?

347

# ACKNOWLEDGEMENTS

I must first thank writer Linda Newbury, who was my first reader, and one whose comments I value. Our conversations about writing are always useful and a very pleasant adjunct to eating lunch, especially when she forgives my tardiness! Thank you too to my other readers, Ruth Clark and Gavin Landless, who always buoy my spirit, and to writer Celia Rees, whose suggestion worked splendidly. Thank you, Celia. Thanks must also go to my agent Jane Conway-Gordon, who is so supportive about my work, and to all at Allison & Busby. It is a pleasure to work with them all.

Many thanks to the Corinium Museum, and in particular James Harris, who gave me access to one of the original accounts of the storming of Cirencester, as well as the petition for forgiveness by some of the prisoners. It is interesting and instructive that eyewitness accounts exist of that event from both sides of the argument. Both accounts are replicated in full in the Cotswold District Council's publication of 1993, written by John Miles Paddock, Keeper of Archaeology at the museum. It was published to accompany a talk given at the time to mark the 350th anniversary of the Civil War. I was lucky enough with my father to attend that very atmospheric event, held in the church where the prisoners had been held.

I wish also to record my gratitude to R. W. Jennings, sometime history teacher at Cirencester Grammar School, who died much too young. He was the only adult to suggest to me, his thirteen-year-old pupil, that I should consider becoming a writer. I was much too shy to tell him that it was my greatest wish to do so. He fostered my love of history, and believed in my potential. This novel in particular would never have been written without his influence.

Some other useful publications were:

*The Cotswolds in the Civil War* by R. W. Jennings

The 1930 edition of the Ordnance Survey map of seventeenth-century England

*The English Civil War* by Philip Haythornthwaite

*The Medieval Traveller* by Norbert Ohler

*Minor Poets of the 17th Century.* Introduction by R. G. Howarth

*The World Turned Upside Down* by Christopher Hill

*The Merchant Venturers of Bristol* by Patrick McGrath

*Charles I* by Christopher Hibbert

*Soul Made Flesh* by Carl Zimmer

*Henrietta Maria* by Alison Plowden

*The Swordsmen in Power* by Roger Hainsworth

*The Last Revolution* by Patrick Dillon

*The English Civil War* by Diane Purkiss

*The Tempest* by William Shakespeare

CYNTHIA JEFFERIES is a long-established writer for children whose work has been translated into more than twenty languages. She was born in Gloucestershire and her love of history was encouraged by regular family outings to anything of interest, from great cathedrals to small museums. Having moved to Scotland and back to Stroud, she has always made time to write and her abiding interest in Restoration England has never left her.

*cynthiajefferies.co.uk*     *@cindyjefferies1*